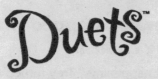

**Two brand-new stories in every volume...
twice a month!**

Duets Vol. #69

Popular Barbara Daly serves up a delightful
Double Duets this month featuring the smart,
sexy, sassy Sumner sisters, Faith and Charity.
The *Telegraph Herald* says this about Barbara's books.
Look for "...a delicious blend of humor, seduction and
romance as refreshing as a day in New England."

Duets Vol. #70

Cheryl Anne Porter returns with the second book
in her humorous miniseries A FUNNY THING
HAPPENED ON THE WAY TO THE DELIVERY ROOM.
This talented writer always delivers "a funny ride—
a roller coaster of fun and adventure." Joining her is
Silhouette author Kate Thomas with a neat premise.
What does an overburdened working woman need
these days? A stay-at-home "wife!"—
in the form of the sexy, ever helpful hero!

Be sure to pick up both Duets volumes today!

The elevator stopped with a sick, grinding crunch.

"This is not happening." Trey turned toward the panel of buttons, pushing every one. Nothing happened. He muttered beneath his breath then started beating on the door with a fist. "Hey, out there! We need help. There's a woman in labor in here—and a man about to have a heart attack. Can anybody hear me?"

Apparently nobody could. Trey turned to Cinda, eyeing her as if he'd known all along that she'd be trouble. "So, how are you feeling right now?" he asked.

"Fine." Trey gave her a doubting stare and Cinda caved. "Okay, so I could explode any minute here. I'm not any happier about this than you are." She bit down on her bottom lip. "Oh, God. A labor pain. I don't think I can hold on. You have to do something."

His eyes widened. "Got any suggestions?"

Was she not busy enough already? Did she have to do everything? Cinda breathed through her physical pain and pointed to the emergency phone behind its glass case. "Try calling someone, Mr. Cooper. Because if my labor progresses much further, the two of us are quickly going to become the three of us...."

For more, turn to page 9

Her Perfect Wife

"Ever heard of a telephone?"

So much for *"Hi, honey! How was your day?"* Melinda thought.

Jack stood in the doorway leading to the living area, and it didn't take much to read his body language—feet apart, chiseled forearms crossed over that hard-muscled, broad chest.

Melinda couldn't help herself. She chuckled.

It was that or cry because *somebody* noticed how hard she worked.

"I don't see what's so funny," he informed her, uncrossing his arms to clamp his hands on his hips. "You're almost two hours late! I was worried—anything could have happened."

The heck with that. "Uh, I don't know what business of yours it—" she began.

"What business?" He interrupted her. "I'm supposed to be taking care of you, remember?"

Flames seemed to flare from his blue eyes—but it was her insides that felt hot. Sexy *and* concerned—an irresistibly attractive combo.

For more, turn to page 197

HARLEQUIN DUETS

ISBN 0-373-44136-3

Copyright in the collection:
Copyright © 2002 by Harlequin Books S.A.

The publisher acknowledges the copyright holders
of the individual works as follows:

DADDY BY DESIGN?
Copyright © 2002 by Cheryl Anne Porter

HER PERFECT WIFE
Copyright © 2002 by Catherine Hudgins

This edition published by arrangement with Harlequin Books S.A.

® and TM are trademarks of the publisher. Trademarks indicated with ® are registered in the United States Patent and Trademark Office, the Canadian Trade Marks Office and in other countries.

Visit us at www.eHarlequin.com

Printed in U.S.A.

Daddy By Design?

CHERYL ANNE PORTER

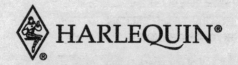

TORONTO • NEW YORK • LONDON
AMSTERDAM • PARIS • SYDNEY • HAMBURG
STOCKHOLM • ATHENS • TOKYO • MILAN • MADRID
PRAGUE • WARSAW • BUDAPEST • AUCKLAND

Dear Reader,

I always love writing books set in the South, because the stories seem to take on a life of their own. The sultry climate and the slow pace of living offer great potential for plot, character and conflict. And with all that in place, all I have to do is write what I know! See, I'm a Southern girl myself, born in Savannah, Georgia. So when I was thinking about writing my second book in the A FUNNY THING HAPPENED ON THE WAY TO THE DELIVERY ROOM miniseries, how could I set it anywhere else?

All I had to come up with was a fictitious small town, a couple of transplanted Yankees, a stuck elevator, a cute baby...and, well, you can read for yourself! I hope you have as much fun reading this story as I did creating it.

Enjoy!

Cheryl Anne Porter

Books by Cheryl Anne Porter

HARLEQUIN DUETS
12—PUPPY LOVE
21—DRIVE-BY DADDY
35—SITTING PRETTY

HARLEQUIN TEMPTATION
818—HER ONLY CHANCE

1

It was January 2. A gray and sleety New York City day, full of traffic gridlock, honking car horns, and short tempers. A day of overworked people in a hurry to get home. What a time for Cinda Cavanaugh to be waiting for the cranky elevator outside her obstetrician's office. She'd just been given the news that she was about to become a mother—soon. Not that she didn't know that. She was, after all, more or less nine months pregnant, the key words being "more or less."

It turned out it was going to be "more." Her routine appointment had suddenly become anything but. In her mind, Cinda could still hear Dr. Butler confirming that Cinda, after many false alarms, was now truly in the early stages of real labor. Only the baby was still in a breach position. So the doctor had promptly sent Cinda on her way to the hospital, promising to follow her as soon as she rearranged her other appointments.

"Ha," Cinda muttered, standing there alone in the long hallway, "I should have taken a rolled-up magazine to those other women and chased them away myself."

Though Cinda felt a little bad about her self-centered, mean-spirited thoughts, she reminded herself that she wasn't always this testy. It was just today. She'd heard that women in labor had a different set of rules. She squeezed her eyes shut and put a hand to her forehead. "So, what made me think I could do this alone?" She opened her eyes, grimacing. "Better yet, what made Dr. Butler think I really needed to be enlightened as to what actually goes on during a Caesarean-section delivery? God, just do it. Don't tell me about it. Ick."

Cinda caressed her swollen abdomen, now directing her conversation to the perfectly formed little girl whose image she'd just seen on the ultrasound screen. *You know what, my little princess? You could really help out. Go ahead—turn. Don't give your mother such a hard time.* Mother? Cinda thought about that. "Oh, God, *I'm* the mother."

She pushed the down button again and suddenly caught her own reflection staring back at her from the polished-metal elevator doors. "Oh, surely not." But, yes, that carnival fun-house reflection was indeed her own. "Are you telling me that I left the house looking like this?"

Obviously she had, because polished metal didn't lie. What she saw was a pale-blond head with angst-widened golden eyes above a swollen body covered by a black-wool winter coat, cream-colored slacks, and black boots. *Well, great. I look like a sheep ready for shearing.* Cinda pursed her lips, transferring her disgust to the elevator. "Come on, what's the problem here? As you can plainly see, I need to get to the hospital. Preferably today."

She pushed the down button firmly again. And then ten more times after that before she caught herself. *Get a grip, Cinda.* She put her fingers to her temples and pressed lightly. "I can do this. I *have* to do this. The nursery's ready. I'm ready. My baby is apparently ready." Cinda put a hand to her swollen belly. "*We* can do this, baby girl."

Just then, an irritatingly pleasant ding alerted Cinda that the contrary elevator car had deigned to arrive. She exhaled her relief. "Oh, thank God."

The doors opened without incident, presenting an empty elevator car. Swallowing back a sudden and uncustomary sense of impending doom, Cinda stepped inside and forced herself to push the button for the lobby. Anticipating the closing of the doors and the pull of gravity on her ride downward, she anchored herself by hanging on to the handrail that girded three sides of the rickety car. Not the least bit reassured, she studied her boxlike surroundings. Had this elevator really been this old and wobbly when she'd used it just an hour ago?

The doors closed. "Oh, calm down. You're getting yourself all worked up," she fussed, breathing in and out, in and out, as she watched the little lights blaze on and then off, indicating the incredibly slow, passage of each floor going by. Fourteen. No thirteen. Twelve. Eleven.

"There. See? It's working fine. You're just being silly." Cinda spoke to herself as if she were her own best friend who needed reassuring. "That whole 'woman in labor stuck inside an elevator' thing is just some silly Hollywood scenario. Or maybe a book. You'd think writers would have more of an imagination these days."

The elevator jerked to a stop. Cinda's heart nearly burst, but the dinging bell alerted her that all was well. Her hands shaking, she clutched at the opening of her woolly black coat as if it could ward off disaster. *This*

*is not a bad thing. It's just somebody on the tenth floor
waiting to be picked up. No problem.*

Confirming her conclusion, the doors opened to reveal a prospective passenger...who just happened to
be an outrageously and ruggedly handsome man.
Cinda's eyes widened with heart-stopping appreciation. *Oh...my...God.*

The man saw her and stopped dead in his tracks.
His eyes widened. Clearly, he was just as affected by
the sight of her as she was by him. No doubt, for
differing reasons. After all, here she was nine months
pregnant, and there he was...well, there he was. He
belonged on a billboard where he'd be engaged in
something really macho that required him to show a
bunch of muscles—and not wear a lot of clothes, if
there was an advertising god.

Those blue eyes and that sandy-brown hair. The
broad and capable shoulders. Movie-star looks. Not
the pretty-boy kind. The serious romantic-lead kind.
The chiseled jaw. And the raised eyebrows, the look
of, yes, dismay as he eyed her. Cinda didn't blame
him a bit. After all, her size rivaled that of a balloon
float in the Macy's Thanksgiving Day Parade. Thinking to put the gorgeous guy at ease, she offered him
a tentative smile.

He grinned back but shook his head. "No thank
you, ma'am, I've seen this movie, and it ends badly."
His accent dripped with knee-weakening, molasses-
thick Southern charm. "I'll just wait for the next car."
He stepped back and waved. "Y'all have a nice day."

She could *not* let him go. That was all she knew.
Cinda held down the door open button. "Wait. You
might as well get in. Trust me, a teenager could qual-

ify for Medicare before it comes back to this floor again.''

He eyed her, the elevator, and then the hallway to either side of him. Cinda waited with the proverbial bated breath. She tried to tell herself that she just didn't want to be alone in the elevator, should it do something heinous like stick between floors. But even she wasn't buying that. The truth was that there was something about this man that affected her, even on today of all days. And she plainly just wanted him in this elevator with her.

And he plainly didn't want to be in here with her. Grimacing with good-natured humor, he eyed Cinda's girth. She would have held her stomach in, but there weren't enough muscles in the human body to make that feat possible.

''I'm pregnant, not contagious,'' she tried helpfully.

That embarrassed him. His color heightened, but he laughed. ''Okay, you win, pretty lady. I may as well chance it.'' With a confident gait that exuded masculine sensuality, he walked into the car, hitting the buttons labeled Lobby and then Door Close.

Nothing happened. Not for several heart-stopping seconds. Cinda froze. The good-looking guy froze. Then, exhibiting a flair for drama, the doors belatedly shut. The elevator, coughing and wheezing like an asthmatic locomotive, begrudgingly set them on a slow-motion downward journey. Cinda clutched at the iron handrails and tried not to look afraid—or like she'd been flattered by the handsome man's calling her a pretty lady. She'd needed that. For a very long time…she had needed that.

Just then her fellow passenger turned to her. With a disarming smile that confirmed his Southern upbringing, he said, "If you don't mind me asking, when's your blessed event due? And don't say yesterday."

"Okay. My due date is a week from today." That was all she meant to say, but his smiling sigh of relief had her conscience railing at her to tell the man the whole truth. "However, I'm in labor right now, so I'm on my way to the hospital."

His expression fell. He looked so disappointed in her. "And we were getting along so well."

"I know. Trust me, it wasn't my idea. Sorry."

"That may be, but I feel it only fair to warn you that, as a pit crew mechanic on the Jude Barrett stock car racing team, I can take an entire car apart and reassemble it in five minutes. But nowhere on my resume does it say anything about delivering babies. So unless you need an oil change and your tires rotated, you just stand over there and behave yourself, you hear?"

Now he'd made her laugh. "You poor man. I'll try to hold on." Now more at ease with the stranger, Cinda heard herself asking *him* a personal question. "You're Southern, aren't you?"

He sent her an arch expression. "What gave me away?"

Cinda pointed to him. "That package of grits sticking out of your coat pocket."

He actually patted down his pocket as humor sparked in his blue eyes. "Damn. I meant to take that out." Then he stuck a hand out for her to shake. "I'm from Atlanta. Well, actually a little town just west of there that nobody's ever heard of called Southwood. My name is George Winston Cooper the Third, but my friends call me Trey. And you are…?"

"Not from Atlanta." Cinda clasped his hand. His flesh was warm, his palm slightly callused. While his grip was firm, he didn't squeeze too hard, and her swollen fingers appreciated that. "I'm Cinda Cavanaugh of Canandaigua, New York. It's just outside of Rochester. But I live here in Manhattan now." He nodded, but didn't let go of her hand. Cinda melted…and added, stupidly, "But I have a house in Atlanta."

As if fate had been waiting only for her to admit that, the diabolically evil elevator stopped dead between floors with a sick grinding crunch of something metallic and a prolonged twanging of cables that just didn't bode well at all. The ensuing lack of movement taunted its passengers. Cinda gasped, clutching harder at the man's hand. "Oh, no."

Trey Cooper voiced her fears. "This is not happening." He untangled his hand from hers and turned to the panel of buttons, every one of which he proceeded to push. And still nothing happened. He glanced balefully at her and then tried to wedge the double doors open. But despite his evident strength and his concerted effort, they wouldn't budge. He muttered beneath his breath and changed tactics, now beating on the doors with a fist. "Hey, out there! We need help. We're stuck. There's a woman in here in labor—and a man about to have a heart attack. Hello! Can anyone hear me?"

Apparently no one could. Trey Cooper turned to her, eyeing her as if he'd known all along that she carried some mutant strain of virus that threatened humankind. Cinda stared soberly back at him. His eyes pleaded for her to reassure him. "So, Mrs. Cavanaugh, how are you feeling right about now?"

Scared, her heart pounding—and her abdomen cramping—Cinda lied. "Fine." The man gave her a doubting stare. She caved. "Okay, so I could explode any minute here. Trust me, I am not any happier about this than you are, Mr. Cooper. We're in real trouble."

"Beyond the obvious, you mean?"

"Way beyond the obvious. My baby is in a breach position, which means I can't deliver her in the normal…well, on my own. I will need help."

His frown deepened. "And me without my toolbox. Darn."

Cinda's fear and pain turned to testiness. "Oh, like you're the one scheduled for a C-section delivery in a nice, safe hospital surrounded by people who know what they're doing…only you can't get there."

"No one wants you to get there more than me, Mrs. Cavanaugh. So you just stand there and keep your baby where it is."

Cinda's retort was on her lips, but then a twinge of building discomfort made her grimace. She bit down on her bottom lip. "Oh, God. A labor pain. I don't think I can hold on. Please. You need to do something—and do it now."

His eyes widened. "Got any suggestions?"

Was she not busy enough already? Did she have to do everything? Cinda clutched reflexively at her abdomen. "You said you know something about cars. This is an elevator car. So do something."

"Ma'am, my expertise is with the four-wheeled variety that tear around racetracks for huge amounts of money."

Suffering a pang of doubt about this heroic-looking man's ability to cope in this situation, Cinda breathed through her physical pain and pointed to the emergency phone behind its glass case. "Try calling some-one, Mr. Cooper." She took a few more puffing breaths. "Because if my labor progresses much fur-ther, the two of us are quickly going to become the three of us."

He blanched. "Then you have got to stop doing that whole labor pains thing."

Cinda tried not to double over. "I would if I could, trust me. My baby's early. We didn't expect this. So *do* something—and do it before I have to name this child Otis."

"Otis?"

"After the man who invented the elevator. Now, do something."

"Good idea." Trey Cooper whipped around, opened the case, and lifted the telephone receiver. But before he put it to his ear, he treated her to a surly "why-me" expression. "So where's your husband? I'm of a mind to throttle him but good for not being the one here with you right now."

Cinda's labor pain receded. She inhaled deeply, re-laxed, leaned against the wall behind her, and said, very matter-of-factly, "It wouldn't do much good. Richard is dead."

Instant dismay and sympathy radiated from Trey Cooper's blue eyes. "Oh, hell, I'm sorry. I didn't mean any disrespect. You're just so young. I never thought you'd be a widow."

She held his gaze. "Neither did I."

"No," he said quietly, "I guess you didn't."

Cinda had no idea what to say next. Apparently, neither did Trey. That left only the obvious between them to fill the gap—a pregnant silence. But as they stared at one another, a totally unexpected jet of sensual awareness sparked between them, catching Cinda off guard. Her gaze met and truly held his. Strangers across a crowded room...or a stuck elevator...whatever. It was as if they were the only two people in the world. The moment got warm, heating up with that whole man/woman thing. That kiss-me-now-big-boy feeling.

Still staring at Trey Cooper, Cinda blinked. She could not believe this. *Who'd have thought that in this ridiculous situation—and with me nine months pregnant—that now I'm going to feel a spark of connection, of attraction with some man?*

"So," Trey said a bit too loudly, breaking the spell between them, "what happened to your husband? Do you mind me asking?"

"No. I don't mind." Surprising her was the realization that she really didn't. In fact, she realized now that she *needed* to tell him, a stranger, about Richard's death, as well as the truth of how she felt about it—a truth she could hardly share with family and friends. "It was all really pretty stupid," she began. "And I'm still mad at him. In fact, I may never forgive him. You see, Richard was trying to go around the world in a hot-air balloon. You know the type—bored multimillionaire adventurer. Almost a cliché nowadays, right?"

"Sure."

He'd agreed with her, but his expression said he didn't have a clue about what she was talking about. Different worlds, she supposed. "Well, anyway, he was ballooning and something happened to the equipment. The sick joke was he finally ran out of hot air. Ha-ha. So there he was over Tibet and going down fast." Cinda paused and eyed Trey Cooper. "I know you're not going to believe this next part. The falling balloon frightened a herd of yaks.''

"Yaks?" Trey looked at her as if she'd said something as absurd as, well, *yaks.* "Those big, hairy buffalo-looking things with the horns, right?"

Cinda nodded. "Right. So, anyway, the basket hit the ground, and—" She inhaled deeply for courage and then pushed out her words. "—Richard spilled out. The impact probably killed him, but the yaks stampeded and...trampled him, pretty much sealing the deal."

Trey Cooper's features contorted with disbelief and horror. "Damn."

"Exactly. It was pretty bad all around."

"I'm sure it was." The man had not yet blinked. "That's quite a story."

"I know. And much stranger than fiction."

"I hear you. Well, still, I'm sorry for your loss."

"Thank you. And I thank you for not laughing. Some people have."

He shook his head. "Hey, I never laugh at death. My job revolves around the daily possibility of taking a permanent dirt nap—" His eyes rounded. "Oh, hell, excuse me. I didn't mean—"

"I know you didn't. It's okay."

"And I was just teasing about throttling your husband, Mrs. Cavanaugh. I'm not the violent type."

"Imagine my relief." Glad to have her story out, Cinda smiled at him. "Would you call me Cinda, please? Every time you say Mrs. Cavanaugh, I think my mother-in-law is behind me. And I have enough trouble right now without that image." Conjuring up Richard's mother sent a pang of disloyalty through Cinda. She looked down and away, then up at Trey

Cooper. "Look, about Richard. Please don't think I didn't care. I did. It's just that I'm mad at him—as silly as that sounds—for being so careless with his life."

"I can see how you would be."

"You're very kind. I keep telling myself I need to get over it. Richard *has* been gone awhile." Trey Cooper raised his eyebrows as he glanced the way of her pregnant belly. Cinda got his drift. "Well, not a *long* while. Nine months."

"Wow. That had to be tough...Cinda."

"It was." Something about the way he said her name sent a thrill rushing through her. He was so easy to talk to, so attentive and sympathetic that she almost forgot she was stuck in an elevator. "Richard was killed before I even realized I was pregnant, so obviously I never got to tell him."

Trey Cooper's expression morphed into the same one worn by people who are unwilling witnesses to a train wreck. "Cinda, does tabloid TV know about you? I swear, you keep this up and *I'm* going to be crying."

Embarrassed, Cinda bit down on her bottom lip. "I'm so sorry. I shouldn't be burdening you with all this." That was all she'd meant to say, but apparently today her psyche had a mind of its own. "Still, even if Richard had known about the baby, I don't think it would have changed anything between us. We were separated. I think. I mean I'd left him, but he didn't even realize it. Not for three days, anyway. But, oh well, that was our life."

The poor man trapped in here with her, a captive audience, just stared at her, his features a mask of sympathy.

Cinda put a hand to her forehead. "There I go again. All this voluntary sharing of mine. Could I *be* more Tennessee Williams? More Blanche DuBois, depending on the kindness of strangers? You'd think this elevator car was named Desire, instead of Otis."

"Hey, don't worry about it. All I want to know is what kind of idiot was Richard Cavanaugh not to have realized a woman like you wasn't around anymore? To me, that would be like not noticing that the sun didn't come up in the morning."

He couldn't be more wonderful. Sudden shyness, and a telling prick of tears, assailed Cinda. "Thank you. I needed that—especially in this condition." She rubbed her rounded belly. Trey Cooper stared at her...warmly, openly. That awareness bug was flying around them again. Cinda quickly pointed to the phone he held in his hand. "Maybe now would be a good time to try that emergency number."

"Right." He put the receiver to his ear, listened, and then shook his head in apparent disbelief. "As long as you live, you are not going to believe this. The line is busy."

"What?"

"I'm not lying. It's busy."

Cinda swallowed the rising panic in her throat. "Busy? How can it be busy? It's the emergency phone for *this* elevator—and we're the only ones in it."

"Believe me, I'm aware of that. Maybe whatever knocked out the elevator, took out the phone, too. Add Edison to your list of inventors to hate right now." He hung up the phone and then stuck his hands in his pants pockets. "Somewhere in here is a...aha, there it is."

He pulled out a pocketknife and held it up for her

inspection. "Never leave home without it." He opened the knife and turned away from her to face the control panel.

This couldn't be good. Cinda peeked around him to see what he might be doing. *Dear God.* He was unscrewing the metal facing plate over the buttons that marked each floor. She put a hand on his arm. "Trey, what are you doing?"

He spared her a glance. "Taking this panel off. Underneath, there should be miles of wiring. Maybe I can figure out which ones to hot-wire and get this elevator back on the fast track again."

Cinda's knees stiffened with her disbelief. "You can't do that."

"Actually, I probably can." His expression radiated confident good humor. "You're the one who told me to do something, remember."

"Well, quit listening to me. What do I know? My point is this is not a '56 Chevy. And I would appreciate it if you would *not* fiddle with the wires. You could blow us up."

He shook his head, unfazed. "That's only if there's a bomb. The worst I could do is fool with the wrong wires and send us hurtling down in a free fall to the basement."

"Well, thank God for that," she said brightly, falsely. Cinda stared at his handsome but possibly crazy profile and retreated to the back wall. "I'm doomed. And so is my baby."

Trey reached out and gave her arm a reassuring squeeze. "Hey, don't give up on me so easily. I have lots of ideas. If I can't hot-wire the thing, I'll remove that ceiling panel up there and climb out on top of the car—"

"*No* you will not." Cinda sternly stared at her companion. "You absolutely *will not*."

He stepped back. "Are you always this bossy, Cinda?"

"Are you always this impractical, Trey?"

A flash of anger sparked in his eyes. "What's so impractical about trying to get us out of here?"

Suddenly, he was acting like Richard Cavanaugh all over again—all strut and no substance, not someone she could rely on. "Look, Trey, there are two things here you are not going to do. One, you are *not* going to do anything to get yourself killed. And two, you are not leaving me here alone. I have been there and done that. And I am not going through it again."

"All right." He flipped his knife closed and shoved it back in his pocket. "You got any better ideas?"

Cinda cast about in her mind—only to suddenly realize that she should have been casting about in her handbag instead. She suddenly brightened. "Yes I do. I can't believe I didn't think of it before now. My cell phone. It's in my purse. We can call someone."

Trey Cooper's suddenly radiant expression said he forgave her doubting him. He stretched his arms wide, as if he meant to hug her. "Bless this technological age. We are saved. I could kiss you, Cinda Cavanaugh. And I just might do it, too."

2

CINDA'S INSIDES FLUTTERED. What would Trey's kiss be like? But then reality—which included her pregnancy, her ill-timed labor, and their current situation—set in and she looked away from his lips. "Not now," she chirped, knowing she didn't really mean it and that he probably hadn't, either. "But I will take a rain check."

His eyes warmed. "You got it."

Her gaze locked with his. That intense, totally inappropriate awareness again flowed between them.

Then, feeling silly in the face of his flirting with her, Cinda busied herself with rummaging around in her purse. "I call my handbag Wonder Purse. Everyone teases me about its size. But every time anyone needs something, it's in here."

"I'll believe you if you pull an obstetrician out of there."

"Wouldn't we both be surprised? But I can do the next best thing. I can call one. My doctor's office is on the fifteenth floor of this very building." Cinda kept up her rummaging, telling herself that she was not undergoing another labor pain. She began to sweat. No such luck. It was a definite labor pain. Her hand closed around her slim cell phone. She pulled it out and shoved it into Trey's hands. "Here. You'll have to dial. Pain. Another one."

"Oh, no. Hang on, Miss Cinda. Hold on to me if it helps." He held his arm out for her. Cinda clutched at him as if he were a life preserver. And in a way, if these pains came any faster, he very well might be. "Squeeze hard," he said. "I don't mind. What's your doctor's number?"

Between shortened breaths, Cinda told him. He dialed, evidently got somebody and began—very calmly and practically—relating the emergency to Dr. Butler's office staff. Cinda's pain receded. Still clutching Trey's arm, she rested her forehead against his muscled bicep. Even through his clothing, she could feel that he was big and strong and warm. Tears of gratitude for a solid, if temporary, presence to lean on, filled her eyes. She'd never had this with Richard, this support, this steadfastness. Not in the five years of their marriage.

Cinda now realized she'd been wrong about this man. He wasn't at all like the late Richard Cavanaugh. Instead, Trey Cooper was a rock, solid and dependable. And kind. She looked up at him, afraid her heart was in her eyes.

"Hey, no crying," he said tenderly, tipping her chin up with his free hand. With great casualness he planted a kiss on her forehead. "The nurse is getting your doctor. Evidently somebody's already called building maintenance about the elevator being stuck. They're working on it now. And the receptionist will call for an ambulance on the other line. So everything is going to be fine, all right?"

Cinda started to thank him, but he gestured for her not to speak as he listened to whatever was being said to him on the phone. Finally, he nodded and said, "Hello, Dr. Butler. Trey Cooper here. Yes, she's right here with me, although I'd venture to say she'd prefer being with you.'' Grinning—a killer one that exposed an expanse of white and even teeth—he handed Cinda the phone.

She took it, putting it to her ear as she pushed her thick shoulder-length hair back. ''Dr. Butler? Oh, thank God. Yes, I'm fine. For the moment, at least. How many pains? Two. Maybe three. No, they're not that bad…I guess. I don't know. I've never had labor pains before. What? No, not very long. But I think they're getting closer and harder. Okay. Here he is.'' She held the phone out to Trey. ''She wants to talk to you.''

''Me?'' Frowning, Trey took the phone. ''Hello?'' As he listened, his eyes widened and he stared at Cinda. ''Her what? Birthing coach, if it comes to that? Oh, ma'am, we can't let it come to that. Miss Cinda told me this baby is breach—what? That means it's turned sideways? It is?'' Sweat broke out on his brow. He ran a hand over his mouth. ''Oh, lordy. No, I'm fine. I'll do it. What? Hold on, and I'll tell her.'' He focused on Cinda. ''She's on her cordless phone. She and her nurse are already taking the stairs to meet us in the lobby when we get there.''

When we get there. Such a wonderful phrase. Still, Cinda had her reservations. ''She's running down fifteen flights of stairs? That poor woman. She ought to be in great shape when she gets to the lobby.''

''She'll be fine, Cinda. And so will we…if there's a God. In the meantime, I'm to relay her instructions to you and, uh, do what she says.''

Knowing what a birth coach had to do—and see— Cinda understood his hesitation and felt her face flame. ''Maybe you won't have to do anything. I haven't had a contraction now for a few—" A sudden, hard pain tore across her abdomen and cut her breath off. She clutched at Trey and the handrail, and began her breathing exercises. "Okay, this one's bad. Talk to her. Tell her. See what to do. Oh, God."

Trey was wild-eyed. "It's bad," he said to the doctor. "She's having a pain. Time it? I can't. She's holding on to my arm. I can't get to my watch and hang on to this phone at the same time. What? Tell her to breathe?" With great pomp and seriousness, he told Cinda, "Breathe."

Feeling as if her insides were being torn apart, Cinda shrieked, "I am, you jackass."

"She is, you jackass," Trey yelled into the cell phone before catching himself. "No. Wait. Sorry. Not you. I didn't mean—do what?" The color drained from the man's face. "Oh, I don't think so. I can't— okay, okay, I will." He focused on Cinda and exhaled. "This is *not* my idea. But your doctor wants you to, uh, disrobe from the waist down. She says I may have to check your—"

"You'll. Check. Nothing," Cinda snarled, her upper lip actually curling. "You tell her I said people in hell want ice water, too, but do they get it? No. Not in a million years."

Trey eyed her warily and spoke into the phone. "She said—oh, you heard that. What? You want *me* to breathe now?" He did. Deeply, slowly.

The elevator car lurched. Cinda gasped. Trey cursed. "It's the elevator," he explained to Dr. Butler on the other end of the line. "It jumped or something. Yes, we're okay. Maybe. Wait. Hold on. I think it's— yes, it is. It's moving."

As if it had never been problematical, the elevator

car began a smooth and controlled descent. With her pain easing, Cinda stared up at Trey, wanting him to corroborate for her that she hadn't lost her mind. "We are moving downward, right? And not in a free fall, right?"

"Right." He then enthusiastically told her doctor, "Yes, Dr. Butler. We're apparently on our way. Where are you now? The fourth floor? Wow. You must be a world-class sprinter. Us?" He looked up to the lighted panel overhead. "Eight...seven. We're on our way. Yeah. See y'all in the lobby." He punched the end button and handed Cinda the cell phone, which she plopped into her purse. "Dr. Butler's meeting us in the lobby," he said, as if reassuring himself as much as her. "With any luck, the ambulance has already arrived."

Another mechanical lurch—a last-gasp one that didn't slow the car down any—had Cinda clumsily falling into Trey's embrace. With his coat open and only his chambray shirt between her and his bare skin, his body felt warm and solid, his scent clean and masculine. His arms about her made her feel the safest she'd felt since before she'd left her parents' home to marry Richard. "I'm sorry for speaking to you like I did. And thank you for staying with me."

His chuckle rumbled in his chest and vibrated pleasantly against her ear. "No apology necessary. But before you get all sentimental, remember that I didn't have any other choices open to me."

Cinda pulled back and looked up at him. "Still, I don't think you're the sort who would have left me even if you'd been able to."

Looking suddenly embarrassed, he said, "You're right. I would have stuck it out." He frowned. "That didn't sound right. What I mean is, I'd have stayed with you.''

AND STAY HE DID. Trey reflected that he'd had no idea, when he'd spoken those words a few moments ago, just how true they'd become. But now he did. The elevator doors opened onto the lobby. A cheering crowd, a virtual welcoming committee, met them. To him, the participants looked more like they belonged at a disaster scene, instead of at the celebration of a new life.

Outside, double-parked in the vehicle-clogged street were the blinking emergency lights of an ambulance, a fire truck, and several police cars—as well as a crowd of curious gawkers, some with cameras. Inside the lobby were several police officers warning people to stay back. Included among the bystanders were two smiling mechanics in greasy overalls. Obviously the heroes who'd fixed the elevator. With them were two emergency medical technicians, one to either side of a waiting gurney. In front of the crowd stood a woman in a white coat—Dr. Butler, presumably—pretty, dark-eyed, blessedly knowledgeable and in charge. A pony-tailed nurse who looked twelve years old but was clad in surgery scrubs stood behind the doctor. The only thing lacking was a partridge in a pear tree.

Though somewhat taken aback by the scene, Trey nevertheless started forward with Cinda at his side. They weren't even out of the car, though, before everyone rushed forward and began talking at once. Cinda was tugged away from him by the paramedics and gently lifted onto the gurney. Then, with Dr. Butler and her nurse pacing alongside, they all hustled toward the exit. Trey stood where he was, just watching, figuring his involvement had ended. He should be glad, he told himself. And he was—for her. But a pang of something inside him told him he wasn't ready for her to leave him just yet.

Just then, one of the mechanics came over and surprised Trey by shaking his hand and congratulating him on his impending fatherhood. Apparently hearing this, one of the police officers pushed him forward— toward the ambulance outside.

"But I'm not—" was all he could get out as he was hustled onward.

Outside, the crowd parted and Cinda was loaded into the ambulance. Dr. Butler climbed in. So did her nurse. One of the paramedics jogged around to the front, obviously the driver. The other EMT—a big guy who could have played football for a pro team— latched on to Trey's arm and cheerfully tried to haul him inside. "Come on, Dad. We're burning daylight here. Get in."

Trey resisted. "But I'm not—"

"It's okay. We've seen this nervousness before. In you go."

And in he went. And away they went, the siren clearing the way for them. Standing at the back of the boxlike interior of the emergency vehicle, Trey tried his level best not to be in the way. He watched as people who knew what they were doing went about doing what they knew to do for Cinda and her baby. Evidently, from Cinda's groaning and Dr. Butler's steady, quiet voice alternately giving orders and soothing her patient, things were progressing a lot quicker than anyone would have liked. Trey realized his mouth was dry and his palms were sweaty. He didn't want to watch such a personal moment for Cinda, but he was pretty much forced to by sheer proximity.

The ride to the hospital, with the ambulance dodging and skirting New York traffic, was, to Trey, like some wild and pitching ride at Six Flags Over Georgia. To keep from being tossed about and becoming the next patient, he hung on to a bolted-down metal shelf about shoulder height to him. In a blessedly few minutes, though each one had seemed like hours to him, they were pulling into the emergency bay of a big hospital. The back doors opened. More medical types in hospital greens reached in and hauled Trey out, again tossing him to one side as they concentrated on assisting Dr. Butler and her nurse with Cinda on the gurney. The EMTs who'd brought them here grabbed Trey up again, calling him Dad and carrying him along in their wake.

Trey was beyond protesting. Instead, he found himself wondering if this much hoopla accompanied every birth…and decided it should. A whole new life was about to happen. A fresh little soul was coming into the world. His stomach knotted with giddy nervousness. He was going to be a father. Wait. No he wasn't. Everyone just thought he was. But it was still exciting—and scary. Cinda was in so much pain. As they all swept along a narrow corridor and through swinging doors, Trey among them, he wanted to shout for them to do something…which of course they were. And very capably.

Suddenly a folded set of surgery greens were shoved into Trey's hands by a short, sturdy nurse with a face that reminded him of a bulldog. Apparently, he'd been handed off. Sure enough, she shunted him down another corridor.

"Put these on in there, Dad." She pointed to a closed door in a wall of doors they were approaching. "Leave on your undershorts and your shoes. You'll find shoe covers and a hair net under the shirt there. Use them. Take off your watch and any jewelry you might have on. Stay here until I come get you. The door will automatically lock when you step out of the dressing room, so don't do that. And once in the surgery room, try to stay out of the way. If you get sick or pass out at a critical moment, you're on your own. You got all that?"

Trey nodded. She reached past him to unlock and open the door. Revealed was a tiny closet of a room with a few pegs for clothes and a wooden ledge for a seat. She firmly ushered him inside it. The overhead light in the claustrophobic cubicle spotlighted him like a trapped insect. He stumbled in, again protesting, "But I'm not the—"

"Save it. You'll be fine. Won't see a thing but your wife's head. Talk nice to her and stay out of our way. I'll give you five minutes to change. My name is Peg. You do everything I tell you, and we'll get along just fine. You got all that?"

What else could he say? "Yes, ma'am...Peg."

"Good." She closed the door.

In the entombing quiet, Trey stared at the shirt and pants he held. This was serious. No way was he going into that room and witness...a birth. He'd only come to New York City to take care of some team business. Didn't it figure that the lawyer's office was in that damned building with the crotchety elevator?

It suddenly occurred to him that he could just leave. In his mind's eye, he saw himself doing that, sneaking out—and getting caught by Peg. That did it. Trey quickly began shedding his clothes and pulling on the hospital garb. He didn't doubt for one minute that the nurse was standing right outside the closed door and would haul him into the delivery suite in his underwear and socks, if he wasn't ready.

In only a couple more minutes, Trey had everything on and was tying the drawstring at his waist when the door unceremoniously opened to reveal Peg standing there. She stared disapprovingly at him. Trey had the absurd notion that he should come to attention, like he had during his stint in the army. Peg gave him a formal once-over. "You'll do. Let's go."

Again Trey hesitated. He took a step back into the safety of his cubicle. "Look, I'm not the father—"

"Right." Peg advanced on him and grabbed his arm, hauling him along after her. "That's what they all say. And everyone in prison is innocent."

Two HOURS LATER, Trey sat glassy-eyed and alone in one of the father's waiting rooms off the wing of delivery suites. He hadn't even bothered yet to take off his paper hair net. Slouching on an ugly vinyl seat, one of many pushed up against a sickly green wall, he stared at a blaring TV suspended in a traylike holder from the ceiling. But he didn't really see or hear a thing that was external. Inside, though, he was humming. He'd seen a baby girl come into the world. He'd never seen anything like that before. Not that there was anything he could compare it to. A whole new and tiny person. And not too happy to be here, either, judging by her squalling when Dr. Butler had held her up.

Chelsi Elise, her groggy mother had named her.

Healthy, chubby, perfect. Honey-gold hair, and a fully functioning set of lungs.

Trey sniffed. Okay, so he'd got caught up in the excitement. So he'd shed a tear and had whooped his joy. That was when Dr. Butler had noticed him and had told everyone he really wasn't the father. Or the husband. Not even the boyfriend. He was just the guy who got stuck in the elevator with the mother. A stranger.

Peg had damn near pinched his head off once she'd gotten him out of the delivery room. She'd told him to stay in the waiting room and not to move. And he hadn't. Not that he was afraid of her. She just reminded him of his drill sergeant from boot camp. Oliver Dimwitty. That man was so mean, not one recruit had ever dared make a joke about the guy's name.

The double doors into the waiting area whooshed open. In walked Dr. Butler, Peg riding shotgun at her hip. Trey sat up straighter, watching the doctor pull her hair cover off and sit down next to him. Peg stood behind the doctor, her arms folded over her chest. Trey focused on the friendlier figure of Cinda's and Chelsi's deliverer. Dr. Butler really was a beautiful woman, he noticed again. Rich chocolate-brown hair. Big brown eyes. An easy smile. But more importantly, a keen intellect shone from her eyes. She grinned at him. "You doing okay? I didn't mean to get you kicked out."

Trey avoided looking at Peg. "I know. So…how're they doing?"

"They're both great. Chelsi weighs seven pounds, eight ounces and is twenty inches long. A healthy little girl who has the good fortune to look like her mother. And Mom's doing well, too. A bit groggy but okay."

Trey realized his heart was hammering and he was eating up every detail…just like a new father. Which he wasn't. "Well, that's good," he said, trying to sound nonchalant. "I'm glad to hear that. It was touch-and-go there for a bit in the elevator. But all's well that ends well, thanks to you."

Dr. Butler smiled. "And to you. You were pretty cool during that emergency in the elevator."

Trey shook his head. "You can say that because you weren't in there when I tried to climb the wall. Literally."

She laughed. "No one would have blamed you, either." Her smile slowly faded into a frankly assessing expression. "But it's not over yet. Not if you don't want it to be."

Trey frowned. "What do you mean?"

"Cinda said she'd like to see you. And thank you."

Trey caught his excited grin before it could come fully to his face. He couldn't become attached here. Cinda was not his wife, and Chelsi was not his baby. A wife and a baby were two things he'd postponed, given all the traveling he had to do. And he'd heard enough from Cinda to know he was the last thing she needed, after her late husband's antics. The truth was, he needed to walk away. Now. So, taking a deep breath and letting go reluctantly, he said, "Well, that's real nice of her, but—"

"Do it. Just get up and let's go." That was, of course, Peg. She held her pudgy hand out to him and waggled her fingers. "Come on. Get up. I'll take you to her."

Trey gaped at the stocky woman and then spoke to Dr. Butler. "I see why you brought her."

Dr. Butler chuckled and glanced up at Peg before

focusing again on Trey. "You'll have to forgive us. Cinda's become quite special to all of us. She's been through a rough time, Mr. Cooper. And I don't mean just today."

His serious expression matched hers. "I know. She told me about her husband. That was tragic."

"Yes, as absurd as the circumstances were, it *was* tragic. I don't know you, but you look like a decent sort. A nice man. We're bending the rules here by allowing you to see her since you're not family. But Cinda asked for you. And I trust her instincts. Just so you'll know, at Cinda's request, the nurses have called her and her late husband's families. They'll all arrive soon. No doubt with enough flowers and toys to spill out into the hallway. But you still have a few minutes of quiet time. That is, if you want to see her."

Trey stood up. "I do. And thank you, Dr. Butler."

She stood along with him. "You're welcome. I've got to go. The pediatrician is checking the baby over, so I'm going to attend that. I'll turn you over to Peg's tender mercies, and she'll take you to Cinda's suite." With that, the doctor strode confidently across the room and out the door.

Arching an eyebrow, Trey eyed Peg. "Lead on. I'd follow you anywhere."

She narrowed her eyes at him. "Hmph. My first husband was a Southerner. Biggest mistake I ever made. North/South marriages never work." She spun around, heading for the same double doors, obviously expecting Trey to follow her, which he wisely did. "So don't you try any of your silver-tongued-devil charm on me because it won't work, Mister Kiss My Grits. Besides, I'm a married woman again."

Trey grinned at the short woman's broad back and

stocky legs. "Yes, ma'am. Just tell me this, please. Why are the good ones always taken?"

Over her shoulder, she said, "They're not. At least, Mrs. Cavanaugh isn't."

COVERED BY BLANKETS, pale and breathing shallowly, Cinda Cavanaugh lay on her back. Her eyes were closed. Faint purple shadows formed half-moon crescents under her eyes. She was still dressed in an unflattering hospital gown that did nothing, in Trey's opinion, to detract from her blond, patrician good looks. There was an IV needle stuck in her arm. A bag of so-labeled glucose hanging from a hook on its wheeled stand slowly dripped the fluid into her system. On her other side, some kind of vital-signs-monitoring machine crouched protectively, ticking and beeping away.

Believing her to be asleep, Trey sat quietly beside the bed, which was the centerpiece in a posh and elegant suite. Well, she *had* said her husband was a millionaire. *Her late husband,* he amended, recalling Peg's parting words. He smiled. Not once had Peg or Dr. Butler asked him if he was "taken." Maybe he gave off "single" vibes accompanied by visible-only-to-females blinking neon arrows that pointed to him.

Just then, Cinda opened her eyes and rolled her head. She caught sight of him. A weak but warm smile came to her generous mouth. She blinked and ran the tip of her tongue over her pink lips. "Hey, you're here," she said, her voice sounding scratchy. "Look at you. You could be a doctor."

A thrill chased through Trey...at her smile for him, at her wanting him to be here. He looked down at the hospital greens he still wore and tugged the hair net off his head. "What? These old things? They were just hanging in the closet."

Cinda managed another smile, this one warmer and saying more than her words. "I'm glad you're here, Mr. Trey Cooper."

His heart fairly leaping now, and more affected than he was willing to admit—he really had to get away from this woman before it was too late to escape—Trey leaned forward. "I'm glad you're glad." Then he didn't know what to say. The silence grew thick. Finally he remembered Peg's parting orders. "Hey, you want some water or something? The nurse said you should drink if you woke up."

Cinda's chuckle instantly became a grimace of pain. She shifted cautiously about in the bed, putting a hand to her much flatter belly. "Ow," was her first comment. Then, after another moment, she said, "I was laughing—or trying to—about the medical confirmation that I should drink. In that case, you got any gin you can put in the water?"

Even now she was witty. Trey liked that. He snapped his fingers. "Darn. I knew I forgot something. You want me to run out and get you a six-pack of beer or a nice wine in a paper bag?"

She offered him a quick grin, then became more sober. "Listen, I really am glad you're here. I was afraid you might have left. I wanted to thank you for everything. I don't know what I would have done without you."

"It was nothing." Trey was as uncomfortable as he was pleased. This woman troubled him. She could make him want something he could never have. He stood up and went to the pitcher of ice water that sat on the bedside tray, grabbed up the plastic cup, and poured the water into it. He stuck the bendy straw into the cup and handed it to her. "Here you go," he said cheerfully…too cheerfully.

He watched her take tiny sips of the cold water and swallow. After a moment, he felt compelled to speak again. "You don't have to thank me, Cinda. I did what anybody would do, which really wasn't anything, if you'll think about it. So please don't read more into it than that."

Cinda's caramel-gold eyes…such unusual coloring…met his gaze and held. In the next few silent seconds she seemed to read his mind. It was as if she could see his hesitation, his wariness of her…his reluctance to become involved with an uptown girl. A wounded smile tilted her lips. She handed him the water cup and rested her hands against her stomach.

As he set the cup down on the table next to her bed, she said, "You're right, of course. Still, I'm grateful for your presence in that elevator, if nothing else. But it could have been a lot worse for me and my baby and you. Had it been, I…well, let me put it this way— if I'm ever stuck on a deserted island, I now know who I'd want to be stranded with."

Trey allowed himself a grin. "Thanks for that. You're a great lady. And a new mother. Congratulations." She beamed a smile his way, making his heart flutter. He looked around the hospital room. "I guess I could have gotten you some flowers or something. Or a stuffed animal for the baby. But Peg wouldn't allow any detours on the way here."

She frowned. "Peg?"

"She's a nurse. And a drill sergeant in a former life. All I can say is do everything she tells you to. Even if it hurts."

"I'll try to remember that."

The moment to leave was here.

"Well," Trey said, "I've got to go. And I'm sure you can do with some sleep. Again, it was..." He was dying inside and couldn't seem to look away from the "please-don't-go" look in her eyes. "It was nice to meet you. I won't ever be able to get into an elevator again without thinking of you and Otis and Wonder Purse."

She blinked and lowered her gaze. When she again met his eyes, her expression was controlled. She lifted a hand and held it out to him. Trey took a deep breath, hating the leave-taking, hating the staying, and then clasped her warm, long fingers in his hand. He had to fight the urge to raise her soft hand to his lips.

"Trey," she said, somehow giving his nickname a depth it had never before possessed, "Thank you. I owe you one, as they say. A big one. You won't ever be able to convince me that you did anything less than save my life and my baby's. I really wish you'd tell me how I can repay you."

He released her hand before things progressed to the point where he wouldn't let go because he couldn't. In his mind's eye, he saw Nurse Peg wielding a scalpel to cut him away from this fabulous woman. "Repay me, huh? Well, I suppose that maybe one day you could save *my* life. That'd be a fair trade."

Cinda surprised him by saying, "You've got a deal. Hand me that notepad and the pen there on the table, please. I want to give you my phone number. One day when you need me, you can call."

Though he really didn't think he should, Trey did as she asked and waited while she wrote down her number. Striving to keep things light, he remarked,

"Will you just look at what's happening here? I swear, all those nights I've wasted in bars. I never once thought to cruise a maternity ward looking to pick up chicks. And now here's a gorgeous one giving me her number."

Shaking her head and, grinning, Cinda folded the piece of paper and handed it to him. "You Southern gentlemen will be the death of me one day. I swear, how anyone could think I could be gorgeous at this moment is beyond me."

Now, flirting he could do. "I've got eyes. I can see. You're gorgeous."

"And you're too kind."

"Never." He fisted his hand protectively around her phone number. He told himself he wouldn't keep it. It wasn't right. She was just emotional right now and had that hero-worship thing going. By tomorrow, she'd probably regret giving her number to him, a grease monkey in a dangerous profession. "Well, Mrs. Cavanaugh, I've got to be going." He forced cheer into his voice. "I think I might drop by the viewing window to peek in at your little girl and then I've got to get back to my hotel. It's late and there's a plane with my name on it leaving early tomorrow morning. You and your daughter take care now, ya hear?"

"I hear," she said.

He met her gaze. Trey feared she could see right into his heart and could see what he didn't want her to know...that already, in only a matter of hours after meeting her, he didn't like the thought of having no part in her life. But when she spoke again, her voice was tinged with finality. "Goodbye, Mr. Trey Cooper."

3

IN THE LAVISH NURSERY of the huge and elegant Atlanta showcase home she'd lived in with Richard, Cinda sat playing with six-month-old Chelsi. The phone rang. Every nerve ending in Cinda's body jumped. This was ridiculous, and she knew it. If the man hadn't called her in the past six months, what made her think he'd choose today to do it? But she'd seen in the paper this morning that the Jude Barrett racing team was back home in Atlanta. That meant Trey Cooper was, too, and could call if he wanted to.

But he hadn't. So obviously, he didn't want to. That knowledge didn't keep Cinda from waiting, her heart thumping heavily, as Major Clovis answered it in the next room. She could hear the older woman talking but couldn't hear what she said. Cinda held her breath. Could this finally be him?

Come on, Cinda, her conscience railed at her. *This is really a bad crush you have here. You'd think that after six months without a call, you'd be over him. And what about you? You can't call? You looked up his number in the phone book, but you haven't used it. So get over it.* But she couldn't. He'd been this nice, handsome guy who'd stood by her during her worst possible moment. So maybe she just had a bad case of hero worship. Maybe. She tried not to look desperately up at her regimentally formal assistant/nurse/social secretary who entered the nursery with the cordless phone in her hand.

The afternoon's late-June sunlight filtered through the sheer curtains at the windows across the room. Major Irene Clovis—a no-nonsense older woman with severely short gray hair—walked in and out of sun and shadow as she approached her employer. "Hate to ruin your day, ma'am, but it's The Real Mrs. Cavanaugh."

Disappointment ate at Cinda. It wasn't him. It was never him. She groaned and slumped over her legs. "Not her again, Major. Not my mother-in-law."

"My apologies," her unsmiling ex-Marine assistant said. "I told Dragon Lady that you'd dyed your hair and the baby's purple and the two of you had run off with the drug-selling leader of a motorcycle gang. I further said the two of you were now known as Hell's Belles. But she didn't believe me."

"I can't imagine why not. But still, you always know just what to say, Major." Cinda's grimace over the caller's identity warred with a grin that tugged at her lips. Major Clovis was the most outrageous and loyal person Cinda had ever met. She also harbored all the love and protective instincts of a lioness toward Cinda and Chelsi. "Thanks for trying."

"Yes, ma'am. Next time, I'll tell her you became a Buddhist monk and sold the only Cavanaugh heir to a zoo in Berlin as part of their mammalian exchange program. That ought to do it." With that, she handed Cinda the phone, did a smart military about-face, and precision-marched toward the door.

Bemused, Cinda watched her go. When Major Clovis reached the open door, she neatly executed a left turn and disappeared from sight around a corner. No doubt she was going to torture poor Marta in the kitchen. Not because the cook had done anything wrong, but simply because the ex-military nurse *could* hassle her—and because the tiny Hispanic woman was terrified of her. Cinda fully expected their wary stand-off to one day erupt into a weapon-based free-for-all. She hoped she wasn't home when it happened.

Sighing over her staff's ongoing bilingual and multicultural altercations, Cinda put a hand over the telephone's speaker and whispered to Chelsi. "It's Grandma. The big scary one in New York City."

The bright-eyed baby girl pulled a face, as if she were about to cry. "Oh, honey, I know," Cinda sympathized, taking a chubby little hand in hers and leaning over to kiss the tiny fingers. "Everyone has that reaction. But she loves you and has your best interest at heart. How many times this week has she told me that, huh?" The baby's expression instantly cleared.

"That's my girl." Then, forcing cheerfulness into her voice for her caller, Cinda spoke into the phone. "Hello, Mother Cavanaugh. How nice to hear from you. How are you?"

Sitting on the carpeted floor of the nursery and listening to her mother-in-law's familiar opening harangue, Cinda winked at her baby, who had her own problems. Perched on her diapered bottom atop a large quilted square of colorful blanket, the blond little girl wobbled tipsily, trying to keep her balance. To Cinda's mother's mind, Chelsi's controlled sitting at six months of age, while a completely normal activity in the development of babies according to the pediatrician, became the newest evidence of her daughter's extreme intelligence and precociousness. A trait she'd inherited from Cinda's side of the family, of course.

Cinda tuned in again to her mother-in-law in time

to hear her ask a question, which Cinda promptly answered. "No, Major Clovis isn't drunk. Or on drugs. But I *didn't* hire her. Richard did. I think. Or she came with the house. One of those. Yes, I'll speak to her about her shocking tales that upset you." But Cinda knew she wouldn't say a word to Major Clovis. Her shocking tales were too funny and too deserved.

The conversation moved on to the weather. "Yes, I've seen the weather report. We do have television in the South now. Yes, it *is* hot in New York City, isn't it? I'm sure you'll be glad to leave next week for the Hamptons. Oh, you're too kind, but we really couldn't join you. *No* we can't. Why?" *Because I flat out don't want to. Because I'm tired of your subtle manipulation of me, your digs at my family, and your blatant disappointment that Chelsi is not a boy.* "I'm afraid something's come up down here," was what she actually said, though, being nice but with an effort. "A thing. Yes. I told you about it." She hadn't. There was no thing. "The important thing with the people I told you about. Over at that place. Yes. That thing."

Cinda silently begged her tiny daughter not to judge her mother too harshly for lying to The Real Mrs. Cavanaugh, as everyone in this household referred to the imperious blue-blooded Ruth Heston Cavanaugh. The woman allowed no one to forget her graciousness in overlooking the fact that the late Richard the Second's only child was female. Oh, the heartbreak of it all. Now there was no one to carry on the Cavanaugh name. As if they were royalty with their own country. Okay, so they owned most of this one. Big deal.

"Oh, I don't believe we can come after the thing is over," Cinda quickly answered the next demand. "Chelsi has a doctor's appointment later this month.

No. Nothing's wrong. There isn't. I'd tell you if there were. I promise. She's fine.'' *If you don't count the fact that she's sprouted another head and gargoyle wings.* It was what she wanted to say, Major Clovis style, but didn't.

"Still, I thank you for inviting us. Yes, I'll keep it in mind if anything changes here. No, I'm not moving back to New York. Because I like it here. I just do. My life is here now. I have friends, social clubs, volunteer work, all that right here. Besides, the weather is better for the baby's health.'' *And my sanity.* "So we'll be staying here. I'm sorry you don't like my decision, but there it is.''

Cinda took the receiver from her ear, gritted her teeth, and took a calming breath. Then smiling determinedly, she resettled the phone to her ear and said, "You give Papa Rick''—her father-in-law, she liked—"our love, okay? Yes, I know I sound 'dreadfully Southern' now. I like that, too. Okay. Talk to *y'all* later.''

Cinda pressed the off button and resisted the urge to toss the cordless phone across the room. Instead, she simply laid it beside her on the rug and smiled at Chelsi, whose blue eyes—so reminiscent of her father's—were rounded as she gnawed at her drool-soaked fist. "Teething is the pits, isn't it? You're going to suck all the good out of that thing, honey. Here.''

Cinda leaned over to pluck a toy—a cloth-covered replica of a stock car—out of the mix of toys surrounding them. She held it out to Chelsi, who batted cheerfully and ineffectually—but better than any other child her age could have done, mind you—at the toy, finally succeeding in getting it in her clutches. Joyously, she instantly stuffed as much of it as she could into her mouth and warily eyed her mother above it, as if she expected the toy to be plucked from her at any second.

Chuckling softly, Cinda stretched out until she was lying on her stomach and supporting her weight on her elbows. She contentedly watched her daughter's antics. "I know. It's your favorite toy," she said wistfully...knowing the baby didn't have a favorite toy at this age but it was Cinda's favorite one to give her. Because Trey Cooper had sent it for Chelsi months ago, along with his very platonic "Hope you're doing well, Trey Cooper" best-wishes card.

"Well, I'm not doing well," she whispered. "I miss you. You're all I think about. And you're home, Trey Cooper. I saw it in the papers." Only recently had Cinda taken to poring over the sports section. "Why don't you call me? Doesn't your life *ever* need saving?"

ON THE OUTSKIRTS of Atlanta, out on a prime piece of land that served as Jude Barrett's elite racing team's headquarters, Trey Cooper was leafing through his mail and frowning. Bill. Bill. Junk mail. Bill. Letter from Mom. Sweepstakes notice. *Finally. I've won ten million dollars.* He tossed it unopened into the wastebasket at his feet.

Still wearing his grimy service overalls, he sat perched atop a wooden stool out in the hangar-like garage. Behind him, up on the lift, being put through a checklist of fine-tuning, was the moneymaker herself. The bright red, shiny, sponsor-decal-covered racing car. Serving as background music was the whine of electric tools, the blare of country music from someone's radio, and the chatter and catcalls of the team members.

It was close to quitting time for the day. Trey's work—including a meeting with the big boss man himself in the front office—was done. He'd cleaned up a bit, got some of the grease off his hands and face, and combed his hair. This was his first chance to check his mail since he'd grabbed up a week's worth of it from his box at the post office earlier that morning. That's how frenetic this time of year was—he only managed to get by the post office about once a week.

Team Leader Mark Mason was on the phone behind Trey. It was a personal call, and Trey tried not to listen. But Mark's voice kept getting louder the longer he talked with his wife. It was a familiar refrain. All the married men here had fielded similar complaints from home. You're never here. The kids hardly know you. I miss you. Your mother's sick. The bills are overdue. On and on with some variation of that song. It was tough and divorces happened. A lot.

Trey felt for his friends and their families. The beefs at both ends were legitimate. But every time he heard them, Trey renewed his promise to himself not to have a family as long as he was on the race circuit. That didn't mean he didn't date and have relationships. He did. Well, he had. Although he hadn't felt too much like making the effort in the past six months or so.

He told himself he was just tired and overworked and thirty years old. All of that was true. But he also couldn't get a certain elegant blonde's face out of his mind. Every other woman had paled in comparison to his few frantic hours with Cinda Cavanaugh. Okay, so he could still see those unique caramel-colored eyes of hers. And, yes, so he still had her phone number folded up and stored in his wallet. He kept meaning to throw it away, but kept forgetting to do it, that was all.

So, why should he call her? What could he offer her that she, a multimillionaire's widow, couldn't get for herself? And, besides, she was probably already surrounded by lots of rich guys anxious to play Papa. So the last thing she needed was someone like him—a high-school-graduate grease monkey. A man with dirt under his fingernails and not enough money in the bank.

At this point in Trey's pity party, Mark hung up the phone...with force. Trey looked up from his stack of remaining mail to see his boss just standing there, his expression thunderous, his complexion red with anger...and worry.

"You okay, Mark?" Trey asked, knowing better but concerned nonetheless.

Mark ran a hand through his brown hair and shook his head. "Hell no. Diane's on a tear, man. All I can say is I'm lucky our team's days off are coming up next month. Everything at home seems to be hitting the fan, you know?"

He didn't—he thought of his quiet bachelor's apartment—but he could sympathize. "I hear ya, good buddy." Then Trey took a chance. "Hey, let me ask you something, Mark. I've been thinking about this. Tell me if it's none of my business. But...how do you do it? I mean the family, the hassles, the fights. The time away and the problems it causes. Here you've got a job you love that's making it all bad at home where you have a wife and kids you love. How do you keep it all together?"

Mark shrugged. Then a slow grin came to his face,

which was streaked with the grease and dirt of his job.
"It's like you said, man. Love. Pure love. Passion. For
your wife. For your job. It's got to be there—at home
and at work. It's like that for me and Diane. Yeah, we
fuss about things, but we always work it out." Mark
picked up a rag and began wiping his hands as he
turned a questioning glance on Trey. "So why you
asking?"

Trey felt his face heat up. He swiped a hand under
his nose and cleared his throat. "No reason. Just thinking, that's all."

Mark tossed the rag into a bin and crossed his arms.
A knowing but friendly smirk lit his fair features. "So
what's her name?"

"She doesn't have a name." Not one he was going
to give, anyway. "I mean there is no 'she.' No special
'she.' No one. Never mind."

Mark grinned devilishly. "Lord above, Trey Cooper's gonna take the bait and settle down. You've been
bitten by the lovebug, haven't you? That's why you've
been moping around since winter."

Trey frowned. "I don't mope. And how'd you get
all that out of what I said? I asked one innocent question. And now I'm in love."

"I didn't say it. You did." Mark crowed with
laughter and went off toward the other mechanics, no
doubt bent on ruining Trey's ladies' man reputation
with the guys. Knowing he'd only make things worse
with his protests, Trey shook his head and told himself
this was why men shouldn't talk about feelings. It
never ended well.

Then he remembered saying something like that,
about things not ending well, to Cinda when he'd first
seen her. Those elevator doors had opened...and there

she'd been. His heart had come close to jumping right out of his chest. He'd seen stars.

And now, six months later, it was like this: *And behind Door Number One, Mr. Trey Cooper, is the most beautiful woman you've ever seen, someone you could come to care deeply about. And she could possibly return your affection if you can answer one simple question. Are you ready, sir? Here's your question: How in the hell do you ever expect to have a chance with her if you don't call her, you big jerk?*

Trey's mood darkened. He'd call her if he had a reason. He knew that much. All he needed was a reason. A good one. Something legitimate, substantial. *Yeah, right.* Feeling deflated, he went back to sorting his mail when, sure enough, the men he worked with began whistling and laughing and calling out his name in a teasing way.

"Why don't y'all just shut up?" he yelled. But they didn't. Pointedly ignoring them, muttering "Bunch of third-graders," he turned over the next envelope…and frowned. The postmark was from his hometown of Southwood. And the return address was that of the Southwood High School Fighting Rebels Reunion Committee.

Reunion? He'd graduated twelve years ago, so this wasn't an anniversary year, like ten or fifteen. What could this be, then? He opened it and read the letter inside. And laughed. This was just like home. They'd let the ten-year mark slip up on them and pass…so they were having their ten-year get-together next month. How messed up was that?

Bemused, Trey read on. According to the letter, the committee hoped to make the reunion into a town-wide celebration by inviting the alumni from every

year of the school's existence to attend. About fifty
years' worth, as near as he could remember. Sounded
like fun. And a nightmare. Trey put the letter down
and caught sight of one he hadn't noticed before in
his pile of mail. The Tampa return address curdled his
stomach and made him want to bang his head on the
workbench in front of him. Bobby Jean Diamante.
Nothing like an old girlfriend to liven things up.

Trey sighed, caught up in kaleidoscopic reflections
of his and Bobby Jean's shared past. In high school,
when she and Trey had been an item, when he'd been
captain of the football team and she'd been head
cheerleader, when they'd both lost their virginity to
each other, she'd been Bobby Jean Nickerson. Then
at eighteen, she'd thrown Trey over and married a rich
man from Atlanta, who'd made her Bobby Jean
Whiteside.

After not too many years of wedded bliss, the much
older man had died. Some said mysteriously. Shortly
afterward, Bobby Jean married a slug who'd run
through her money. So she'd left him and had been
forced to marry again. The last Trey had heard—his
source being his mother—Bobby Jean had taken up
with, then married, some really rich but hard-nosed
guy from up north. His mother kept saying Mr. Rocco
Diamante had mob connections. Lovely.

Between husbands, Bobby Jean was hell-bent on
starting up again with Trey. She always called him her
one true love. And somehow, although he never intended to get sucked in by her scheming, he did.
Maybe it was the way she went about it that left him
no choice. She always involved his poor mother or
pulled some public stunt that left him no choice except
to get involved on some level. Some stunt like at the

upcoming reunion, maybe? How perfect would that be? Trey grimaced. He could see this one coming. Like a freight train. He really, really didn't want to be involved with Bobby Jean. But she went after him whole-hog and it never ended well. Once he disentangled himself and his family from her clutches, only embarrassment and gossip were left behind.

So what was she up to now? Trey picked up the scented envelope and opened it. On flower-embossed stationery, Bobby Jean—a staggeringly beautiful redhead, no doubt about it, but an overblown magnolia of a woman—told Trey how very excited she was to learn of the reunion. He read about how she was separated now and how her husband wasn't taking it very well. He was harassing her, she said. So she was looking forward to getting away from Tampa and going home for a weekend…the weekend of the reunion.

Trey cursed out loud, wondering what size concrete shoes he might wear. Bobby Jean was on the run from an unhappy mobster husband. Who didn't know he'd follow her right to Southwood—and right to Trey? He repeated his curse, only this time more emphatically. Life was no longer good. It was also about to become very short, if Bobby Jean had her way. But her next sentence curdled Trey's blood. She wrote that she understood from talking with Trey's mother last year that he—meaning Trey—still hadn't married. *Aw, man, not my poor mother.* The mobster husband didn't have to be a genius to trace that call and get the name and number.

Trey had to go home. He couldn't leave his mother to face that alone. He could just see her now, a petite, brown-haired woman who wore glasses, worked at the local bowling alley, and loved to bake and do needlepoint. She'd become a mother at the age of thirty-eight and a widow at the age of fifty, due to an unfortunate farming accident. Her only child was Trey, and she'd never lived anywhere but in Southwood, Georgia.

It was no wonder, then, that her life revolved around him and the many goings-on in her hometown. She was a goodhearted soul. To Trey, she had only one flaw. She liked Bobby Jean. She always said what pretty babies Trey and Bobby Jean could make together. Dorinda Cooper, Trey's mother, just thought it was so sad, the run of bad luck that poor Bobby Jean always seemed to have with men. Trey could only stare at her when she said that. *Run of bad luck? The woman was a black widow.*

Sitting there on the stool, Trey shook his head and refocused on the perfumed letter he held in his hand. No surprise here. Bobby Jean wrote that his mother was just the sweetest thing who thought Bobby Jean would make such a wonderful mother. Trey's old girlfriend then chastised him for not giving his mama grandbabies and went on to say how she sincerely hoped that the reason he'd never married had nothing to do with any lingering feelings he might harbor for her. She ended the letter by saying she was very excited about seeing him at the reunion. Trey could only wonder if she'd told her husband that, too. He scrubbed a hand over his face. *Oh, lordy. Between the two women, they're going to get me killed.*

Then, because he was sane, and because he was human, Trey considered not going to the reunion. Wouldn't that be the simplest solution? Sure. Until that irate mobster husband showed up on Trey's mother's doorstep. Just the thought of that had every protective fiber in Trey's body raising its hackles. *Aw, damn it all to hell. I've got to go. That damned Bobby Jean.* Trey knew in his bones that she'd use the reunion to make yet another disastrous play for him. That wasn't conceit on his part. It was knowing Bobby Jean. The woman could not be without a man. And Trey knew he was the man she didn't want to be without. In fact, she'd always let him know, even when she'd been married, that she wouldn't mind seeing him on the side.

Trey had never taken her up on that offer for a lot of reasons. For one, because she'd never wanted to marry him. She just wanted to sleep with him. To Trey's way of thinking, that type of relationship—using the term loosely—would cheapen them both. He also hadn't taken her up on her offer because he wasn't the type to get involved with a married woman. Even if her vows meant nothing to her, they did to him.

He was no saint. But he did respect marriage. Still, if he'd felt for her what she said she felt for him, he couldn't say that he might not have jumped at the chance to be with her. But he hadn't because he didn't have feelings for Bobby Jean. Not the ones she wanted him to have, at any rate. Trey actually felt sorry for her on some level. He supposed that meant he did care about her in a "childhood sweetheart" way. After all, she had been a big part of his youthful history and glory. Trey believed he owed her respect, if nothing else—respect she didn't ever seem to accord herself.

But all of that aside, he was in big trouble here. Trey eyed his mother's unopened letter. Even as he opened it, he felt certain he already knew what she'd written. He unfolded her letter and started reading. *Yep, I was right.* She wrote that he hadn't been home for any length of time in almost two years, and that she really wanted him to come home for this event. All his friends would be there, people he hadn't seen in years. Including Bobby Jean Diamante, who was separated now. Trey sighed and shook his head. *I'm a dead man.*

He picked up his reading again. The rest was haranguing him, in a loving way, yet again for not having a family. His mother always did this, bless her good heart, saying she hated to think of him being alone now because when she died, he'd be truly alone with no one to love him. How could she rest in her grave knowing that? Trey chuckled, recalling his mother's lecture the last time he'd been home. It had been more to the point of why she wanted him married.

You're thirty years old, Trey, and I'm not even a grandmother yet. How am I supposed to hold my head up at the bowling alley and, worse, the beauty shop? Every lady there except me has a string of grandbaby pictures to wag around and stick under my nose. And me sitting there under the dryer with not the first picture of a child to brag over. How am I supposed to feel when Lula Johnston says "Dorinda, that boy of yours hasn't made you a grandmother yet? What's wrong with him?"

Nothing, was Trey's answer to himself. He just hadn't met the right woman yet. The one who filled him with passion, like Mark Mason had just said. Suddenly the image of one Cinda Cavanaugh came to mind. Blond, delicate, beautiful. Warm, funny, witty. Rich, out of his league, as good as locked away in a tower, for all the access he had to her. All right, so maybe he had met a possible candidate for "the right one." But maybe he was trapped in one of those "in another time, another place" deals. Because there she was, a chic millionaire New York woman. And here he was...he looked down at himself, at his greasy dirty mechanic's coveralls. Yeah, here he was. Damned depressing was what it was.

Trey shrugged his shoulders, as much to exercise cramped muscles as to shake loose his bothersome thoughts. Still, he decided, wouldn't it be funny if he just waltzed into town with a family? Yeah, real funny. Ha-ha. His mother would kill him. But that was exactly what he needed, if he had any hope of quickly derailing Bobby Jean Diamante's shallowly disguised plot to catch him in her web. The more Trey thought about it, the better he liked the idea. An instant family. Then he heard himself and shook his head. *Like you can pick one of those up on any aisle in a grocery store.*

Sudden inspiration dawned. Trey jerked his head up and stared unseeing at the stock-car calendar hanging on the wall in front of him. He knew exactly where to get an instant family. Hadn't she said to call her if his life needed saving? Trey nodded to himself. His life most definitely needed saving. Or did it? After all, he had no proof that the disgruntled Rocco Diamante would follow his wife to Southwood. Not that Trey wanted Cinda to handle the man for him. Or even Bobby Jean. He had always handled her before, and he could do it again this time.

And there was no real danger here, except to him. Still, it wasn't as if Trey thought the man would come in shooting the whole town up like in some old mobster movie. And who said the guy was in the mob, anyway? It wasn't like they advertised that. A more likely story was this was one of Bobby Jean's drama-queen spoutings of organized crime connections, just to make her life look more exciting. Still, if it was true, Trey figured the guy would load him down with chain, sink him in the lake, and then take Bobby Jean home. He wouldn't mess with anyone else. He'd have no reason to. Problem solved.

For Rocco maybe. Certainly not for Trey. Okay, that was a pretty scary thought. Trey preferred to think of this from another angle. The one where his ex-girlfriend had maybe just handed him a golden opportunity to reconnect with Cinda Cavanaugh.

Trey chuckled. Yes, if this worked out, he'd have to remember to thank Bobby Jean. She'd love that—about like a hornet did someone stomping on its hive. That quick-tempered redhead would probably react in much the same way, he figured. And then, having created sufficient hoopla and having gotten all the attention she wanted, she'd blow out of town and go right back to her husband.

And everyone would be happy. Then it was decided, right?

Yep. Grinning, Trey reached into his back pocket and pulled out his wallet. Before he could change his mind, he lifted out the folded piece of paper and opened it. Staring at Cinda's handwriting and her phone number, he remembered that day as if it had been yesterday. Even after just having a baby, she'd been the most beautiful woman he'd ever seen. Certainly the classiest. Yeah, he'd been smitten. Since that day, he'd carried this piece of paper in his wallet like a good-luck charm. It had served as a concrete link to her, a slim possibility that the two of them might become something more to each other some day.

And now, maybe that day was here. Trey took a deep breath. This was a big step. And wasn't this using her and her baby, somehow? Maybe, but not really. She'd know up front what was going on. So if she agreed, there'd be no harm. After all he only wanted one weekend out of her life. Nothing more. The worst she could do was say no.

Trey focused on the wall-mounted phone next to the calendar and simply stared at it. He admitted to himself now that one of the reasons he hadn't called her yet was that if he didn't, she couldn't reject him. And if she couldn't reject him, then he wasn't out of her life. *Oh hell, man, that's stupid. She couldn't be more out of your life than she is right now this minute. You don't see her or talk to her. She probably doesn't even think about you anymore.*

Great. So he was going to reject *himself* before he even gave her a chance to do it. This was messed up. He was a thirty-year-old man who was experienced with women. *So act like it,* he told himself. Trey reached for the phone but caught himself. The guys he worked with would just love this conversation, wouldn't they? Trey lowered his hand. *Forget it.* If he was going to put his heart and pride on the line, then he'd do it from the privacy of his own home. That way, if she said no, he could immediately go drown himself in his shower.

That sounded like a plan. Trey folded the note Cinda had given him and stuck it back in his wallet. He'd call her later.

4

FRESHLY BATHED and clad in her nightgown and robe, Cinda sat curled up on the sofa in the family room. The large-screen TV was turned off, and the built-in stereo system softly played jazz in the background. Cinda was tired but it was too early in the evening to go to bed. She'd already nursed and rocked Chelsi to sleep and this was Major Clovis's and Marta's night out. So Cinda essentially had the place to herself.

She loved moments like this. Yet she also hated them. They were too quiet, too ripe for reflection. Her mind insisted on wandering from the book she'd picked up, to center itself on Trey Cooper. She supposed it was only natural. After all, he'd been a major player in a really big moment in her life, the birth of her daughter. *Oh, nice try, Cinda. It was more than that and you know it. Much more.* Okay, so there had been attraction. She hadn't imagined that. Something chemical had happened between them. He'd made quite the impression on her senses. A lingering impression.

Feeling all dreamy, like a lovesick teenager, Cinda allowed her hardcover mystery to flop onto her lap as she gave in to thoughts of Trey Cooper. Such a handsome, virile man. Cinda sat up, hearing herself and looking around guiltily. *What am I thinking? Here I am a widow with a six-month-old baby acting as if I have my first crush.* Now she was sounding like her mother-in-law. The woman would have a stroke if Cinda even thought of seeing someone, much less marrying anyone else. The Real Mrs. Cavanaugh, as Major Clovis called her because of her condescending airs, talked as if she believed Cinda should remain chaste in loving memory of Richard the Second.

Frowning, Cinda spared a moment for her complicated relationship with Ruth Cavanaugh. She supposed she loved the difficult woman, who could be overbearing and opinionated. Okay, so she could be a battering ram. Most days, though, and on most issues, Cinda simply didn't give in to her. In disagreements with Ruth, Cinda tried to remain firm but respectful. After all, Ruth was Chelsi's grandmother, which meant she would always be a part of her life. And, Cinda knew Ruth had it hard. After all, she'd lost her only child.

Oh, Richard. Cinda's eyes grew damp. She had loved him. Well, she'd tried to. But he wouldn't allow it. He hadn't wanted a wife, just a child, an heir. And now he was gone. But wasn't life for the living? Cinda asked herself. She'd always heard that, and now she understood what it meant. She was alive. And so was Trey Cooper. In light of that, what was she supposed to do with all the hormones that still drove her, as well as the fifty or so years of life still ahead of her? Just sit here and vegetate? She didn't think so.

So why didn't she just get over it and call Trey Cooper? Where was the harm? Women called men all the time now. She had, before she'd met Richard. In fact, that was how she'd met Richard. She'd called him. Okay, so she'd been a reporter assigned to do a story on him. But still, she'd made the first move. And that had worked out well, hadn't it? For a while, anyway. It had certainly worked out better for her than it had for Richard. Poor Richard. He got the yaks, and she got Chelsi.

Just then, the phone rang, shattering the silence. Nearly jumping out of her skin, Cinda tossed her book aside and scrambled up onto her knees. Reaching over the back of the sofa, she plucked up the cordless handset from atop the long narrow table that reposed there. A quick check of the caller ID had her groaning as she sank back onto the plush cushions. *Speak of the devil.* Her in-laws' name and number graced the tiny glowing screen. So why couldn't she just be "not at home" and let the machine get it? Tempting. But no. Ever dutiful, Cinda depressed the talk button and put the phone to her ear.

"Hello, Mother Cavanaugh," she said in a pleasant voice.

"Sorry to disappoint you, sweetie, but this is Grandpa Rick."

Cinda's mood instantly lifted. Richard's father. She loved this man. "Papa Rick! How are you?" He hardly ever called. Couldn't wrest the phone from his wife's hands, no doubt.

"The Dragon Lady fell asleep in her lair, so I snatched up the phone when it rang an hour or so ago. And it's lucky for you I did."

"For me? Why? Is something wrong?"

"Only if you don't like the young man who called for you."

Cinda sat bolt upright on the sofa. Her pulse picked up. Anticipation flitted through her, drying her mouth. "A young man called for me?"

"He did. And like I said, it was a good thing I answered and not Ruth."

"No kidding." She and Papa Rick were in this conspiracy together to survive the Dragon Lady. "But why would the, uh, young man call you? You're in the Hamptons. And I certainly haven't given anybody your number there. This doesn't make sense."

"Cinda, slow down. All I know is he sounded Southern."

"S-Southern?" Cinda could have kicked herself for that stutter in her voice. Thank God, Papa Rick couldn't know how her heart was leaping right now. Only two days ago she'd been wishing every call was Trey's. And now, just maybe, here it was.

"So," she said, trying to play it cool, "Who was he? What'd he say? What'd he want? Why did he call you?"

Okay, so she blew the cool part.

Rick Cavanaugh chuckled in her ear. "My, don't you sound eager."

Cinda took a deep breath. She wasn't certain yet that she wanted to confide in Papa Rick, or if she even should. After all, Richard had been his son, too. "Eager? No. Just curious is all. Like I said, I can't imagine why anyone would call you looking for me."

"It wasn't exactly your young man who called—"

"I don't have a young man." Immediately, Cinda grimaced, rapping her forehead with her knuckles. She'd been too quick to protest.

"Of course you don't." Papa Rick's voice remained friendly and teasing. "You should have one, you know, honey."

Cinda was pleasantly taken aback. Papa Rick

thought she should have a young man? That was enlightening.

"At any rate," her father-in-law was saying, "our Miss Reeves—oh, you remember our Miss Reeves, don't you?"

Cinda gave an indelicate snort. He may as well have asked her if she remembered the axe-wielding monster she'd felt certain had resided in her bedroom closet when she'd been a child. "Yes. Tall. Big hair. Humorless. The saint and scourge of social secretaries. The one everyone is afraid of. Well, except Major Clovis, who isn't afraid of anyone. You mean that Miss Reeves?"

"Yes. Well, our Miss Reeves was at your apartment earlier this evening, making her rounds, as it were, checking on things—"

"She was? Why?"

"The Dragon Lady thought it would be a good thing to do."

"I see." So The Real Mrs. Cavanaugh had her spy snooping around in Cinda's absence. There wasn't much Cinda could say about it. The penthouse was in the elder Cavanaughs' names. "So what did she find?"

"A blinking phone message, actually. From two days ago."

"Two days ago?"

"According to the date and time on your voice mail."

"Oh, I can't believe this. I have been so lax about checking it up there. Every time I did, it seemed like there were no messages. And then I got busy here and just stopped thinking about it. I figured by now everyone knew I was in Atlanta."

"Well, not everyone, I'd say."

Suddenly it all made sense. Her caller was Southern and last January she'd given Trey Cooper her New York number. Despite her excitement, Cinda wanted to groan. Trey probably believed that she had no intention of returning his call. What must he think? Putting that aside for the moment she concentrated on Papa Rick. "Hey, have I told you lately that I love you?"

"No. I don't think you have."

Cinda grinned at the mock hurt in his voice. "I love you."

"That's nice to know. I love you, too."

"Then it's mutual." Though warmed by his affection, Cinda worked to get them back on track. "All right, so your Miss Reeves took down this phone message for me and called to tell the Drag—I mean Mother Cavanaugh about it, but got you instead. So, what did you tell her to do?"

"You know it doesn't work like that. Our Miss Reeves instructed me to call you to see if you know this man. Do you?"

Well, obviously, it wasn't only in her home where control over the staff had long since been ceded. "I don't know, Papa Rick. You haven't told me who called."

"Well, that makes it hard then, doesn't it? Let's see. It was... Oh, for the love of Mike. Where did it get to? Hold on. I seem to have misplaced the note."

He'd lost the note. Cinda pitched over onto the sofa's cushions while she listened to sounds of fumbling and searching at the other end. *Please, God, let him find the—*

"Aha, here it is. Oh, wait a minute. Now I have to find my glasses."

Cinda vaulted up to a sitting position and shoved her hair back from her too-warm face. "Papa Rick? Look in your shirt pocket. Your reading glasses are always in your shirt pocket."

Silence. Then… "Well, I'll be darned. What do you know? There they are. Now let me put them on."

Cinda put her free hand to her aching forehead. God love Papa Rick, the big old bear of a man. It was a good thing this kind and sweet gentleman had inherited his vast wealth and hadn't had to earn it because he would have ended up on the street.

"Okay, I think I'm ready now. Do you have something to write with, dear?"

Cinda gasped. She didn't.

"I'll give you his number. Oh, wait, how's my beautiful granddaughter, the light of my life—after you, of course?"

"Thank you. She's fine. Chubby. Happy. Healthy. She can sit up on her own now." Cinda fumbled for paper and pen. Until this very moment, there had always been a pen and a notepad of paper on this end table. But not tonight. Cinda scurried around the room, looking. Opening cabinets. Searching through drawers. "I expect she'll be crawling in a few months, if not heading up her own corporation."

"Oh, that's wonderful. I really miss seeing her."

The wistful note in his voice caused Cinda to slow down. Her features crumpled into a sympathetic mask. "I know you miss her. I *swear* I'll bring her up to see you." She bit the bullet. "Or why don't y'all come down here?"

"Ruth won't cross the Mason-Dixon Line. You know that."

"Then come without her." As she listened to Papa Rick telling her all the reasons why he couldn't come without his wife, Cinda rushed into her gourmet kitchen and snatched a paper towel off the roll. She next opened a drawer of the built-in desk and found a permanent laundry marker. "Oh, sure you can. Just tell your pilot where you want to go, and he'll fly you here."

"That's true. I could do that."

"See?" Using her teeth, and praying she didn't get the indelible ink all over her face in the process—she could see a dermatologist having to sand that off—she bit down on the pen, spit the lid out, and said, "Okay, I'm ready. Go ahead." She smoothed the paper towel atop the granite breakfast bar and waited. "Papa Rick?"

"Shh. Hold on. I think I hear Ruth coming downstairs."

Dread swept through Cinda and had her gripping the phone tighter. It was like they were conspirators in the French Resistance. "Then hurry, Papa Rick. Give me the name and the number really quick, okay?"

Talking to this dear man was like trying to communicate with a cat—you could, but you had to do it carefully and patiently and with a lot of cajoling. Yet it still might not work, anyway.

"No. It wasn't her. Must have been the dog."

Cinda grimaced her distaste. Calling Ruth's nasty-tempered little dust-mop of a yappy, biting lap ornament a "dog" was really using the term loosely. "So who was this Southern gentleman who called for me, Papa Rick?''

''I hate that dog. It bites my ankles and shreds all the hems in my pants—while I'm wearing them.''

''I know. I hate Empress, too. She's got an attitude problem. Now, who was it you said phoned me?'' Much more of this, Cinda knew, and it would be three days since Trey had called. If it had been Trey who had called at all.

''Oh, I'm sorry. I haven't told you yet, have I? Okay, here it is. Let me see now. A Mr. Trey—now, that can't be right. People in the South don't name their children after parts of the silver service, do they?''

It was Trey. Dear God, it was Trey. Cinda feared she would burst into flames, she was so giddy with excitement. Still she managed to sound sane when she replied. ''Yes. Down here they do. I know actual children named Cream and Sugar.'' Of course it wasn't true, but it was a shorter explanation—and one this blue-blooded, harmless Yankee would believe. ''So...Trey who?'' she added to maintain her air of innocence.

''Cooper is what I wrote down. And this next part is serious. Miss Reeves said to tell you that Mr. Cooper said his life needed to be saved. Does that mean anything to you?''

Cinda barely covered her gasp. Trey Cooper was calling in his favor. ''Uh, maybe. Give me his number, and I'll try him right now, okay?''

''That's a good idea. I just hope it's not too late. He could be dead by now. But anyway, here it is.'' He finally read her the telephone number.

Maddeningly, Cinda's fingers didn't want to work

in concert with her brain. She was too excited, too nervous. She had to ask Papa Rick three times to repeat the numbers to her, but finally she got them in the correct sequence. Relief coursed through her. Short-lived relief.

"Wait a minute," Papa Rick said. "Trey Cooper. That name sounds familiar. This isn't the nice young man who was stuck in the elevator with you last January, is it? The one you told us about?"

Oh sure, now his mind clears. "Yes. But don't tell Mother Cavanaugh, all right? I don't want her jumping to any conclusions that would have her taking to her bed for a week and making your life unbearable."

"Oh. I see your point, although I can't vouch for our Miss Reeves. No doubt, she'll tattle. But anyway, good luck, dear. I'll let you go so you can call your young man."

"He's not my young man."

"Well, go see that he is. Goodbye. And kiss that baby for me."

"I will. And I love you. Goodbye, Papa Rick."

Cinda disconnected the call, then stared at the paper towel she held and on which she'd scrawled the phone number with the Atlanta area code. Her heart and her mind were singing. Trey Cooper had called her. And his life needed to be saved. Oh, happy day.

Then she sobered. Surely, he didn't mean that literally. So this could only be a good thing, right? A social call, as in "how are you doing, I meant to call you before now."

That had to be it. She eyed the phone still in her other hand…then the phone number. The phone…the number. Then the kitchen clock. It wasn't even nine yet. She could call right now. Cinda took a deep breath for courage, swallowed her heart back down into her chest, and began dialing Trey Cooper's number. Right then, she couldn't have said if she wanted him to be home or not. After all, this could be a good thing—or it could be opening a Pandora's box of emotions best left unexplored. She just didn't know which.

Somehow, though, the number was dialed and the phone at the other end was ringing. Hearing it, Cinda was seized by a sudden spate of panic that shrieked at her to hang up. Her hand tightened on the phone—

STARTLED AWAKE, Trey grabbed his phone off the hook on the second ring and put it to his ear. "Hello?" No one said anything. "Hello?" He listened. "I can hear you breathing. I know you're there. You might as well say something."

"Oh. Trey, is that you? This is Cinda Cooper—I mean Cavanaugh. Cinda Cavanaugh."

Trey sat bolt upright on his couch, where he'd been about half asleep as the TV blared some mindless nonsense. "Cinda?" Had he heard her right? Had she really said Cooper? Surely not. That was just wistful thinking on his part. "Hi. I didn't think you were going to call me back."

"I'm sure you didn't, but I just now got your message. By a very roundabout way, too."

"Really?" He grabbed the remote and turned the TV off. The sudden quiet was a blessing. "Been away from the house?"

"It's an apartment, actually. In New York. But yes I have been away. In fact, I'm back in Atlanta now."

Excitement quickened in him. "Are you serious? You're here in Atlanta? Just visiting, or what?"

"Or what. I moved back here a few months ago, into my old house. The same one I lived in before."

"Before what?"

"The yaks."

"Oh, hell. Right. But, hey, this is great. If I'd known you were in town, I'd have come by to see the baby. How is she?"

"Asleep, blessedly. But she's fine. Absolutely beautiful, of course, and the smartest child in the world. Just ask her mother."

Trey chuckled. Then he was silent, gathering his thoughts as he ran a hand through his hair. "So, how are you doing, Cinda? I mean really."

"I'm good. You?"

"I'm good." He wasn't. He'd been a wreck since he'd called her and hadn't received a call back. He'd put himself through hell with all the reasons why she might not be going to call him back. In none of the scenarios had he come off well. In none of them, either, had he assigned such a simple reason as she simply no longer lived at that number.

Suddenly Trey realized there was a silence between them. He opened his mouth to say something, but Cinda beat him to it.

"Well, this is certainly awkward," she said.

"I know. Hard to believe, isn't it? Especially after what we shared together in that stupid elevator—for which I'm eternally grateful, by the way."

"Oh really? Why is that?"

"Because otherwise I never would have met you."
Trey applauded his boldness, on the one hand. But on the other, he wanted to kick himself. He held his breath, wondering just how old a man had to be before

he no longer felt like a fool just for calling a woman and saying what he really felt.

"Well."

Trey died inside...fourteen times, to be exact.

Finally she saved him. "That's certainly a nice thing to say. You're being very charming, you know."

He exhaled, fully expecting his heart and lungs to whoosh out along with his relief. But boldness had brought him this far. So, ever one to keep crashing onward, even if it was into brick walls, he decided to try again. "You say that like it's a bad thing."

"It might be." Her tone of voice was clearly teasing. "You see, I'm very susceptible to charming Southern men and have to watch myself around them."

"And yet, now that you are in Atlanta, you're surrounded by them."

She hesitated a moment. "Not so many as you'd think."

"Really?" Encouraged to know that she wasn't inundated with men, Trey's heart stepped out onto the romantic-risk-taking high-dive and took the plunge. "Good. Because I have a proposition for you."

"Is this the part where I save your life?"

"Pretty much. If you're willing, that is."

"As long as it doesn't include a stalled elevator, I probably am."

"I can guarantee there are no elevators, stuck or otherwise, involved. In fact, I'm not even sure there's a building in Southwood with an elevator."

"Southwood?"

"My hometown. Just west of here."

"That's right. Now I remember. I'm still trying to

figure out why I've never heard of it, though, if it's that close to Atlanta."

"No reason why you should have. We didn't produce any Confederate generals or Olympic medalists. Just a dusty little town planning a big celebration."

"I see. Of what?"

"My high-school class reunion. Our tenth, even though it was actually twelve years ago."

"I wish I could say that made sense."

"So do I, but that's Southwood for you. It's a long story."

"Let me guess. You need a date, right?"

"Worse. Or better, depending on how you look at it. I need a wife and a child."

Silence ensued. Trey held his breath, not knowing if he should say something to assure her he wasn't joking, or if he should just wait and see what her reaction would be.

"You're not going to tell me this is some sort of crazy scavenger hunt, are you?" she said a moment later.

Trey grinned. "No. But you may wish that before I'm done here."

"Wow. Sounds really intriguing. Go ahead. I'm listening."

Trey exhaled and ran a hand through his hair. "Intrigue may not be the half of it. And I don't like asking you this over the phone, but—"

"But your life needs to be saved and I owe you, right?"

"Yes and no. Yes my life needs to be saved. And no I don't feel that you owe me. I meant this to be— I just thought maybe—Oh, hell, never mind, Cinda. Look, I'm sorry. Forget it. This didn't sound so nuts to me the other day when I called you with this idea of mine. But now, hearing it out loud and asking you, or trying to ask you, well, it sounds stupid. Just never mind. I'm sorry I bothered you. I can go by my—''

''Wait, Trey. Give me a chance here. I didn't say no, did I? Just tell me what's going on, and we'll go from there.''

Hope bloomed in his heart. ''You sure?''

She chuckled. ''I think I am. Maybe.''

''An open mind. That's a good beginning. So, here's the deal...'' Trey launched into his predicament, hitting the highlights, as if there were any, of his upcoming reunion weekend and what role he needed her and Chelsi to play. He worked hard to make it sound sane and logical when, in fact, it was neither. He didn't tell her about Rocco Diamante, though, thinking there was no reason to needlessly scare her. If the man showed up and made trouble, Trey would call his friend, the police chief, and then get Cinda, the baby, and his mother out of town. But, still, the longer he talked, the more he was convinced Cinda would not only say no, but she would probably also hang up on him and change her phone number.

But finally, he was through telling his tale. ''So, what do you think? You don't have to say yes, Cinda. Seriously. No harm, no foul. Because I think it's a crazy plan, and it's *my* plan.'' She didn't say anything. Trey sighed. ''You think I'm nuts, don't you?''

''No. I probably should, but I don't. You know what? It sounds fun and crazy. And maybe that's exactly what I need right now. So...yes, Trey Cooper, I'll do it. Well, we'll do it—Chelsi and I.''

Trey bolted to his feet, narrowly avoiding colliding

with his coffee table, and paced excitedly across the carpet. "You will? You'll be my wife?"

There was a moment's hesitation. "Well, let's keep our heads here. I'm saying that I'll be your wife and Chelsi will be your daughter...but only for that one weekend, of course."

"Yeah. Of course," Trey echoed. "One weekend. That's all I need."

He just wished he could be sure about that. Because he wasn't. Not at all. And that couldn't be good.

5

JUST AFTER NOON on the following Saturday, Cinda waited nervously for Trey's arrival at her Atlanta home. His high-school reunion was the next weekend, the Fourth of July, so she'd invited him over to discuss the details of their ruse and to allow him and Chelsi to get acquainted. After all, it wouldn't do to pose as a loving couple with a young baby if the baby would have nothing to do with her "father."

But those combined reasons, while valid, weren't the whole truth. Cinda forced herself to admit that she *wanted* to see Trey Cooper and couldn't wait another week to do so. She wanted to know if he could still affect her as he had that January day in the elevator. The evidence—her never-ending thoughts of him, her incredible excitement that he had finally called, and her giddiness at the prospect of seeing him again—already pointed to the fact that he could, he would, and he did.

As if that weren't enough to stress over, Cinda feared that she wasn't yet ready to act on that speeding bullet of awareness between them. It could turn out that she just thought she was ready and that she'd back off when—if—things heated up between her and Trey. And if she let it get that far and then backed off? Well, it wouldn't be fair to him. Or to herself. So here she was, not completely in touch with her emotions beyond the recognition of a confused mishmash of desire and restraint.

And none of that altered the fact that Trey was due at any moment. Cinda had already changed outfits— hers and the baby's—no less than four times. Right now she had on a new flower-sprigged sundress, but she had yet to call it her final decision. Nor was she satisfied with Chelsi's outfit. But her daughter wore a mutinous expression that promised a tantrum of diva proportions should her mother try yet again to poke her chubby arms and legs through one more article of complicated baby clothing.

Respecting Chelsi's stubbornly poked-out bottom lip, Cinda dropped the dress issue and set about making everyone else in the house miserable. With Chelsi in her arms, and with Major Clovis on their heels, Cinda now flitted through every room of the two-story Southern Colonial mansion, conducting an inspection tour. She told herself she simply needed to make certain everything was cleaned and straightened. She wanted to make a good impression. Was that so awful? She stopped in the richly decorated, sunny formal living room and looked around appraisingly.

"Begging your pardon, ma'am," Major Clovis said, "but we didn't go to this much trouble for the IG's visit back during my days in the military."

"The IG?" Cinda asked distractedly, balancing Chelsi carefully while fluffing a throw pillow on the sofa. "What's an IG?"

"Inspector General, ma'am." Major Clovis put the pillow back where it had been. "A high mucketymuck with the power to make your life a living meat grinder if he found so much as one speck of dirt on the ground outside."

Pinched by the comparison, Cinda began to feel a bit surly. "I hardly think I'm going that far. And I wouldn't define Mr. Cooper as a mucketymuck. I just want everything to be nice for his visit."

"I understand. I believe the barracks will pass muster, ma'am. I hired three extra maids for this major field day."

Long ago Cinda had given up trying to get Major Clovis to call her anything except ma'am or to forego the use of military jargon. Still, as she inspected the hang of the curtains Cinda remained distracted. "What's a major field day, again? Some sort of military maneuvers?"

"In a way of speaking." Major Clovis reached around Cinda to shake out the folds she'd just shaken in. "It's when everyone falls out under orders to clean an entire installation from top to bottom."

"I see." Cinda flitted to an end table and ran her fingers over a lampshade. She checked it for dust. There wasn't any. "Sounds like a worthwhile thing."

"It's meant as a punishment, ma'am."

Cinda faced her adjutant, who stood at ease with her hands behind her back. "Well, that's not what we're doing here, Major Clovis. Certainly no one is being punished."

"Yes, ma'am."

As much put out with herself for caring so much how everything looked as she was with Major Clovis's hovering, Cinda clung stubbornly to her defensive mood. She stood back from the gilt-framed beveled-glass mirror that hung over the fireplace and gave it the once-over. "Will you look at that? Why haven't I ever noticed before that it's hanging crookedly?"

Mindful of her daughter on her hip, she reached up on tiptoes to straighten the mirror's edge.

"Here. Allow me, ma'am." Major Clovis leaped to help, essentially swinging the mirror's position back to where it had been a moment ago. She then stood back with Cinda to inspect their counterproductive handiwork. "There. Good as new."

Assessing the frame, tilting her head this way and that, Cinda frowned, "I suppose." She then focused on Major Clovis. "Mr. Cooper will be staying for lunch. Has Marta prepared the menu I requested?"

Major Clovis executed a sharp nod of military precision. "Yes, ma'am. I told her she'd be court-martialed if she failed to please."

Already hating herself for asking, Cinda eyed her aide. "How exactly did you say that to her since you don't speak Spanish?"

The beginnings of a smug little grin became a self-satisfied pursing of the major's lips. "I know a few words, ma'am. But I believe my exact word this time was *muerte*."

Cinda could only stare without blinking. "Dead? You told her she'd be killed, didn't you?"

"At sunrise." The major's light gray eyes swam with feigned innocence. "Was that too much, ma'am?"

"If it explains the shrieking commotion I heard last night, yes it was."

"I wasn't aware of any such—"

The front doorbell rang, playing a melodious tune. A least, it was supposed to play a melodious tune. Cinda directed an exasperated how-could-you look the major's way. Obviously the woman had reprogrammed the door chimes. To wit, a very patriotic and rousing rendition of the "Battle Hymn of the Republic" rang out through the house.

Over the booming tune, which had baby Chelsi blinking rapidly and screwing up her face as if she weren't sure if she was supposed to cry, Major Clovis said, "If you'll excuse me, ma'am. Your guest appears to have arrived."

My guest. The full implication of those words ran through Cinda, weakening her knees. Forgetting all else, she shot a hand out to stop her assistant from leaving. "Wait. Bring him to me in the family room. And not in chains or with his head on a platter, do you understand?"

"Whatever you say, ma'am." The wiry woman, dressed in olive-drab belted slacks, a light green button-down blouse and sensible shoes, then performed a sharp about-face and, marching in time to the music, headed for the front door.

In a complete fluster, Cinda walked rapidly toward the back of the house to the family room. She pinched her cheeks to bring more color to them and smoothed a hand through her hair. She pulled a thick lock of it into her view, studied it, and wanted to groan. Just as she'd feared. It looked dull, like dirty dishwater. What had happened to the blondeness? To the highlights? She hated her hair. It just hung there straight. It had no body. Could it be more stringy and lifeless?

Great. Well, if she couldn't be gorgeous, she could at least be gracious.

Once in the family room, Cinda sat on the sofa and perched her daughter next to her so she could give her a final going-over. Chelsi's dark-blond hair stood up at right angles from her head. The child looked like a little blue-eyed baby monkey. When had that happened? Horrified, Cinda quickly moistened her fingers by dabbing them against her tongue. Then, utilizing a time-honored mothering technique, she applied her wet fingertips to Chelsi's hair and tried to fashion attractive feather-soft curls out of the dandelion fluff that was the baby's hair.

Cinda just wanted the darling little dumpling to shine. Was that so awful? It was to Chelsi, who had not been consulted. This latest act of her mother's was apparently the last straw for the little girl. As if totally over it with the demands of feminine vanity, she stiffened and began screaming her protest.

ALL TREY HAD DONE was push the doorbell. But now, standing outside the impressive and intimidating redbrick Southern Colonial mansion that reposed in a neighborhood of such magnificence that Cinda's house actually seemed small by comparison, he stood stiffly at attention. Four years of military training were hard to overcome. So was the "Battle Hymn of the Republic."

But if Trey thought that tune had given him a terrifying flashback of boot camp proportions, it was nothing compared to the woman who opened the door. Tall, slender, with short hair the color of steel, and dressed in an approximation of an army uniform, she eyed him like the lowly enlisted man he'd been. "Yes?"

Trey told himself that this feeling that he'd strayed onto top-secret, off-limits property was ridiculous. He forced a smile and put his best mannerly foot forward. "Hi. I'm Trey Cooper. Mrs. Cavanaugh is expecting me...ma'am."

With the doorbell music dying out, the only sound

Trey heard now was a baby crying in the background. It didn't faze the middle-aged woman standing in front of him, though. She slowly roved her gaze up and down him. No doubt about it—this was an inspection. Trey thought of his khaki slacks and light blue knit golf shirt, neatly tucked in and belted…thank God. As he'd had a haircut only this morning, it should pass muster. When the silent woman's gaze lowered to his feet, Trey fought a nearly overwhelming urge to look down to see if his loafers had the appropriate shine.

The woman's gaze flicked back to his face. Trey met her eyes. She never smiled. "You'll do. Come in."

Exhaling as if his life had just been spared, Trey stepped over the threshold and inside the home's grand and tiled foyer. He heard the door—one of a set made of highly polished wood—close behind him. But he forgot the intimidating woman and the crying baby as he looked around, barely biting back a low whistle of appreciation for the grandeur of Cinda's home. He had one conclusion only. He was in over his head here.

The only house he'd ever seen that he could compare this one to was Jude Barrett's own. Other than his boss's place, Trey had never seen anything like this. His parents' home, where his mother still lived, was a five-room, white wood square of a house with a screened-in front porch, big trees outside and a neglected flower bed. And his apartment here in Atlanta was a nondescript, one-bedroom, furnished box in a complex of over one hundred units skirted by concrete and parking spaces.

Trey tried to picture himself coming home here, closing a door behind him, and calling out, "Hi, honey, I'm home." And then Cinda, smiling, would come greet him—

Someone touched his elbow. Trey jumped and whipped around. His escort was there, right at his back. But she was smiling—about like he expected a praying mantis would before it devoured its prey. The woman leaned in toward him and looked him right in the eye as she whispered, "If you hurt her, I'll hunt you down and rip your beating heart right out of your chest, do you hear me?"

The skin on the back of Trey's neck crawled. He swallowed. "Yes, ma'am. Loud and clear."

She stepped back. "Good. Then we understand each other." With that, she did an about-face and began walking away. Trey put a protective hand over his heart. "Follow me," the woman said over her shoulder. "Mrs. Cavanaugh awaits you in the family room."

The queen has granted you an audience, peasant, was how she said it.

Feeling way off his game here but committed to the course, Trey fell in step, thinking this gray-haired character would even scare Peg the Nurse up in New York City. Down a wood-floored hallway they traveled, sweeping past the wide stairs that obviously led up to a second floor. Trey finally found himself in a room that alone had to be bigger than his mother's entire home.

So this was what it was like to be a millionaire. The room demanded his attention. It was all windows and open spaces and white carpet and big pieces of furniture. Big paintings and sculptures, too. And flowers. Fresh ones. Everywhere. Beautiful. Colors impinged on his senses. He called them red, white and blue, but no doubt some interior decorator had fancy names for them that Trey would never be able to wrap his tongue around.

Just then, he became aware that the crying baby was close by and that the crying was subsiding into hiccups and sniffling. Trey looked around but didn't see anyone else. Then...Cinda stood up from where she'd obviously been sitting on the other side of a big cushy beige-colored sofa.

Catching sight of her, locking gazes with her, Trey's breath caught. He forgot his surroundings and his escort. His mouth was suddenly dry, his palms sweaty. For him, no one existed except Cinda. She filled the room with her smiling warmth and her beauty. She lit up the—

Pow! Trey was smacked hard in the middle of his back, hard enough to rock him off his feet. He tripped forward, gasping, and heard Cinda do the same. She put a hand to her mouth and looked as surprised as he was.

From Trey's left, the austere, serious-minded woman who'd brought him this far said, "Breathe, soldier. You forgot to breathe."

Ever dutiful, Trey breathed. In and out. In and out. And stared at his...what? Assailant? Arch-enemy? Someone to whom he'd forgotten he owed a huge amount of money? "Thanks," he managed to croak out. "I'll try to remember that from now on."

"Good. It makes life a whole lot easier." She got in his face. "And I want you to enjoy what you have left of it, son." Leaving him with that cheery thought, the woman zipped around on her heel and marched out of the room.

Swallowing hard, Trey watched her go. He made

certain that the woman was gone before he turned to Cinda and remarked, "She loves me. We're engaged."

Cinda laughed. "Well, I'll certainly look forward to *that* wedding."

Grinning, Trey noticed how much Cinda had changed in the last six months. Not surprising that she would, since she'd been nine months pregnant when first he saw her. Though beautiful even then, she was more so now. Motherhood agreed with her. Slender and tanned, she stood there in a dress that showed off her figure. Her face was thinner, too, highlighting her cheekbones and sensual mouth. And those wonderful amber eyes. They were enough to stop a man's heart from beating.

Trey realized he was staring. He also knew that Cinda was watching him do so. He inhaled, trying to rouse himself to action. The polite thing to do was go over to her, sit and visit and make a fuss over the baby. But he'd be damned if he could get his legs to cooperate. That was when it hit him. *Wait a minute. Baby? She has a baby in her arms.* How had he not noticed before now? He pointed to the child. "Have you always been holding her?"

Cinda raised her eyebrows. "It seems like it some days, but I've only had her for six months, remember? You were there." She pointed to her child. "This is Chelsi Elise."

"She certainly is," Trey said, thinking himself ridiculous. "And she's beautiful. But I must be losing it. I didn't even notice you were holding her when you stood up. All I saw were stars."

Cinda's expression melted into one of apologetic sympathy. "Oh, I know. You poor man. I should tell you that was Major Clovis—the woman who brought you in here and smacked you on the back. She's my nurse, assistant, secretary...bulldog.''

Trey had meant Cinda. All he'd seen were stars when he saw her. But it had been a pretty hokey thing to say once, much less twice. "Ah. Major Clovis."

"She came with the house."

"Chained up in the basement, no doubt."

Cinda laughed, and it was magic. "Exactly right. How'd you know?"

"A lucky guess. I like her. I think she's nice." God, how he wanted Cinda.

"You're being kind." Cinda patted the happily gurgling blond baby girl in her arms. "The truth is, if you're not me or Chelsi, she won't like you. Ever. Now, tell me, what hideous thing did she say to you on the way in here? And don't tell me she didn't because she always does."

She did? Did that mean there had been a procession of men through those front doors? Trey instantly hated that idea—and now truly liked Major Clovis for doing her best to run them off. One thing Trey knew was she wouldn't run him off. But in answer to Cinda's question, Trey shrugged. "Nothing much. Ripping my heart out. Things like that. At least she's up-front about how she feels. I can respect that."

"Oh, you poor thing. But speaking of respect, come over here and pay yours to my daughter, a little girl you almost had to bring into this world, Mr. Trey Cooper." Cinda's eyes shone with maternal pride.

Trey loved the way she said his name. *Mr. Trey Cooper.* Like she was trying it out for size. *Mrs. Trey Cooper.* But wait a minute, he chided himself, shouldn't he hate that whole idea? Shouldn't he be running away, instead of steadily walking toward her? As he approached where she still stood, he reminded himself of his own rule: no wife and kids while on the race circuit. Sure, he knew that intellectually, but another part of his psyche, the part that reported directly to his heart, said…maybe, maybe not. Oh, this wasn't good. This woman had danger written all over her. She was the yellow flag that warned the drivers to slow down when there was trouble ahead on the course.

And yet, here he was standing in front of her as close as propriety and the baby's presence between them would allow. He looked into Cinda's golden eyes, caught the scent of her perfume, and smiled. Awareness flashed and caught him off-guard. His heart beat faster, harder. Cinda's lips parted slightly, as if she thought he was about to kiss her. As if she was about to allow him to kiss her. And oh, he wanted to, all right. Trey leaned in toward her. She leaned in toward him. He reached out, putting his hand lightly on her back as he lowered his head to capture her mouth.

He heard her little gasp…of passion for him? No, of pain because the baby had yanked a handful of her mother's hair. And Cinda was pulling away from him and looking embarrassed and disconcerted. Feeling much the same, Trey cleared his throat and retreated a step or two. Still, despite the "kissus interruptus," the good news here was Cinda was obviously as affected by him as he was by her.

"So," Trey remarked, striving to get nonchalant as he pointed to the baby, "tell me about this little lady here who likes to pull hair and ruin tender moments between two adults."

Trey grinned at the child and turned to mush. He

was a total sap for babies. The little girl was beautiful. Healthy chubby-baby round. Pretty pink skin. Blue eyes. She had dark blond curly fuzzy hair that looked…Trey fought a bemused grin…spiky and wet or something. Dressed in a one-piece ruffled pink baby-girl-outfit thingie with snaps, she clung to her mother and eyed him warily as her mother set about making the introductions.

"Mr. Trey Cooper," Cinda said, "I'd like you to meet my daughter, Miss Chelsi Elise Cavanaugh."

As Cinda reassured the little girl that it was okay for the big and smiling man to talk to her, Trey suddenly realized something amazing. Chelsi could be his daughter. Not in the biological sense. But in the physical traits department, she looked just like him. Her eyes were blue like his, and her hair was a sandy blond, again like his. He fought to keep the shock off his face, even as he heard himself engaging in the simpleton banter adults employ with babies.

Still, he couldn't get past it. Anyone who saw the two of them together would have no trouble believing that he was Chelsi's father. Of course, that was what he wanted people in Southwood to think. But this was pretty upsetting. It bothered him, and he couldn't figure out why. So she looked like him. So what? His looks and coloring, unlike Cinda's, weren't all that unique.

Then Trey realized what had him upset. It wasn't just that Chelsi looked like him. It was that he was proud she did. As if he'd had something to do with her creation. Well, that did it. Trey's single-male-and-liking-it genes rose up in protest. *Easy, buddy. With this kind of thinking, can pushing a baby buggy be far behind? Or the tan minivan? And holding your wife's purse in the mall while she shops for bras? Remember the race circuit. That's your first love. Always will be. Run, man. Just hightail it out of here, dude, I'm telling ya.*

Trey knew he wouldn't do that, but a more upsetting realization had just smacked him between the eyes: if Cinda's baby looked so much like him, then that meant he looked a lot like the baby's father, right? Okay, now here was some tricky ground. Trey pretty much believed that Cinda was attracted to him. He knew the signs. But could it be, at least in part, because he reminded her of her deceased husband? Oh, that would really suck.

Trey told himself that he needed to know what Richard Cavanaugh had looked like. Just to put his mind at ease. Just so he'd know that Cinda wasn't a vulnerable widow, one he was taking advantage of. But how the hell was he supposed to go about finding out what her husband had looked like? He couldn't just, out of the blue, ask her. What reason would he give? Nor could he demand that Cinda produce a picture of the man. And he certainly didn't think it would go over very well if he set out on a photograph-hunting safari of his own throughout her house. No doubt, Major Clovis would skewer him before he got to the stairs.

Though still chuckling at the baby who refused to come to him, on the inside Trey was beating himself up. What the hell was he even doing thinking he had a right to question Cinda about her feelings about anything? He barely knew the woman. Only it didn't feel that way.

So here was the thing: He wanted to see her and get to know her. Yet he didn't. If he did and came to really like her, which he thought he pretty much already did, then he'd have to confront and possibly abandon his own conviction about not being in a committed relationship right now because of the demands of his profession.

Or he could not see her at all. Too late. Here he was in her family room and that was her standing in front of him. All right, so he couldn't stop thinking about her and, yes, he had initiated this meeting between them. But now that he had, he was sorry—not because he didn't feel anything for her, but because he did. And he didn't like that. But since he did, it would really hurt now to find out that he reminded her of her deceased husband.

Damn, this was like a splash of cold water in the face. He'd gone down roads and pathways here in the past few moments that were really not called for. After all, what the two of them were doing here was trying to even a score. That was it. So he was attracted to her. So he'd gone to some lengths to see her. So what? He'd been here before in his thinking with other women.

No he hadn't, Trey realized. Not even close. The way he felt about Cinda was new and different from anything he'd ever felt before. Hell, he'd only seen her twice in six months, but she'd filled every thought he'd had in that half a year. There was no denying that.

So stick to the script, Trey told himself. *What difference does it make who you might remind her of? You didn't come here to ask her to marry you. You came here because she agreed to pretend to be married to you.* So get over yourself.

But he couldn't. He realized that this ruse of his

could work too darned well. After all, if he could see the resemblance between him and Chelsi, then so would everyone else, which, again, was what he wanted. But—and it was a big but—could he take a whole weekend of being told what a beautiful wife and daughter he had, with him already this attracted to Cinda and smitten with her baby? Wouldn't that fill him with joy and pride? *Oh, yeah, no doubt about that.* All right, then, wasn't it possible that he would then want to have that feeling permanently?

Extremely possible. And it wasn't fair to either one of them. He had his life on the circuit, and she had her baby and memories of her deceased husband.

Very troubled now, Trey focused on Cinda, who was fussing with the baby's outfit as he stood in front of her and watched. He put his hand on her bare arm. "Cinda, look at me." She did, her expression sweet and expectant. Trey felt like such a jackass. "I don't know how to tell you this, but I think I've made a big mistake in coming here. I don't think this whole thing was a good idea at all. I think I should just leave."

6

Trey watched Cinda for the effect of his words on her.

"Leave? But why? Because you almost kissed me? Or because I almost let you? I admit it was sudden. And unexpected. But—" Her expression mirrored her sudden concern for him. "Trey, are you all right? You look a little pale."

"I feel a little pale, but it has nothing to do with our ill-fated kiss. May I sit down?" He was already lowering himself onto the sofa's cushions.

"Of course." Cinda sat with him, perching her daughter on her lap. The baby immediately clutched her mother's heavy gold chain necklace in both fists and tried to stuff it in her mouth. Cinda held on to her daughter's fists and turned to him. "Tell me what's wrong. Should I call for Major Clovis? She *is* a nurse."

"No. God, no. I don't need a nurse. I just need to get a grip." Trey sank back against the supporting comfort of the sofa cushions. His knees apart, his hands resting lightly on his thighs, he stared into Cinda's mesmerizing golden eyes. "Cinda, I think we should—"

Chelsi let out a squawk, cutting Trey's words off. She then pitched herself over in his direction, dragging her mother, via her gold chain, with her. "Oops."

Cinda righted herself and her daughter. "I think she wants you to hold her, Trey. You don't have to—"

"No. Let me see her." This was perfect. Exactly what he needed to do. "I love babies," he said holding his hands out. "And I never miss an opportunity to hold one when offered."

Cinda looked enormously pleased. "Okay. If you're sure. Just let me get my necklace untangled from her fists."

As she gently pried her daughter's fingers open, Trey realized that he already felt a sort of kinship with this baby. After all, he'd been there when she came into the world. But right now, Trey wanted to hold the little girl for a reason not having to do with her own preciousness. Despite his misgivings of a few minutes ago, his not seeing how he could just blatantly ask Cinda what Richard had looked like, he decided that maybe one live picture—of himself and Chelsi together—was worth a thousand words. What he wanted to witness was Cinda's first and honest reaction upon seeing him and her baby together. He felt certain her face would reveal her emotions, and he might as well know them now as later.

"Okay. There we go. Finally." Cinda had untangled herself from her child. "I should know better than to wear anything she can get her little paws on." With that, she scooped up her baby, holding the child up and out to him. "Ready? Be careful. She can be a handful."

"About like her mother, I suspect," Trey quipped, striving to sound light and humorous, even though that wasn't how he felt.

Not yet handing the dangling baby over, Cinda

looked at him questioningly. "No one's ever said that to me before. Richard thought I was boring."

"Which is why the yaks got him." Trey heard himself—and saw Cinda's startled expression. "I'm sorry. That was out of line."

With a smile tugging at her lips, Cinda shook her head. "Actually, it was more funny than out of line."

"Whew. Dodged that bullet." Trey took hold of the soft and chubby little girl whose limbs were flailing wildly. "Come here, you." He turned her in his arms and greeted her. "Why, hello there, Chelsi. How you doing, huh?"

The baby stuck out her tongue and gave him the raspberries, a rousing Bronx cheer, and chortled her happiness with her efforts.

"I think I deserved that," Trey said mock seriously.

"Oh, God." Cinda covered her eyes with a hand. "I am so embarrassed. Major Clovis taught her that."

"Why am I not surprised?" Grinning, Trey focused on the baby. She was killer cute. He held her close to his face and turned toward Cinda. But the baby promptly grabbed two handfuls of his hair and, with more strength than he would have credited her with, pulled herself forward, her mouth open as if she meant to gnaw on his scalp. Making a sound of protest, Trey did his best to hold her at bay.

"You'll have to excuse her. She's teething," Cinda explained benignly, not offering him any help. "Either that or there are cannibals in the Cavanaugh bloodlines."

Trey was still fighting for his scalp, but this was just the opening he wanted. "Speaking of the Cavanaugh's, what do you think? Do you see here the same thing that I do, Cinda?"

"If you mean a man trying to keep a baby from snacking on his head, then yes I do."

"Not that. I meant not just any man and not just any baby."

Shaking her head, Cinda gestured her confusion. "Okay, specifically it's you and Chelsi."

"That's right. Me and Chelsi. And...?"

"Me?"

"Look again. Look closer. Do you see any resemblance here? Maybe between me and Chelsi and someone you knew and loved?"

Cinda's frown deepened. "What are you talking about?"

She really didn't see anything. A bit heartened but still stubbornly pressing his point, Trey finally disentangled his hair and sat the chortling baby on his lap, facing her mother. "Are you going to tell me that you don't see the resemblance here, Cinda? Look at us." Trey divided his attention between mother and daughter. "Chelsi looks just like me."

Cinda cocked her head, now looking from him to her daughter and back to him. "Do you really think so? I admit your coloring is the same. I mean your skin tone. But that's about it."

"Yeah? And our hair color?"

She considered them both. "Your hair color is about the same, too."

"And our eyes?"

"Blue. Oh, I get it. This is good since everyone in Southwood will believe she truly *is* your daughter, right?"

This was very good. She was going nowhere near Richard. But Trey had to be certain. "That's one way of looking at it. But I was talking about something else here.''

Looking perplexed Cinda crossed her arms over her chest. ''Something that made you want to leave, you mean? Maybe you'd better just tell me what it is, Trey. In plain English.''

Inhaling for courage, he plunged ahead. ''What did Richard look like?''

''Richard?'' She stared a bit blankly at him. Then suddenly she sobered. ''Ah. I see. I can't believe I was so slow. You and Chelsi look alike, so you're wondering if you and Richard bear any resemblance, right?''

''Yeah. I guess I am.'' Now Trey felt deflated. He'd brought her to this point, only now he didn't want her to think about it.

But Cinda looked just as pained as he felt. ''I don't really know what to say here, Trey, except I don't know why it would matter. After all, we are just talking about one weekend of the three of us posing as a family. I mean, that's all there is to this you-and-me thing, right?''

''Maybe.'' Trey held on to Chelsi and found he couldn't look the little girl's mother in the eye right now. The air between them seemed to settle, as if the air conditioner had just shut off. Hell, he'd opened this can of worms, so now he had to go fishing—and risk getting stuck on his own hook. He settled his gaze on her and opened his mouth to speak. ''Look, Cinda, I didn't mean to—''

She'd held her hand up to stop him. ''No. Allow me. Okay, look, I'm just going to say this. There is more going on here than your reunion. Between us, I mean. At least I hope there is, or I'm going to feel pretty stupid.''

''No need. I feel it, too.''

She nodded. ''I want to say 'good,' but it's obviously got you spooked, I can see that. Well, guess what? Me, too. Yet I'm thinking this topic, what Richard looks like, might be a bit premature. I mean, despite what this thing is between us, the truth is we hardly know each other. So wouldn't it make more sense to postpone this until we see if we even like each other?''

She was right, of course. And he was an ass. ''Cinda, I didn't mean to put this out there like that. There's a reason why women shouldn't ever talk to men. We're clueless.''

Finally she smiled. ''No, you're not. You're actually very sweet. And I guess I should be flattered that you'd already be so far along in your thinking.'' But then her expression crumpled, putting the lie to her words. ''However, this has nothing to do with—''

Leaving her thought unspoken, she abruptly stood up. She held her hands out for her daughter. ''Will you excuse us a moment, please?''

He wanted to say no he wouldn't. He had a feeling he wouldn't see her again if she left the room now. No doubt, Major Clovis would then come in, skewer him on a spit, and javelin-toss him out into the street. ''Cinda, I didn't mean anything by that. I really—''

''No, it's okay. I get it, Trey. You want to be certain that I, in my delusional grieving-widow state, don't think of you as a substitute for Richard. Am I right?''

Well, there it was. Everything he feared, and he had only himself to blame. ''Boy, that sucks when said out loud, huh? Look, I'm sorry if I hurt you or insulted you, Cinda. It was the last thing I wanted to do.''

"I think on some level I know that, Trey." She still held her hands out for her child. "It's just that I, well, I need to put Chelsi down for a nap."

"Oh." Coddling the baby, Trey stood and handed her over to her mother. "Listen, if you want me to leave, Cinda, just say so. Maybe it would be best if I did, if we just forget everything and I go."

She took her daughter from him and kissed the top of the child's head. Then she looked up into his eyes. Trey's heart thumped dully as he met Cinda's gaze. A sudden instinct had him wanting to gather her and her daughter into his arms, hold them forever, and tell them that everything would be all right. But that wasn't his job or his privilege, he quickly reminded himself.

Cinda inhaled and opened her mouth to speak. "No," she said. "Don't leave, Trey. That's the last thing I want you to do. Please wait for me. I want to show you something."

"All right."

She turned away and Trey watched her go. She moved her slender body with ladylike grace that was somehow very sensuous. Just the way she walked, the gentle sway of her hips and the way her long, blond hair moved with each step…it was very affecting. It made Trey want to run after her and take her in his arms and tell her everything he was thinking. He made a tiny sound of self-deprecation. Hadn't he just done that and with these wonderful results?

Wait for me, she'd said. He watched her turn a corner out of the room, leaving him there alone. Feeling very much out of place, Trey shoved his hands in his pants pockets and looked around. The room's very quietness accused him. But off to his right were French doors that looked out onto an expanse of immaculate lawn bordered by friendly looking beds of healthy blooming flowers. Trey walked over to the closed, beveled-glass doors and stared out. *Wait for me.*

Should he? he wondered. Maybe it would be best for them both if he made his apologies and just left. He didn't like to think he was chickening out, but, hell, it was obvious that Cinda was still vulnerable here. And he, well, he was awash in conflicting emotions himself regarding her. Trey shook his head. Teach him to get involved. Well, he wasn't yet. Not much.

UPSTAIRS, CINDA SOFTLY CLOSED the door to Chelsi's bedroom. The drowsy little girl was more asleep than awake. Cinda stood in the hall, listening to see if her daughter would fuss or take her nap. Waiting and listening, she leaned back against the wall, which had her facing three decoratively shaped windows across the way. Cinda planted her hands at her waist and studied her sandals. *I could hardly wait to see Trey today. And he is every bit as gorgeous and nice as I remembered him to be. Yet he thinks I'm a pathetic widow who has him confused with her dearly departed husband.*

Of course, Cinda realized, she had done nothing downstairs to dispel that notion. Again she saw herself making that pretty speech and then essentially fleeing with her daughter. Cinda winced at her own behavior. What must Trey think? This was not going the way she'd seen it in her mind. And, darn it, she had such a nice lunch planned for the two of them.

A happy gurgle of sound had Cinda listening again at the baby's door. The little stinker was playing. Smiling, Cinda resumed her wait. She'd give the baby a few more minutes to settle in. As she did, she thought again about her dilemma. On the one hand, she didn't owe him any explanations at all. They had no agreement, no arrangement. But on the other hand, it wouldn't be so awful if they could come to one. She considered that, wondering how it would feel to have something real with a heart-stopping guy like Trey. An impromptu poll of her senses told Cinda she liked that idea.

But this Richard thing was evidently a stumbling block for him. A valid one, she had to admit, because she knew firsthand how it felt to be second-best in someone's heart. Richard had been a man's man, a person more at ease with a life of masculine pursuits and testosterone-laden adventures than he had been with home and hearth. And her. So maybe she owed it to Trey to show him that in the nearly year and a half since her husband's death, she'd worked through all those feelings and had done her grieving.

She hated to admit it, but it hadn't been all that hard. Not that she was coldhearted. And certainly, she was sad about his death. But she and Richard just hadn't loved each other like they should have. That was probably the saddest part of it all. Still, Richard had seemed to have a pretty good handle on what he'd wanted from her. Loyalty and an heir. A good, quiet wife he didn't have to worry about. A woman who would uncomplainingly keep his home fires burning while he globe-trotted from one adventure to the next.

He hadn't been mean or even unkind. More like benignly neglectful. But once she'd realized that he would never be involved with her, that he might be fulfilled but she wasn't, she'd retreated into her happiness at the prospect of having a child. But even that hadn't been able to keep her satisfied. So she'd left. And then Richard had been killed. It was sad, she was sorry, and she had mourned him. But now, fifteen months later, she had it all in perspective and she could even think kindly of Richard.

So today was a little ironic, Cinda decided. Her greatest fear in the past six months had been that she, in her new-mother reluctance to get back out there and date, would become some needy, clingy female who glommed on to the first eligible male who crossed her path and would make him want to run. And that seemed to be happening because Trey had been in her company less than thirty minutes, and he already wanted to leave. Cinda thumped the heel of her hand against her forehead. *Good, Cinda. You're doing great here, girlfriend.*

Totally demoralized now, Cinda twisted her lips. *Maybe I'm not ready for this. Maybe Trey's right. We should call this whole thing off. It's only fair to us both. And to Chelsi. The last thing she needs is to get attached to a man who won't be around long. And that's the last thing I need, too.*

There. That was good and healthy. Cinda pushed away from the wall at her back and listened yet again at the door. All was quiet. Good. Cinda turned to face the stairs at the end of the hall. If Trey Cooper was still downstairs, then she owed him hospitality, if nothing else. Cinda smoothed her hands down the front of her flower-sprigged summer dress and fussed with her hair. And stopped. And entertained second thoughts. *You know what? Forget that. He's not getting out of this so easily. I want to do this. So we are going to do this—whether he likes it or not. He made an invitation and I accepted it.*

Now, that felt better. A whole lot better. Squaring her shoulders, Cinda marched with resolute steps toward the sweep of stairs that would carry her down to risk and adventure—and fun and laughter. Just what she needed. She started down the steps, her tread light and bouncy. She couldn't have felt more giddy, more adrenalin-pumped—

"No." Cinda stalled out, stopping on the stairs. "I can't make him do something he doesn't want to do any longer." She turned and fled back up the stairs. She stood at the head of them, one hand gripping the banister as she faced the second floor hall. "Wait a minute," she said softly to herself, a frown capturing her features. "He has to go through with this. He still needs us." Cinda saw herself standing there in the empty hallway. "And maybe I need to quit standing here talking to myself."

And maybe she needed, too, to quit being such a timid little mouse about men. Just because Richard hadn't valued her didn't mean no man would. Sure, he'd shaken her with his careless affection, but she knew how to live, how to have fun. Certainly her family was big and raucous and outgoing. Her father was an investment banker and her mother an attorney. Cinda thought of her three older brothers. Jeff was a pilot. Tim a policeman. And John, perhaps the bravest of them all, was the mayor of Canandaigua. And her? She was a journalist. Or had been. Still, no timid mice there in her bloodlines.

And it wasn't as if Trey was asking her to rappel down the Matterhorn with the baby strapped to her back. Richard might have wanted her to do that. But not Trey. Still, what they were going to attempt to pull off could prove to be just as tricky. But at least it wouldn't be physically dangerous. Certainly, Richard's derring-do and the fact that it had finally killed him had made her gun-shy, but only to physical danger. And that was only smart, she supposed.

Then why didn't Trey's occupation concern her? Well, it did. She had been concerned for him every time she'd read the sports section of the paper during the racing season. Stock car racing certainly had its share of tragedies. *But Trey isn't a driver,* she would always remind herself. He was a mechanic. So unless he dropped a lug wrench or a power drill on his head, he wasn't in the line of fire. She could live with that.

Happy again, her resolve renewed, Cinda once again took to the stairs. She could now face Trey with an open heart and a clear conscience. And now she could also show him a picture of her husband and laugh with him when he saw Richard's black hair. Chelsi didn't resemble her father at all. She looked more like a Mayes, Cinda's side of the family. Of course, she could have told Trey that downstairs, but she hadn't been ready then and, besides, what better proof than a picture?

"Which I can't show him without an actual picture in my hand. Hello." She stopped on the stairs. "Oh, Cinda. Go get the picture. Duh." She whipped around and scrambled back up the steps. A part of her mind wondered if Trey could hear all the noise she was making. Well, if he could, it was on his behalf, she reassured herself.

Cinda hurried to the closed door to Chelsi's room and put her ear to it. Thankfully, no fussing sounds came from that direction. *Good.* Cinda smiled. Now she could turn her full attention to safely and sanely pretending to be Trey Cooper's real-life wife in order to help him avoid the clutches of an over-sexed former girlfriend.

Cinda thought of the woman, a faceless stranger to her, and made a face of her own. What had she thought only a moment ago about this not being physically dangerous? What if the woman got violent? *Oh, surely not. Please. Certainly we're all mature adults here.*

Or…maybe not. Cinda treated herself to the mental image of her and some Southwood honey going at it tooth, nail and claw over Trey Cooper. Of course, Cinda saw herself getting the best of the woman. After all, she did have those three older brothers…. Suddenly, that prospect was funny—her in a catfight over a man who wasn't really hers.

She chuckled…then slowly sobered.

Still standing outside her daughter's room, Cinda crossed her arms under her breasts. She kept thinking words like "pretend" and "false scenario" and "for one weekend only." She didn't like the sounds of those. What she felt inside didn't feel false. Or like it would or should be short-lived. It felt more promising than that. At least to her, it did. Did it to Trey? Was he thinking past the weekend? Or would he just drop her and Chelsi off at the end of forty-eight hours, thank her, and drive happily away?

She'd kill him.

No, wait. Why would he be so upset that she might be looking for Richard in him if all he wanted was a wham-bam-thank-you-wife for forty-eight hours? In that case, it wouldn't matter what she might be thinking. And hadn't he said something about there being a possibility of something between them that would outlive their weekend together? Why, yes he had. Joyful again, Cinda wanted to cheer out loud but didn't dare. Still she pumped the air with a celebratory fist, mouthing, "Whoopee. He likes me."

Then didn't she need to get back downstairs before he gave up on her and left? Yes, she did. Cinda grinned diabolically. She was going to go get her a man. The thought became action. She turned and hurried back to the stairs and started down to the first floor. But then she turned right back around and charged back up them. "The picture, the picture, the picture, Cinda. God, think, girlfriend."

Suddenly she knew exactly which one to show Trey. It was in the home theater. In this particular snapshot, Richard was riding a camel in Egypt. He was tanned and swarthy and turbaned and looked like no one in this house. That ought to convince Trey that in her eyes he was his own man. A tiny little part of Cinda's woman's heart whispered, *With any luck, he'll be your own man, too.*

Luck, phooey. Cinda's snort was indelicate. What female needed luck when she possessed feminine wiles? So, there it was, her plan. Once they got to Southwood, Georgia, next weekend, she promised herself, she would play the role of Mrs. Trey Cooper to the hilt. But not only to fool, or to foil, the scheming ex-girlfriend's plotting. No, Cinda now had an agenda of her own with regard to Mr. Trey Cooper—a man who didn't know it yet, but a man who had just leaped from the frying pan...right into the fire.

Feeling good, feeling healthy and aware, Cinda told

herself she almost felt sorry for Trey. But only almost. Because by the time she was through with him, the man would be thinking he'd been trampled by his very own herd of stampeding yaks. But in a good way, of course.

Cinda hurried into the home theater, snatched up the framed picture, and again took to the stairs. This time, she made it all the way down them and through the house and back to the family room...where her guest awaited her. When her heart tripped happily at the sight of him standing there with his back to her, his hands in his pants pockets as he stared out her French doors onto the garden, Cinda knew she was right to pursue this with him.

"Trey?" she called out softly. He turned to her, a framed picture himself of masculine beauty all his own. Cinda's breath caught in her throat. Recovering, she said, "I want to show you this picture and tell you why you have nothing to worry about here. At least, not from Richard."

7

SO THIS WAS SOUTHWOOD. It was late in the afternoon on the following Friday, when Cinda got her first look at Trey's hometown. Through the car's windows, as they motored toward his mother's house on the other side of the small, quaint town, Cinda noted the passing sights. Decked out in its patriotic Fourth of July bunting, the place looked like a throwback to the nineteen-fifties. Unpaved roads met main streets. A redbrick schoolhouse sat happily closed for the summer. A drive-in hamburger place featured carhops and cars full of teenagers. A bowling alley sat surrounded by cars big enough to be called land yachts. Well-used pickup trucks kept them company.

A brick theater's old-time marquee advertised a two-year-old romantic comedy now showing on its one screen. They next drove past a soda fountain, then a drugstore, a clothing and furniture resale shop, a farm equipment dealership, a barbershop and of course, a beauty shop. And they had grabbed a soda at the greasy-spoon diner where the town's men probably gathered every morning for coffee and gossip and politics.

Cinda smiled. She loved it. She was glad she'd convinced Trey that she saw him for himself and that she was here with him. She'd broken free of the shackles of wealth. More than once, she'd felt she was as sheltered and coddled and restricted as any medieval princess in her castle tower. But not here. She was her own woman. Not Richard Cavanaugh's widow. Not Ruth Cavanaugh of the Long Island Cavanaughs' daughter-in-law. Here she was…pretending to be Trey Cooper's wife. Cinda came back to earth with a wry grin. Okay, so she wasn't exactly her own woman.

"And here's Main Street," Trey said, capturing her attention as he made a right turn. "The nerve center of town. City Hall and the rest of the bastions of local government."

Sure enough, official-looking buildings from another era, perhaps another century, held captive a town square, complete with a cannon at its grassy center. Scattered around under the trees were park benches populated by old-timers. Off to one side resided a bronze statue of what was no doubt a war hero.

Cinda pointed to it. "Trey, that statue there." She looked over at him. "Didn't you tell me once that Southwood had no war heroes?"

A teasing light in his blue eyes rewarded her when he flashed her a grin carrying enough sensual wattage to light up a Christmas tree. "We don't. He's a borrowed Civil War hero. Belongs to the next town over."

"Are you pulling my leg?"

"No, but I can if you want me to." He made a playful feint in her direction, as if to grab her thigh.

Ticklish, Cinda squawked and grabbed his muscled forearm. "You stop that. You're going to make me wake up Chelsi."

Still looking devilish, Trey settled back into his driving. "Hey, look there," he said, pointing ahead.

Cinda saw a big banner strung high up between

street lamps on opposites sides of the road. Waving in the slight breeze, it announced the town's high-school reunion and welcomed all the alumni back to town. To her surprise, Cinda was overcome with a warm but inexplicable feeling of actually coming home. "I like this town. It's like a Norman Rockwell painting of small-town America."

Trey's expression mixed doubt with hope. "You're just being nice. This is Hicksville, Nowhere, USA."

"It is not. Quit saying that." Turning toward her passenger-side window, Cinda smiled a secret smile at the note of boyish pride in his voice that put the lie to his words. This was the same man who'd spent the past hour telling her how much she was going to hate it here and how glad he was that he didn't live here anymore.

And all of *that* from the same excited man who had shown up at her house today an hour earlier than their agreed-upon time. He'd calmed down quite a bit, though, after Major Clovis took him aside and told him—to use Trey's exact words—how the cow ate the cabbage. As near as Cinda could tell, that came close to meaning the same thing as having been read the riot act. Or being threatened with a guillotine.

"You'll notice this street is actually paved," Trey observed dryly. "And that, unlike on Elm Street, there are no dogs sitting in the middle of the road licking their, uh, private parts."

"Hey, I was impressed that you knew the dog's name and who he belonged to," Cinda quipped. "Mr. Cheevers's old mutt named Ed, right?"

"Right." Again he glanced over at her. "You hate it here, don't you?"

He wanted so much for her to like Southwood that

he didn't believe her when she said she did. "I don't hate it here, Trey. In fact, I was just thinking how much I like it. How unlike Atlanta it is."

"I thought you liked living in Atlanta."

Cinda shrugged. "I do. But it doesn't feel like home." Not like it did here, either.

Trey made a left onto a residential street—Maple Avenue. As Trey drove slowly down it, Cinda caught sight of a few brick homes interspersed with the mostly wood-framed ones. The houses were well-kept, modest, and sported cyclone fences that enclosed grassy backyards.

Gravel driveways were laid out beside each house. Some led to attached single-car garages. Others ended at former garages that had been enclosed at some point for extra room in the house. Shading everything in a friendly manner were tall, leafy oaks and pecan trees. Also scattered in the area were various running, playing children, and a few mothers chatting on the sidewalk amid toddlers and their toys.

Excitement coursed through Cinda. She sat up straighter, thinking this was how life was supposed to be. "Oh, Trey, this is so great. If Chelsi were older, she would love all this." Cinda turned in her seat as best she could, given the constraints of her seat belt, to see what her daughter was doing. Still sleeping. Cinda again faced forward. "What a great place to grow up. Why did you ever leave here?"

He chuckled as he pulled into a gravel drive that ended at a small wood-frame house surrounded by tall trees and fronted by a neglected flower bed. "Why did I leave? Ask me that again after this weekend."

"You keep saying that."

"I mean it, too." Trey pulled up to the closed gate

to the backyard and stopped his red, shiny American-made muscle car. "Here we are. All safe and sound." Leaving the engine and the air conditioner running, he looked over at her. "So. Let the games begin...Mrs. Cooper."

Cinda looked around. "Your mother? Where?"

Trey gripped her arm. "Cinda, that's you. Don't forget."

Cinda's heart thumped with apprehension. "Ohmigod, that's right. I'm sorry. I'll get better at this, I swear. I guess it was just being here at your mother's house that threw me for a second. I'm okay. Really."

"You sure?"

It was there in his raised eyebrows and doubting look. This whole weekend could blow up in their faces if she didn't remember her role here. What had she been thinking to agree to such a thing as this? "What are we doing? This is wrong. I mean...look at this."

By looking down at her hands in her lap, she directed Trey's gaze there as well. Circling her ring finger was a fake gold wedding band. Once again, in her mind's eye, she saw Trey's reddening face earlier when he'd unceremoniously presented it to her and had put a matching cheap band on his own ring finger. "Trey, we can't do this. You have to think of something else. We'll be lying to your family and friends. I don't think I can—"

"Hey," he said softly. From the corner of her eye, she saw him undo his seat belt and reach out to her. Before she could even hold her breath in anticipation of his touch, he tucked a finger under her chin and turned her head until her gaze met his. A thrill chased through her. The merest touch from him, the briefest of glances, and she was mush, even now.

To her utter surprise, he then leaned over and gently kissed her on the lips. Tiny shocks of electricity skated over Cinda's lips. She barely had time to close her eyes before Trey pulled back. "I wondered when this reaction was going to set in. If it makes you feel any better, I've had second thoughts about all this, too. I think it's a little late now for backing out, but just say the word, Cinda, and I'll take you back to Atlanta."

He gently caressed her cheek and then took his hand away, resting it on his thigh. Cinda stared at his work-roughened, capable hand and wished she had the courage to reach over and take it in hers and guide it back to her cheek and nuzzle it, like a cat would. Exhaling, she said, "No. I promised you I'd do this, and I will. Just call it a case of, I don't know, new-bride jitters, I guess."

"I like that. New-bride jitters, huh?" His smile was warm and sympathetic—and sensual.

But then his expression became serious. Cinda held her breath. Trey was giving every appearance that an admission of some sort was coming.

Sure enough, he said, "Cinda, I just…" He glanced at her and then away. "I want you to know—" Again he stopped himself. He ran a hand through his hair, exhaled, and then looked over at her. "You know, I'm a grown man and this shouldn't be so hard. But what I'm stumbling through trying to tell you is I want you to know that the *only* reason I asked you to come with me this weekend was…so I could spend time with you."

Cinda exhaled her relief. She'd had no idea what he might have been about to say. But this was good. Very good. As if to prove it, a jet of desire flitted through her veins, carried by steadily warming blood. She found she had to swallow before she could speak. "I don't know what to say, except thank you."

Trey chuckled as if she'd said something funny. "You're welcome. I didn't mean to make such a big deal of it. I just wanted you to know. I mean, after you cleared up that do-I-look-like-Richard thing for me, I find I...just want to be with you. And there it is again. All of a sudden, I can't stop saying it."

"No one says you have to," Cinda rushed to assure him. Could his eyes be more blue? That was all she could think about—that and how much she wanted him to kiss her again. He was so wonderful. But then, she had a sobering thought. Their pretense wasn't only about some sensual game between them. There were consequences for other people as well. "But Trey, what about your ex-girlfriend? That Bobby Sue woman?"

"Jean. Bobby Jean. She doesn't scare me."

Finding this topic to be safer, firmer ground, Cinda stood on it. "Well, she ought to, from everything you've told me about her."

"That's true. But I didn't tell you everything."

Cinda's firm ground felt suddenly soft and marshy. "Oh, I don't like the sound of that at all. What is she—?" Cinda cast about for the worst thing she could think of. "—the mother of your child?"

"Ha. Hardly. No."

Thank God. "Then what? Is she in the Mafia?"

Trey didn't laugh. And then he made it worse. "No. But her estranged husband, one Mr. Rocco Diamante from New Jersey, is reputed to be. Very strongly reputed."

Cinda's heart turned to stone. Gone was her excitement for the coming weekend. In its place were anger and a sense of having been set up. "Oh, God, Trey, where there's smoke there's fire. Why didn't you tell me this before?"

Trey shot her a sidelong glance. "Would you have come with me if I'd told you that part?"

"No, Trey, I wouldn't have. I have a daughter to protect."

"And I have a wife and a daughter and a mother to protect."

"A pretend wife and daughter."

"Okay. Pretend. But three women, at any rate."

"I can protect myself."

"All right. I have a baby and my mother—"

"I can take care of my baby, too."

Trey exhaled loudly. "Fine. I have my mother to protect."

"I'll bet she can take care of herself just fine."

Trey frowned. "Will you leave me someone to protect, please?"

Cinda crossed her arms over her chest. "Fine. Keep your mother. And if I were you, I'd watch my own behind, too."

"Thanks for the advice. I will." Then he became explanatory. "Look, Cinda, you have to know that I wouldn't have brought you and Chelsi here if I'd thought there was the slightest danger. Besides, there's nothing to say that Bobby Jean's husband will even show up—"

Cinda's abrupt move to turn toward him cut off his words. "Trey, two words." She held up two fingers. "Estranged." She crooked one finger. "Mafia." She crooked the other one. She now had a fist. "He'll show up. Here's another word—Headlines. I was a reporter. This is a story. He'll show up and he'll kill us all."

"I don't think so." Trey stopped the engine and opened his door. "But thank God you're here to report it, if it does happen. Which it won't."

Cinda was right behind him, releasing her seat belt and preparing to exit the car. "How could I report it if I was dead?"

"I don't know. You're the one who's the reporter. But for crying out loud, you won't be dead."

"Oh, you can guarantee that?" Assaulted by the summer's sticky heat, made worse by her escalating anger, Cinda stepped out of the car and opened the back door where Chelsi slept on in her car seat. Cinda leaned over, poking her head and upper body into the car's interior, thinking to undo and then extract her little girl from the NASA-worthy contraption. But then she realized that Trey hadn't answered her. She retreated from the car and found him just then coming around to the vehicle's trunk.

He met her gaze, then hit the remote button on his key chain to pop the trunk lid. "I heard you. And yes I can guarantee that you won't be dead. Don't you think I've thought this through, Cinda? If the guy shows up—and I still think it's a big if—I know the police chief. Bubba Mahaffey and I went to high school together."

Cinda put her hands to her waist. "Bubba Mahaffey? *Bubba?* Well, there's a name that will strike terror into a Mafioso's heart. I think I'd feel better if his name was something like Killer."

"You obviously haven't seen Bubba yet." His mouth pursed, Trey began tossing their luggage out of the trunk and onto the grass.

Two pieces of her top-end designer-label bags went flying by. Mouth agape with outrage, Cinda glared at Trey. "Do you mind not throwing my luggage about? There are things in there that could break."

Without a word, Trey raised an eyebrow and tossed her makeup kit on top of the sorry heap he'd already made of their weekend things.

This meant war. Cinda eyed him. "Lovely. We're not here five minutes and we're already fighting. I knew I shouldn't have come. Major Clovis told me this would end badly. So did Marta."

"Oh really? What exactly did Marta have to say?"

Cinda couldn't quite hold his gaze. "I don't know. Something rapid-fire in Spanish that required a lot of gestures. She even did that slitting your throat thing with her finger across her neck."

"You sure she wasn't talking about Major Clovis?"

"She could have been. I don't know." Cinda adopted a defensive posture, crossing her arms over her chest. She stared at her "husband" standing next to the raised trunk lid. With his chambray shirt highlighting his broad shoulders, as well as his blue eyes, Trey Cooper could not have been more handsome, damn him.

Then, suddenly, it was just funny, the two of them standing there in his mother's front yard and fussing just like they'd been married forever. It was funny and silly. The Mafia? As if. Cinda popped a hand over her mouth, bound and determined not to be the first or the only one to laugh.

But apparently Trey had come to the same conclusions as she had because he chuckled. "I can't believe this. What were we fighting about?"

"I don't know. The Mafia, I think."

"Well, as long as it wasn't politics or religion."

"Or sex and kids. Or money or the in-laws."

The humor fled in Trey. Suddenly he looked a bit sickly.

Without even knowing what was wrong, Cinda caved right along with him. "Oh, no, Trey, what now?"

"I have something else to tell you."

She put a hand to her forehead. "Dear God. What now?"

He took a deep breath. "Okay. It's my mother."

"Your mother? Great. What about her?"

"You made me think of it when you named those things that married couples fight about."

Married couples. But they weren't a married couple. Cinda pondered that, then feared she knew where this was going. "Trey, if you tell me that you didn't tell her the truth here—"

"I did." He raised a hand to halt her objections. "I told her. Only she doesn't believe me."

"She doesn't—what does that mean?" Cinda's next thought stiffened her knees. "Are you telling me that she thinks we're really married?"

He shook his head. "No. She doesn't just *think* it. She chooses to believe we're really married and I just didn't tell her we were getting married. Or having a baby."

"What possible reason would you have *not* to tell her?"

Trey was looking more and more uncomfortable here. "That's what I told her."

"And she said…?" Not that Cinda really wanted to know. "Based on your having told her the truth, of course."

Now he looked defensive. Big, handsome, manly…and little-boy defensive. He couldn't have been more endearing—if Cinda had been less angry with him, that is.

"I told her," he said stubbornly. "But she thinks we didn't tell her because we—you and I—*had* to get married, if you get my drift."

Cinda could only stare at him. "We *had* to get married? Trey, does your mother *know* how old you are? I mean you're not a kid. It's not like you wouldn't be allowed to go on the senior trip because of an unplanned pregnancy. Besides, it's not a big deal today anyway…" Cinda stopped herself. "Will you listen to me? Now I'm preaching. None of that relates to us."

"No it doesn't. But the important thing here is my mother has it in her head that I've made up this cockamamie story—her words—to cover my butt and keep her from getting mad or being hurt."

There was absolutely nowhere Cinda could go with this. "Well? Did it at least work? Is she mad or hurt now?"

"Yes. She's both."

Cinda clapped her hands to her aching head. "I do not believe this. What must your mother think? That you're ashamed of me? That I'm some kind of…easy woman or something? Someone you don't love and who trapped you?"

"I don't think she thinks any of that, Cinda. It's me she's mad at, not you. See, she wanted me to marry Bobby Jean."

Cinda dropped her arms to her sides. "Oh, that's perfect. It doesn't get any better than this."

Trey kept talking as if Cinda hadn't interrupted him. "But once she meets you, she'll forget about all that.

Which is also part of my plan. But come on, Cinda, she could hardly think you're easy. Everything about you says class. The way you dress. The way you look, talk, carry yourself. Hell, you scream respectability.''

"So that makes me about as exciting as an old-maid schoolteacher.''

"Man, I am losing here. Big time.''

"No, you're not," Cinda said, relenting some. "But you know, Trey, just once I would like to have a mother-in-law—real or pretend—who actually likes me.''

His frown mirrored disbelief. "Richard's mother doesn't like you?''

Cinda made a face. "Yeah, I guess she does. Probably even loves me in her own way. But I took her baby from her.''

"No you didn't. The yaks did. Wait. You mean Chelsi, right?''

"No, I meant Richard. He was her everything, her whole reason for living, despite having a wonderful husband. That's Papa Rick. A sweetheart of a man. But then Richard married me. And we didn't really love each other, and she knew it. And then I left and he was killed and then Chelsi— Would you listen to me? You know this story. And I certainly do, too.''

"Hey, Cinda, listen," Trey said, his expression sympathetic, "it's going to be okay. I can feel it.''

She smiled but she didn't believe him. "Good. I'm over it. I really am. So your mother thinks I'm some trashy something you have to keep hidden. Whatever.'' She quickly bent over to undo Chelsi from her car seat.

The baby was awake now and chewing on a fist.

That meant one thing. She was hungry. In about five minutes she could be screaming.

Cinda believed that she just might join her daughter, too. Especially when the sound of a car turning into the gravel driveway behind Trey's car could only mean one thing.

Her "mother-in-law" was home.

8

THERE'S NOTHING LIKE A POTLUCK DINNER. Why the reunion committee had decided to hold this Friday-night event in the too-warm, too-small veterans' meeting hall in the center of town was beyond Trey. At least the food was great and plentiful. And the three-piece band of old coots with fiddles was jubilant if off-key. Adding to the general celebration, the crowd proved noisy and friendly.

Trailing docilely behind Cinda and his mother, who had Chelsi in her arms, Trey held on to their plates of food as they searched for three empty chairs together. Trey had no idea how he'd survived that afternoon and his mother meeting Cinda and Chelsi, but he had, and he was grateful for that. But, to his horror, because nothing good for him could come out of this, his mother and "wife" were now best friends and were both mad at him. Why, he had no idea. He couldn't think what he'd done...except to maybe lie to them both to get them to this point. But that had been for a good cause. And now they liked each other. So what was the problem?

Being a smart man, Trey remained quiet as they threaded their way through the happy crowd and toward the far tables and chairs set up all around the walls. But he couldn't get more than two feet, it seemed, before someone else recognized him and just had to clap him on the back and bend his ear about old times and glory days. He'd be more than happy to swap lies with them, he told his old friends, once he could set down the two overflowing heavy-duty paper plates of food from the unbelievable spread at the front of the meeting hall. He'd made it this far with everything from chicken to chocolate cake piled atop the plates. And despite the best efforts of the jostling, churning crowd, he was determined not to drop or spill anything now.

But of more immediate concern to him was the fact that the two women had their heads together and were nodding conspiratorially. That didn't bode well. He needed to listen in on them. But once he got close Trey heard, to his relief, that he and his sins weren't, for once this evening, the subjects of discussion. Instead, his mother was regaling Cinda with her take on the town gossip.

"Oh, honey, over there that's old Mrs. Ledbetter. She's a hundred and five years old and deaf as a doornail. You got to yell to get her to understand you. Come on, go this way before she sees us. She hasn't shaved her chin lately and hasn't got a tooth in her head, but she'll want to kiss this baby. And that could scare the child into raising a permanent birthmark. Excuse me. Lady with a baby coming through. Trey, be careful with those plates. I don't want banana pudding smeared on my back. Oh, Cinda, honey, do you see that woman over yonder with the ugly eyeglasses and yellow dress? That's Pearl Thompson. Her husband's the preacher hereabouts. The man's a drinker, I tell you. I haven't ever caught him at it, but he has the look about him.

"Now wait here a minute while I see if I can spot—

Aha, there she is. The old biddy by the potted plant. See her? I do want you to meet her, Cinda. She's always bragging about her grandkids. Ugliest children you ever saw in your life. Not that the poor things can help it. The little girl's got the lazy eye and the boy's a bit simple. Anyway, the old sow's name is Lula Johnston. Once we get to a place where we can sit down and eat, providing Trey doesn't drop those plates first, I'll take you around to meet her. Yes, ma'am, I want her to meet *my* daughter-in-law and *my* grandbaby. We'll tell her the reason you and the baby haven't been around before is because you were in some place like Germany."

Over her shoulder, Cinda arrowed a pointed this-is-all-your-fault glare at Trey, and he winced. His mother was telling a different story each time she introduced Cinda and Chelsi. So far they'd lived in five different countries. And once they'd been in the witness protection plan. Like you could get out of that. And, oh yes, they'd been lost in a canyon out West, only to be discovered by a passing band of kindly Indians. But Trey's personal favorite was they'd been living in a commune in northern California. Anything but the truth, which, he had to admit, his mother really couldn't tell, even if she had believed him. Which she didn't.

But even if she did, what could she say? *Trey's pretending to be married to this widow so he can keep Bobby Jean's mobster husband from killing him?* As if his mother believed that. What sane person would? Who cared if it was the truth? Sometimes the truth just wouldn't cut it.

Even more importantly to Trey, he wondered what Cinda was thinking about all this. She was certainly being a damned good trouper about everything. He had to respect that. And, God bless her, here she was smiling and being sweet to everyone who—Trey now good-naturedly mimicked his Southwood friends—just had to meet Trey Cooper's wife. *Why we never thought he'd settle down and aren't you just the prettiest thing and my, my what a pretty baby. Looks just like Trey, doesn't she? How come we didn't know about you before tonight? Trey, why are you keeping this sweet girl a secret?*

Which resulted in his mother's varying stories, all of which she would deny saying at a later date. With an affectionate smile on his face as he walked behind his family, real and otherwise, Trey still couldn't say if he was blessed or cursed. It was hard to tell, given the scene from earlier that afternoon that had resembled a female version of an Old West gunfight when his mother and Cinda had met.

In a nutshell, his mother had come home from work at the bowling alley, and as she'd climbed out of her car, she saw Cinda, and had just stood there. Then Cinda had lifted Chelsi out of her car seat and the two of them had faced his mother. Then the baby began to cry, followed by Cinda bursting into tears. Then so had his mother. And finally—what man on this green earth understood women?—they had rushed toward each other, only to fall, sobbing, into each other's arms as they cradled the squalling baby between them.

Again Trey saw his mother turning to him and smacking his arm for making them all cry. What was wrong with him, anyway, she'd wanted to know, for keeping them all apart like he had?

While he was happy that his mother and Cinda had—Trey grimaced at his use of the politically correct word—"bonded," all he could think was what he wouldn't give right now for something he truly did have a prayer of understanding. Like a lube rack. Or a power drill. Or a life-sized poster of the Andretti racing team. Or a map of the layout of the track at Darlington. A stopwatch. A checkered flag. All those things were easy. And they weren't women.

In the interest of self-preservation, however, Trey kept his wits about him. His mother, so far, was content to fill Cinda in on all the town gossip regarding essentially everyone in attendance. That amounted to over two hundred noisy people. And by the time they got to the long cloth-covered picnic tables set up along the walls and found some empty seats together, Cinda had been given the scoop on everyone. She had the blank stare to prove it.

All Trey knew was that not for all the money in the world would he try again to convince his mother that he and Cinda really, *weren't* married. The woman had loved her "daughter-in-law" and "grandbaby" on sight. There was only one thing to do. If things didn't work out between him and Cinda, Trey knew he would have to stage a divorce and set up fake child visitation privileges. The thought made Trey's stomach hurt. Damn, it would just be easier to marry Cinda for real—and kiss the ground she walked on for the rest of their lives for having him—than it would be to explain to his mother that he had always been telling the truth.

But Dorinda Sue Cooper wouldn't hear it, believe it, or accept it. Besides, she'd already made up the pointedly double bed in what she now called her guest room—Trey's old bedroom—for the two of them and had bought a crib for the baby. One big happy family in a room the size, no doubt, of Cinda's walk-in clothes-closet at her home in Atlanta. And yes, of course, he'd gotten The Look from Cinda when she'd seen his mother's plans for their sleeping arrangements. Her expression had clearly conveyed that he'd be sleeping on the floor for the next two nights.

No more than he deserved, he supposed. Trey set the plates on the table and, in his continuing effort to keep his scalp by being a gentleman, he turned to Cinda and held his hands out. "Here, let me have those."

"With pleasure." She handed over the three cold cans of soda and the plastic forks and spoons she had clutched in her arms.

Trey set them all down and then again held out a hand to her. "And the diaper bag."

"It's all yours." She had it slung over her shoulder with her purse. How such a small woman could tote all that without falling over, he'd never know. But she gave it to him, too, and then they settled into their chairs and began arranging their places.

Within seconds, a group of Trey's rowdy friends from high school exploded out of the milling crowd and accosted him. Loud craziness prevailed. High fives. Old memories. New families. Who was bald, who wasn't. Who'd put on weight, seemed shorter. All the have-you-seens and where's-old-so-and-sos were interspersed with handshakes and bear hugs. Trey loved every bit of it. He hadn't seen some of these guys for years. And he was more than proud, as well as a bit guilty, knowing the truth of his "marriage," to include Cinda and call her over to be introduced and to show off Chelsi.

As Cinda excused herself to go sit with his mother

at the table while he relived old times with his friends, every nerve ending in Trey's body was on red-alert for trouble. After all, here he was with his "wife" and "daughter" and mother…and Bobby Jean Diamante was nowhere in sight.

Trey kept a close watch out for the firebrand troublemaker. No matter who he was talking to, he was looking over their shoulder or his own. Bobby Jean was not the type of person you'd want to have sneak up on you. So where could she be? What could she be planning? A grand entrance? That was her style. Everyone knew she was in town and took great pains to tell Trey so. On just the one trip across the crowded room, he'd been pulled aside countless times by friends who had whispered in his ear that Bobby Jean had blown into town earlier this afternoon. In a black stretch limousine, no less, the excited conspirators had told him. *A limo. You know what that means. The mob.* Trey wasn't so sure that's what it meant, but he was relieved to learn she'd come to town alone.

Just then, Trey's arm was grabbed by the one man here he really wanted to talk to. Southwood's police chief, Bubba Mahaffey, pulled Trey away from his waiting family as the milling crowd closed between him and them.

"Bubba, you old son of a gun," Trey greeted him. "How you doing, boy? Damn, look at you. You still growing, or what?"

The police chief, dressed in a suit and cowboy boots, was a six-foot-five florid man with a barrel chest, a quick smile, and big hammy fists that no one challenged. A former classmate and football-team member of Trey's, he clasped Trey to him in a back-pounding hug that nearly deflated Trey's lungs. "Trey, you dog, you. How the hell are you, old son?"

"Never better. Still on the race circuit. How about you? How's crime?"

"Can't find none to speak of. Got a nice new jail I'm just itching to try out, though, if you'd care to break a law or two. But what about you? I heard you got married and had a baby girl."

"Yeah, that's the rumor," Trey answered. "They're back there at a table with Mama. I'll take you around and introduce you in a minute." Trey grinned gratefully at his friend. Bubba was playing this to the hilt. Of course Trey had called last week to tell the sheriff what he was doing and why. It never hurt to have the law on your side. And he'd also asked Bubba to check up on that husband of Bobby Jean's. "So, Bubba, how are Marlee and the kids?"

"Sassy as ever. Just the way I like 'em. They're up front somewhere filling their plates. They should be along directly." Then suddenly the man was serious and quiet. "You know Bobby Jean's already in town?"

Trey sobered right along with him. "I've been told a couple hundred times already this evening."

"I bet you have. I called up to New York City and checked that ole boy out that Bobby Jean married. The police there haven't heard anything about him. Don't have him in their system. There could be a lot of reasons why not. It could be that he's really high up. Or he could be small-fry, a new player, someone they just haven't caught in their net so far."

"In other words, Bubba, nothing can be proved or disproved, right?"

"That's right."

"That damn Bobby Jean," Trey fumed, shaking his head.

"That's the truth. I swear that gal's got the whole town in an uproar. The wife says Bobby Jean put in an appearance at Ramona's Salon of Beauty this afternoon and told everyone she was separated from her husband and said how she'd told him he couldn't compare to one Trey Cooper."

Feeling knotted up inside, Trey grimaced at Bubba's broad grin. "You're enjoying this, aren't you, Bubba?"

"I sure as hell am. Anyway, your old girlfriend caused quite the scene, Marlee says, when the ladies told her you were a married man and a daddy."

Trey nodded. "I knew I could count on Mama to do a good job of telling everyone in town that bit of news." *A married man and a daddy.* Only temporarily and by design. What upset Trey was how bad he felt that it was so. Or maybe he just felt bad about lying to everyone. At least Bubba knew the truth.

"She sure did," Bubba was saying. "Now, Bobby Jean, according to Marlee, said that made no difference to her because everyone knows you're hers. Then she flounced out, telling them to just stand back and see if she didn't have her way with you."

Feeling like death warmed over, Trey ran a hand over his chin. "Man, Bubba, what the hell. I've got to set that girl straight before she messes around and gets me killed."

"That's no lie, buddy. Listen, after Marlee told me about the beauty shop set-to, I paid Bobby Jean a visit at her daddy's hardware store. And damned if she isn't as beautiful as ever. Still has that stop-you-in-your-tracks figure of hers. And all that red hair. Hard to think of her as conniving. But anyway, I told her I didn't want no trouble this weekend.''

''How'd she take that?''

Looking sheepish, Bubba scratched at his head. ''She pretty much told me to mind my own business and stay out of hers.''

Alarm spread through Trey. ''So, of course, you told her that keeping the peace here *is* your business, right?''

''I did.'' Then Bubba, his expression desperate, moved in close to Trey. ''Damned if she didn't tell me that if I messed with her she'd tell Marlee and my mother about that time in the eighth grade—before you and Bobby Jean were together—that she and I got caught by the coach in the locker room after football practice….'' Bubba's voice trailed off, his face turned red.

''It's cool, Bubba. I knew about that. I was on the team, too, remember?'' This was why Trey didn't live in Southwood. Being here was like being back in high school. In so many ways, his friends had never moved on. Trey shook his head over this Bobby Jean silliness that could easily turn into seriousness. ''Go on. What happened then?''

''Nothing. We left it at that. And now I'm telling *you* that I don't want any trouble this weekend.''

Trey pulled back sharply. ''Wait a minute. You're warning *me* now?''

''No, no, not warning, buddy. Just asking you to try to keep a lid on things, if you can. Otherwise, the Fourth of July celebration won't be the only fireworks we have.''

Bubba was clearly out of his league here. Bobby Jean had that effect on people, Trey knew. Even someone as big and as official as the sheriff wasn't immune to her scheming. Trey didn't know whether to laugh or cry. "Bubba, I'll do what I can. After all, this mess is partly of my making. I've ignored Bobby Jean's maneuverings when I should have told her but good to lay off. Maybe I can do that this weekend. And out of earshot of everybody else."

Obviously relieved, Bubba cuffed Trey's arm playfully. "I'm glad for your help is all I'm saying."

Trey nodded. "I tell you what, though, Bubba. It's a boneheaded thing I did bringing Cinda and her baby here. This could be a real disaster. I don't know what the hell I was thinking."

"You weren't thinking with the right part of your anatomy is the problem." Bubba clapped a big hand on Trey's shoulder with such friendly force that Trey nearly went to his knees. "The good thing is Bobby Jean's here alone, and I don't expect she'll do much more than make a scene. Marlee says all Bobby Jean needs to settle her down some is a baby." A wicked glint came into Bubba's eyes and pulled his grin up suggestively.

"Don't you even say it, Carter Raymond Mahaffey," Trey warned. "You might have five inches and about fifty pounds on me, you old tin badge, but I've beat up on that thick head of yours more than once when we were growing up. And I can do it again."

Bubba's good humor was unfazed. "Take your best shot, friend. But Marlee says Bobby Jean wants a baby. And she wants her high-school sweetheart to be its daddy. Now who could that be? Let me see. Oh, I know. The captain of the state-champion football team his senior year in high school. One George Winston Cooper the Third. You know him?"

His eyes narrowed in warning, Trey crossed his arms over his chest. "Never met the man."

"Is that so? Well, if you do meet him, give him some advice for me, will you?" Bubba pulled Trey in so close to him that their noses almost met. "Tell him he'd better marry that little blond girl of his for real because Bobby Jean has her sights set on him. And what Bobby Jean wants, Bobby Jean gets."

How well Trey knew that. Dread washed over him as he stepped back from Bubba. "Look, I'll worry about Bobby Jean. You worry about her husband showing up and looking for her."

"I've got your back, Trey. You can count on me," the police chief said as he moved away through the crowd.

"I always do, Bubba," Trey called out, wondering when the next shot would be fired.

He didn't have long to wait. A commotion at the front of the meeting hall captured his and everyone else's attention. He heard loud greetings and happy feminine shrieks of recognition and reunion. Then, a tense, suspenseful silence rolled like a wave through the crowd. When all was dead quiet, everyone turned Trey's way. He swallowed. As long as he lived, he would swear that the crowd parted—to a man, woman, and child, half on either side of the room—until there was nothing but floor space between him at the back of the hall and Bobby Jean Diamante at the front.

And then, she caught sight of him. Grinning evilly, she vamped his way. Trey exhaled softly in a low whistle. *Here comes trouble.*

"WHAT'S WRONG? What's going on? Why did everyone get so quiet?" Cinda craned her neck and looked toward the small stage area where the awful little trio was, or had been, playing. "Is some sort of program going to start?"

Dorinda Cooper handed Chelsi off to Cinda and stood up, looking around. "Lord above, honey, it's not a program. More like a spectacle, I'll warrant."

Cinda knew immediately what, or who, Dorinda meant. Her heart rate picked up, and she knew a moment of fear. "Bobby Jean's here, right?"

"In all her radiant glory, honey. And she's alone." Dorinda, a small woman with stiffly styled brown hair and thick eyeglasses, turned to Cinda. "Give me that baby back and you go save your husband."

"I don't have a—oh, my husband. Trey. Of course." Cinda died a thousand times in the next few seconds before she realized, with tremendous relief, that Dorinda Cooper had apparently not registered Cinda's confused yet honest response. As her "mother-in-law" pulled Chelsi out of Cinda's ams and held her, Cinda cleared her throat and tried again. "What am I supposed to do to save him?"

Dorinda Cooper's expression was stubborn. "You're a woman. You'll think of something, honey. You just go out there and stake your claim, girl. And don't you take any guff off Bobby Jean, you hear me?"

"Yes, ma'am," Cinda heard herself saying, even when she had no idea yet what exactly was expected of her.

"Good. Now, I need to tell you something, just so's you'll know. I used to think Bobby Jean and Trey were meant for each other. But not anymore. He's a married man now, and my allegiance is to you. So you listen to me. Bobby Jean is a sweet child, but she can also be like a little animal. If she smells fear, she will turn on you in an instant. Takes after that lazy mother of hers. Got a tongue like a viper, and she's not afraid to use it.'' Dorinda tugged at Cinda's arm, wanting her to stand. ''Come on now. You're burning daylight here. You've got to go out there right now and stop her.''

Dear God. Shaking with the fear that she was actually going to have to do something here, something possibly humiliating if not downright dangerous, Cinda stood and tugged at her stylish denim dress. ''How do I look?'' She smoothed her hair back, feeling more like a prizefighter in her corner of the ring with her trainer than she did an allegedly jealous wife at a potluck dinner.

''You look fine. No. Wait.'' Wearing a blue polyester skirt and pink cotton blouse, and holding Chelsi on her narrow hip, Dorinda Cooper used her free hand to fluff and primp Cinda wherever she felt she needed it. ''Look her in the eye, honey, and smile. Hang on to Trey's arm and just out-charm her. Use your Southern graces. You live in the South now. So act like it. At least you look like a graduate of a finishing school, so go with that. Ooze sugar and molasses and manners. That brassy girl won't know what hit her.'' She shoved Cinda forward. ''Now, go get her, champ.''

No one in the course of human history had ever felt less like a champ than Cinda did. A chump, maybe. With her knees all but knocking together, she walked the gauntlet of wide-eyed smirking bystanders who happily parted in front of her as if at the passage of a pro-wrestling upstart. Clearly, they couldn't wait to see what happened next. Pride had Cinda raising her chin and smoothing out her stride. She may not be the hometown favorite, but she was a finishing school graduate. No, actually, she wasn't. But she was a transplanted Southern lady full of grace and charm. Soft-spoken and feminine. Demure. Quiet. Mannerly.

Then she saw what everyone else had already seen. Her shocked and disbelieving senses tried valiantly to take in the garbled mess that presented itself for consideration. There stood Trey Cooper's feet and legs facing toward her. But above them, and as if the result of some horrible genetic experiment gone awry, was the butt, back, and long and curling red hair of what had to be a woman. Apparently a female octopus had her tentacles—no, her arms and legs—wrapped around Trey's neck and waist. And apparently she was kissing him. Hard. Judging from the noises, it was a face-sucking kiss of no uncertain lust and yearning.

It was a bit frightening to witness. And infuriating. And humiliating. After all, everyone here thought Trey was married to her. So here she was, Cinda told herself—the wronged wife. The wronged and very jealous wife. *I don't like this one bit.* She didn't like the competition, either. Titian hair. Milky white skin. A spaghetti-strapped sundress hiked up to her behind. Strappy spiked heels. Well-muscled, firm legs that probably went all the way up to her neck. *Fine. The woman is a knockout. So she'd make a superstar underwear model look like a loser at a dog show. So what?*

The important thing here, to Cinda, was this Bobby Jean Diamante creature had herself wrapped around Cinda's "husband." Even if she and Trey weren't actually married, the potential existed between them. And that was what Cinda realized she really wanted to preserve here. Not an actual marriage or relationship, but the potential for one.

Thus fired up, Cinda figured her first course of action should be to disembowel—no, to *disengage* the female sucker fish from Trey's face. She had to save his life. And from where she was standing, it certainly looked as if his life, if not his reputation, needed saving.

Cinda exhaled. This was going to require some courage, some adrenaline…some psyching up. Cinda gave herself over to the only thing she had going for her at the moment. Jealous anger. She curled her hands into fists. What with everyone's heads whipping so fast from her standing there by herself…to the embracing couple…and back to her alone…and then the kissing couple…and then to her standing there solo, why, there was enough of a wind created that it ruffled Cinda's hair.

She moved into the arena. So, okay, she was going to do something. She didn't know what yet…but something. If only she didn't feel like a plucked chicken trying to compete in a beauty contest with an Arabian mare. But she did, and this situation was awful, especially so because the entire population of Southwood was present to witness her betrayal, her humiliation—and her revenge. All of that implied a plan that Cinda didn't have. Nevertheless, she was determined to rely on inspiration and to see this soap opera through to the bitter end.

She stopped beside the still embracing couple. Screwing up her courage with another deep breath and a lift of her chin, she tapped the encroaching female on her bare arm. "Excuse me."

Politely, Cinda waited. But in vain. There was no

break in the action, no response. Now what? Only too aware of the crowd's hushed whisperings, Cinda tapped a little harder on the woman's arm and said softly, "Excuse me." *Bitch.* "But I need to break in here, if you don't mind."

Again, nothing. The kiss went on. But now that she was this close, Cinda was encouraged to realize that what had looked from afar like him returning the woman's embrace was now revealed to be him trying to push the trashy woman off him. Cinda's heart melted. *What a sweetheart.* The poor guy was trying to break Bobby Jean's lip-lock and the death grip she had on his neck and waist. But his efforts were in vain as Cinda personally believed a fire department's jaws-of-life couldn't separate the two.

What chance, then, did she stand? Cinda looked around sheepishly at the interested bystanders. Her gaze lit on her "mother-in-law" who stood on the fringes of the crowd with Chelsi still on her hip. Dorinda Sue Cooper flapped her free hand at Cinda, urging her into the fray. *Great.* Cinda squared her shoulders, wondering just what the heck else she was supposed to do here. Maybe she should try the arm-tapping thing again. Maybe the third time really was the charm.

So, she tapped, being sure to use a good bit of fingernail this time. She also decided to include a loud speech. "Pardon me, Bobby Jean, I know you're busy. I mean I can *see* you're busy. So can the whole town. Which brings me to my point. You don't know me, but the man stuck to your face happens to be mine. And I would appreciate it if you would *not* continue to kiss him and rub yourself all over him."

Cinda waited. No response. Nothing. She exhaled

her frustration. Clearly, something drastic was called for. Maybe if she spoke louder and issued a warning. "Okay, stop it right now, lady," Cinda barked. "You don't want to make me angry here."

Finally, at long last, Bobby Jean broke off kissing Cinda's man, who gasped and looked wild-eyed as the redhead unpeeled herself from his body and turned to face Cinda, who gulped. Bobby Jean was tall. Almost as tall as Trey, who was being steadied on his feet by two guys who held onto his arms.

Bobby Jean got in Cinda's face and poked one of those long-fingered hands with the orange-painted nails at Cinda's chest.

"Honey," Bobby Jean said, her voice magnolia-sweet and husky as her green eyes sparked serious warnings Cinda's way, "I'm only going to say this once, so you listen up real good, you hear? Married or not, this man is *not* yours, sugar. He's mine. He always has been. And he always will be. So you just back off right now and we'll call it all a big mistake."

The crowd oohed. Cinda felt her cheeks flame. Then...she lost it. "Oh, it's a mistake all right," she said. "But *you* made it, sister."

Lost to the moment, Cinda—the wealthy and demure alleged charm school graduate who despised violence of any kind—pulled her fist back, bunched her muscles, and, hard as she could, socked Bobby Jean Diamante right in the kisser.

9

IT TOOK TREY AND HIS MOTHER and baby Chelsi a good two hours to bail Cinda out of Bubba Mahaffey's shiny new jail. The police chief had abandoned his earlier sympathy for Trey's dilemma. Utter joy in having an actual prisoner had replaced it. And what a notorious prisoner she was, too. It just didn't get any better than this: A female incarcerated on charges of assault and battery, a crime committed in front of no less than two hundred witnesses, himself included.

Yes, sir, an open-and-shut case of violence by an outsider against a favorite daughter of Southwood. Yessir, blood had been shed and charges had been brought, all by Bobby Jean Diamante—the injured party with the fat lip and the bruised pride. While Chief Mahaffey personally deemed the events that had transpired in the veterans' hall one helluva show, he told Trey that officially he could not allow his personal feelings to intervene with his duties as a sworn officer of the law.

Trey's response had been a roll of his eyes and an "Oh, criminy. Give me a break here, Bubba. Cinda was obviously provoked."

Bubba's expression had become pugnacious and Trey had given up any hope of reasoning his high-school friend out of his precious prisoner. So he'd resorted to threatening to take the police chief out back of the station, if he didn't release Cinda, and, just for old times' sake, personally stomp Bubba into a mud hole. When Bubba threatened to oblige and began coming out of his uniform, Trey had quickly reminded his friend that he was a father who was holding his baby. The police chief wouldn't hit a man who was holding a baby, would he?

Well, that had stopped Bubba—and given Trey the idea to inform the chief that Cinda's incarceration constituted cruel and unusual punishment for her baby—her *nursing* baby, who Trey had held up as Exhibit A.

As if on cue, baby Chelsi caught sight of her mother peering forlornly at her from behind the iron bars of a jail cell, just visible through the open doorway behind Bubba. The baby wailed like a siren and fought Trey's hold on her. Over Chelsi's heart-wrenching shrieks for her mother—or for her next meal, who knew?—Trey had told Bubba either to release Cinda to his custody or to stick the baby in the cell with her mother.

That is, unless the police chief thought he could feed the child himself. Wouldn't that make a great picture in the *Southwood Tattler?* Trey had pointedly added. He'd assured Bubba that he wasn't above calling reporter Gerrie Ann Fenwick right now and telling her to bring her camera to the police station.

Worked like a charm. Though clearly despondent over losing his prize, Bubba had agreed to release Cinda into Trey's custody with a warning that she was not to leave town. The legal system would have to work before she could take off for Atlanta. Fine. Whatever. They'd worry about it tomorrow.

Right now tomorrow seemed a long way off to Trey because he finally had Cinda at his childhood home with him. His mother, though inordinately proud of her daughter-in-law, had called herself winded and had already gone to bed. And Chelsi, after Trey helped bathe her, had been fed and laid down for the night. Life was again good.

Or would be if he and Cinda could get the sleeping arrangements ironed out. On the surface, it was easy. They could simply adjourn to the double bed in Trey's old bedroom that his mother had designated as theirs. "Theirs" as in a married couple's. Which of course they weren't. Only his mother still wouldn't believe that. And besides, the baby was sleeping in the crib in there. So, what if things—*please, God* was Trey's prayer—progressed between him and Cinda and got a little warm? *Come on, not with a baby in the room, one who could wake up at any moment,* his conscience railed.

So, okay, even if things didn't or weren't going to heat up, the two of them still couldn't just nonchalantly go to bed. Hell, they'd barely hugged or kissed yet. So it would be too awkward to undress in front of each other, climb into the same bed, say good-night, and then lie there next to each other. Two wide-awake and sensually aware adults who wanted each other but couldn't find their way across a narrow bed to the other one. How stupid was that?

Pretty damned. But effective in keeping them up half the night in the low-lit living room because neither one wanted to call it. Trey gave up thinking about it as he sprawled at one end of the couch and eyed Cinda sitting primly at the other end. Only the width of the middle cushion separated them from each other. But the distance, though measurable in inches, yawned like a chasm.

Exhaling his amorous frustrations and his tiredness, Trey watched Cinda, his favorite thing to do. Her hair—so soft-looking, so blond—had fallen forward, effectively shielding most of her face from him. But it didn't matter. In his mind's eye, he could see her features. High forehead. Amber eyes. Prominent cheekbones. The perfect nose. A pink and sensual rosebud mouth that he wanted more than anything in this world to fully kiss. And he didn't mean the pecks like they'd had up to now.

As he watched, Cinda flexed her right hand and rubbed it. Though still totally entranced by her, Trey couldn't help his chuckle. She was such a mixture of everything he liked and admired. Intelligent. Educated. Funny. Brave. And a complete surprise around every emotional turn. "Your hand hurting you, champ?" he teased.

She flipped her hair over her shoulder and showed him her narrowed eyes. "Yes. It hurts like crazy."

"Want me to get some ice for it?"

"No. I deserve for it to hurt."

"Come on, don't be so hard on yourself."

"I need to be. Trey, I am appalled at myself. I don't know what came over me. I've never hit anybody before. I mean I'm a *mother.* And Chelsi witnessed me attacking someone. What am I teaching my daughter?"

"She's six months old. She won't remember any of this. But since you asked me, couldn't you be teaching her to stand up for herself?"

She pursed her lips. "I wasn't standing up for myself. I was standing up for you."

"And may I just thank you right now for doing so? I really thought I was going to die. Doesn't that count for something? You know…fight if the cause is right?''

''Maybe,'' Cinda grumbled. ''But still, it was an awful thing to do. I had no idea I was capable of punching someone out like that.''

''We're all capable, Cinda, under the right circumstances. And you found what they are for you. Namely, me.'' He couldn't help the grin that followed his words.

''You're just full of yourself, aren't you?'' She fought a grin, he could see that. She returned her attention to her hand, rubbing it and shaking it.

Trey couldn't keep his eyes off her. She was so damned funny. Here she was, this petite blond woman…the embodiment of a lady, the object of his burgeoning desire, the one who made his heart go pit-a-pat…and she was talking about punching someone's lights out. The world had gone crazy. But maybe in a good way.

Trey had thought before tonight that she was such a refined person that his blue-collar ways and rowdy friends might put her off, might show her their two worlds would collide. Well, they had in a way, he supposed. But it hadn't been his doing, and she'd hung right in there. He could respect that. But could he afford a relationship with her? *Oh, the hell with it,* he decided. Tonight he refused to overthink things. All it did was make his head and his stomach hurt. Couldn't the simple truth be that when the right one came along, nothing else mattered? That was what his teammates told him. Nothing else mattered.

''Trey, quit staring at me. I said I'm sorry if I embarrassed you tonight in front of your friends.''

''Embarrass me? Hell, you made me a legend. I can

now tell everybody that my wife can beat up your wife. But I could tell you'd never hit anyone before. The way you came around with that roundhouse punch? All wrong.'' He shook his head as if at a serious no-no and sat up to give his ''wife'' a boxing lesson. ''See? This is what you did.'' He put his fists up. ''Like this. And it left you wide open. Bobby Jean could have sucker punched you in the belly. You want to avoid that. It hurts like hell.''

Cinda batted at his fists. ''Stop that. Are you making fun of me?''

''Making fun of *you*—Sugar Ray Cavanaugh? Uh-uh. Not now, not ever. I've seen you in action. You're a contender, baby.''

''Quit saying things like that.'' She held her right hand out to him. ''Look at my knuckles. They're skinned and swollen.''

Jumping at this opportunity to hold on to any part of her, Trey took her fingers in his and rubbed them gently. He didn't even try to deny that a nervy tingle was running up his arm. He could only wonder if she felt it, too. ''Yeah, I see that. The skinned places would be from Bobby Jean's teeth. Hey, you've had a recent tetanus shot, right?''

Cinda's expression blanked. She slid her fingers out of his grasp. ''Ohmigod, I never thought of that. But yes, I have.'' A second's silence followed, then her features showed her escalating panic. ''Bobby Jean's brought me up on charges of assault and battery. Not that I blame her. But what am I going to do? I can't go to jail. What about Chelsi? I just don't know what came over me—''

''Hey, hold on.'' Trey rubbed her arm sympathetically. It was soft yet firm, warm yet cooled by the air-conditioning. "Come on, it's not as if you're locked away in the big house." Then he couldn't resist. "Well, not yet."

Cinda's posture crumpled. "You are *so* not helping here."

"Aw, I'm sorry. Come here." Trey pulled her into his embrace and held her close. God, she felt good against him. His pulse picked up...and it wasn't the only thing. "I was trying to tease you out of your fears, and I should know better." Encouraging to him was that she didn't resist him or try to pull away. Trey rested his cheek against her hair. "I wouldn't be teasing you if I didn't think that by tomorrow Bobby Jean will cool down and drop the charges."

With her head still against his chest, Cinda nodded. Hopefully she was considering what he'd said. But all he could think about was now nice she smelled, how warm she was, how right she felt in his arms.

Cinda suddenly looked up at him. Trey met her gaze, saw her frown. He wanted so much at this moment to kiss her. A scant few inches away from his, her soft, pink lips were parted, showing a glimpse of white teeth. She tilted her head. A perfect invitation. Trey leaned toward her....

"No," Cinda said sharply.

Shot down, Trey sat back, embarrassed and self-conscious.

"No, I don't think she'll drop the charges," Cinda said. "I pulled out a hunk of her hair and gave her a fat lip. In front of the whole town. I think she'll prosecute me to the fullest extent of the law. I would if the situation was reversed."

Trey didn't know whether to laugh or cry. Or just give up. Here it was late at night, they were the only two awake, and they were as good as cuddling on the couch. Add to that, they were two healthy adults attracted to each other. Then he berated himself. *What kind of a jerk am I to be thinking about the bedroom when she's so scared about the courtroom?* What he needed to do here was help her past her fears. At least, maybe then they could get some sleep.

"Cinda, don't worry about tomorrow. Really. For one thing, it's Saturday and the Fourth of July. No one will be sending you up the river on a national holiday. What I can do is call Tommy Milton. He's a lawyer here in Southwood, and I trust him. We'll get him on the case. Or better yet, I'll go around first thing in the morning and talk to Bobby Jean myself, see if I can't get her to drop the charges."

Frowning, Cinda abruptly sat up. "You are not going over there alone. I mean it. And drop the charges? Ha. She'd be more likely to try to get you to drop your pants. And then I'd have to hit her again."

Trey stared in wonderment at Cinda. She was jealous. He grinned and took complete advantage of the fact that her feminine hackles were up. "Hey, how about giving me some credit here, okay? So what if *she* wants me to drop my pants? That doesn't mean I will." Then, because he had a devilish spirit that wanted to get a further rise out of Cinda, Trey added, "Although, I would be willing to put my body on the line for you, if that's what it took."

Her eyebrows arched dangerously. "Oh, you poor brave man, I just bet you would."

Grinning, Trey wanted nothing more than to grab her up and make love to her. She was so damned cute and desirable. She made him want to laugh and sing and shout. Could it be worse?

"I haven't thanked you for threatening to beat up your friend Bubba if he didn't let me out of that jail cell, Trey. That was sweet."

Mugging a face, Trey shrugged. "Sweet, hell. I was just trying to keep up. You'd already beaten up my ex-girlfriend. I thought pounding Bubba was the least I could do to save face. Oh, and thank you again for defending my honor in front of the whole town. You know, a boy's reputation is all he has and once that's gone—"

"Oh, shut up," Cinda said, grinning, looking a bit embarrassed. "You will never let me live that down, will you?"

"No. Come on, it was great. There you were, this tiny little blond thing, all lace and ladyhood. And there Bobby Jean was, some tall overgrown showgirl-looking thing. And you just haul off and *pow!* You made me proud, girl. 'That's *my* woman,' I was thinking."

Cinda tucked a lock of hair behind her ear. "You were thinking of me as…your woman? Really?"

Her expression could only be called shy. And flattered. And hopeful. Trey knew it was time, right now, to tell her how he felt. "Cinda, I think I have been thinking of you as, well, I hate to say 'my woman' in seriousness, but yeah, there it is. Those elevator doors opened last January and, wow, it was you. Like some fabulous prize behind Door Number One that I just had to have."

She sent him a sidelong glance. "Fabulous prize? Oh, please, I looked like some huge sheep that day."

"Never. You were beautiful and desirable even then. All I could think was 'Thank you, God.' I still do. Cinda, I've never met anyone I've wanted more.

Women like you don't run in my world of grease pits and grinding gears. You're refined and educated. So smart. And so far above anything I ever thought—''

Cinda had put a hand over his mouth. "Don't, Trey. Please don't put me on a pedestal. I couldn't take that. I want real life. Intimacy and rumpled sheets and lying close at night. I want someone to hunger for me. Someone I feel the same way about. But more than anything, I want a face I can see in my mind when a love song plays. Do you understand?''

Trey covered her hand with his and kissed her palm. "I think I do. You want the white picket fence and worrying about what's for supper and the laundry still to do. And for the first time in my life, Cinda, I'm beginning to think I do, too.''

Her voice softened. "And don't you dare tear down yourself or what you do, Trey. Stock car racing is very exciting. And it requires a tremendous amount of specialized knowledge and skill to do what you do. Don't think I don't know that. And you—you're the kindest, most thoughtful man I've ever met. And I can tell you're a good son to your mother. And you're fabulous with Chelsi—''

"How am I with you?'' His sidelong glance met her heated gaze.

Cinda's amber eyes darkened. Finally, the words came out. "You're awful.''

Trey's heart damn near stopped. Still holding her hand, he lowered it with his to his thigh. "Awful? How?''

"You waltz into my life on a cold day in January and then I don't hear from you for six months.''

"I wasn't sure I should call you. I didn't know what to say.''

"How hard is 'I want to see you'?"

"Real hard. A guy could get shot down."

"And yet I gave you my phone number, Trey. Didn't that tell you anything?"

He nodded, feeling troubled. "Look, this is hard, Cinda. Yeah, I wanted to call you and see you. I just...couldn't. No matter what you say, your world is really different from mine. And everyday, with the men I work with, I see love going sour. I promised myself I wouldn't get caught in that trap, Cinda. I just said, 'No way, man, not for me.' And then I met you and I knew it could all fall apart. I got scared..."

Looking down at her hand in his, Cinda said, "Then why *did* you call me?"

Trey inhaled, then let out a slow breath. "Because I thought I could fool myself into thinking this was just a pretend thing. Just one weekend. To see what it felt like."

Cinda puckered her mouth. "Oh, thanks. So you're just shopping? Trying on a family to see if it fit? But not buying?"

"No, I didn't mean it like that." Trey frowned. "Or maybe I did. Maybe that is what I was doing." He sent Cinda a look of troubled sincerity. "If it is, it sucks when you say it out loud. But no matter what it was, I don't mean it now."

"But that still scares you, doesn't it? I understand. I mean here I am, this rich widow with a baby. That's a lot of baggage."

Warming to her, Trey reached out and caressed her shoulder. "I don't think of you that way at all, Cinda. Not as baggage. Not as a burden. If anything, you're a sweet, sweet gift."

She smiled. "Trey, I'm going to go out on a limb here, okay? I'm just going to say this."

"All right." His heart thumped leadenly in his chest as he watched the play of emotions over her face.

She leaned in toward him and put her hand on his knee. "Trey, Cooper, you are the sexiest man I have ever met. Ever. I can't get enough of looking at you. And you excite me and make me laugh. And I love that. But you also make me crazy. You make me behave in ways I never have before. I mean I haven't even been around you for a total of twenty-four hours, but I... Well, I want...." She stopped, smiling at him, wide-eyed...and yearning.

In awe, Trey stared at her, his gaze roving over her features. Could it be that, after being stuck in neutral for so long, their gears had finally engaged? The edginess he felt right now, the tension, the dry mouth and tightening muscles were the same things he experienced right before the starter's flag came down on a big race. He loved that adrenaline-pumped feeling. Lived for it. Or he had. Until now. Until Cinda. Now she was the source of his excitement and the one who consumed his thoughts. "What are you saying to me? I want to be sure."

Her expression was troubled, vulnerable. "Trey, I just need to know something, all right? I need to know if there is an...us. Or I guess a chance of an 'us.' I'm not a casual person, and I don't think you are, either. But I—" Her expression became plaintive. "*Is* there an us?"

Trey's heart thumped happily. "God, I hope so."

She didn't say anything, just stared at him. Without thinking about it—and damned tired of thinking about it and dodging it—Trey said, "So, you wanna make out?"

Surprised, Cinda sat back, her face alight with humor. "What? Are you serious? Make out? We're not in high school, Trey."

He shrugged. "Okay, we're not. But this *is* my high-school reunion. I thought we might as well act like it." He added an evil, suggestive grin.

Cinda smacked playfully at his arm. "You're not serious."

He grabbed her hand, holding her as he leaned in close. "Am so. We could even go outside to my car and get in the back seat, if you want."

Her mouth gaped open, but then she grinned and arched her eyebrows, sending him a speculative, suggestive look. He couldn't believe it. She was actually thinking about it. Not wanting to lose her or the moment, Trey arched his eyebrows in answer. "Yeah? You want to?"

"You know…I do." She said it like she couldn't believe it, either. "But first I have to tell you something." She leaned toward him, her mouth almost touching his. "When Bobby Jean kissed you, Trey, I wanted to do more than hit her. I wanted to scratch her eyes out." She kissed the corner of his mouth. "And right now I want to wash away her kiss on your mouth." She tipped her tongue out against his lips. "I want you to have only my kiss, my taste, in your mouth. Do you mind so much if I do that?"

Trey could barely breathe, much less shake his head. His limbs felt heavy, and all of his blood had left his head. This woman was going to kill him with sensuality right here tonight on his mother's couch. Then she surprised him by grabbing him around the neck and pulling him to her. "You owe me this." Without further preamble, she took his mouth in a deep, heartfelt, wet and hungry kiss.

She was right. He did owe her. Trey's heart leaped and his body responded. Without breaking their kiss, Cinda pressed herself to him and he toppled over backward onto the cushions, taking her with him. He wrapped his arms around her slender body and held her tight. She stretched out atop him, along his length, and their kiss became little biting moans and tugging on lips and delicious swirls of passionate heat.

When it finally ended, Trey was in a sweat and breathing hard. And Cinda's face was only inches from his. In her eyes he saw awareness and need and everything he'd ever wanted. She lowered her head to him again and placed a tender, nibbling kiss on his chin. Her long blond hair tickled his face. "So. Why don't you show me the back seat of your car, Mr. Trey Cooper?"

CINDA COULDN'T BELIEVE their boldness. After checking on Chelsi and getting the necessary condoms from Trey's suitcase, they'd actually crept out of his mother's house, across the dewy grass, and, with the neighbor's dog barking at them, unlocked Trey's car. He'd rolled the windows down while she'd taken Chelsi's car seat out of the back and propped it up on the front floorboard. And then they'd both silently slipped into the back seat. Right there in the driveway. In the middle of a neighborhood. Oh, it was wonderful!

They'd looked at each other and laughed. "We'll probably get eaten alive by mosquitoes," Trey had said. And she'd answered, "So?" And then they'd come together for more of those passionate kisses and heated embraces, which had quickly led to just plain groping and moaning and tugging off of the necessary clothes to accomplish the deed. The car was hot and uncomfortable. The vinyl back seat sticky. And their love-slick bodies made funny, sucking noises every time they tried to switch positions or figure out how they were going to get "what" where "it" needed to be. A time or two, when it proved impossible, they'd ended up laughing out loud and then shushing each other.

Every now and then, Trey poked his head up to look out a window or the back windshield. He'd keep saying, "Did you hear that? What was that? Was it the cops? Or my mom?" And Cinda, who knew he was just trying to scare her, would pull him back down to her and say, "Oh, shut up. Who cares who it is?" And then they'd go at it again. Just like two damned teenagers in heat.

Finally, they'd sat up. And, breathless, sweating, not quite really sated yet, they'd stared at each other.

"You know what? This sucks. How did we do this when we were kids? I still can't honestly say yet if I've made love to you or not. I mean, how sure can you be in the back seat of a car this size?" Trey said.

"True. I guess we could go back inside to the couch," Cinda said seriously.

He'd nodded. "Or I could get a blanket out of the trunk and we could go out to the backyard to the gazebo and do this under the stars."

And Cinda had melted. "Oh, that sounds wonderful, Trey. What with the full moon and all. I'd like that."

And so they had. They'd put on enough of their clothes for the sake of decency and, carrying the rest, had sneaked back into the house, where they'd checked again on Chelsi, who blessedly slept on. Then they'd treated themselves to big drinks of water, enjoyed the air-conditioning for a minute or two...and then their eyes had met and awareness had again flared. Then out the back door they'd gone.

And now, here they were...their bodies bared to each other, their hearts open, and the two of them atop a blanket under the stars. The wood gazebo floor had proved too hard. So onto the more forgiving grass they'd moved.

With Trey's hard-muscled, exciting weight atop her, Cinda still could not believe her hunger for the man. Or the sweet intensity of his kiss as his arms again went around her. Trey was everything she'd known he would be. A thrill right to her toes. His lips fit hers perfectly. His breath was warm, his arms around her strong and supporting. His body was hungry and insistent. And he was inside her, trying to hold back. She felt it in the bunching of his muscles. He was waiting for her, even as he broke their kiss to trace tiny kisses over the outline of her mouth, even as he ever so gently held her bottom lip between his teeth and sucked softly. He was waiting for her.

Then he was tracing kisses down her jaw, her neck, up to her ear, where he whispered, "Bobby Jean means nothing to me, Cinda. You have to know that." With his nose, he nuzzled the sensitive spot behind her ear and traced her skin with his tongue. Shivers ran over Cinda. Trey spoke again, his voice low and husky. "That kiss wasn't my idea. I had no idea she was going to do that."

"I know." Cinda loved the feel of his chest pressed against hers. He was solid as a rock, just as she remembered from when he held her on that cold day last January when Chelsi had been born. And now he was smiling down at her, his blue eyes so dark they looked black. "Take me, Trey. Love me."

"That's all I've ever wanted to hear from you, Cinda." Trey pushed fully into her. How he filled her. How gentle yet insistent his strokes were. How wonderful the play of his muscles as Cinda freely ran her hands over his body, over the broad expanse of his back. As he kissed her deeply, she wrapped her arms and legs around his neck and waist, banishing forever the sight of Bobby Jean Diamante's pose that had mocked this intimacy.

In only moments, Trey's pace became rapid, more plunging. The good sweetness was tightening, building deep inside Cinda. She was very close. So was he. Right then, the demanding urgency of the love act took over, robbing her of conscious thought and taking Cinda to a place she'd never gone before, not even in her marriage…the place where her heart was at one with the act of loving someone.

10

CINDA AWOKE the next morning to the soft grays of curtain-filtered daylight. And to a soft whispering her sleep-fogged brain couldn't identify. She lay still, not quite oriented to time and place, and frowned. Okay, she was not in her bed and was facing a wall. Aha. She was in the double bed in Trey's old room at his mother's house. And he'd slept with her. He'd more than slept with her. There'd been the car, the back-yard...and the bed. Cinda smiled. Her senses told her he was not in the bed with her at this moment, but that was okay. He certainly had been in the bed last night. He'd held her close, they'd made love, and then they had gone to sleep like two spoons in a drawer, his arms around her, his knees bent to hers.

How wonderful that had been. And now it was Saturday, the Fourth of July. For some silly reason it felt like the first day of the rest of her life. Always before, that sappy saying had made her roll her eyes. But now, today, she really understood it. And love poetry. She now got that, too. All the yearnings and the hunger that the poets wrote about. The desperation to be together, to see your loved one's face. To wax maudlin over the color of someone's eyes, his hair. But best of all, she told herself, she now had a face to put to the love songs.

So today, couldn't she begin marking time on a future brighter than it had been yesterday? Yes she could. A secret grin captured her mouth and Cinda stretched in what promised to be a luxurious loosening of love-sore muscles—

Then she heard it again, behind her, the whispering. She held still, listening. Low talking. Like love talk, only not love talk…like someone talking to a baby. Her mind put two and two together, and Cinda's expression brightened. Ever so carefully, not wanting to disturb the scene she felt certain was playing out behind her, she rolled over in the bed. And was rewarded. The sight that greeted her melted her mother's heart and brought tears to her eyes. She felt so silly, so emotional. After all, hadn't she ever seen a man wearing only his pajama bottoms and sitting in a rocking chair and holding a baby before?

No. She hadn't. Not in real life. And not this man with her baby. It struck Cinda then that Trey was the only man to hold Chelsi—one who could possibly qualify as a father figure, that is. Of course, her own father and Papa Rick and her brothers had held Chelsi. But they weren't, well, *her* man, someone who could play a significant role in her daughter's life as well as her own.

Wishing she could paint, could sculpt…heck, just wishing for a camera so she could preserve this scene forever, Cinda lay on her side and tucked her hands under her cheek. She couldn't get enough of watching Trey with Chelsi. Holding the little girl under her arms, his fingers interlocking over the baby's back, he had her in his lap, facing him. Dandelion-fluff baby hair stuck up all over Chelsi's round head. Still in her little pajamas, she was cooing and flailing about happily and trying to stand on Trey's knees. He was talking softly to her and chuckling at her antics. He then leaned forward and kissed the baby on the forehead. "Look at you. Such a big girl. So damn—uh, darned cute. Would you want to be my little girl? Would you like that?" he whispered.

Had there ever been a more poignant, heart-warming scene in the history of humanity? The bonding of a man with a child. It was beautiful.

Hot tears of strong emotion pricked at Cinda's eyes. She spoke up almost before she realized she was going to. "I know I would. I'd like it very much for her to be your little girl."

Trey looked up, meeting her gaze. His blue eyes were soft and bright with welcome. "Hi. You're awake."

"It would seem so." Cinda smiled, wondering if he too was playing back in his head their funny, tender, and sweaty lovemaking scenes from last night. She ran her proprietary gaze up and down him, noting things like his bared chest, those broad shoulders. This morning she knew every masculine inch of him. She knew his kiss, what it felt like to run her hands over the crisp and curling hair on his chest, how his weight felt atop her, what it was like to sleep with him. She knew the scent of his skin, how he tasted, and the love sounds he made. Cinda let out a sigh of yearning and contentment.

Trey raised his eyebrows. "You sound like a contented cat."

"I feel like a contented cat."

His grin was cocky, sure of himself. "Can I take any credit for that?"

"You can take all the credit for that."

"Good." Then he suddenly looked unsure of himself, as if he didn't know what came next in this scenario. He resorted to the baby. He turned Chelsi in his arms until she faced Cinda. "Look," he said, putting his face next to the little girl's, "Mama's awake."

"Hey, sweetie," Cinda greeted her daughter. Chelsi caught sight of her and immediately began fussing for her breakfast. With a sigh for having to give up lying in her—their—rumpled love nest, Cinda dutifully sat up and arranged herself on the bed. "Bring her to me and I'll nurse her."

With the baby held securely in his arms, Trey got up and approached Cinda. "Good. It's only fair. I had to change her morning diaper."

"You poor, poor man."

"It was awful." He handed the baby over to Cinda.

She took her fretting daughter and settled her in place. "I can imagine," she told Trey, looking up. "You're very brave."

He leaned over and kissed her on the mouth. "I do what I can."

"And you do it so well."

Cinda knew it was silly, inane even, this morning banter. Yet it was intimate somehow. Private. The language of couples. The building blocks of a relationship. A time and a scene not open to the public. Could it be that this whole morning was enchanted? And if it was, could it please last?

It did, for about twenty minutes of solitude. Then the door to the bedroom jerked open with a suddenness that had Trey whipping around and Cinda gasping. Chelsi even let go of her "breakfast" to see what was up. There, in the doorway, wearing a high-necked nightgown and with her tornado-resistant hairdo wrapped protectively in toilet paper and held in place with little metal clips, stood Cinda's "mother-in-law."

With a plastic flyswatter in her hand, and squinting through the thick lenses of her eyeglasses, the older woman took in their one-big-happy-family and highly domestic scene. "Trey, how come that old blanket I gave you to keep in the trunk of your car is all grassy and draped over the gazebo railing out back?"

The flames of embarrassment burned up Cinda's cheeks, and she absolutely refused to look at Trey. Or to help him. Instead, and studiously, she focused on her darling tiny baby daughter, just fluffing the child's hair and playing with her sweet little fingers…and leaving Trey to the wolves.

"Oh, never mind." Dorinda Cooper sighed. "You never could keep up with your things. Besides, we've got us some serious trouble here this morning."

Cinda looked up, exchanging a glance with Trey. Frowning, he'd come to attention and had his hands planted at his waist. "What do you mean, Mother?"

"Well, here I haven't even had my coffee yet and there's a gangster on the front doorstep."

Not surprisingly, nobody said anything. All Cinda could do was squint back at the older woman and think *You mean instead of a newspaper?*

Chelsi, apparently unimpressed, glommed back on to her breakfast. Cinda divided her attention among her nursing daughter, Trey, and his mother. Just then, Mrs. Cooper waved the flyswatter in their direction. "I knew it, I knew it. Just look at y'all in here. You *are* really married."

Trey finally found his voice. "We're not, Mother. I keep telling you that. But what did you say about a gangster?"

"He's on the front stoop. I guess you didn't hear him knock. I peeked through the living room curtains and saw him out there. I'm not about to answer that door. But someone needs to go out there and talk to that man." She used the flyswatter much like an orchestra's conductor would his baton. "He has goons with him and a black stretch limo. Right out there in the driveway where all the neighbors and especially that nosy Lula Johnston can see. Scared me to death, the sight did, so I grabbed up this fly swatter for my own personal protection."

Well, that explained the flyswatter, but not much else. Cinda looked to Trey when he spoke. "Goons, Mother? A black stretch limo? Are you sure?"

Dorinda Cooper pursed her lips. "I think I know goons and gangsters when I see them. I watch the daytime TV when I'm working at the bowling alley."

Trey snatched up his T-shirt from the arm of the rocking chair and began pulling it on. "Then I know what this is. This is one of Bobby Jean's tricks, a scare tactic. I'm going to—"

"I don't think so, son." Mrs. Cooper slowly shook her head. Given the white toilet paper wrapped around her hair, the older woman's movements reminded Cinda of a revolving satellite dish, the kind that searched for signs of intelligent life in outer space. "By the looks of things outside," she was saying, "I'd say there's no Bobby Jean to it. I think it's really her husband."

Trey said something that sounded like a curse, but his actual words were muffled by his shirt not being fully over his head. When he had it on, he turned to Cinda. "Rocco Diamante is here."

Fear shot through Cinda, shredding her nerve endings. "Ohmigod," she barely got out in a whisper, seeing herself last night at the potluck dinner and smacking—hello!—*Mrs. Diamante* in the kisser. Right now, Cinda figured, prison was the least of her worries, and perhaps one of her better options. She turned a pleading expression up to Trey. "What am I going to do?"

He looked so fierce standing there frowning and with his hands planted at his waist. Like a general. A man with a plan. Getting ready to direct his troops. "We. What are *we* going to do, Cinda? You're not in this alone."

That did it for her. The whole world seemed to recede, leaving Trey standing in the forefront. The man was a rock. Her hero. Staunch in the face of danger. Someone who would put her first, who would stand beside her, no matter what. Cinda's fear fled. She would be okay as long as Trey was with her. If she hadn't already suspected she loved him, she told herself, she would have after this. Her vision misted over as she stared at this wonderful man. "You are so good to me, Trey. I mean that. What are *we* going to do, then?"

"*We're* not going to do anything," he said emphatically. "*I'm* going to go out there and talk to this joker."

As he headed for the bedroom door where his mother still stood, Cinda's lofty heroic thoughts came to a screeching halt. Her love-misted eyes dried and her stomach plummeted. She felt sick. Instantly gone were Trey's superhero cape and his special powers. "No you are not," she called out, stopping him.

Trey turned to her, a surprised and questioning look

on his face. "Well, I'm certainly not going to send my mother out there."

"That's for damned sure." This was Dorinda Cooper.

"You're not going out there, either, Cinda," Trey said.

"Trey, he's here because of me. I'll go." Brave words for a woman in her nightgown and with a nursing baby at her breast.

"You will not. And we don't know he's here because of you. Knowing Bobby Jean, he's probably here for me."

"Personally, I think he's here for the both of you." Again, Dorinda Cooper.

Trey turned to his mother, giving her an encouraging look full of affection. "Mom, honey, why don't you go make that coffee. I think we can all use a cup."

"And bullet-proof vests." She didn't budge from the doorway.

Exhaling sharply, the sound carrying a load of frustration, Trey turned to Cinda. "I have to go to the door. I'm the only one who can. Look at you there. You're a small woman and you're nursing a baby."

"And look at you there, Trey." Cinda couldn't help the accusation in her voice, any more than she could the scared waver it held. "You're only one man. And you're acting just like Richard. All you need is a herd of yaks."

"Yaks?" Dorinda Cooper weighed in.

"It's a long story," Trey told his mother as he turned again to Cinda. "How is my talking to this guy anything at all like Richard?"

"Who's Richard?"

Again Trey turned to his mother. "Chelsi's father."

His words hung in the air like psychically suspended knives. Sharp ones. Exchanging a look with Trey, Cinda tried to silently communicate… *Here we go.*

Dorinda Cooper's eyes rounded. "But you're Chelsi's father."

Trey shook his head. "No I'm not. A man named Richard Cavanaugh is. Was. Cinda's husband. Late husband. He was killed by yaks while hot-air ballooning in Tibet."

Cinda wished he'd stop. He kept making it worse.

Dorinda Cooper's gaze darted from her son to Cinda—sitting there, embarrassed now, in her son's rumpled bed—and back to Trey. "You lied to me," she said, waving her flyswatter about threateningly, as if she meant to spank Trey with it.

He chuckled but it wasn't meant completely as humor. "No, Mother, I didn't. Remember? I told you the truth, only you didn't believe me."

"And now I'm supposed to believe a story about balloons and yaks? On the Fourth of July with gangsters at my door?"

Trey turned to Cinda. "Tell her."

Cinda exhaled her breath and faced the older woman. "It's true. My husband was killed by yaks. Trey is not my baby's father. And we are not married."

"You're both lying," Dorinda Cooper said without hesitation. "You're married and that's your baby. She looks just like you, Trey. And the two of you have on matching wedding bands. Explain that."

Cinda pointed to Trey, who said, "We did that to fool Bobby Jean."

And that was when, collectively Cinda joined Trey

and his mother in remembering *Mr.* Bobby Jean still stood on the stoop outside—with goons…no doubt, armed and impatient ones.

Trey took charge. "Okay, we'll talk about this later. Right now I'm going to go out there and—"

"No you're not."

"Cinda, this is where I came in," Trey warned, his chin edging up a stubborn notch.

"That might be." Cinda's anger got the better of her. "But I will *not* sit here helpless while you rush right into danger without a thought to anyone else who loves you or how your actions might affect them, Trey Cooper. I have had my fill of that. So you mark my words, I will take this baby and go home if you so much as leave this room right now."

"You tell him, sister." Dorinda Cooper was all but crowing.

This was insane, was Cinda's thought. Just then, obviously now full as a little tick, Chelsi popped herself off her mother's breast and clutched at Cinda's gown, wanting to right herself. Cinda pulled at her gown, restoring her modesty. She sat her daughter up, kissed the little cherub's cheek, and turned her to face Trey. She rubbed Chelsi's back. The baby burped. Then the two females, mother and daughter, presented a united front to Trey.

"Oh, y'all are so married." Dorinda Cooper leaned against the doorjamb and crossed her arms over her chest. In her fist, the flyswatter waved about like a scepter.

"We are *not*," Trey denied, turning his attention back to Cinda and softening his voice as well as his stance. "What is really wrong here, Cinda? What are you afraid of? And I don't mean the guy at the door."

"Neither do I. The truth is I think I'm suffering flashback emotions having to do with Richard. How he wasn't reliable. How I couldn't count on him in any crisis. Not when my father had his heart attack or my brother was running for office. I think I'm afraid, Trey, that you'll go do something silly and get yourself killed and leave me here alone." She heard how that sounded and hung her head. "I'm sorry. I think I slipped back into some old behaviors. I was putting things on you that I shouldn't have."

Out of the corner of her eye, Cinda saw Trey moving toward the bed. He sat on the side of it, facing her and being careful of the baby, who contented herself with a slightly spastic, if not thoroughly delightful, round of pat-a-cake. Trey smoothed Cinda's hair back from her face. "It's okay, honey." She met his sympathetic, blue-eyed gaze. "Look, I'm not Richard, and I'm not going to do anything dumb or rash here. I'm just going to go talk to the man. That's all."

Cinda sniffed back her tears. "What if he's not here just to talk, Trey?"

"Well, I won't know until I go out there and see, now will I?"

"No. But I want to go out there with you." She could see that Trey's protest was coming, so she spoke quickly. "I need to do this, Trey. I'll feel better if we face this together." He was shaking his head but Cinda rushed on. "With Richard, I would never face anything with him. I see that now. I don't want to make that mistake with you. It's hard for me to say this, but it is different with you, Trey. I care about you in ways I don't think I did with Richard. And I don't want to make old mistakes again."

Trey's gaze roved over her face. He seemed to be

considering what she'd said. But still, when he opened his mouth to speak, Cinda put her fingers over his lips. "Please? I need to do this with you. No matter the outcome here, it will be a big step for me toward trusting again. I swear it will."

There. That was what she'd wanted to say. Cinda lowered her hand from Trey's mouth and watched his eyes. She knew the moment he gave in because he slumped and then smiled, like a man resigned to his fate. "You know that I hate this, don't you? My every instinct is to protect you."

Cinda nodded. "I know. But I happen to feel the same way about you. If you'll remember, it's what got us into this mess with the goons at the door."

Trey chuckled and shook his head. "Can't argue with you there. Okay. Give me Chelsi and pull yourself together. I'll wait for you, and we'll go to the door together." He stood up and took Chelsi from Cinda's lap. "Come here, sweetie. Let's go see your Grandma Cooper."

Grandma Cooper jumped on that. "See there? That proves it. If I'm the grandma, y'all are married."

"All right, Mother," Trey said. "Have it your way. We're married. But take this baby and go into the kitchen, okay? And stay there until I come to get you."

Trey's mother raised an eyebrow at her son and then turned to Cinda. "I didn't raise him to act this bossy. Don't you let him get away with that."

"Yes, ma'am," Cinda said, ever obedient.

Apparently satisfied with that, and looking for all the world like a British general handling a riding crop, Dorinda Cooper stuffed her flyswatter under her arm and took the baby from her son. "Come here, punkin, come to Grandma. These silly old parents of yours are trying to tell me you're not my grandbaby.'' Chelsi cooed and gurgled. ''That's right. You are. I knew that. You look just like a Cooper.'' With that she turned around, apparently heading for the kitchen.

Cinda had straightened her garments while Trey had dealt with his mother and Chelsi. She now scooted off the bed and stood, tugging her knee-length gown around her. Wordlessly, Trey handed her the matching robe to her silky set and she put it on, belting the waist. She couldn't help feeling like a knight putting on protective armor. Right now she wished she had protective armor. Two suits of it, one for each of them. And those long lances. Weapons of any sort. And lots of people on their side. Help.

She said none of this and hoped it didn't show on her face. The lesson, however, was brought home to her: deliberate bravery was a lot scarier than the spur-of-the-moment stuff, the kind where you could randomly poke someone in the mouth. But when you *knew* beforehand that you were putting yourself in harm's way and had time to think about it, it was like *yikes*. Cinda grabbed Trey's hand with both of hers to keep herself from climbing out of a window and bolting for the highway.

''Ready?'' Trey asked, his eyebrows raised, his expression saying she could back out if she wanted.

Cinda took a deep breath. ''Ready.''

Trey squeezed her hand. ''Okay. Then let's go, slugger.''

With that, they set off, walking down the short hallway, past an array of pictures that showed Trey as a baby, a toddler, a kid, an adolescent, a teenager, and finally the man he was today. That took them into the living room, where the draperies were still drawn against the morning light. Trey stopped in front of the door and looked down at Cinda. "I just want to tell you now, in case I can't later, that I think I love you."

"I think I love you, too," Cinda blurted.

"Good." Trey inhaled, squeezed her hand, stepped in front of her—and opened the door with a vengeance. "Yes? Can I help—" Silence. Then, "What the hell?"

Cinda peeked out, feeling the morning sunshine on her face. She squinted against its brightness and suddenly realized that no one was there. The front stoop was empty. The only cars in the driveway were Trey's and his mother's. No goons. No limos. No Mafia dons dressed in black. Nobody. Cinda exchanged a glance with Trey. He looked as befuddled by their lack of visitors as she felt.

"I don't think my mother made them up," he said, stepping off the stoop and walking barefoot through the grass to look up and down the tree-shaded neighborhood street.

Cinda was right behind him. "Neither do I." The dewy grass was cold and tickled her feet as she tugged Trey back with her to the dubious protection of the porch. "Could you be a bigger target, Trey? They could be anywhere. I think they just thought no one was home and left."

"I agree. But they could come back at any minute. That's what worries me."

"Ohmigod, you're right. It was better when we knew where they were. This is awful. Now what?"

"We come up with a plan," he said very simply,

as if every day he waged war on the mob. Indeed, his gaze was focused on the near distance.

Cinda whimpered. ''Oh, Trey, it is the Fourth of July and we're all going to die.''

11

TREY'S PLAN WAS SIMPLE—he would take the bull by the horns. Face the lion in its den. In other words, get in his car and go find those damned goons and straighten this whole mess out. It was a good plan. Risky, yeah. But straightforward. A plan whereby Trey could respect himself in the morning…if he lived to see it.

But then, once he'd told his mother and Cinda what he intended to do, his plan had been shot to hell. And now, it was just embarrassing. Because his mother, Cinda, and Chelsi were now all piled in his car and they were on their stubborn, collective way to Bobby Jean Diamante's parents' house. That had to be where her shady husband had gone: where Bobby Jean would be staying. It made sense.

Just like his going to Bobby Jean's alone made sense to Trey. A man had a problem, he took care of it himself. Stood his ground. A lone wolf. Facing the odds. Yeah, that's right. A man didn't take his mother along. Or his sweetheart and her baby girl. Yet, here they were. So how seriously would a bunch of bad guys consider him once they caught sight of his posse?

His posse. His dust-mote-sized mother with her thick glasses and stiff brown hair and flyswatter—who'd wanted to know why the baby's car seat was in the front seat. Cinda, a sweet, slender blonde whom he hoped to have something permanent with, and for reasons other than her vicious right hook. And Chelsi, a six-month-old little girl who looked just like him by some happy coincidence, a child who was strapped into her car seat and was busy cooing and drooling.

Boy, the four of them would scare the pants right off those tough New York types, wouldn't they? Trey figured the wise guys would take one look at his backup and would shoot him just to put him out of his misery. And right now, as ticked off and embarrassed as he was at the women for coming along, Trey thought he just might welcome a bullet or two.

"This isn't a good idea, Trey."

"Oh, you think?" Trey spared a glance for Cinda, who sat in the front passenger's seat. Her bottom lip was poked out stubbornly, and she had her arms crossed over her sleeveless blue-linen shirt. Could she be cuter? Or more exasperating? "Cinda, I *know* it's not a good idea. I didn't want you—any of you—to come, remember?"

"That's not what I meant. Watch the road. I think you should have called Bubba. He has a gun."

"He also has a town overloaded with happy revelers and only one officer to help him with crowd control. I'll take care of this myself."

"Oh, that reminds me," This came from the back seat where Dorinda Cooper sat next to Chelsi. "We need to be back by noon. I've got a pie in the oven. I'm taking it to the picnic this afternoon, and I don't want it to burn."

Where could he go with that? Nowhere. But it was a good example of exactly what he meant. His entourage had no concept of the danger here. Trey fumed and drove and refrained from mentioning the obvious—a pie and a picnic were the least of their worries. As if they would live long enough to even see the damned thing thoroughly baked, much less burned.

Cinda made the mistake of commenting on the obvious. "How did my comment about Bubba having a gun remind you of a pie, Dorinda?"

"Well, you put a gun in a holster, right? And a pie in the oven. Seems clear to me, honey. Turn left up here at Mimosa Place, son."

Trey looked in the rearview mirror at his mother's reflection. "I know where the Nickersons live, Mother. Bobby Jean's parents have lived in this house since before I was born. But thank you."

"You're welcome. Use your blinker this time. You didn't on that last turn. I'd think a man who works with cars for a living would know to use his blinker."

"Not much use for a turn signal, Mother, on an oval track," Trey commented patiently. "Unless you want it blinking a continuous left turn."

"Well, I still don't get the connection," Cinda persisted. "About the pie and the gun, I mean. One has nothing to do—"

Trey's lowered eyebrows and frowning expression as he shook his head at Cinda, giving her a clear don't-go-there signal, cut off her words. Not that she appreciated it. Looking peeved, Cinda wrinkled her nose at him and turned away, looking out her side window. *Well, good, now Cinda isn't talking to me. This is perfect. Just perfect.* Trey made a promise to himself right then that never again would he go to another reunion. Not for as long as he lived. Trey turned left onto Mimosa Place. He used his blinker.

"Oh, no," Cinda intoned. "Oh, Trey, I don't like the looks of this."

Trey knew exactly what she meant. He didn't like it, either. The Nickersons' property, still several houses away, occupied about two wooded acres in a nicer part of town. But right now it looked like a used-car lot. Maybe twenty cars were parked in the driveway and up and down the street. And a crowd was milling around out front of the two-story Southern Colonial house. Trey frowned, wondering what was going on and why all these people would be here. A private party, maybe, before the town party?

Then, through a break in the gathering, Trey spotted a big black limo parked in the yard, parallel to the house. That explained the gathering. Curiosity had gotten the better of folks. The doors to the vehicle were open. And big ugly men dressed in black stood in front of it, their eyes hidden behind reflective sunglasses, their hands folded together in front of them. There were four of them, each one the size of a professional wrestler. Trey's gut tightened. Cinda's words from earlier that morning came back to him. *We're all going to die.*

Then his mother, who'd obviously undone her seat belt and scooted forward to peer between his bucket seat and Cinda's, sized up the situation admirably. "Ha. Look at that. There's four of them and four of us. At least we aren't outnumbered, son."

Trey didn't know whether to laugh or beat his forehead against the steering wheel. But since Cinda laughed, he joined her. God love her, his mother was ever the optimist. "That's exactly what I was thinking, Mom. At least we're not outnumbered." He was trying to picture baby Chelsi's part in all this when it came to a brawl, as it very well could. What could she do? Bite an ankle? Toss up her breakfast onto a goon's shoes?

Trey parked his red machine at the curb about three houses away from the Nickersons'. It was the closest he could get. He cut off the engine, undid his seat belt, and turned to face his posse. "Okay, here's the deal. Yes, you tricked me into bringing you along by piling into the car while I was still inside. By the way, which one of you hid my car keys in the freezer? Not funny. Anyway, I may have lost the battle to get you to stay at home, but I'm not going to lose the war. By that I mean you all are staying right here in this very car while I go sort this mess out. I mean that. And I don't want any arguments. You're not to get out of this car. Do you hear me?"

Trey looked from one face to the next, seeking a sign of intention to comply. Cinda nodded. His mother nodded. Chelsi, who was happily occupied with chewing on a chubby little fist, just stared at him, her blue eyes big and round. Forcing himself to maintain his stern expression in the face of their wide-eyed sincerity, Trey called the nodding and the gnawing full compliance. Well, finally. He'd actually won one. Maybe the sight of the big men had brought them to their senses. This was a man's job. "All right then, good," he said. "We understand each other."

With that, Trey opened his door, got out, and closed it with a solid thunk. His mother promptly followed suit. Thunk. Then Cinda. Thunk. She opened the fourth door, got the baby out of her car seat, and closed the door. Thunk. The three women—or rather, two women and a baby held in her mother's arms— converged like planets aligning and stood together in a knot of solidarity. They stared at him, three sets of widened, imploring eyes.

"Dammit," Trey commented, planting his hands at his waist. "I thought you agreed with what I said."

Trey saw his mother elbow Cinda into speaking. "We did. You asked us if we heard you, and we nodded that yes we had."

"That wasn't what I meant, and you all know it."

"We want to go with you, Trey. We *are* going with you."

Completely exasperated now, Trey jerked his thumb toward the goons. "Did you see the size of those guys, Cinda? What do you think you're going to do? Pinch 'em? Pull their hair?"

"No. I'm going to stand with you and dare them to shoot you in front of your mother and your wife and child."

"See there?" his mother piped in. "I knew you two were married."

"We're not married, Mother." Trey hooked his thumbs into the belt loops of his denims and shifted his weight to one leg. He stared at his posse. And got tickled. Hell, it just might work. Chuckling, he waved his hand before him in a sweeping gesture to indicate they should precede him. "All right. Come on. Let's go. We've got a pie in the oven we don't want to get burned."

Grinning their triumph, his posse stepped through the neighbor's grass to join Trey. When Cinda pulled even with him, he took her elbow and drew her attention. "If you ever tell that Major Clovis of yours about this, she won't hesitate to make me a soprano."

"I know," Cinda said cheerfully. "She's very good with a knife."

Trey felt sick, then fatalistic. "Then I'd give ten years off my life to see her riding up about now."

With that, he fell in between his mother and Cinda, easing their way across the uneven lawns and driveways with a hand at each of their elbows. Impressed on Trey's consciousness was the mood of the crowd ahead. They were jovial, celebratory. Friendly. At ease. Even at a glance he realized he knew everybody here. Once they'd achieved party ground-zero, his friends greeted him, offering him and his entourage a beer or a handshake or a clap on the back. Men, women, children everywhere—all of them agog at the sight of the limo and its occupants. Just as he'd figured. An impromptu gathering of the curious that had quickly become an event.

Just then, as Trey was figuring it out, the hometown crowd, the same people who had cheered him on and made him a football god in his high-school days...well, the rotten turncoats now parted for him just as they'd done last night for Bobby Jean. And it was "déjà vu all over again," to quote Yogi Berra. There she was, Bobby Jean Diamante, not ten feet away. Stunning, as always, the redhead was dressed in white short-shorts and a red, white and blue striped tank top. Her heavy jewelry patriotically bore the stars-and-stripes, too.

"Wow," Cinda said quietly. "I feel like I should salute her or something."

"I heard that, honey," Trey's mother whispered loudly. "That girl looks like the Statue of Liberty after a cheap makeover."

"I'll say," Cinda followed up, tugging self-consciously at her own modest khaki shorts, as if by doing so she could make Bobby Jean's shorts longer.

Trey wisely had no response. For one thing, Bobby Jean had spotted him... Okay, them. Trey tensed, trying to watch everyone at once. "Everyone" being defined here as the four big and silent men by the limo, who had yet to move. The crowd quieted. So did the birds in the trees. The dogs in the yards. The kids running around. Everybody.

"Hello, Trey," Bobby Jean drawled, or tried to. Not even her heavy makeup could hide her fat lip, which also made her speech sound like that of a novacaine-induced lisp. Her gaze slipped to Cinda, and she sniffed, raising her chin a notch.

At his side, Trey felt more than saw his sweetie tense. Then she handed Chelsi off to his mother and all but flexed her muscles. Oh, hell, a catfight was brewing.

Trey quickly greeted his childhood friend. "How ya doing, Bobby Jean?" Then, hoping to head World War III off at the pass, he said, "Bobby Jean, I've known you since you were a baby. We had our times together. And they meant something to me. Something good. But what I feel for you now is friendship, one that stretches back a long time. But that's all. Friendship. I'm with Cinda now. And that's the way it's going to be." Trey firmed his stance in the well-tended Nickerson lawn. "I had some visitors this morning. But they left before I could speak with them. The trail led here. So I came by to see what they wanted. Is your husband around?"

In the silence that followed what was essentially him calling the man out, Trey heard in his head the haunting music from Clint Eastwood's spaghetti Western, *The Good, the Bad, and the Ugly.*

Bobby Jean remained unsmiling, her stance as unyielding as Trey's. "Yes. My husband is here."

"I'd like to speak with him, if I could. Maybe clear this up right here before things get out of hand."

Bobby Jean crossed her arms over her ample and almost exposed bosom. "Things are already out of hand. I've got a lawsuit against your little wife there."

"'Little wife?'" Cinda all but snarled as she took a step forward. "Who are you calling a 'little wife,' you big, overgrown—"

"Cinda." Trey put a restraining hand on her arm.

"Well, she is," Cinda hissed at him.

"And I agree. But...look, will you?" He nodded his head in the direction of the four goons.

The big bodyguards were shifting their considerable weight about as if preparing to go into action on Bobby Jean's behalf. But then they looked toward the front door of the Nickerson house. A muttering went up from the crowd...about like it had last night at the veteran's hall just before the two women had started to rumble. Trey thought he knew who'd be in the doorway, had a bunch of bodies not been blocking his view.

With his hand still on Cinda's arm, Trey spoke quietly to her. "Don't let her bait you, honey. Let me take care of this." Though her mouth was set in a pugnacious pucker, Cinda retreated. Exhaling a modicum of relief, Trey focused again on Bobby Jean. "Look, if you won't be reasonable, then my business here is with your husband. I don't want to disrupt your party, but can I see him please?"

As she was the center of attention, something she loved, Bobby Jean shrugged, her features in a pretty pout. "I don't see why not. He wanted to see you, too.

That's why he came to y'all's house this morning.'' Her expression became catty, her voice a purr. "Only no one would answer the door.''

Snorting her apparent outrage, Trey's mother shifted Chelsi to her hip, leaned toward him, and spoke out the side of her mouth. "I believe she's calling us cowards, son.''

Trey leaned down to her. "I believe we were, Mother.''

Just then, the crowd shifted and people were craning their necks. The four pillar-sized goons left the flashy car and walked, two-abreast, toward the house. Trey swallowed, flexed his hands, and exhaled slowly out his mouth. No one had to tell him that the man himself, Rocco Diamante, was putting in an appearance. Adrenaline pumped through Trey's bloodstream, readying him for fight or flight. Given his druthers, and being the smart man that he was, Trey knew which one he'd choose. But not in front of this many witnesses.

"I think something's happening,'' his mother said. She bobbed and weaved in place, trying to see around everyone. "Can you see what's going on?''

Without losing his focus, Trey answered her. "No. But I think we'll know soon enough.''

He wasn't wrong. The goons came back into view. A short, heavyset man in a black suit, shirt and tie was in their midst. The five of them were headed in Trey's direction. All of a sudden this confrontation didn't seem like such a good idea. "You and Cinda get behind me, Mother. And stay there.''

Neither woman moved. However, his mother did see fit to announce loudly, "Lord, he looks just like the real Mafia men I've seen on the TV.''

Trey glanced at Cinda and saw her frowning at the man in the middle. "Yes, he does, Dorinda. A little too much like one, actually."

BEFORE CINDA COULD do anything, Trey stepped forward, leaving her and his mother to huddle behind him. Peeking around his beloved shoulder, Cinda watched and listened. The men, ever so polite, were introducing themselves, shaking hands, and warily sizing each other up. Cinda looked the goons over...and frowned. Why did they seem familiar?

More than curious now, she settled her attention on the alleged Mafia don. Something about him, too, was naggingly familiar. She couldn't be sure...because his hair was dyed. It had to be. That color of shoe-polish black simply didn't occur in nature. And he was heavier, a lot heavier, than the man she was thinking of. And she couldn't see his eyes because of the sunglasses.

But...could it be? It wasn't as if she could afford to make a mistake here. That could really cost them big time. She settled on listening to the short, fat man talk. Maybe his voice would give him away.

"...Understand my problem here, Mr. Cooper. I had to come all this way to deal with this situation. I don't like getting a call from my wife, hearing about her being knocked around," the mobster said—using a lot of subtly threatening gestures. "You know what I mean, Mr. Cooper?"

Mr. Diamante's voice was rasping, husky. New York. He spoke slowly. To Cinda's ear, a poor imitation of Marlon Brando in *The Godfather*. Or not. She had to be sure. Still, there was something there, something nagging at her.

"I understand," Trey said levelly, not the least bit subservient as he stared down at the Mafioso. "I guess Bobby Jean told you what happened? Or should I say *why* it happened?"

"You just hush yourself up, Trey Cooper, you dog you." Looking alarmed, Bobby Jean rushed over in a jiggling run and latched on to her husband's arm, rubbing herself suggestively against him. "Don't listen to him, honey. All I did was say hello to Trey, and I got attacked. Look at me. I'm the one with the bruises and the split lip."

Rocco Diamante patted his wife's hand but otherwise ignored her in favor of concentrating on Trey. "You see what I mean, Mr. Cooper? We got a problem. Where I come from, we don't look none too kindly on men who hit their women, much less *our* women."

"We don't either down here." Trey's voice was a growl. "But I didn't hit her. I've never hit a woman in my life."

Rocco Diamante bristled. "You calling my wife a liar, Mr. Cooper? Because I'm standing here looking at her fat lip. How'd she get that, huh?"

Oh, boy, this was getting serious. Cinda looked up at Trey. He crossed his arms over his chest. His mouth was set in a line of stubborn determination. Alarm shot through Cinda. He wasn't going to say anything—and she knew why. He was protecting her. She couldn't let him do that. The same instinct that had a parent throwing herself in front of a bus to save her child had Cinda out from behind Trey and in plain view of the Mafia guys.

Trey gasped and grabbed her arm, but Cinda resisted his tug on her and faced the dangerous don. "I did it. I hit her."

You could have heard a Georgia pine needle drop right there on Mimosa Place.

But the effect of her words—or her mere presence—on the short and stocky man in the expensive suit was astounding. He dropped his tough-guy pose and his mouth rounded with surprise. His cheeks turned red—and his voice changed. It went up about an octave. "Cinda? Cinda Mayes? Is that you?"

"You know her?" Bobby Jean cried, letting go of her husband.

"You know him?" Trey cried.

"He knows her," spread through the crowd. "They know each other."

Cinda shrugged out of Trey's grasp and approached Mr. Rocco Diamante, Mafia don. As if. Angry, upset, and relieved in the extreme, Cinda stopped in front of the man. "Tommy Jenkins, is that you? It is, isn't it?" She reached out and pulled the sunglasses off the man. And gasped. "Why, you little stink, I thought I recognized you. Does your father know you took his limo and his bodyguards out for a drive down South?"

Tommy Jenkins, aka Rocco Diamante, looked like he was about to cry. "Can I see you over here a minute, Cinda?" She consented and stepped to one side with him. Tommy immediately began to whine. "Don't tell my father, Cinda. Please? I did it for a good reason." He leaned in toward her and lowered his voice. "I want my wife back."

Cinda's whisper matched his. "Well, there she is. Take her. Please. With my blessings."

"I can't. She won't go."

"Oh, for God's sake, Tommy, why not?"

"Look at her, Cinda."

"Uh-uh. I've seen all of her I want to, trust me."

"No, I mean really look at her. And now look at me. I'm a short, fat kid from suburbia. She'd never go for a guy like me. But I love her. So I made up this story about me being in the Mafia, and she fell for me. But then I never did anything dangerous or scary and she got bored and left me. So now here I am like some big man with some clout and she's buying it. Please help me out here, Cinda. Please? Besides, I have something to tell her."

Before Cinda could really process that, Trey stepped up to stand at her side. "What is going on here, Cinda?"

She shook her head, signalling for Trey to speak quietly. Then she brought her own voice down to a whisper. "Trey Cooper, meet Tommy Jenkins. Tommy and I went to the same high school. Do I even need to tell you that he was the president of the drama club and he's not in the Mafia?"

"Get outta here," Trey said, sounding more like a Mafioso than Tommy ever would.

Bobby Jean flounced over and gripped her husband's arm. The woman stood a head taller than Tommy. She looked from him to Trey to Cinda. "What are y'all whispering about over here?"

Tommy looked a bit ill. Cinda raised an eyebrow at him and then turned to her nemesis. "Look, Bobby Jean, I'm going to be straight with you. I knew your husband as Tommy Jenkins when he was a kid. But that was before he was...inducted into the Mafia as Rocco Diamante. He's a big man now in the organization. But don't worry." She turned to Tommy and winked, making sure Bobby Jean didn't see it. "His secret is safe with me."

Tommy puckered his bottom lip and sent Cinda a silent, wide-eyed thank-you.

"Oh, baby," Bobby Jean cooed, at her husband. "You never told me that name. I like it better. Tommy. It's much nicer, you know. It sounds like the name of someone I could cuddle up to at night."

Tommy puffed up like the big man he so badly wanted to be, turned to his wife, and blurted, "You're pregnant, honey. Your test results came back. And that's why you've been feeling bad. We're going to have a baby."

The crowd sent up a collective and happy gasp. The facts made the rounds in loud whispers. "She's going to have a baby." "The Mafia don got her pregnant." "Who got her pregnant?" "Don somebody." "Who's pregnant?"

Bobby Jean's expression was pretty much the shocked one she'd worn when Cinda had smacked her last night. "What? Rocco—I mean Tommy—a baby? We're going to have a baby?" She let go of her husband and began squealing and jumping up and down in place. Her tube top had a tough time keeping up. "We've got to go tell Mama and Daddy. Right now. We're going to have a baby! Omigod! A baby!"

Then she set her sights on Cinda. "Oh, sugar, I'm going to have a baby. I'm so happy. I can't believe it. And here you are—darned near family since you knew my Tommy when he was a boy. Look, I'll call you. You've already had a baby, so you can tell me what all to expect, okay?"

Cinda couldn't believe it. *Good God, we're girl-*

friends. "But what about the lawsuit?" was all she could get out.

Bobby Jean waved that away. "Oh, shoot, honey, I was just kidding y'all. I already forgot about that. Now, I'm going to need to know everything from you, okay? Like about breast-feeding and such. We'll get together." She then turned to Trey and, to everyone's surprise, looked suddenly shy. She fiddled with her fingers as she talked. "Trey, I've been awful to you. I'm sorry. You're such a good friend to me. I think…well, I'll always love you. But like a friend."

Cinda realized she was actually moved. Someone took her hand. It was Dorinda Cooper. "I told you she was a good girl at heart."

Cinda nodded and smiled, believing anything today. She listened as Trey said, "I love you, too, Bobby Jean. And congratulations, honey." He hugged her.

Everyone sighed and aahed. Then Bobby Jean grabbed her husband again by the hand and took off for the house. "Come on, baby. Wait until I tell Mama and Daddy they're going to be grandparents of a future Mafia don."

Though he looked a little sick at that, Tommy/ Rocco asked plaintively, "Then we aren't separated anymore?"

"Of course not, doll. What made you think we were separated?"

The four goons closed ranks around Bobby Jean and her hapless but adoring husband and blocked them from sight. The happy crowd was pleased to follow after them, apparently wanting to see firsthand the elder Nickersons' response to the joyous news. That left Cinda and Trey and Dorinda and Chelsi standing there alone.

"Well, that's it," Dorinda declared. "Let's go see about that pecan pie. It ought to be done by the time we get home."

So that was it. Cinda couldn't believe it. It was over. She looked up at Trey. Ever handsome, the poor man looked shell-shocked. "Are you all right, Trey?"

"I think so," he said, taking Chelsi from his mother and holding her as the foursome headed back toward Trey's car.

"So you really knew him in high school?" Trey asked Cinda as he put his arm around her shoulder.

"Yeah. I thought I recognized him when he came outside, but I wasn't sure. I would have hated to be wrong."

"I guess. Damn. That ended with a fizzle, didn't it?"

"Not really," Cinda said. "I'm happy for Bobby Jean and Tommy. Or Rocco. What a name. That crazy guy. He said he put on that big show to impress Bobby Jean when he met her. And then, when she fell for it, he had to keep it up. But I'm telling you, she's not the worst of Tommy's problems. His father is going to kill him."

"Yeah, that's what you said. What's his father do that he needs those guys and that black limo?"

"Oh, he's in the Mafia."

Trey stopped. Cinda looked up at him. "What?"

"His *father* is in the Mafia? The man's name is Jenkins and he's Mafia?"

Cinda gently reproved Trey. "The Mafia's equal opportunity, honey. Anybody can join. You don't have to be Italian. I guess I was just around it more than you, so I understand it better. A lot of the kids in high school's dads' were reportedly mobsters."

"Child, where'd you go to high school that so many Mafia children were running around loose?" Dorinda chimed in.

"A private one in New York City. Tommy and I were in the same class."

They started walking again toward the red muscle machine that was Trey's car. "Then you're really a Yankee?" Dorinda asked a few steps later.

"Afraid so," Cinda had to tell her.

"Well, what do you know. My son married a Yankee." Dorinda didn't sound happy, just resigned. "I never thought I'd live to see the day."

"Take heart, Mother. We're not really married."

"You are so."

"We're not, Dorinda. But we will be," Cinda boldly announced, feeling her face—and her heart—warming up as she stared into Trey's eyes.

"We will?" Trey made the mistake of asking. "I mean…we *will*. We will."

"Yes, we will. We have to be. And soon, too."

Trey frowned at her. "I'm not following. I love you and want to marry you. Damn. It's true. I do. But…what are you talking about?"

Cinda smiled broadly. "*My* high-school reunion is next month."

Trey stopped them again. "No. Sorry. Only today I made a promise to myself that I was never going to another reunion ever again."

Undaunted, happier than she'd been in a long, long time, Cinda shrugged. "Well, you'll have to break it. Because we're going. I already sent in my RSVP."

Cinda watched as Trey tried to look displeased, but he couldn't. There was too much love radiating her way from his blue eyes. He chuckled happily and kissed Chelsi on her sweet chubby baby cheek. "You hear that, gal? We're going to New York for a reunion. Yippee. I'll show you where your mama and I met and where you were almost born."

So it was settled. They headed again for the car, in no real hurry. They hadn't gone more than ten steps before Trey broke the silence. "I have to break more than one promise to myself today, I suppose."

"Really? What promise is that?" Cinda put her arm around his waist, walking easily at his side even though her heart was doing ecstatic loops of sheer joy just knowing that Trey was going to be a real part of her life.

"Well, I promised myself years ago that I'd never marry while I was working on the race car circuit. Too many problems. I see it all the time. The travel. The hours. The divorces. It's rough, Cinda. I want you to know that."

"I understand, Trey. I wouldn't ask you to give up something so important to you."

"I appreciate that, honey. But it still worries me. I don't want those things—the fighting, the hurting—to happen to us. I don't know what to do. Except quit."

Cinda hated the wistful, resigned note in his voice. Hated even worse that his loving her was causing it. She thought about what to do and came up with a compromise by the time they reached the car. "Trey, maybe you don't have to break that promise. And maybe you can stay in racing."

He frowned. "I don't see how. It's a very demanding lifestyle. And Jude Barrett doesn't cut anybody any slack. No, I'll just have to quit. Because you come first. That's just the way it is."

"I really needed to know you believe that. But, listen. For one thing, you're not married to Jude Barrett. You'll be married to me. Have you ever thought of sponsoring a car yourself, Trey? Or starting your own team? Then you'd be in control and could set the hours or whatever.''

''Hell, yes, I've thought of it. For years. It's been like a dream of mine. Shoot, I even know which of the guys on the team I'd ask to go with me. But I'll never have the money.''

Cinda smiled. ''Well, I do.'' She saw Trey's protests coming and rushed on. ''Don't let your pride answer for you, Trey. We can do this. I think Richard would approve, too. He was such a daredevil himself that I think he'd love my idea. I personally can't think of a better way to invest some of his money, can you?''

Trey looked thunderstruck as all the possibilities sunk in. ''My God, my own team? Wow.'' Then he sobered. ''If I went along with this, I'd want to pay you back all the money you'd put in up front.''

Cinda laughed. ''You silly thing. When we're married, it will be *our* money. So if you want to pay yourself back, go ahead.''

''Well, I'm going to. But I don't know what to say, Cinda.''

Well, if he didn't, his mother did. ''For corn's sake, son, say yes.''

Trey laughed and then bent over Cinda to kiss her. When he pulled back from her, he said, ''Okay. Yes, I accept.''

''Then it's settled. Good.'' Cinda thought she would faint from so much love and happiness. This was how it was supposed to be. This was how she was supposed to feel. Happy. Complete. Like she was going to die from it.

Trey handed her Chelsi and walked with her around the back of the car to open the door where the baby's car seat was. "So tell me about this reunion of yours. Oh, jeez, we'll probably see Rocco—or Tommy—and Bobby Jean there, won't we?"

Cinda grimaced. "Oh, that's right. God, Trey, Bobby Jean thinks she and I are friends now." Trey laughed at her chagrin, so Cinda had to get him back. "What's so funny, mister? Guess who's going to the reunion with us?"

Dorinda Cooper's head popped up on the other side of the car where she'd been about to pile into the back seat. "Besides me, you mean?"

"Besides you, of course." Cinda turned to Trey. "Well? Are you going to guess?"

He looked suddenly sullen. "I don't want to."

Cinda could have devoured him right there, he was so cute. "Okay, I'll tell you. Major Clovis."

"Who's he?" Dorinda asked.

"She," Cinda corrected. "And you know, Dorinda, I can't wait to see the two of you together. That ought to be interesting."

"Ha," Trey griped, crossing his arms protectively over his chest. "I don't like her. She threatened to hurt me."

Balancing Chelsi on a hip, Cinda rubbed Trey's arm affectionately. "And she will, too, honey. She wasn't teasing you." Then Cinda remembered something else. "Oh, and Richard's parents will be there, too."

"No."

"Yes. They're big contributors to the school. Richard also graduated from my high school, but I didn't know him back then. He was four years older than I was. Anyway, you'll love Papa Rick. That's Richard's father. Oh, you know what, Trey? I bet he will want to invest in your car, too. Oh, that is perfect. You'll be so good for him. Oh, but then there's the Dragon Lady, Richard's mother. She's a huge pain, but I love her. I'm afraid they're just going to be in our lives, Trey.''

Looking ill, Trey braced his butt against his car. "Lovely." Then he smiled at her. "I'm kidding you. That's fine with me, Cinda. I'll love whoever you love. But is there anything else I should know?"

Time to come clean. "Yes. I have three brothers. They're all older than I am, and they'll be there, too. And my parents. Everyone will be there." Cinda smiled encouragingly. "Do you still want to marry me?"

Trey reached out for her, drawing Chelsi and Cinda into his embrace. He kissed her forehead lightly. "Yes," Trey said, "I do. I have since that day I saw you in that elevator."

"What elevator?" Dorinda Cooper asked.

Cinda and Trey disengaged from their hug and turned to face Trey's mother on the other side of the car. Trey answered her for them both. "We need to go rescue that pie, so we'll tell you about it on the way home, Mother. But this elevator is a very important one. So important that if Cinda and I should ever have a son, we'll have to name him Otis."

Her Perfect Wife

KATE THOMAS

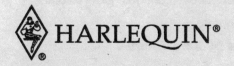

TORONTO • NEW YORK • LONDON
AMSTERDAM • PARIS • SYDNEY • HAMBURG
STOCKHOLM • ATHENS • TOKYO • MILAN • MADRID
PRAGUE • WARSAW • BUDAPEST • AUCKLAND

Dear Reader,

Long ago, a friend of mine was working full-time for a law firm and going to medical school. When I voiced admiration for her industriousness, she launched into a semi-hysterical recitation of all the things she wasn't getting done, things her stay-at-home mother did for her father: picking up dry cleaning, grocery shopping, sending out birthday cards....

She ended with a summation I've never forgotten. (That's what writers do: listen, look, remember and ask "what if?") "What I need is a wife," my friend said with a sigh.

Today, as I kick my way past a mound of laundry that's escaped its container again so I can shove a handful of receipts into the bulging "To Be Filed" file—while ignoring the answer machine's impatiently blinking light and hoping the allergy-shot clinic is open tomorrow—I have to agree with her.

All of which explains the premise of my latest Duets novel. These days, *everyone* could benefit from having a "wife" whose main job is to make life run smoother.

I hope you enjoy *Her Perfect Wife*. And may yours be as hot and sexy as Melinda's—the adorable though occasionally overconfident Jack Halloran!

Kate Thomas

Books by Kate Thomas

HARLEQUIN DUETS	SILHOUETTE ROMANCE
18—TOO LUCKY FOR LOVE	1023—THE TEXAS TOUCH
	1123—JINGLE BELL BRIDE
	1357—TEXAS BRIDE

My thanks to Pat Rush for the sentiment,
to Jean Price for her integrity
and to my great editors at Harlequin/Silhouette
for their enthusiasm and expertise.

1

As the two friends emerged from the chiffon and cummerbund gauntlet, their polite smiles faded like goodwill in the Middle East and they got down to business.

"You grab the food," instructed the redhead, whose name was Sherry. "I'll snag the champagne. Meet at the usual table."

"Gotcha." Sketching a brotherly salute, Jack Halloran, the taller half of the duo, turned toward the buffet.

Separately but equally efficiently, the childhood pals worked their way through the crowded reception hall, resurrecting the paste-on smiles for strangers, exchanging slightly warmer greetings with wedding guests they knew from work.

Ten minutes later, Jack plunked two plates piled with finger sandwiches and sundry toothpicked items on the corner table and dropped into one of the chairs against the wall. "Whew—what a mob! The far table has shrimp and a big bowl of strawberries, but I couldn't get near it. You'd think these people hadn't eaten in months."

Sherry, his champagne-wrangling compadre, pushed a stemmed glass across the table. "They always go nuts when it's free. Hope Deb's braced for a hefty bar tab."

"No sweat," Jack assured his best friend since third grade. "The groom's father owns a liquor distributorship."

"To Brad's dad." Silence reigned as two champagne glasses were raised and tilted. Toothpicks were lifted.

A few minutes later, Sherry suspended her grazing to watch the bride and groom shuffle around on the dance floor. "Very Fred and Ginger," she commented before switching her gaze to her companion. "You gonna dance if somebody asks you?"

Jack shrugged. "Moot question, probably. Nobody even asked at Anne-Marie's last week. Maybe I need a new outfit."

"It's not the outfit," Sherry countered with the bluntness only possible between longtime friends. "It's the haggard, grim expression you wear with it. Drives people away."

Haggard became an outright scowl. "Sorry. I'll try to be more glowing in the future." Jack's sarcastic tone warned against further discussion.

After shooting him a return glare, Sherry obligingly shifted the focus of the conversation. "Well, *nobody* danced at Anne-Marie's wedding—except the bride and groom. And they had to."

"Yeah, why was that reception so dead?"

"Accordion music, that's why."

The two shared a shudder, then Sherry pushed back her folding chair and stood. "Want some more champagne?"

Jack nodded. Then, thinking the noise level around them would drown it, he gave a sigh that seemed to come from his toenails. "What I really want…"

Instantly abandoning interest in bubbling alcohol, Sherry dropped back into her seat.

With a glance at the milling reception crowd as if to check that nobody was paying the slightest attention to the two old pals in the corner behind the deejay's setup, she tapped her friend's knuckles with the back of her hand. "I *knew* something was bugging you! You've been OTL for weeks. Spill it, Halloran. What is it you really want?''

After a moment's hesitation, Jack let the answer out in a rush. "I want to do what Deb's doing—get married, quit work and stay home.''

Sherry's eyes bugged out. "You can't be serious! Have you flipped?''

"Oh, don't get the wrong idea, Downe,'' Jack assured her. "I'm not looking for brain-blasting, from-here-to-eternity love.''

That earned a fervent nod of agreement. They both thought love was a four-letter word.

"It's just...ever since my brother-in-law cashed out with cancer...well, I've been thinking about my life.''

"What about it?'' Sherry asked, totally dumbfounded.

"What about—? I want one!'' Jack exclaimed. "I'm burned-out, Sher. I'm tired of seventy-hour weeks. I want to go to the movies in the afternoon once in a while. I want to eat real food, not microwaved boxes and fast-fat concoctions.''

"Who doesn't?'' Sherry retorted, playing devil's advocate as usual. "If only we didn't have all those stupid bills to pay.''

Jack ignored her lame attempt at humor. "Look, I want to open my own investment counseling firm, set my own hours. Actually help people. I've finally completed the education program, now I've got to take the Certified Financial Planner Certification Examination. But there are still some topics I'm weak on—like insurance and trust law. If I was a stay-at-home wife, I'd have plenty of time to review all that stuff. And I could nail the test on the first try.''

Sherry shook her head. "B-but you can't just...just get married and quit your job!''

A blare of disco music nearly drowned his response. "Why not?''

"Well...because you're a stockbroker!"

Halloran snorted. "So's Deb. If she can give it up to sit home being a wife, why can't I?"

His redheaded friend waved a hand in frustration. "What kind of wife would *you* make? Aren't they supposed to at least be able to cook and clean?"

"Can Deb?"

Sherry conceded the point. "She can't even make popcorn. She blew up the microwave in the break room last month, didn't she?"

Jack jabbed the air with a finger. "Exactly. So if it's okay for her to stay home when she can't do anything useful there, why can't I?"

"Because you're as straight as a West Texas highway, Jack! And I don't know too many women in the market for a wife."

"All I need is one," he pointed out.

"It's Jensen, isn't it?" Without waiting for his answer, Sherry said, "So transfer to the Richardson office."

Jack shook his head. While their boss was a bozo, he wasn't the problem. His best friend and fellow stockbroker, Sherry Downe still had all the driving ambition they'd shared when they swept out of college and plunged into work at Loeb-Weinstein.

His own interest in the job, on the other hand, had dried up like the Texas Panhandle in the eleventh year of a ten-year drought. Every day was a battle now. He could barely dial up enough enthusiasm to make himself show up, let alone function.

Investment counseling, where you got to draw up a comprehensive, personalized plan and help someone carry it out... That sounded so much more interesting than hunting down today's hot stock for the Beemer set. His brother-in-law's death had convinced Jack that life was too short to dread each morning's sunrise.

"Take a vacation," Sherry suggested. "Ross and Kilmer are going fishing in the Gulf next week. Go with 'em.''

"No way." A week with those margin-trading maniacs and he'd go postal for sure. "What I need is a break so I can bone up on all the ins and outs of insurance and trust law and taxation scenarios." No lie. He had to have some saturation review time. The Certification Exam for CFPs covered a hell of a lot more than the equity instruments he'd worked with the past ten years.

"Well, then—sit by the pool at your apartment for a couple of weeks."

"It'll take longer than that," Jack admitted gloomily. Studying aside, he needed some serious downtime. Enough to clear his head so he could map a real future for himself. One that appealed rather than appalled.

"Quit, then," Sherry snapped. "Walk away. You've got some bucks stashed, don't you?"

"Not enough," Jack said with a grimace. "Besides—remember that ski trip we took a couple of years ago?"

Puzzled, Sherry nodded.

"And the little, ah, problem I encountered the second day."

"I think they called it a pine tree."

Jack threw her a disgusted look. "Ha, ha, Downe. Well, that put me in the high-risk health insurance pool."

"But they fixed your bulging disk! You ran a 10K last week."

"Doesn't matter. I'm in, period. Only zillionaires can afford *those* premiums." He raked fingers through his hair in disgust. "Hell, I can't afford even to pay for COBRA if I leave Loeb-Weinstein. And if I *don't* keep up continuous coverage, nobody will insure me in the future. They don't have to—and they won't. I checked.

"Which makes Deb's trick the best solution to all my

problems. Get married, get spousal coverage, stay home and study."

Jack's jaw jutted out. "Besides, if it's okay for her to do it, why isn't it okay for me? Because I'm a guy? That's sex discrimination."

Raising her hands in surrender, Sherry stood and smoothed down her dress. "Okay, Halloran, chill. I know that tone when I hear it. Spare me the crusade speech. Please. I'll go get us some more champagne," she went on. "And if I run into a female looking for a stay-at-home wife with marginal homemaking skills, I'll give her your number."

Jack Halloran spied one last meatball on his plate. He picked it up by its toothpick. "You do that, Sher." He waved the meat-capped stick in the air. "I'd be as good a 'wife' as ol' Deb's gonna be," he declared. "At least I can microwave popcorn."

As his friend disappeared into the reception throng, Jack stared moodily at the scene before him. How many of these shindigs had he and Sherry attended—or, worse, participated in—over the past ten years? Fifty? A hundred? Two hundred?

"I am so tired of this," he muttered, drumming the fingers of his free hand on the table. And he didn't only mean these stupid weddings.

At thirty-one, he felt ninety-one. Drained. Burned-out. All the time.

For months now, he'd longed to escape from the grind of tracking IPOs and global hedge funds dawn to dusk, minute by minute.

He'd noticed the same desire in many of his co-workers.

And that the only ones who escaped with their sanity were people who became independent financial advisors—and women who married their way out of the rat race.

So why couldn't he use the same tactics? One to get to the other.

Because men aren't supposed to? Jack bit into the meatball. What a crock.

A stay-at-home "wife" would have a shipload of time to review all those arcane things he needed to know to pass the CFP test.

And it wasn't as if he needed to delay marriage until he fell in love. He wasn't going there, not after seeing the wreckage it could cause. His sister's husband had died almost a year ago; Tess was still so devastated she could hardly function.

Jack's fingers tightened, snapping the little stick he held. *Tess...* That was another reason he needed a life away from that fast-lane, high-pressure brokerage job: he had to get Tess out of her apartment and back into the land of the living. Pete had been a great guy, but he was gone. It was time for his sister to move on—only she apparently wasn't going to do it without help.

And since he was the oldest Halloran sib and the only other one currently living in Dallas, Jack had appointed himself to provide it.

AT HIS INSISTENCE, they left the wedding early, reclaiming Sherry's car from the parking valet.

This being Jack's turn as designated driver, Sherry kicked off her shoes as she slid into the passenger seat.

Jack loosened his tie before maneuvering the vehicle out of the country-club parking lot and through the surrounding maze of dark streets until he found the highway. Once on the interstate going north, he put on the cruise control.

After fifteen minutes of the kind of comfortable silence only two very old friends can enjoy, Sherry shifted sideways on the seat.

Jack lifted an eyebrow, but kept his eyes on the road. "What?"

"That wife stuff you were ranting about earlier—you weren't serious, were you?"

Jack sighed. "Look, Sher, I know how you feel about marriage." Hell, if he'd grown up in her family, he'd feel the same way.

And aside from love being a generally *baaad* idea, who in his right mind would sign up for the traditional husband role: slaving away at a cutthroat career just to support a wife and kids you never spent any time with?

Being a wife, on the other hand…man, what a deal. Read the mail, buy a few groceries and you're done. Take the rest of the day off.

He exited the highway and made the turn into Sherry's apartment complex. "I'm wiped, Sher. I want to slow down for a while," he said. "Housewifery would sure as hell be more relaxing, more enjoyable than churning accounts to make Jensen happy."

Sherry snorted. "You think laundry's relaxing? Dusting's enjoyable? You *are* nuts."

Jack snorted right back. Those simple housekeeping tasks sounded like heaven after ten years of chasing the Dow, the S&P, the NASDAQ and assorted overseas bloodbaths, but he didn't expect Sherry to understand.

She still had the market in her blood. He didn't. Maybe he'd have to wipe out his 401(k) after all to buy medical coverage.

"Trust me. The way I feel these days—anything's better than paving Jugular Jensen's path to the top," Jack insisted, slotting her car into its assigned space. He followed her out of the vehicle and tossed her the keys before climbing into his Jeep, parked nearby.

"You want to do brunch at Smitty's tomorrow?" he asked as he cranked the engine.

"Can't," Sherry said, tucking her shoes under her arm as she searched the ring for her house key. "I have to meet a new client at noon."

"On Sunday?" Jack shook his head. See? That's exactly what he wanted to bail on.

"Her aunt—who's been a client of mine for years—is giving her some stock to fund a retirement account. And Sunday's the only time she can meet with me to go over it.

"Don't worry." Sherry smiled wryly as her best friend put the Jeep into gear. "If she looks like she needs a wife, I'll give her your name."

"SORRY...SORRY...EXCUSE ME...SORRY..." Melinda muttered the apologies automatically as she followed the stiff-backed maître d' through a sea of linen-draped tables to a booth along the far wall.

Her glasses slipped down her nose, creating two maître d's. Impatiently Mel pushed the center of the frame back up on the bridge of her nose. The arm movement caught her lab coat on the back of a chair. As she yanked it loose with another apology, her pocket crackled. The notice from the city's code compliance division. Frustration rolled through her.

Failure to mow, for God's sake! How had things gotten so out of control?

And how the heck was she going to get them back under it? Frustration morphed into desperation. She had to regain manageability—somehow!

"Your party, madam." Monsieur Snobby waggled his fingers toward the booth, then flounced away.

"Ms. Downe?" Melinda extended her hand to the woman seated in the booth, who was properly outfitted for the occasion in a tailored silk outfit and polite smile. *Unlike me,* Mel groused to herself. *Wearing one of Mom's old dresses because nothing I own is clean.* "Melinda Burke. Sorry I'm late—we had to stop some bleeding in a three-year-old."

"Medical emergencies come first," the stockbroker

agreed, shaking hands, then indicating the banquette opposite her. "Please. Have a seat. And call me Sherry."

"And I'm Melinda or Mel or 'Hey, Burke!'" Melinda said half-jokingly, remembering to smile as she slid into the booth and accepted a leather-bound menu.

"I went ahead and ordered," Sherry said. "I hope you don't mind."

"That's fine. I'll have whatever she's having," Mel told the waiter who'd materialized beside the booth.

With a murmur that might have been "Very good, madam," he plucked the menu from her hands and disappeared again.

As Melinda shifted on the padded bench, the notice in her pocket crackled again. *"Creating a public health menace."* Another wave of panicked fury broke over her.

Darn it, for the first time in her adult life, she was at a loss. And that alone had her freaking. She'd just spent twenty minutes stitching up a toddler's artery, for crying out loud, but this daily-living stuff—not being able to just resolve these ridiculous situations and move on was driving her nuts!

The woman across from her, ah, Sherry, pulled a stack of brochures from the briefcase at her side. "We can eat first, if you like," she said pleasantly, "but I brought you some fund materials to look over."

Mel could feel her blood pressure jump. Then, without warning, tears started streaming down her face. She pressed her napkin against the stupid things. "Sorry," she said as she immediately brought herself under control. Ridiculous! "I just—"

"—hate financial reports," Sherry finished for her. "I understand."

"Oh, no. I'm sure they're...fascinating," Melinda finally managed, which only made the other woman grin knowingly.

Melinda found herself smiling back. "Okay, they

might put me to sleep,'' she admitted as the waiter brought salads, offered to grind pepper, then whisked himself away. ''If I had time to read them.''

Sherry looked at her through narrowed eyes. ''You're too busy to plan for your future?''

That notice from the city crackled in her pocket again as Melinda replaced her napkin in her lap and picked up her fork. ''I'm too busy to go to the bathroom,'' she declared, frustration and fatigue lowering her guard. Normally she handled everything the way surgeons were taught: don't complain, *fix*.

But these days, there was too much to fix. ''If the discount store near the hospital wasn't open 24/7, I wouldn't be wearing clean underwear,'' she confessed, ''because I can't get to the Laundromat to drop off for wash-and-fold service. I've tried for a month now.''

Putting down her fork, Mel jerked the final straw from her lab coat. ''In fact, my work demands are so overwhelming right now that I'm about to be arrested for criminal lawn neglect!''

During Mel's outburst, Sherry had laid her fork on her salad plate, placed her elbow on the table, bent her arm and cupped her chin in her palm. Now she stared at Melinda as if fascinated. ''Do tell,'' she said softly.

Mel pushed the confounded glasses back up the bridge of her nose. She'd abandoned her contacts weeks ago due to lack of sleep.

Unfolding the official notice, she tossed it onto the table. ''Last night, about midnight, I managed to look through a week's worth of mail. Included was this—it's a notice from the city citing my parents' lawn as a public health hazard.''

Sherry freed her chin to spread her hands wide, palms up. ''What does that have to do with you?'' she asked.

''I'm supposed to be taking care of the place for them while they're in Oman,'' Mel explained. ''Dad's working on an oil project over there.'' Pushing aside her barely touched salad, she thrust her fingers into her hair. "I've tried, really I have, but…" She swore under her breath. "I'm in a pediatric-surgery fellowship program at Southwestern Medical Center. Intense is an understatement. The program head, Dr. Bowen, is one of the top surgeons in the field. He's completely focused on his work and he expects us to be the same.

"I've worked my whole life for this," Mel continued, "and I *will* meet his expectations." Meet, hell. She'd surpass them.

Since the age of ten, she'd devoted all her time and energy, her whole life, to becoming a pediatric surgeon. To save other families the pain hers had endured when her little brother had died needlessly. And she was so close!

"I'm guessing you have a lot of demands on your time," Sherry said, her head tipped to one side.

"Too many," Melinda grumbled. "I was holding my own in my apartment. Then my parents handed over the keys to their three-thousand-foot house—with its felonious yard. And a pool, for God's sake."

Mel shoved the perpetually sliding glasses back up in frustration. "My folks always supported my drive to be a doctor. They've never asked me for anything until now." More stupid tears threatened; Mel dashed them away with the back of her hand. "I feel like I'm letting them down, but I—I just can't keep up with everything!"

"Besides laundry and sleep, you mean?" Sherry asked, leaning forward.

"Ha!" Mel began ticking off items on fingertips. "The pool hasn't been cleaned since they left six weeks ago. I haven't deposited my last two paychecks. I've got a stack of unpaid bills because I *cannot* find the time to sit down and write out the checks! The water company's pretty frosted about that—they're threatening to turn off service. And now this—" She indicated the code-compliance notice, then swore under her breath again as she buried her head in her hands. "I need help, but I don't even have time to contact all the different services I need!"

"You're not talking about a permanent arrangement, are you?" Sherry wanted to know.

"No, just till my folks get back. Six months, max."

The waiter suddenly manifested in corporeal form, replaced the salads with entrées, then dematerialized.

Melinda eyed the cross-hatched chicken breast. "I think I'd kill for a home-cooked meal," she said sorrowfully. "And clean laundry."

"How about dust?" Sherry asked with an odd little smile. "That a problem, too?"

"Bah. The dust is so thick, I write notes to myself in it." Melinda reached for her fork. "I guess I need a time management course. Or—"

"What you *need*," Sherry interrupted her firmly, "is a wife. And I know just the man for the job."

2

MELINDA TOLD HERSELF to close her mouth and disregard what was going on inside her head: a lot of jumping up and down, yelling about the cavalry coming.

"I need a wife," she echoed finally. "You're not serious, are you?"

"Serious as an IRS audit," the woman across from her said, with that half smile still in place. "You need one of those fifties-television wives, right? The kind nobody really wants to be anymore? Someone who keeps house and takes care of your personal life while you're out becoming a doctor."

"And you know the man for the job."

"Since third grade."

Well, shoot—it *was* tempting. A simple, efficient solution to a whole bunch of problems. Melinda raised her hand, got the waiter's attention, pointed to the short, businesslike drink on a nearby table, then touched the tabletop in front of her.

"How much does he charge?" she asked as the waiter flicked his order pad in the air and scurried away.

Sherry grinned. "The man I'm talking about will work for marriage. And health insurance."

"Huh?"

"He's really a stockbroker with a case of job burnout, not a housekeeper," Sherry explained. "He wants some time off to study for his financial planner's exam, but he needs to stay insured while he's not working. Plus he thinks that a guy quitting to get married will make a statement about gender inequality or something.''

"Oh," Melinda said, regretfully discarding what was really a brilliant way to slide out of dealing with all that daily domestic drone stuff that was ruining her life. "He's crazy. Well, never—"

"I'll admit I thought the same thing when he first brought up the idea, but now…" Sherry looked thoughtful, the odd little smile returning. "Now I think it's the perfect solution for you both."

Melinda prodded her chicken slab. Had they both lost their minds? She couldn't marry somebody she'd never met. Could she? No, she should drop the whole crazy subject and get back to the hospital. Back to reality. She had ten charts to work up before Bowen came in for evening rounds. "What if I'm already involved with somebody?"

"You're not," Sherry replied knowingly. "Your aunt Gertrude told me all about you, except the criminal lawn bit."

The waiter brought Melinda's drink. She took a healthy sip. "Just how well do you know my aunt?" she asked.

"She's been a client of mine for almost ten years."

Ten years? Aunt Gertrude didn't go to the same hairdresser twice. She must really trust Sherry Downe and her judgment.

So maybe it wasn't such a crazy idea. "And this guy who wants to be a wife. You've known him since third grade?"

"Yep," Sherry said. "You couldn't do better than Jack Halloran. He's smart, responsible, trustworthy—and a natural-born caretaker."

Jack Halloran. He had a name. It made the whole idea more real somehow, but… "If he's so wonderful, why doesn't he have someone already lined up to marry?"

"Because Jack's not interested in true romance—or any other kind," Sherry declared in a tone too positive to doubt.

"Is he gay?" Melinda asked, taking another sip of whatever she'd ordered. Not that his sexual orientation mattered, of course. Even if she did marry this stranger, she wouldn't consider having sex with him...would she?

Sherry shook her head.

Right. As if she had time for *that,* anyway.

"Meet him," Sherry suggested, "then make up your mind. But I promise you, if you marry Jack Halloran, your problems are over." She gestured at the city code violation notice. "By the time they get back, he'll have your parents' yard looking like a golf course. And you'll have clean clothes all the time. Home-cooked meals...."

God, it was tempting. So tempting. The perfect answer to a prayer she hadn't even known she'd been praying.

Still, she would have never made such a snap decision, she told herself later, if she hadn't been working the ER that month. It put her in crisis management mode.

Draining her drink, Melinda plunked the glass on the table and grinned at the woman across from her.

A surge of elation and hope and plain old adrenaline-fueled daring pushed its way through her guilt and frustration and exhaustion. This was what surgeons do, she told herself. Define the problem, determine the solution and *do* it. "Your friend Jack would really be up for this? Being a 'wife' for six months while I finish my surgical fellowship, then...well, riding off into the sunset?"

Sherry looked at Melinda for a long moment.

Tension built.

Then the stockbroker pulled her briefcase onto her lap and stuck her hand inside.

"Let's ask him," she said as she retrieved a cell phone and flipped it open.

WITH A SHUDDER, Jack slammed the bedroom door on the disaster. Thank God the woman wouldn't be inspecting his apartment as part of the selection process.

But he'd had to scramble. *And what the heck* do *you wear to a "wife" interview?* he wondered as he gathered his keys and wallet from the breakfast bar and headed for the door. Not the boxers and ragged Rangers T-shirt he'd been working out in when the phone rang.

After a quick shower, shave and some hair gel, he'd finally settled on a business-casual outfit of khakis and a purply blue shirt Sherry called indigo.

He still wasn't sure why he'd agreed to meet this doctor who must be nuttier than a San Saba pecan grove. Except that women shouldn't get all the equal rights; he loathed his job the way environmentalists despise strip miners; and he needed to commit beaucoup time to study if he wanted to pass that bleeping CFP exam.

Besides, Sherry had dared him to put up or shut up, and dammit, it would be nice to meet somebody who *wanted* his help for a change.

Unlike Tess. Who'd hung up on him just before Sherry called.

Jack growled with frustration as he left the apartment and loped down the outside stairs. Dammit, he knew Tess missed Pete. Hadn't he envied the way they'd been crazy about each other from the get-go?

But it just proved his theory. The only safe way to approach marriage was this way—as a compensation package.

Pleased with the analogy, Jack climbed into his Jeep and headed for the restaurant. *'Cuz I'm so never falling in love.*

Too freaking dangerous.

At twenty-seven, Pete Malloy had been diagnosed with cancer; in eight months he was gone.

And a year later, Tess still claimed she wasn't ready to get on with her life—as in, start dating again.

No way I'm opening myself to that kind of grief.

Of course, in thirty-one years, he hadn't met anyone who knocked his socks off like with Pete and Tess, so he was probably immune. Another reason he might as well marry this doctor.

If he didn't, he'd have to keep working for Go-For-The-Jugular Jensen.

Hell, the overnight shift in the most dangerous convenience store in south Dallas was more appealing than *that,* Jack thought as he pulled into the restaurant's parking lot and killed the engine.

He sat there a moment, absentmindedly raking wind knots out of his hair, wondering exactly what the doctor expected in the way of wifely duties.

She wouldn't demand that I be her boy-toy, would she?

It's not that he had to love a woman to make love *with* her, of course, but sex under those conditions, on demand…?

"Glaack," Jack muttered, and leaped from the Jeep.

Still figuring he was as loony as a New Yorker who'd been riding the subway too long, Jack strode into the restaurant, gave his name to the guy holding menus and followed him through the after-church throng filling the place.

What if this Dr. Burke turned him down?

She couldn't! Jack came to a halt in mid-restaurant as he faced facts: it was marry the doc or bag beer at the Stop-n-Sip. He'd taken all of Jugular Jensen—and equity trading—he could take, but he wasn't naive enough any longer to think that a guy his age couldn't need medical insurance. Hell, just driving the Dallas freeways was a health risk these days.

"SHE'S ANSWERING A PAGE," Sherry said when he arrived boothside to find her alone. "She'll be back."

Jack felt a bead of sweat form between his shoulder blades as he slid in opposite her. "Tell me again which one of us is crazier, Downe—you, me or the sawbones?"

Sherry refused to be drawn. "How's Tess?" she asked after they'd ordered coffee from a waiter lurking behind a nearby ficus tree.

Jack frowned. "The same," he admitted gloomily. "She goes to work, but that's it. She won't even come over and watch a video with me."

Sherry made an irritating, Bronx-raspberry sound. "Maybe because you had that guy waiting the last time she did."

"Bailey's a perfectly nice guy," Jack shot back defensively. Was he the only person in Dallas who gave a rat's behind that his sister was stuck in a solitude rut? "I'm just trying to help."

"Obviously, Tess doesn't want your help," Sherry pointed out patiently. "But here comes someone who does."

The someone wore thick-rimmed Elvis Costello glasses and had shoulder-length dark hair. Pulled back by some headband contraption.

Normal size, normal height. About his age.

Hard to tell about her body—a white lab coat billowed over something dark and baggy. Not that her shape mattered, of course.

Jack rose to his feet as the woman approached.

"Melinda, allow me to introdu—" Sherry began.

"Jack Halloran," he interrupted, frowning at his friend. Enough with the polite manners. Couldn't she see this woman was at the end of her rope?

It didn't take Hercule Poirot to detect the bone-deep fatigue in the sag of her shoulders, the droop at the corners of her mouth. The way she propped her hands in the pockets of her coat. The way she just stood there, staring at him.

"Jack, Dr. Melinda Burke," Sherry finished dryly.

"Pleased to meet you," the woman said.

"Yeah, yeah. Me, too," he responded impatiently but she remained motionless. "Dammit, woman—sit down before you fall down!" he suggested. Okay, maybe he sort of shouted it, but only because she was actually swaying on her feet. Damn—she *did* need a caretaker.

Sherry chuckled softly.

The glasses winked at him a few seconds longer, then Dr. Burke slid into the booth.

Her hair gleamed like a ribbon of dark chocolate as it swung over her shoulder. Jack felt a sudden urge to touch it. Instead, he fisted his hands and quickly sat next to Downe.

"Okay, where do we start?" Sherry asked when nobody else spoke. "Questions, I guess. Mel, do you want to start?"

Melinda's head jerked upward; the sudden motion made her glasses slip down her nose.

And Jack found himself lost in twin pools of smoky jade, which revealed more than exhaustion. The green depths held desperation and a tinge of sorrow, the same things he saw sometimes in his sister's eyes.

Jack rubbed his jaw, then curled his fingers around his coffee cup as the waiter set it down and whirled off. Dammit, maybe he couldn't force his sister into resuming her social life, but he could, he *would* help this doctor stay functional for the next few months while she finished her training deal.

"Well," Sherry said with a chuckle, "I see Halloran's made up his mind. That leaves you, Dr. Burke. Will you take this man to be your short-term wife? To feed and shelter while he dusts and launders?"

"Food, shelter and health insurance," Jack corrected.

Melinda nodded. "Sherry told me your...ah, conditions. As a spouse, you'd be covered under the fellow-ship program's group policy," she assured him, pushing her glasses up again as she spoke.

"That works," Jack said, then they all sipped their coffee in silence.

Mel knew she should take the time to question the man thoroughly and check some references, but hello!— that's why she was actually considering this wacko idea: she didn't *have* time for normal activities!

She did need a wife. And what a deal if it looked like Jack Halloran.

The guy was a certified stud! Tall—six-two, maybe. Lean, rangy build: linebacker's shoulders, six-pack stomach, trim hips. Firm jaw, chiseled mouth. Thick, well-cut hair—brown with golden highlights. Man, even the Martin Sheen cowlick above his left eyebrow, mak-ing a strand of hair shoot straight up from his hairline, was sexy.

And those deep-blue eyes. Like those shoes Elvis didn't want anyone to step on.

Melinda imagined herself gazing into those glorious, sensual eyes while she coolly told their owner to mop the kitchen floor or wash a load of clothes.

Hmm. Now that she thought about it, Jack Halloran looked more like the trophy-wife type. High mainte-nance. Completely not the point.

"A maid. That's what I need. Not a wife." Mel fum-bled for her purse while the other two sat frozen. Okay, she was chickening out, but come on—how could this harebrained scheme work? "I'll just...call a service." Scooping up the criminal-lawn notice with one hand, touching her pocket with the other to make sure she still had her beeper, she scooted toward the edge of the ban-quette. "Sorry I wasted your time."

"No." With the kind of natural grace that had always eluded her, Jack unfolded his athletic body and came around to block her exit as he shook his head gently.

She caught a whiff of some understated, woodsy cologne. "Excuse me?"

"You need more than just standard housecleaning services," Jack informed her, his eyes mesmerizing. "You need somebody—*me*—to handle everything you don't have time for. Like, ah…cook and, ah…do windows and…stuff."

"You'd pay the bills?" she asked, feeling tempted. Very tempted. "Clean the pool?"

"Sure. Yeah. All that stuff. Rotate tires, trim shrubs, change lightbulbs." His voice was deep and soothing, the list almost erotically hypnotic. "Whatever you need. I'll even bring you coffee in bed."

Her favorite fantasy. "You'd do that?" she asked, tempted again. Sorely tempted. "I have to be up by five."

"No problem," he assured her. "I'm a morning person."

"What about sex?" Sherry croaked after a brief coughing fit, then held up her hands when Jack and Melinda turned to stare at her. "Hey, just trying to help. Thought you'd want everything settled up front."

Melinda waited. Knowing what he would say.

He did. "No sex. Of course."

"Of course," Mel agreed. She didn't think sex without love was all that satisfying. And she certainly had no time for love. Not yet, anyway. Maybe next year.

"At least, not right away," Jack added.

Her head snapped up, leaving her glasses at the end of her nose again.

"We can always reopen the topic for discussion later, if we change our minds." His bored tone clearly indicated he thought that about as likely as a politician being altruistic.

"Then it's decided," Sherry said triumphantly. "Unless—any more questions, Melinda?"

Yeah. Who's the psychotic one here? Or is it an epidemic?

Mel looked at Jack. "How long are we talking about?"

"Six months, Sherry said." Jack shrugged one of those broad shoulders. "Then we bail."

Another question occurred to her. "How much time off do you want for studying?"

The man waved a large, square hand nonchalantly. "We can play it by ear. I'll get everything done that needs doing."

Irresistible. But...married? Not that she had anything to lose when they divorced—except half of a staggering pile of student loans. "Sure you can't just move in and—"

"No." Jack's jaw hardened as he shook his head. Obviously, the man could be implacable when he wanted to be. "Health insurance, remember? Besides—" he twinkled those lapis eyes at her "—I want to make a statement about gender stereotypes."

Melinda touched her pager. "And what exactly is your position on that?" she asked. *This oughta be good.*

"If a woman can be a doctor instead of cooking and cleaning," Jack said, his voice quiet but intense, "a man ought to be able to stay home and do housework without being looked upon as a slacker."

How could she disagree? Melinda thought as she chewed on her lip, trying to make a thoughtful decision. The nutcase in her head was shouting, "Do it, do it, do it!"

Sherry stirred her coffee absently, her gaze shifting between the doctor and her potential wife. A muscle twitched along Jack's jaw, but he sat silently. *Waiting for me to make him an offer,* Melinda suddenly realized.

Well, shoot. She needed help. He was available—and way cheaper than hiring who knew how many people to do all the things she needed done. And he seemed nice. Sherry vouched for him. Aunt Gertrude's decade of loyalty vouched for Sherry....

"Okay," she said, instantly light-headed at having her biggest headache removed. "Let's go down to the courthouse tomorrow and—"

"No!" Jack and Sherry shouted in chorus.

"No?" Melinda shook her head to clear it. "But I thought—"

"Well, yes," Jack said, reaching across the table to take her hand and squeeze it gently. An odd, electrical tingle skittered through her. "I'll be happy to marry you, Melinda."

For safety's sake, she reclaimed her hand. "Then what—?"

"No courthouse quickies," Sherry insisted.

Jack nodded his concurrence. "That's no way to make a statement," he began, then gave her a sheepish grin. "And besides—for the past ten years, for co-workers we barely know and generally don't even like, Sherry and I have dressed up on weekends, eaten stale canapés, danced with too many drunken relatives of the bridal couple, bought enough place settings of ugly, expensive china to outfit our own banquet hall—"

"I get it," Melinda interrupted. "You're talking payback, right?"

"Right," Jack agreed, grinning at her. It was like sunshine slicing through thunderclouds. It made her dizzy.

"But...I need—" Melinda clamped her mouth shut on *help now, dammit!* According to Dr. Bowen, surgeons never showed emotion. "Ah, doesn't putting on a big wedding take months?"

"Don't worry," Jack said, reclaiming her hand. Same electric tingle. Weird. "Sherry and I can throw one together in no time."

His matchmaker friend nodded. "Sure. And we'll get

the grass cut right away—I'll explain later," she told Jack when he grunted questioningly.

"I've got to give two weeks notice," Jack said, shooting Sherry another puzzled glance. "If you can hold out till then, we can put together a prenup, too, so we both just walk away when it's over."

A weird feeling rippled along her spine at the words. Mel shrugged it off. *Until then, coffee in bed. Clean underwear. No more nasty citations.*

"Okay," she said. "Two weeks it is."

THEY ADJOURNED to the bar after the waiter threw a series of vicious glares in their direction. After all, turn-over meant more tips.

Sherry ordered champagne and offered a toast to a mutually beneficial arrangement.

After a quick sip, Mel asked if they needed anything from her to plan the wedding. Otherwise, she'd head back to the hospital and her stack of patient files.

Jack turned those deep-blue eyes on her. "Do you have a church or a minister you prefer?"

For some reason, Mel's hand twitched, spilling champagne on the table. *Don't be a numskull,* she told herself, shaking her head as she mopped up the wine. *There's nothing romantic about this. It's a clever solution to a nagging problem, that's all.*

Jack locked gazes with his old friend. "So whaddaya think?"

Sherry shrugged. "The Empire Club. Three o'clock."

"If we can get it," Jack said, touching his shirt pocket, then his thighs.

Melinda pulled a pen and pad from her lab coat and handed them over.

"Thanks," he said absently, making a note. "I'll try to get Father Bernard, but you'll probably have to call that justice of the peace you know."

Sherry nodded, pulling a leather-bound notebook from her briefcase and making a note of her own.

"Flowers?" Jack asked.

Melinda sipped champagne; he wasn't asking her.

"Fanny's. She needs the business, she'll give us a great deal."

Jack nodded again. Made another note. "Music?"

"Jazzy Jake. Easy eighties."

Another nod, another note. "Food?"

"Cake, hors d'oeuvres, cash bar."

Not exactly the way I'd imagine my wedding taking shape, but... Mel smiled as the two friends continued their machine-gun planning. *They were getting the job done.*

"Speaking of cake, where should we—?" Jack broke off to grin. Sherry grinned back. Together they chanted, "Austin's!"

More jotting, then, "Tuxes?"

"First Night—I get this one free."

"They rent bridal gowns, too," Sherry said. "No sense buying one. I'll check there tomorrow. What size are you?"

Melinda jerked as she realized the woman was addressing her. Before she could answer, Sherry said, "A six, right?"

See? They don't need my input, Mel thought, nodding politely. *Not even for my dress size.* Just as well. She wouldn't have much to add. She'd given up silly "girl" things like dates and proms and romantic wedding fantasies years ago to achieve her goal in medicine. And now she had an M.D. after her name.

Which meant a lot more than having a Mrs. in front of it, Mel reminded herself. Not just to her, but to all the little kids like her brother, kids who needed the special skills of a pediatric surgeon.

Dodging a familiar stab of sorrow, Mel returned her

attention to the wedding planners as Sherry pointed her pen at Jack, who responded with, "Decorations?"

"How about balloon ropes? Confetti on the tables."

"Gifts for the wedding party—what did Sam give out?"

"Business card cases."

"That's good." Nod. Note. "No videographer, right?"

"Right. Dave'll take photos."

Jack jotted as he muttered, "Music for the ceremony—the usual." He looked up. At Sherry, naturally. "Should we have a soloist?"

"No!" they shouted together, then laughed companionably.

Melinda touched her pager. She wasn't jealous of their friendship. All she wanted out of this was the help she needed with her parents' house. And clean laundry—no matter how late she worked.

"Groomsmen?" Sherry asked.

"My brothers, I gue—"

"You have brothers?" Melinda interjected, the old, familiar heavy feeling settling in her chest again. "Plural?"

"Yeah." Jack sounded so casual she wanted to hit him. "Three of 'em. And a sister."

Unbelievable. Better-looking than a *GQ* model *and* siblings. The man's middle name must be Lucky.

"As usual, Mike's out of the country," Jack went on. Addressing Sherry, of course. "Maybe if we ignore the other two…"

"Dream on," his friend said. "Those bozos will *insist* on participating. You Hallorans make the Brady Bunch look like a collection of introverted loners."

"Bridesmaids."

Melinda felt her toe nudged. "Bridesmaids," Jack repeated. "How many do you want?"

The real question was how many women did she know well enough to ask. "Oh, um, Sherry, of course."

The woman rewarded her with a smile.

Mel looked at Jack. "Your sister?"

After a second's thought, he shook his head. "She's...no." When Sherry uttered a sound of protest, he jutted his jaw. "She needs to get back in the swim, but that's too much," he said fiercely. "She's not ready."

"My sister lost her husband last year," he told Mel with a crooked smile that made her heart valves flutter. "She's...having a hard time pulling out of it."

"Anybody else?" Sherry asked, giving Jack a frown he ignored. "We've still got one more Halloran."

"Well...my cousin, maybe." They weren't particularly close, but since Aunt Gertrude only attended funerals and her parents were in Oman, Noreen was all the family she had. "If she's available. She has a pretty small baby—"

"Give Sherry her phone number and she'll find out."

Obediently Melinda scribbled Noreen's name and phone number in Sherry's notebook.

"Are we gonna have a theme color?" Sherry asked Jack.

Melinda checked her pager again. *Oh, stop it. Stop pretending you're too busy to feel left out.*

She *was* too busy. She *didn't* feel left out. The wedding thing was their idea, not hers. Her priority was becoming the best pediatric surgeon Leo Bowen ever trained. She was twenty-eight, not seventy-eight. She'd get a personal life later.

"Bronze would be interesting," Sherry suggested, one hand going to her dark auburn curls.

"British racing green," Jack countered, making a note. "The color of Melinda's eyes. Let's see...oh, yeah—caterer?"

"My friend Bernice'll do it for cost," Sherry said,

scooting closer to Jack to compare notes. "What have we forgotten?"

Using one fingertip, Melinda pushed aside her glass of champagne. She refused to go all giddy just because Jack Halloran had noticed the color of her eyes. What mattered was—could he iron?

"This'll get us started," Jack declared, ripping out his pages of notes, then sliding the pad and pen back toward Melinda. "Anything else comes up, Sher and I can touch base at work."

His grin heated Melinda's insides, even though it wasn't aimed at her. "After all, we're Jensen's top producers. What's he going to do, *fire* us?"

The two friends laughed. Together. Easily.

Melinda touched her beeper.

She wanted to save kids' lives—and she'd be ready to do that, finally, if she survived this fellowship under Dr. Bowen.

With Jack Halloran's help, she'd achieve the goal she'd set for herself eighteen years ago.

And her parents would have a house left to come home to.

"Ready, Melinda?" At the sound of Jack's deep, smooth voice, she looked up. Straight into his blue eyes.

Wow, those babies were spellbinding! "Ready?" she repeated. Like a moron.

"To leave." Jack tossed aside his napkin and reached for the check as he stood.

"Yes." Melinda pushed back her chair. "Yes," she repeated. "I have to get back to the hospital."

"I'll start looking at dresses this week," Sherry said. "Do you want to go with me, Melinda?"

"The big public statement is y'all's idea," she reminded Sherry. "I'll wear whatever you pick out." *If I stay nuts long enough to go through with this.* Doubts were already snowballing like government cost overruns.

While Jack paid the bar tab, Sherry pulled Melinda across the restaurant's foyer. "You *will* take the whole day off for the wedding, right?" she asked in a low voice.

"I could probably trade an ER rotation with somebody," Melinda admitted, "but why? I thought the ceremony was at three."

Sherry picked up Melinda's hand and studied her fingernails. "I'll make appointments with my stylist Raoul and the nail tech. She does facials, too."

Before Mel could decide if she'd just been insulted, Sherry grinned. "A little makeup, the right dress—I can't wait to see Jack's face when you come down the aisle. He'll never know what hit him."

"Come on, Sher," the babe magnet in question interrupted, strolling over from the cashier. "Dr. Burke's a busy woman. Find somebody else to micromanage."

He turned warm, cobalt eyes on Mel and handed her a business card. "Call me when you're free to get the license."

How could such a simple solution suddenly feel so complicated? Melinda wondered as she fled.

TODAY. MEL STOOD beside the other fellow, Dan Something, waiting to assist Dr. Bowen. *I'll call today. Tell him I'm sorry, but I've thought it over and—*

Melinda sighed. She'd told herself this every day since Sunday, but she still hadn't called. Hadn't explained to Jack Halloran that she couldn't marry him, she didn't even know him!

There was just one reason she hadn't picked up the phone. Not the pathetic suspicion that a strictly business marriage was the only kind she could handle. And definitely not the daydreamy fantasy of a hottie like Jack serving her coffee in bed every morning.

She hadn't called because someone had mowed the lawn on Tuesday or Wednesday—she'd slept at the hospital both nights on orders from Bowen to monitor the telemetry on a critical four-year-old.

"Will you be joining us today, Dr. Burke, or are you too busy formulating your strategy for the next Neiman Marcus sale?" Bowen's barb cut through the classical music pouring from the operating room's speakers.

Okay, *that* was the real reason she hadn't called off the marriage-for-her-convenience: the short, balding, caustic Dr. Bowen. Who delighted in torturing his fellowship trainees, especially the females.

Melinda forced herself to answer the program director calmly. "I'm ready when you are, Dr. Bowen."

"You'd better be, Burke. I tolerate no woolgathering in my OR." The man glared at her over his mask.

How dare this man question her devotion to excellence? Hadn't she given her whole life to medicine? No friends, no hobbies, no—

"As long as you understand the sacrifices I require, we'll get along fine." His eyes doubted it—and promised additional sacrifices. "Now, Dr. Burke. If you'd care to make a lateral incision approximately eight centimeters below and to the—"

Mel selected a scalpel. She'd call Jack today all right—to set a time to get the license, not to bail. Clearly Bowen's attitude meant she was going to need a wife now more than ever.

Taking a deep breath, she made a swift and perfect incision, then helped retract the ten-year-old's skin and external muscle sheath. As Dr. Bowen bent forward to access the polyp, she nudged Dan Something with her foot.

"Would you take my ER rotation next Saturday?" she whispered beneath the soaring tones of Handel's *Water Music*. "I'll take your next holiday."

Dan thought a minute, then nodded. "Big plans?" he asked.

"Not really." Mel tried to sound offhanded. "I'm getting married."

Unless Jack has changed his mind, she thought as Dan's eyebrows rose.

"Suction! No—" Dr. Bowen stopped the surgical nursing assistant with an imperious gloved hand. "Let's observe Burke's technique." Mel stepped forward, grateful for the distraction as well as the chance to be guided by one of the foremost experts in pediatric surgery. Even if he did have the charm and personality of a hungover rat.

"OH, HI, MELINDA!" Grabbing a pen, Jack twirled it so fast it flew out of his hand. Landed two desks down. The broker there, glued to his monitor, didn't even flinch. "Uh, can I put you on hold for a minute?" Without waiting for a reply, he punched the hold button.

Then he lowered his forehead to his desk.

He'd been expecting this. The kiss-off. After almost a week of silence—and *after* he'd submitted his resignation to ol' Jugular.

No surprise, really—why *would* a smart, ambitious surgeon marry a burned-out-at-thirty-one stockbroker who wanted to freeload on her and her insurance plan so he could study annuities at his leisure?

In spare moments since their meeting, he'd been optimistic. And haunted by Melinda Burke's faint air of desperation and fatigue.

He'd become almost obsessed with the crazy idea of showing the world that he, Jack Halloran, could be a perfect wife. *Her* perfect wife.

Dammit, the woman needed him. And he needed—

Aw, get it over with, he told himself and depressed the blinking button.

"Thanks for waiting," he said, keeping his voice steady. "What can I do for you?"

"Well, first, what do you tell people when they ask how we, you know, got together?"

"The truth," Jack said with a shrug. "That Sherry introduced us."

"Of course!" Delight warmed her voice and made his insides kind of knot up.

Jensen came out of his office to glare in Jack's direction.

Jack glared back. What the hell—he was out of a job, anyway. "And second?" he prompted.

"When can we get our license?" Melinda's words were brisk, though her voice was suddenly as soft as kitten fur. "If we need blood tests, I can get them run here at the hospital."

Jack imagined that velvety voice murmuring endearments against his skin. In the dark. Between the sheets.

Put a lid on it, Halloran. Dark-rimmed glasses, shapeless clothes, no sex, remember? So just stick to business.

After clearing his throat, Jack said, "We have to go to the county clerk's office. Together."

"Noon tomorrow?" Mel asked.

"Fine with me." Hanging up a minute later, Jack told himself there was nothing about Melinda Burke to make him think their relationship would or should be anything other than platonic.

Nothing except a pair of smoky green eyes. A velvet voice. And hair the color of dark chocolate.

Jack gave Jensen another glare for the heck of it. Then, resuming his stock tracking, he decided it was a Martha Stewart good thing he had no interest in a real relationship. Just as well, though, that there wasn't going to be a doctor in the house.

At least, not often enough to worry about.

3

JACK SHIFTED HIS WEIGHT from one foot to the other. The permit-to-wed line was moving about as fast as granite.

Giving him way too much time to watch the couples bracketing them smooch and drape around each other like Confederate jasmine.

Hell, the pair in front were going to have each other completely disrobed by the time they reached the head of the line.

Which made it damned near impossible to not think about the one aspect of marriage he and his virtual-fiancée, Dr. Burke, had agreed their relationship would *not* include: intimacy.

A surprisingly dangerous thing to contemplate, with Melinda's scent—something sweet yet spicy—filtering subtly into his lungs.

So don't. Distract yourself.

"What made you decide to be a doctor?" he asked in a low voice.

"Um…" Melinda paused, as if choosing her words carefully.

One half of the couple ahead of them was sucking the earring right off the other. That left Jack unmoved, but Mel wet her full lips and his male equipment stirred in response.

"Go ahead," he urged, turning the inappropriate de-sire into something safer: childish irritation. "Use multisyllabic words. I have a college degree—I'll get the gist of it.''

"I'm not worried about your comprehension," she snapped.

Jack hardly heard. He was noticing how soft-looking her mouth was. Wondering how it would feel beneath his. How she would taste.

"It's just—" she raised and lowered a shoulder "—hard to talk about." She looked down the bland hallway. "I was ten when my brother died. Harry was only six."

He couldn't imagine her pain, but instinctively Jack moved closer. "Oh, Mel…I'm so sorry."

For a minute, she seemed to lean toward him, then Melinda stepped back. Jack let her have the space. *It's not that kind of relationship,* he reminded himself. And that's the way he wanted it.

Because he knew what happened when people started caring about each other. All he had to do was think of his sister to remember the wreckage love could leave behind.

Melinda shook her hair; it fanned forward over her shoulder and tumbled onto her breast. "A good pediatric surgeon might have saved Harry's life."

Desire bloomed again thick and hot. Jack stuffed it down, ordering his mind to stay off soft green eyes, sexy perfume and the mystery of what lay under today's shapeless outfit.

She shrugged; her hair rippled again. "That's why I became a doctor. And this fellowship is the last of the training I need to save other Harrys. And their families."

Without thinking, Jack captured her hand and squeezed it. "And I'm going to help you do it."

"Next!"

Smiling at the bored bureaucrat behind the counter, he stepped forward. It wouldn't take *that* much effort—

How hard was dusting?—but he was more than willing now to fulfill his end of the bargain.

After a second's hesitation, Mel joined him.

Within minutes, they'd completed the process and were doing an Elvis: leaving the building. As Melinda checked her pager and rummaged in her lab-coat pocket for her keys, Jack tucked the license into his shirt pocket, then halted her departure activity by placing his big hands on her shoulders.

"Hang in there, Doc," he said, trying to ignore the sensual pleasure his palms derived from molding themselves around her softness. "Your worries are almost over."

"Is that a promise?" she asked, lips curving in a brief smile. A flicker of green glinted behind the thick lenses covering her face.

And Jack felt…odd. As if the earth's axis had, like, shifted or something. "Yes," he vowed. "I couldn't promise to love you forever and mean it, but I *will* take care of you for the next six months while you finish this surgery deal."

"And my parents' house, right?" Mel asked after a moment of chewing on her lush lower lip. "I do owe them a lot."

"The house, too," Jack said firmly, stuffing his hands into his pockets, because the damned things wanted to revisit Melinda's shoulders. "Look, I'll see you Saturday. We'll get married. Then you'll focus on your fellowship, I'll keep house and prep for the Certified Financial Planner's exam. Everything will work out great. You'll see."

"I…I'll hold you to that, Jack." Mel looked at her watch. "I've got to go now." Her chocolate hair flared like an opening silk fan as she turned away. "See you Saturday," she called.

Jack watched her go. This hair thing was becoming

an obsession. Maybe he ought to encourage her to braid it. Or cut it. Better yet, shave it.

For the next week, wedding logistics and Jensen's transition demands kept Jack occupied. Too occupied to worry about the recurring jolts of lust that hit him just before he fell asleep, when his hands recalled the curve of her shoulders and his nostrils remembered her scent. And his mind's eye saw again that chocolate silk spill over her breast....

"Ow!" MELINDA WINCED as Sherry and Noreen took turns ramming hairpins into her head. *I should have let Raoul attach the veil,* she thought as another pin pierced her skull.

Foolishly, she'd declined the hairdresser's offer, unwilling to leave the salon in jeans, T-shirt and a cloud of tulle. They'd had to cut the T-shirt off to avoid disturbing Raoul's artful creation of curls.

Then Sherry had applied makeup while Noreen supervised. Finally they'd helped her step into the foaming pool of white that was her rented wedding dress. The two women had taken turns working the aspirin-sized buttons through their loops.

And she still hadn't seen herself in it. "Wait till we're done," Sherry had insisted. "I want you to get the full effect."

Melinda feared she'd never make it down the aisle once that happened. How could she plausibly portray the happy bride of a handsome hunk like Jack Halloran if she knew she looked like a nearsighted geek playing dress-up?

Noreen plowed a furrow in her scalp with another hairpin.

The dress rustled as she jumped. It felt heavy and rich and elegant. Add in the satin pumps, her mom's pearl drop nestling just above the edge of the bodice.

Even though she knew better, it all made Melinda feel special, beautiful, feminine.

Feelings she'd given up to pursue her medical degree and surgical training.

For the first time in years, Melinda wondered if she'd missed out on anything important by focusing so exclusively on grades and her career goals.

Holy organdy! Mel shook her head in disgust. *Slap a bridal gown on me and suddenly I want to be Snow White or whoever married the prince and lived happily ever after.*

Sherry tugged on the veil cloud, then reached for another pin.

It might be interesting, though, to talk to a noncolleague about something besides fracture displacement and suture techniques.

A platonic marriage like this offered just such an opportunity, Mel reflected as the two bridesmaids finally abandoned the hairpin torture and stood back to study their handiwork.

Matching frowns appeared as they tilted their heads to one side, stepped back, tilted the other way, stepped forward.

"What's wrong?" Melinda asked. *Is it that obvious I belong in scrubs rather than this dress?*

"Well…" Noreen said, one perfectly manicured nail tapping her cheek.

"Aha!" Sherry snapped her fingers, then leaned forward. Carefully she removed Melinda's dark-rimmed glasses.

Noreen's hand moved to cover her mouth. "Ooh," she breathed.

"I knew it," Sherry declared as she turned Melinda toward the mirror. "Take a look," she invited, "at the most beautiful bride in Dallas."

It must be the dress, Mel thought dazedly. With its plunging sweetheart neckline, beaded bodice, lace cut-outs covering the full skirt—anyone would look gorgeous. *And Raoul's hair magic, of course.*

And a couple of gallons of under-eye concealer.

Because aside from the usual grind of sixteen-hour days, she'd been up until three that morning, stupidly attempting to minimize Jack's inevitable initial shock when he saw the place. Cleaning the house for the maid—how idiotic.

"Have you seen your flowers yet, Mel?" Noreen asked as she reached into the florist's box.

As Melinda shook her head, unable to speak, the tulle they'd nailed to her scalp floated back and forth across her shoulders like winter mist.

Noreen held out a big spray of orchids and roses and baby's breath encircled by assorted greenery—just as her husband poked his head around the door. "Y'all about ready?" he asked.

Melinda's cousin smiled sappily. "Sure are, darlin'. How's my angel?" she cooed.

Bobby swung a baby carrier into sight. "Still sleeping," he reported, "but who knows for how long. Come on, ladies, show time." With that, he disappeared.

"Go ahead, Noreen." Shoving Melinda's glasses into the woman's hand, Sherry pushed her gently toward the exit. "Give 'em back after they cut the cake," she instructed, then, when they were alone, addressed Mel solemnly. "There's nothing to worry about, you know."

Melinda nodded. *Duh.* She wasn't marrying some adorable hunk who loved her madly and wanted to sweep her off her feet and carry her away to his castle.

It was her castle—and it needed cleaning. Either that or the immediate application of a smallish nuclear device.

"You're just going to walk down that aisle," Sherry reminded her, "say a few words—and take Jack Halloran to be your perfect, homemaking wife." With a last look in the mirror, the maid of honor picked up her bouquet and headed for the exit.

"Coming?" she asked as she paused in the doorway.

Melinda took a deep breath. What the heck. She needed Jack's domestic help. And he wanted her insurance plan. Without her glasses, everything was a blur. She'd just pretend she was playing life-size Barbies. In an hour or so, when they were done here, she'd do the Cinderella thing and turn back into Dr. Bowen's pet surgical slave.

But with clean underwear to look forward to!

"Right," she said, curling her fingers around her bouquet. "Let's do it."

Sherry led the way from the dressing room down the hall to another room, stopping at the end of an aisle running between rows of white folding chairs—all of them occupied by strangers. And "cousin" Bobby.

Taped organ music flowed from speakers near the ceiling.

"When you hear the Wedding March," Sherry instructed in an undertone, "just walk slowly forward. Stop when you get to the tuxedos."

Jack in a tux. Melinda's eyes flew open.

She didn't need glasses to see her groom. In sharp, perfect detail: the crisp white and tailored black outfit adorning his magnificently masculine form—and every handsome, craggy feature above those football shoulders, too. The rich golden-brown hair with its adorable cowlick. The chiseled mouth. Those cobalt-blue eyes.

In a few minutes, the guy in the judge's robe was going to ask her if she took this man.

Who wouldn't? She might be busier than a honeybee in a field of wildflowers and as socially inexperienced as a cloistered monk, but she wasn't *crazy*. Somewhere inside, what felt like a full liter of estrogen stirred to life.

"Okay, Noreen," Sherry whispered. "Whenever you're ready."

With a final tug on her neckline, Mel's cousin stepped forward.

JACK TWEAKED HIS CUFF, then let his arm fall to his side. Tried to look appropriately solemn, but man, he wanted to grin like a fool!

'Cuz here he was, standing at the head of the line, in front of an ornately carved fireplace, which Sherry's florist friend had decorated with greenery, flowers and ribbon-dripping candle stands. And if he turned his head a degree to the left, he'd see his sister, Tess, sitting in the front row.

Life was great and for once, he had the easiest job in the wedding: repeat some vows, cut the cake and dance once with the bride.

No worrying he'd lost the ring. No having to come up with a clever toast. No concern over who and how many he had to partner when the dancing started.

No more Jugular Jensen and the grind of Loeb-Weinstein, either.

Just dust something once in a while, pay a bill, do a little laundry. Study, relax.

Kevan leaned around Geoff. "Tell us again why you're suddenly getting married. When...where... how'd you meet this babe, anyway?"

"I told ya," Jack said out of the side of his mouth, "Sherry introduced us."

Kevan guffawed—loudly enough to make Tess frown at the trio. "Pull my other leg, bro. You and Sherry quit fixing each other up in high sch—"

"Shh." Geoff nudged Kevan to silence. "Here comes bridesmaid number one."

"Cute," the youngest Halloran assessed sotto voce, then informed his brother, "but she's already married. I checked."

Folding his hands in front of him, Jack hummed along with the music as first Noreen, then Sherry strolled down the aisle and stood opposite him and his groomsmen. *Real wedding, fake marriage,* he thought smugly. *The only way to go.* The only way to avoid the unhappiness Tess had experienced.

He flashed a gentle smile at his sister just as the familiar fanfare sounded.

"No wonder you took the fall!" Kevan exclaimed under his breath.

Geoff whistled softly and dug his elbow into Jack's side. "Tell me she has a twin sister," he begged.

Confused, Jack looked first at his brothers, then followed their gaze to the doorway.

Oh. My. God. A gigawatt of pure, full-potency lust hit him in the chest. Then lower as he gazed at, at...*a female goddess with curves a man could embarrass himself over in public.*

It's the dress, he told himself.

He'd better hope it was, Jack thought dazedly as he watched the beautiful, dark-haired angel float down the aisle toward him, or this business arrangement was in deep dirt.

Because any male with a pulse would want this woman in the snowy, dream-princess outfit. Want to woo and win her, then possess her in the most primitive, elemental way.

Melinda halted as she reached him, smiling faintly up at him as the music swelled, then died.

In slow motion, as if in a dream, Jack offered his arm to his bride.

Her right hand held a huge bouquet. Attempting to switch it to her left, Melinda lost her grip on the flowers.

She and Jack bent to retrieve the nosegay-on-steroids at the same time.

That darned physics! The nitpicky law stating that two solid objects cannot occupy the same space at the same time did not take Saturday off: the bride and groom cracked heads.

Pain, always a valuable tool, tried to recall Jack to his duty. Unfortunately, as he took a deep breath to control said pain, he inhaled his bride's perfume. With the same enticing, erotic effect as before.

He forgot where they were, and that they had an audience.

"Jack..." Her velvet-soft voice further heightened his arousal.

He wrenched his gaze from the breathtaking focal point of that wicked, curved neckline—right into smoky-green eyes, fringed with thick lashes the same strong-coffee color as the lustrous bundle of hair twisted up in some tantalizing concoction that simply begged a man to find and remove the hidden pins holding it hostage so it could spill loose from that puffy white cloud hovering around it and cascade over his hands onto her creamy—

"Your foot is on my flowers."

Jack continued staring at the vision of feminine loveliness. Marry her, yes, he thought hazily. Live with her. Yes.

Ignore traditional marital activities?

Noo—

"Jack?" Her eyes darkened. His fingers moved to thread their way into that silky, chocolate hair.

The justice of the peace squatted to join their conference on the floor.

"Could we get started, folks?" the JP asked.

Moving his black wing tip, Jack freed the bouquet and handed it to Melinda. "Sorry," he mumbled as he helped his bride to her feet.

Without looking at him, she gave a silent nod, then stood there fiddling with the flowers he'd crushed.

"Dearly beloved..." the judge began.

Jack let the familiar opening phrases of the wedding

ceremony flow over him. He damned well wasn't going to *love* this or any other woman, but now that he—*and everyone here, dammit*—knew what those shapeless outfits had been hiding, he wouldn't mind cherishing Melinda a little. *Worship her with my body?* Oh yeah.

Like heck, moron. They'd made a bargain and he'd keep his end of it. But being married to Melinda Burke in name only might not be as easy as he'd thought. Or as enjoyable.

"Who gives—?" The JP stuttered to a halt, apparently only now remembering Melinda's solo walk down the aisle.

"The woman's twenty-eight, for God's sake," Jack growled protectively at the be-robed idiot when a pink flush crept up her neck and over her cheeks. "She's giving herself away."

The audience tittered behind him.

"That's not— Oh, just skip that part," he ordered the JP, who cleared his throat and obediently moved on.

They took turns making the forever promises they only meant to keep for six months and exchanging the rings he'd picked out with Sherry's help. Melinda stared at the narrow band with beaded edging as he slid it onto her finger.

After a little prodding from Sherry, she returned the favor.

Jack wiggled his finger, wondering how soon he'd adjust to wearing the gold symbol he'd insisted was part of his "statement"—and then suddenly all his careful planning went to hell in an express mailing tube.

"I now pronounce you husband and wife," the justice of the peace intoned. "You may kiss the bride."

Jack bent to deliver a quick, G-rated peck, but Melinda tilted her face upward. Wide misty-green eyes blinked at him, and his simmering desire simply exploded.

With a soft growl, his mouth covered hers.

The room, the building, hell, the *planet* disappeared as their lips met, molded, melted. He deepened the kiss. She let him. One of them moaned. Flames licked his body, her fingers clutched his arms, slid up to circle his neck and bury themselves in his hair.

His arms tightened, slid downward to bring her closer. He moved a hip to tuck her—

"Whoa, there, big brother." Hands gripped his upper arms, tugging to loosen the embrace.

What? Who? Jack blinked. "Geoff?"

"Save it for the honeymoon," the grinning brother advised.

"Although we do understand now why the short notice," Kevan added with a wink as he peered around Geoff.

"Ahem." With a repressive frown, the JP took charge. Turning them to face the guests, he intoned, "Ladies and gentlemen, may I present Mr. and Mrs. Jack Halloran."

The audience's applause covered Jack's fairly unsuccessful attempt to regain his equilibrium. "Di-didn't we decide you were k-keeping your own name?"

"Yes." Melinda sounded completely calm as she reclaimed her flowers from Sherry. "But right now, I imagine our guests are more interested in food than nomenclature."

Was he the only one blown out of the water by that incendiary kiss? Jack wondered as he watched his wife carefully settle the bouquet in front of her, then daintily tuck her free hand in the crook of his elbow.

Sherry gave them a nudge. Jack obediently started forward, then staggered to a halt.

My God. What if the sex was as good as that kiss?

"Move it, Halloran," Sherry urged in an undertone. "We're finally getting to the good part."

Jack groaned.

STRUGGLING TO HIDE how that incredible kiss affected her—*pretty much the same way a match affects gasoline*—Melinda smiled and nodded like a robot through the receiving line, the pictures and the paperwork. She cut and fed cake mechanically and entwined her arm as directed for the toasts.

Even when Jack led her out to the center of the reception hall for the first dance...

Melinda wondered if she was having an out-of-body experience. Instead of being a bundle of impatience or twitching when the heat of his hand splayed on her back or even simply stumbling blindly around the dance floor, she bonelessly spun and glided and twirled in perfect time to the music.

"See? Payback can be fun." Jack's deep, smooth drawl penetrated her sensual fog. Making an idle comment. In a cool, laconic tone.

Right. To someone as obviously expert in kissing as her new "wife," their little lip-lock ending the ceremony probably rated one star. Or less.

So keep your head straight, Burke. This was still and only an efficient business solution—even if it looked like a fantasy, danced like a dream and kissed like an X-rated film.

"I suppose it has its points." Mel thought she managed blasé pretty well.

The music ended and Jack stopped in mid-glide. His eyes were perfect sapphires as his head bent toward—

"Now you get to dance with the *real* best man here." A shorter Jack—without the cowlick—grinned down at her as he pried her fingers from her husband's grasp. "Geoff, remember?"

"Go mingle," he ordered the groom. "Kev and I'll take care of the missus for a while."

Mel danced with Geoff and traded a few sallies with the other brother, Kevan. Both men had Jack's blue eyes and different shades of his honey-brown hair. One of them said the absent brother was another chip off the block; they all took after their father.

Jack's children will probably look like him, too.

Don't even go there, Burke. The only connection she'd ever have—or want—with Jack Halloran's offspring would be doctor-patient.

As the music started up again, Melinda told Kevan she needed to powder her nose. He joined Geoff; she watched them put their heads together a moment, then saunter toward the nearest clump of giggling, hair-tossing females.

Jack stood near the hors d'oeuvres table, laughing and chatting with a band of former co-workers. Sherry had a similar group around her at the bar.

Noreen had rushed off with her husband and baby.

Nobody approached Melinda; she couldn't make herself push her way into any of the groups.

So much for practicing social skills, Mel noted ruefully. *Here I am—a wallflower at my own wedding.* And what was the point of trying not to be? *I'll stick to medicine,* she decided. Meanwhile, she'd fade into the woodwork until it was time to go home.

Spying an unobtrusive alcove, she drifted across the room to take refuge there. Reaching her chosen retreat, Mel turned to gaze at the celebrating crowd.

"You're very lovely," a female voice said from behind her.

Melinda spun. The woman curled up in an overstuffed armchair in the farthest corner of the alcove looked vaguely familiar.

"But I'm still miffed that Jack didn't bring you home to meet the family before the wedding. He makes everyone else do it."

That's where she'd seen those blue eyes and brown hair. "You must be Jack's sister."

"Tess Malloy," the woman agreed, extending her

hand. "Welcome to the family," she added with a sweet smile.

Melinda hated withholding the truth about their marriage, but explaining was not an option. "Your brother sure is protective of you," she blurted.

A sigh replaced Tess's smile. "I'm not diving into the singles scene, so Jack thinks I'm taking too long getting over my husband's death," she said matter-of-factly, her lips resuming their upward curve.

"Too long?" Melinda echoed, then bit her lip. Jack knew his sister better than she did, of course, but... "You never get over missing someone you love, do you?"

"No," Tess agreed, her smile wobbling a bit, then firming again. "I don't think you do."

The two women shared a moment of companionable silence. Then Tess asked, "So, how *did* you meet my brother?"

"Through Sherry," Melinda answered mechanically.

Jack's sister remained silent, apparently waiting for nonexistent courtship details.

Okay, now *I understand the value of chat,* Mel thought, as her mind went blank and the silence grew awkward.

Finally she had to resort to the one subject she knew something about. "So, um, how did your husband die?" she asked.

"Cancer," Tess said. "Pancreatic."

"That's a tough one," Melinda commiserated. "Too often asymptomatic until it's already late-stage."

Tess nodded. "We only had eight months after Pete's diagnosis, but he never suffered much pain. That's a blessing."

Mel's own buried sorrow threatened to choke her, but she managed a smile instead. Hell, it was a wedding, right? "And at least you had time to say goodbye."

The other woman's head jerked up to study Mel.

"That's true," she said slowly. "Not everybody gets that lux—"

"There you are!" Appearing out of nowhere, Jack towered over the two women. As he wrapped an arm around Tess's shoulders, a frown marred his handsome features and he addressed Melinda with all the warmth of a prison guard. "I'd like to talk to my sister alone for a minute. If you don't mind." It wasn't a question, but a dismissal.

Tess is family. You're not. Melinda nodded to show she got Jack's message. Turning to leave, she smiled at the woman in his embrace. "It was nice to meet you, Mrs. Malloy."

Jack's sister smiled back. "Call me Tess," she urged. "And it was nice to meet you, too."

When they were alone, Jack gave Tess a comforting squeeze. "Whatever she said, Sis, don't let it upse—"

"Jack Halloran, you have the intelligence and sensitivity of a cement block," his sister retorted, shrugging off his arm. With that puzzling pronouncement, Tess gathered up her purse and wrap. "I'm going home now."

After a couple of steps, she turned back, her eyes blazing with Halloran temper. "I hope your marriage makes you happy, Jack. So happy that you stop trying to make me forget mine."

Following that strange remark, his sister stalked away, leaving Jack totally confused.

He still hadn't figured out what the heck she was talking about—Had widowhood finally sent her bonkers?—when he saw Sherry pointing to her watch. Oh, yeah, time to leave.

Well, just to avoid any future misunderstandings, he'd explain to Melinda why Tess needed careful handling, he decided as he strode toward the exit to change out of his tuxedo.

And he'd work on expunging that sock-singeing kiss from his memory, too.

GOOD PLAN.

Except that his smart-aleck brothers had moved his going-away clothes into Melinda's changing room, and with a crowd of chortling witnesses—including Jugular Jensen—hanging in the vicinity, good old-fashioned male pride left Jack no choice but to knock on the damned door and smile cockily when Mel called "Come in."

It's no big deal, he told himself as he turned the knob. *She's a doctor; you're an adult.*

Stepping inside, he closed the door.

His throat went dry. His pulse went haywire.

The woman he'd married strictly for business purposes had her back to him, revealing a sliver of flawless, creamy-smooth skin where she'd managed to unfasten the first twenty of about a thousand tiny buttons running down the center of her back. *All the way* down her back.

"Thank heavens," Melinda purred in that velvety voice. "I can't get myself out of this dress." Her left hand, the one wearing the gold band, waggled at the buttons. "Would you mind?"

Mind? No. He had no mind left. None. Just desire. Growing, throbbing, damned near ready to explode.

Silently, Jack crossed the room and forced his trembling fingers to slide little round buttons through narrow satin loops. As he worked, the snowy silk bodice fell open, exposing—millimeter by tempting millimeter— the sexiest, most enticing, most *feminine* back in North America.

At least.

"Th-there," he said hoarsely as the last button slipped free and the exquisite curve between waist and hip begged to be stroked by an appreciative male hand.

Jack jerked away, then pivoted and flung himself across the room.

"Thanks," Melinda said over the rustle of falling fabric.

Oh, God. They were alone. They were married. She was taking off her clothes.

And he wasn't supposed to touch her. Not until they discussed it—and in his present state he couldn't have stated his own name correctly.

Determined to get out of this room before his control broke and he took her—*right here, right now!*—Jack jerked loose his bow tie, fumbled with his shirt. As rapidly as possible with hands shaking like an addict's on the first day in rehab, he stripped off the monkey suit and donned jeans, polo shirt, and sport coat, practically ripping the latter's lining in his haste to shove his arm into the sleeve.

He transferred wallet and keys. Toed off the dress shoes and jammed his feet into high-top hiking shoes.

"You ready yet, Doc?" he asked the wicker-framed flower print on the wall in front of him when he'd gotten the darned laces tied. Probably to each other.

"Mm-mm-mmhum-mm."

At the odd sound, Jack turned cautiously. Thank God. She was safely back inside a dark, loose dress, wrestling with her veil—her moist, warm mouth full of hairpins.

Before he could stop himself, he said, "Let me."

And then he was touching her again. Turning her by the shoulders so he could take over the veil-removal operation.

"Again—thanks," she said with a grateful sigh after she transferred the hairpins from her mouth to a tissue. "My head feels like a pincushion. I must say, I never realized how complicated a wedding could be."

"Complicated?" Jack echoed in surprise. "This one was about as no-frills as it gets outside of Las Vegas."

Freed of her veil, Melinda turned around. Her glasses

were back in place, but somehow no longer hid her green eyes—or the patent disbelief they held.

"Why don't you know about weddings?" Jack blurted. "I thought all women did."

Mel's chin went up, her voice chilled. "I had other priorities after Harry died. I read science books, not bridal magazines."

Well, that little ice bath cooled his blazing libido, but Jack still wasn't going anyplace that included a bed just yet. So he insisted on taking her to dinner at one of the latest chic spots in the Deep Ellum area of Dallas.

Because he had one other thing to say to her and a restaurant seemed like a good, neutral place to say it.

"ABOUT TESS..." Jack began, as they pretended to study the menu's paragraph-long descriptions of the American-eclectic entrées.

"She's very lucky," Melinda said quietly, then gave him a smile that did weird things to his heart rate. "You obviously care about her very much."

Well, jeez. Who expected a doctor raised on science books to understand his intentions so swiftly? Especially when his own family didn't. Jack switched to football—even Mel had heard of the Cowboys—and somehow they got through dinner.

It was dark by the time he followed Melinda's directions to her parents' home in Merriman Park.

"That's it," she said with a yawn, indicating an older, two-story brick home much like its neighbors.

Jack parked the Jeep in front of the garage, lifted his overnight bag from the back of the vehicle as he came around to help Mel out, then trailed her into the house. He nodded when she asked if he'd like to see his room and went upstairs behind a swirl of chocolate hair and the world's sexiest back. Even hidden in shapeless knit.

"This is my room," she said, opening the first door

on the right. When he arched a brow, she merely blinked before adding, "For the coffee."

"Right, 5:00 a.m. It'll be there," he promised, trying to block the delicious, erotic images filling his head. Of that satiny hair spread across pillows. Of his hands sliding along her curves. Of hot, deep kisses picking up where their first one left off.

"And that's your room." She pointed to the door at the far end of the hall, then yawned again. "Sorry. Guess I didn't realize getting married would be so exhausting. Is there anything you need before I turn in?"

Proving, you idiot, that you're the only one hot to trot around here. "I'll be fine," Jack assured his it's-just-business bride as he stepped past her carefully. "See you in the morning."

With a nod, Melinda turned away. "Right. Good night."

Jack strode down the hallway to the room she'd indicated. After carrying only his luggage—not a willing woman—across the threshold, he flipped on the overhead, closed the door behind him and eyeballed his domain for the coming months. Nice enough, he supposed. Own bath, own TV...own bed. Big enough for two interactive people.

Stop it. She married an on-site domestic engineer, not a lover.

Jack snapped on the television, located a sports channel and half listened to a recitation of college scores as he unpacked, took a quick shower, set the alarm for four-thirty—God help him—and went to bed.

Not to sleep, though. He lay there in the dark, staring at the ceiling, willing himself to forget every creamy, satiny inch of Melinda's back and the explosive heat of their kiss.

Tomorrow'll be easier, he assured himself, turning and punching the pillow. He'd be busy moving in, getting settled.

And Melinda would be back at work. Before sunrise. Lord, the woman worked more hours than an ambitious stockbroker.

Tonight he was grateful for her killer schedule. Not only because it let him leave Loeb-Weinstein to study for his CFP exam and catch his breath, fully insured.

But because, as everybody knew—out of sight, out of mind....

4

_____

THE STUPID CLOCK RADIO blared to life without warning, rattling Jack's sleep-logged brain like a jet's sonic boom slapping a single-pane window.

He opened one eye to check the time. 4:30! Jack hit the snooze button before Britney hit the first note of the second line. Jensen and the Nikkei could just wait ten min—

Hold it. He wasn't covering the overseas markets this week.

He was free! No, he was married.

And in thirty minutes, he was supposed to serve Melinda Burke coffee in bed. Hers, not his.

"I must have been nuts," Jack muttered as he pushed aside the covers and headed for the bathroom. "Loony. Insane. Whacked out of my mind."

Three minutes into a four-minute shower, his mind and a certain southerly body part were replaying wedding highlights, featuring vivid close-ups of that erotic, feminine back he'd undressed yesterday. And that turbocharged kiss!

Like he needed help being aroused in the morning, Jack grumbled, spinning the water regulator to chill before shutting it off. As he reached for a towel, he looked at the shaving kit he'd dumped on the vanity. No way he was scraping off whiskers before the sun came up.

Okay, so this wife thing was his job now. That didn't mean he had to set himself a high-performance standard first thing. The whole point of this escapade was R and R, after all.

Stalking jaybird-naked into the bedroom, Jack jerked on underwear, a pair of jeans and last night's polo shirt, then, ignoring the rumpled bedclothes, he strapped on his watch and headed out to discharge his first duty as Melinda Burke's wife.

He'd make the bed later. He had all day for it. Right now—*make like Starbucks, Halloran, and brew up some coffee.* A simple chore, he thought as he loped downstairs to the kitchen, even at—he looked over at the microwave—4:39 a.m.

Congratulating himself on his perfect timing, Jack opened the cabinet above the coffeemaker. Not there.

He opened another cabinet. Then another...

At 4:47, he halted his frenzied search.

Just stood there, motionless, gazing at the ranks of opened cabinets. He'd discovered plates, glasses, mixing bowls, casserole dishes and every small kitchen appliance known to man—including two types of coffeemakers.

But no coffee. None. No beans, no ground, no instant.

The Burkes' kitchen apparently didn't contain anything else edible, either. The pantry held only a dried macaroni elbow, a canister of salt, three packets of fake sugar and a box of crackers that looked old enough to qualify as historical artifacts.

The fridge contained a pile of fast-food ketchup packs and a jar of mustard.

Moron—thinking he could just marry himself onto easy street! He was screwed.

Jack growled with frustration, then his jaw and his determination, which Sherry and his sibs uncharitably referred to as stubbornness, hardened. *No!* He'd promised Mel coffee. She'd damned well get coffee. In bed, by five.

How, brainiac?

Out of the corner of his eye, Jack caught a turquoise flicker; the rightmost number on the microwave's clock had changed to an eight.

Ha. The one thing he wasn't out of—not yet, anyway. Time.

Jack sprinted back upstairs for keys and wallet. Shoved his feet into flip-flops. Raced out to his car and leaped behind the wheel like a NASCAR veteran.

"Okay. If I was a convenience store, where would I be?" Jack wondered aloud as he jammed the key into the ignition, fired the engine and backed out of the driveway. He had less than twelve minutes to find, purchase and return triumphantly with hot coffee.

Or he could just keep driving, he thought as he dodged some old codger in a pickup delivering newspapers that would be yesterday's if he drove any slower, and an appalling number of joggers trotting through the dark.

Yeah, just drive till he ran out of gas. Start a new life—and a new career—there. Counter help at a dry cleaners. Fast-food driveup window. Something so simple even ol' burned-out Halloran couldn't screw it up.

Slowing to avoid wiping out a whole clot of jabber-walkers crossing the street, Jack noticed a line of bright light glowing behind the houses a few blocks down. His brain cells sluggishly processed the information: main drag…commercial enterprises…java!

The clock on the Jeep's dash glowed nastily: 4:50.

Ten minutes. Dammit, he was *not* blowing his first wifely assignment.

Tapping his horn to motivate the dawdlers, Jack threaded his way through the neighborhood, heading for the lights. While his hands gripped and spun the steering wheel, lingering memories of Mel's creamy-skinned, feminine curves altered the fit of his jeans.

Don't waste the testosterone, Jack advised himself.

Dr. Burke was trading health insurance and study time for domestic assistance. Period.

That sexy back and silky chocolate hair and hot, melting kiss were not part of the—

Pancake house!

Grinning at the tangerine and blue sign glowing through the predawn darkness, Jack turned left onto a major artery lined with all the usual retail stores, spun a ninety into the restaurant's parking lot and hit the sidewalk running.

Though he delivered the order with barely restrained urgency, the plus-size waitress, wearing limp brown polyester and a can or two of hairspray, only trudged toward the six-pot brew station near the kitchen pass-through.

To avoid making the situational slowdown worse by betraying any sign of impatience, Jack spun around and leaned his backside against the edge of the counter.

The place was pure pancake house: cracked, orange vinyl bathed in harsh fluorescent light. Laminated menus, laminated tables, even the food looked vaguely laminated. The air hung thick with cigarette smoke and old grease.

It was packed, too, mostly with customers in uniform, grouped by employer. They sat talking and smoking over plates sucked clean, only the occasional grease glob, yellow smear or puddle of syrup offering a clue to the thick china's former contents.

Jack shuddered. What would Melinda say if she knew her coffee was coming from a place like this?

Oh, ha. Even at—he checked the clock on the wall—4:54 in the gad-awful a.m., he wasn't letting something that simple trip him up. Any fool knew to transfer the java to a mug before presenting it to his new wife. Who'd be in bed. Undressed.

Jack closed his eyes against the image. It had haunted him last night, too. Kept him awake through two

SportsCenters and an hour of grizzlies waiting around a stream for salmon....

Melinda Burke in bed, her glorious feminine back and—if that bride dress could be believed—an equally glorious front. Clad only in a wisp of sheer lingerie and tangled sheets....

"Here ya go, hon."

Jack jerked around as the waitress set a large coffee on the counter. Retaining its lid in her other hand, the Hairspray Queen pressed buttons on the cash register with majestic deliberation—while he stared at the pearlescent sheen of oil spots floating atop the black liquid they called coffee.

Beverage beggars couldn't be choosers, Jack reminded himself sharply. It was hot and contained caffeine. Close enough for today.

"Dollar thirty-nine, hon," the waitress growled, her voice a testament to too many years spent inhaling secondhand smoke and grease.

Pulling two dollars out of his wallet, Jack flashed Polyester Patty a grateful smile as he slid the bills across the countertop.

Thanks to her, and if he hauled serious butt, he'd be back at the house with time to spare before Mel's alarm went off.

"Keep the change," he said, reaching for the coffee.

"Much obliged, hon." Ignoring his outstretched hand, the waitress proceeded to carefully—meaning so slowly Jack thought he'd scream, except his nerves probably couldn't take the noise for another hour or two—clamp the lid on the to-go cup.

Eventually, satisfied she'd secured it against any attack up to and including a well-armed rebel insurgency, she pushed the sealed drink toward him. "You have a nice day, now. 'N come back 'n see us, y'hear?"

Yeah, he heard. As the glass and aluminum door swung shut behind him.

Then he did a one-eighty and reentered the grease pit.

"Have you got any little cartons of milk?" he asked, digging for his wallet again.

The waitress, who hadn't left her position at the register yet, pressed her chin into her neck.

Jack took that for a yes. "Great. Let me have a skim, please." Growing up with a sister had taught him that much. "And one of those." He pointed to a rack of single serving boxes of cereal. "Any kind."

Too darned many minutes later, Jack threw himself and his booty into his car, cranked the engine, dropped the transmission into drive and floored the gas pedal.

As he shot out of the lot and roared down the street, he revised his schedule for his first day of wifely leisure.

Somewhere between "a little dusting" and "survey daytime television schedule," he'd better hustle on over to a grocery store. How on earth had those cupboards gotten so bare?

Taking a corner on two wheels, Jack pondered that.

Hell, even *he* usually stocked some OJ in the ol' icebox along with the beer and leftover pizza. And everybody kept cereal around!

Despite the early hour, he could draw the proper conclusion from the facts.

Melinda Burke had definitely not married him out of pity, or as a lark, he reminded himself as he parked, ran inside, poured the coffee into a Dallas Stars mug and nuked it—just in case.

Having proof that she really did need his wifely help restored Jack's good mood. As long as he was earning his vacation, he could enjoy it. But first...

Jack tore open the cereal, dumped it into the first bowl he found, then rummaged through drawers for silverware. Snagging a spoon, he glanced up. 4:59.

He swore; the microwave beeped. Grabbing the coffee, he sped upstairs, halting only at Melinda's door to rake fingers through his hair, then knock once. Softly.

No answer.

Another knock. Another no answer.

Dammit. He'd have to go in there.

For a second, Jack hesitated. Okay, he chickened. Then, dredging motivation from his memory bank, he curled fingers around the doorknob, twisted, opened the door and walked into Mel's bedroom.

See? The perfect wife. Perfectly willing to carry out his duties.

All it took was remembering that *anything*—even waking the gorgeous woman he'd married but agreed not to touch—was better than working for Jugular Jensen again.

The rest will be a piece of cake, Jack told himself as he crossed the room toward the sleeping figure tucked neatly under the covers of an Early American twin bed. Just make sure she's awake. Deposit the steaming mug on the nightstand. Get the hell out of here.

Light from the hallway revealed a plastic skeleton loitering near the closet and a disgusting anatomy poster hanging above a student desk piled high with medical journals.

Okay, Doc, he rehearsed silently, *rise and shine.*

MEL SMILED. She felt, *mmm,* sooo relaxed and she was having a really good dream for a change. There was soft music playing somewhere in the background as a wonderful, sexy man's voice caressed her name....

She burrowed deeper into the pillow, hoping the dream guy would keep talking sweet, and look as great as he sounded.

"Come on, Melinda," her dream man coaxed. "Here, take a whiff...."

He's bringing me flowers? Excellent.

Mel sniffed obediently. What the—? Nothing floral about *that* scent. Her nose wrinkled as her eyes flew open.

Well, he did look as great as he sounded, Mel thought ruefully as she stared up at her brand-new husband...wife...whatever. Damn, the man's looks got more appealing by the encounter.

That morning stubble alone promoted him from hunk to heartthrob!

"Your coffee. Oh, hell," Jack added conversationally. "I forgot to ask how you take it."

"Just plain."

"Great. Black it is."

Mel started to sit up to take the steaming mug being held out, then thought better of it.

Then thought better of *that*. Let him get used to it, she told herself as she scooted into an upright position. She'd married the man to simplify her life, not complicate it.

Besides, she wore a T-shirt to sleep in. Nothing indecent about it. And they were both of legal age, anyway.

Mel wrapped her fingers carefully around the mug. As she lifted it to her lips, she studied Jack Halloran through her eyelashes.

Oh, yeah, her myopia notwithstanding, the man's wake-up quotient beat the Weather Channel crew any day.

Get a grip, Burke. The human body holds no secret allure, remember? A dedicated doctor wouldn't wonder about his...well, uh, how well endowed he is.

"There's cereal and milk downstairs," Jack said, inching backward. Away from the bed. Toward the door. As if he was—

"Breakfast!" Mel exclaimed, inwardly jeering at her lunacy. No way a guy this hot would get nervous being in *her* bedroom.

Any man who looked like Jack Halloran damned sure knew his way around plenty of bedrooms.

Still...he'd brought the coffee as promised. And

made breakfast. Bonus! "Careful, you'll spoil me," she said with a smile. For a moment, she thought the man she'd married practically sight unseen looked dazzled.

Dazed, Burke, dazed. It's five o'clock in the morning.

"Actually," she mused after another sip of café oily, "I can't remember the last time I ate something *before* traffic instead of *in* it."

Jack jammed his hands into his pockets. Which only made the anatomical area behind his fly more spectacularly noticeable. "Is there, ah...anything special you want me to do today?" he asked.

How about joining me for a quick roll in the hay?

Mel choked at her own audacity, then downed another gulp of coffee, flung herself out of bed and marched herself toward the bathroom. Get real, she told herself. She didn't know one thing about this man that made him beddable.

Well, okay, she didn't know *another* thing....

But this wasn't that kind of relationship, and Dr. Bowen had scheduled rounds for six. Sharp.

Flipping on the bathroom light, Mel made herself say, "There's some, ah, laundry in the utility room."

"No problem." He was scuttling backward again.

Which behavior Mel still didn't get as she watched him pivot and head for the exit about as fast as that Indiana Jones guy vacating the booby-trapped ruin with the big rock chasing him.

Then she caught a glimpse of herself in the bathroom mirror.

Oh. No wonder. She looked like a street freak, her hair every which way, her eyes like a raccoon's—apparently she'd missed the tenth layer of mascara when she'd scrubbed off Raoul's makeup last night. And the T-shirt was way old. Not quite as "decent" as she'd thought, maybe.

And here she stood, ordering the man around like a War College general just off Prozac. *So? We made a deal,* she reminded herself. *He agreed.* And she was desperate. "If you wouldn't mind—"

"'Swhat I'm here for." He'd paused in the doorway but hadn't turned around.

Just as well—easier to say the rest of this to his tapering, muscular back than to his too attractively masculine face.

"Could you, um, do some underwear...ah, in the first load, I mean?"

"Right! Sure! Will do." With that, Jack threw himself out of the room.

Thanks to her years of medical training, after a nonplussed second, Mel set aside the puzzle of his odd behavior for later consideration; she went into make-ready mode: start the shower, gather clothes and finish off the Juan Valdez while the water heated.

Not that the coffee had been exactly gourmet, but she did appreciate the gesture. And the feeling that she wasn't the only person who cared if she was up at this unearthly hour.

Shucking her T-shirt, Mel climbed into the shower.

As she sped through the wet-soap-rinse routine, she imagined clean underwear. And wearing her own clothes again.

And eating breakfast. In the morning. Every day.

She'd died and gone to heaven, Mel decided as she toweled off.

Now if she could just forget that incendiary ceremonial kiss and get herself inured to the bold male aura that hung around Jack like groupies stalking a pop star.

It'd be nice knowing there was someone here for her, Mel thought as she pulled on the last clean underwear she had, clunky shoes and another of her mother's old dresses, even if *she* mostly wasn't. *Someone more interested in solving her problems than creating them, which seemed to be Dr. Bowen's favorite hobby...*

"Come on, Burke. It's a little late for the helpless

female routine.'' She rounded up her lab coat, stethoscope and pager. ''You couldn't pull it off anyway. So just go to work, where you've got tougher things to face than a gorgeous babe magnet who's pleasing you for reasons of his own.''

And who was lurking, she discovered when she got there, in the kitchen. Ready to pull out a chair for her before moving to sit across from her.

Eat with him? Make conversation? N-not yet.

''Darn!'' Mel exclaimed, pretending to look at her watch. ''Gotta run. I'll take it with me.''

Her glasses slipped down her nose as she leaned forward to scoop up the bowl of garishly colored grain blobs and the spoon. Giving her two Jack Hallorans to try to ignore.

They were both frowning, but all he said was, ''What time will you be home?''

Leapin' liposuction! His deep male voice touched off another round of X-rated anatomical exploratory ideas.

''I'll, uh…'' Mel grabbed the mini milk carton. It reminded her of elementary school, and her brother Harry. The familiar stab of loss managed to reorient her enfeebled brain from its sudden, inexplicable lapse. Momentarily, at least.

''Don't expect me before ten.'' There. Nice and cool, professional.

Then Jack blinked his dark blue eyes at her and all traces of professionalism fled.

So did she.

JACK GAZED after her. *What an incredible woman!* Melinda Burke made that whole caterpillar-to-butterfly thing look like a slacker activity.

She'd transformed herself from seductive bed-nymph to professional superdoctor in—what?—ten minutes?

A yawn intervened. He should have gotten two coffees at the pancake house, Jack realized. Oh well, maybe he'd go out to breakfast. Celebrate his retirement.

Grinning, he pumped his fist in a victory gesture. He was a free man!

Oh, he'd do all the stuff he'd promised Mel, but in his own sweet time, according to his own sweet schedule. With plenty of breaks to study for his CFP exam and to coax Tess back to the land of the living.

Plenty of breaks. Jack gave a hoot of laughter. What a scam this housewife stuff was! Cup o' coffee, a load o' laundry and he'd be done for the day.

Still chuckling about the "demands" of his new position, Jack strolled over and gave the utility-room door a push. It refused to open.

He frowned briefly, then, in typical male problem-solving fashion, put his shoulder to the door and forced it open.

Some laundry? Jack felt his jaw drop.

Pediatric surgeon, my derriere, he thought as he stared at the mountain of fabric filling the small room. Melinda Burke was the queen of understatement!

Fine. He'd still keep his part of the deal. Be her perfect wife—no matter how much TV he had to miss. Virtuously, Jack kicked aside enough clothes to reach the washer.

He knew how to do this, even if he'd always sent his dress shirts and slacks to the cleaners. Locating detergent in the cabinet above it, he poured in a generous capful.

There. Now just throw in the clothes and start the machine.

Jack looked at the vast pile of laundry.

Hmm. Real wives sort. He was sure of it. But how? On what basis?

Size of garment? Nah, he washed socks with jeans; they all came out fine.

Style? Doubtful. Too hard to categorize, even for

women. Every year, the fems at Loeb-Weinstein spent hours discussing the Christmas party dress code—like they needed a Rosetta Stone or Oprah to explain the true meaning of "semiformal."

For a second, he considered calling Sherry for advice, but she was even less domestic than he was.

His sister? At dawn?

No way. This was laundry, for cryin' out loud.

Sure he could figure out something so simple, Jack plucked an item off the top of Laundry Mountain.

Oh. My. God.

His throat tightened. So did his jeans—again—as he stared at the tiny scrap of silk and lace dangling from his fingers.

This was not his sister's underwear.

And he sure as hell wasn't picturing his sister in it.

He was picturing those mile-long legs Mel had flaunted less than thirty minutes ago as she sashayed across her bedroom on her way to…*being wet and naked. After which she slid one of these hot little confections up those columns of smooth female flesh to—*

"Chill, Halloran!" Jack ordered himself. This was a platonic, business relationship, with no room for erotic fantasies. Besides… "The sun's not even up yet."

But something else was—the old divining rod was way up! Much more of this unauthorized fantasizing and he'd explode.

Jack dropped the lingerie like a hot CheezPocket. Only the darned thing was so weightless, it didn't even *fall.* More like *drifted* downward to join its fellows, nestling amidst thick terry towels, worn jeans, sleek short skirts and slinky silk blou—

"Eureka!" Jack whispered shakily, suddenly inspired by his desperation to get this task done. Before he suffered some kind of testosterone meltdown.

A glance at the washer and dryer controls confirmed

the validity of his newborn theory. *Delicate, Regular, Heavy.*

Professional wives sorted laundry by fabric weight. As his heart rate returned to normal, Jack grinned victoriously.

He'd solved his first housework mystery without any help.

Scooping up an armful of laundry, he divided it rapidly, tossing delicate—as in thin and slippery—stuff into the washer, dropping the rest back on the floor. When the machine looked pretty full, he slammed down the lid, pulled out the knob and booked.

Now what? Jack wondered.

The microwave reported the time was only 5:42. In the *morning.*

Sunday morning, at that. Nuts. Jack headed upstairs to rest on his laurels, leaving the washer chugging away, doing its thing.

WHEN DR. BOWEN APPEARED around the corner, marching toward the small group of surgical residents like Sherman heading for Georgia, Mel breathed a sigh of relief. Now all those unnerving thoughts of hunky husbands and bone-melting kisses would vanish. *Like ice cubes.*

"I sure as hell hope nobody's missing," Bowen snarled.

On asphalt. In August.

The program chief's bald head swiveled, glistening as he scanned the group. Choosing today's ambushee, no doubt. "Who's first? Let's go."

So much for chitchat.

As she trailed the others down the corridor, Mel recalled that awkward scene with Jack's sister at the reception. Light social conversation did have its uses, she conceded.

Not that she'd ever need chat skills with Bowen. The

man was all business all the time, Mel reminded herself as the group crowded into a room with two small patients in two large beds. The business of saving lives.

One of the residents—Simmons?—indicated the first bed. In a rapid monotone, he began to read from a color-coded chart. "...seven-year-old male, unrestrained MVA, surgically repaired damage to lower intestine..."

Mel's attention drifted to the patient. Oh, no—the kid was taking in every word Simmons rattled off, understanding none of them and getting more scared by the minute.

His eyes were huge. They were also dark blue. *Like Jack's.*

Without thinking, Mel slipped around the other students. Reaching the bed, she squeezed the child's hand. "What's your name?" she whispered.

"Eddie," the boy whispered back.

"Well, don't worry, Eddie. The man using the big words is a very good doctor who only lets his patients get better."

The youngster's rigid form relaxed as he gave Mel a grateful smile.

She smiled back. It was always good to remember why she was here. Not to impress Dr. Bowen. To learn how to help children heal.

That's why she'd married Jack Halloran. Not to jump-start her previously flatlining erotic imagination. To help her survive this fellowship.

A minute later, as they all filed out of the room and headed down the hall, Dr. Bowen dropped back to walk beside her.

"Heartwarming, Dr. Burke." His tone missed being scathing by a mosquito's eyelash. "But don't make promises to these kids that other doctors have to keep. And don't get distracted during rounds."

With that, Bowen strode forward, leaving Mel to

grind her teeth in peace. Lordy, the man made piranha look like Easter pets.

Is that how Tess—and Jack, and Sherry—saw *her?* Mel wondered, touching her pager as she followed the other white coats into the next patient's room. So dedicated to medicine, she'd lost touch with humanity?

It's not that she didn't *want* to have friends, a social life, some fun once in a while.

But everyone had to make a choice, and she'd chosen medicine. Six short months from now, her years of personal sacrifices would start paying off. Soon she'd be saving children like Eddie, like her brother, sending them back to their families healthy and whole and alive.

That would make every solitary, dateless Saturday night, every clueless social situation worthwhile. It would even, Mel assured herself as the group squirted back into the hallway and headed to the third patient, make marrying a stranger for the purpose of housework seem like a good idea.

Which it hadn't this morning. Not when she'd awakened to that sexy stubble and hard, hot body looming above her. She'd wanted to ditch everything except coaxing him into bed for a real honeymoon.

Mel shook her head. Where was this mushy female stuff coming from?

She'd have plenty of time for all that personal stuff later. Now she'd just have to watch herself around him. Yeah, keep her distance, so she didn't do something career-damaging stupid. Like throw her socially inept self at her hottie of a husband. Er, wife. Er—

"Does your silence mean you're unprepared, Dr. Burke?" Bowen's sharp-edged question cut through Mel's self-lecture like one of those lasers used for vision correction surgery.

"Of course not, Dr. Bowen," she replied calmly, ignoring the weasel's patently skeptical expression as she mentally assembled her case's information into coherent order.

"Good." Bowen's silky purr grated like nails on a blackboard. "We were afraid you were lost in a romantic haze."

"Excuse me?" Mel fingered the pager clipped to her pocket.

"I understand you took the weekend off to get married."

Mel shot a glare at ol' Dan Something. Dan Blabbermouth, apparently. "Saturday, sir," she replied quietly, her fingers sliding past her beeper to form a fist in her pocket. "One day. I can assure you that my full attention remains focused on pediatric surgery."

"It better, Burke," Dr. Bowen snapped. "Because only those willing to give 110% can hope to complete this program."

Taking a deep breath to avoid shouting at him that she was already giving 150%, Mel nodded, then began her presentation.

No question she'd made the right decision, marrying Jack. The next six months might be hard on her hormones, but with his help, she and her parents' house would survive this surgical residency from hell. Run by the devil himself.

AMAZING WHAT A three-hour nap could do for a man's outlook on life, Jack thought as he shambled into the kitchen. He was good to go now. Ravenous, too.

He headed for the refrigerator, ready to chow down.

Oh, yeah. No food. And fixing that was his job.

For the second time that morning, Jack retrieved his keys and wallet and headed for the supermarket he'd seen near the pancake house.

A woman in Mel's high-stress profession needed to eat right; he should stock up on healthy, nutritious foods. Like what? Tofu patties or fruit-flavored sports drinks or something?

Trying to guess Mel's likes and dislikes, Jack cruised the aisles, filling his cart. The meat department was a little confusing, but he emerged from it with hamburger meat and something called a roast. He'd make that for dinner, he decided as he ate a bag of pork rinds on the way home.

The snack restored his good spirits—so much that when the retiree across the street came over to introduce himself, Jack accepted his offer to help carry in the sacks of food.

Ol' Bob seemed okay. A little talkative...

Now who's making understatements, Halloran? The guy hung around for thirty minutes, blabbing nonstop.

Once the old geezer left, Jack opened a can of ravioli. As he forked out the first bite, he remembered the laundry needed drying.

Man, this housework was just one thing after another.

Setting aside Chef B's creation, Jack went into the utility room and lifted the washer's lid. He reached in and pulled out some tiny wet feminine coverings.

Pink, tiny, wet feminine coverings.

Mystified, Jack gave a shrug, then transferred them to the dryer.

Back at the washer, he picked out more pink little bits of clothing.

"What the—?" This time, Jack reached in with both hands and pulled out a whole wad of wet laundry. Also pink. Weird, he thought as he tossed them into the dryer with the other stuff. He could have sworn she didn't have so many p—

"Oh, hell." Spying the explanation, Jack snatched it out.

With a sinking feeling, he draped the red silk blouse atop the dryer, then dug through the washer.

Dammit! The whole load was pink.

And he was toast.

So now what, imbecile? Jack asked himself, perusing the culprit blouse gloomily. That, of course, was when he noticed the label.

Not that the instructions it contained were much help. "Wash with like colors."

Colors like what?

He was guessing not ivory. Or pale blue. Or yellow. Great. Now he remembered their original colors.

The real question *du jour* was—how chapped would Mel be when she discovered he'd ruined her underwear?

Not that any of it was shredded. If it was his stuff, he'd just figure "no harm, no foul." But women, he knew, looked at these things totally differently.

Refusing to let himself picture even that crimson blouse against Mel's pale skin and dark hair, Jack grimly read labels and resorted everything he'd turned pink.

He ended up with a "do not bleach" bunch—consisting of the lacy little lingerie confections that made his palms sweat—and a "use only color-safe bleach" group.

Wasn't that an oxymoron? Jack wondered as he began the rewashing process.

Two hours later, both batches were still pink. Glumly he folded it all and took it upstairs, leaving it piled pinkly on her bed.

Then he clomped back downstairs, determined to do *something* right today.

He'd dust, he decided, heading for the den. Catch the end of the Rangers game, get a saner—i.e., less erotically charged—perspective on the woman he'd married...and dust.

Any moron, he assured himself—even an ex-stockbroker—could dust.

5

Mel let herself into the house quietly. Not that she expected a little noise in the kitchen to disturb her new…wife?…husband?…maid-by-marriage? *Jack, just call him Jack.* His room was at the far end of the house and upstairs to boot. And it was way late. Closing in on midnight.

The guy's in dreamland, Burke.

Which was where she needed to be. Mel pushed her glasses up onto her hair so she could rub her tired eyes.

"You call this ten o'clock?"

Mel jumped. Who the—?

Oh, my. There was no "just" about the Jack who stood in the doorway leading to the living area, and it didn't take corrective lenses to read his body language—feet apart, chiseled forearms crossed over that hard-muscled, broad chest.

The man looked like a slightly overdressed but still lethally attractive pirate, straight off the cover of one of those torrid historical romances she sometimes wished she had time to read.

"Ever heard of a telephone?"

So much for *"Hi, honey! How was your day?"*

"Do you even own a watch?" Somehow he managed to inject the question with the same blend of astonishment, worry and mild disappointment her mother always had when Mel had first started working at the hospital during med school.

Mel couldn't help herself. She chuckled.

It was that or cry because somebody noticed how hard she worked.

"I don't see what's so funny," Jack informed her, uncrossing his arms to clamp his hands on his hips. "You're almost two hours late! I was worried—anything could have happened."

Mel lowered her glasses to bring him into focus and felt her jaw drop. The man was scowling at her?

The heck with that. Bowen's criticism she *had* to take, but not Jack Halloran's nagging. "I don't know what business of yours it—" she began.

"What business?" He interrupted her, just like Bowen always did. Was that a man thing or what?

If she wasn't too exhausted to spare the energy, Mel decided, she'd get PO'd about it.

"I'm supposed to be taking care of you, remember?" Flames seemed to flare from his blue eyes, but it was *her* insides that felt hot.

Sexy and concerned—an irresistibly attractive combo.

And that's exactly why she'd dawdled at the hospital, gathering nurses' observations instead of rushing right home after she finished charting her patients.

"For all I knew," Jack was ranting on, "you wrecked your car or got mugged in the hospital parking lot or—" his arms waved through most of the kitchen's air space "—or something."

The man certainly had a vivid imagination, Mel thought as she struggled to ignore the way her pulse spiked when Jack rebulged—er, recrossed his arms.

"Okay, I'm sorry." Mel offered a smile as a peacemaking gesture. "This—" she did her own arm-waving "—is all new to me. I—"

Don't explain, Burke. Inform. "I mean, I don't expect you to greet me at the door with my pipe and slippers."

"Fine." Jack's voice dropped to its normal, still dangerously sexy level. "But feeding you *is* part of my job.

And if I'd had something ready for you at ten, it would be totally ruined by now.''

It would? Mel thought pizza could stay warm in the oven indefinitely.

Wait a minute. "*If* you'd made something?"

"Don't change the subject."

Mel felt her eyelids retract. Her eyeballs were probably popping out of their orbital sockets.

Halloran, however, didn't seem to have heard what he'd just said. Instead—as if *she* was the one with the reasoning impairment!—he blithely continued, "I agreed to take over all homemaking chores—including cooking meals—but I can't do it without your cooperation."

That sensual idiot who'd taken up residence in her brain immediately suggested a few delicious—and deliciously indecent—cooperative "chores" they could do. Together.

Maybe her reasoning *was* impaired.

"Again, I'm sorry. I'm not used to having a wife yet." Mel started forward, then stopped. His large male body blocked her path. Like Hoover Dam blocking whatever river that was.

"I'll, uh, call next time," she promised, trying to edge around him so she could escape upstairs. Before she did something stupid, like blurt out one of those X-rated suggestions. Or heave a sigh of pleasure as she plastered herself against that big, hard chest wall.

"Dinner's no big deal," she said, to clarify to herself, at least, that *she* wasn't needy, not really. She'd married him for the house.

Yeah. And Bowen's a marshmallow inside his cactuslike exterior. "I had a piece of somebody's birthday cake this afternoon."

Jack shook his head at her like she'd given the wrong answer to a test question. The little strand of hair shooting out into space from the cowlick above his eyebrow waggled at her.

"That's not eating, Melinda," Jack's disapproving-mom voice instructed. "That's snacking. Nobody who works as long and hard as you do can survive on cake." Brushing past her, he headed for the refrigerator. "Good thing I went to the supermarket today. Twice."

If it was such a good thing, why did he sound so annoyed?

"I'll microwave you something."

"Oh, I can nuke boxes," Mel said cheerfully, following him across the kitchen. Hell-bent on getting him out of the room. Out of pheromone range. "Let me—"

Pirouetting with the grace of one of those Russian ballet-athletes, Jack planted a rock-hard arm against an upper cabinet, blocking her progress like a railroad crossing gate. She could go through it if she had the guts, but something told her it might be a bad idea.

"I'll prepare your dinner, Melinda," he insisted softly, jutting his jaw at her. "It's what I do now, remember?"

Between the man's force field of sheer maleness and the goofy pronouncements coming out of his mouth, Mel was beginning to feel light-headed.

Or maybe she *was* hungry.

"I think we need to set some ground rules," Mel declared, then her gaze came to rest on the crinkly hair covering his forearm just inches away. Her brain quit thinking—its synapses shorting out under a flood of glandular secretions aimed at species' continuity.

"I thought we had," Jack claimed, adding piously, "I do the cooking and cleaning."

"But you don't have to wait on me hand and foot." *Jack's hands on her. Mmm.* Mel struggled to resist the image. "You see, Dr. Bowen—that's my boss—he's very dedicated—"

"He's a slave driver."

Well, yeah. That's why she'd married this hunk.

She *hadn't* married him to get into domestic arguments like this, but she was at a complete loss about how to wrap it up. How *did* couples stop wrangling once they got started?

"I'm just saying, my hours are crazy—"

"I noticed."

Mel grinned. "That doesn't mean I expect you to keep crazy hours, too."

"No sweat," Jack said, then grinned sheepishly. Even that did something very somersaultish to Mel's insides. "I, ah, took a little nap after you left this morning," he confessed.

Then, before she could congratulate him, he scowled. "But I still pulled my weight today. Hell, I spent all afternoon at the supermarket. Bought nearly three hundred dollars' worth of groceries."

"H-how much?" Whoa! Had she married a compulsive shopper?

"Two hundred, thirty-nine dollars and seventeen cents, to be exact."

Huh? "I thought you rounded down below fifty," she said faintly.

"Not if you're making a point."

Mel closed her eyes. So gorgeous, so male, so *nuts.* "The point being—?"

"You do need me, Melinda." His voice caressed her name. His hands cupped her shoulders gently. Oh, she wanted to lean into him, to press against that solid chest, to rest in his arms....

Puh-leeze, Burke. He wants your insurance, not your body draping all over his like burn dressings. He said so, remember?

"And I'm going to help you." His hands left her shoulders, which wanted to veto the departure. "But you have to let me. I admit—" Now he held out open palms. "It's going to take me a while to whip this place into shape and for us to develop routines that work—for both of us. All I'm asking is that you do your part. Just communicate, okay?''

Mel nodded, mesmerized by such sweet reasonableness. That woodsy, understated cologne he wore didn't hurt either.

Her stomach, however, wasn't quite as impressed; it growled.

Jack's hands returned to her shoulders. But only to turn and aim her toward the breakfast nook. ''Go sit down.'' He opened the freezer. ''Chicken marsala okay?''

''Sure.'' Relieved they'd resolved their differences so easily, Mel imitated that bobbing-headed doll Aunt Gertrude's husband used to set in the rear window of his '57 Chevy. ''Fine. Great.''

Whatever. She'd just as soon go upstairs and crash, but he sounded so intense about his wife-ing, she was afraid he'd suffer severe emotional distress or something if she bailed on dinner.

So she sat as ordered and let herself enjoy the appetizing view as Jack unboxed and vented the meal.

''Did you know your stove doesn't work?'' he asked as he popped it into the microwave.

Why would she? ''No.''

''That's why there's no real dinner,'' he explained, stabbing the key pad. ''I called a repair service, but....''

''On Sunday?'' Even *she* knew real businesses weren't open then.

''They advertised 24/7 service.'' Jack frowned at the now-revolving carousel. ''Which is bull! They said they can't send anyone out until Tuesday—at the earliest!''

Mel realized her limited experience with interpersonal relations was hampering her again. She didn't have the faintest glimmer of how to assure him that the delay wasn't a personal affront.

Or a national disaster. "So we eat fast food or frozen dinners for a few days. No biggie."

"But I promised you home-cooked meals."

The man actually looked distraught. And Mel felt an inexplicable and totally inappropriate urge to fly across the room into his arms to comfort him.

Comfort, my—

The microwave dinged.

Desperate to distract her mind from its obsession with matters they'd agreed to ignore, Mel sought her purse. "Let me reimburse you for the groceries." She extracted her checkbook, still babbling. "Two-thirty-nine-seventeen, right? My, you must have bought a lot of food."

Jack shrugged as he pulled the plastic cover off the formerly frozen dinner, releasing a cloud of steam. Groceries, yes.

But food? He looked at the geometrically shaped blobs in the tray's compartments. He wasn't so sure. Maybe they'd look better on some nice china?

Sometime between his first and second trips up and down the wide, friendly aisles, he'd realized that he didn't know squat about real cooking.

As a result, he'd practically kissed the stove when it refused to work. Thanking God, he'd gone back to the supermarket to stock up on microwavable stuff.

Deciding that the bubbling globs would look even less like real food on an actual plate, Jack plunked the tray down on the table. "Other than restocking your kitchen, I didn't get much done today," he said, changing the subject since he couldn't manage *"Bon appetit."*

Not that an army of experienced hotel maids would have made much of a dent. Ordinary swiping and sweeping weren't even on the event horizon yet.

The den looked like a college fraternity of geeks had held a rave in there. The formal living and dining rooms were world-class museums of fossilized dust. Run, it appeared, by a colony of confirmed pack rats.

And the yard…Jack shuddered. The grass needed cutting again, the shrubbery qualified as a small rain forest and the pool was only two-thirds full. Of greenish swamp water.

Yeah, Halloran, the place is a disaster. But for the next six months, it's your disaster.

"No rush," Mel said quickly, then cleared her throat. "You, um, you didn't get a chance to do any laundry, I guess." She sounded crestfallen.

Nailed. Hell. "Yeah, I did a load," he admitted grudgingly.

"Oh, that's wonderful!"

Jack stared. Costello glasses and a shapeless dress didn't hide Mel's beauty now. Not while that beaming smile lit the room like a solar flare. And her green eyes danced.

Which, of course, reminded him of that enticing back and the intoxicating wedding kiss they'd shared. He only kept from grabbing her and going in for Round Two by remembering what he'd done to her laundry.

"Ah…you might want to hold that thought," he cautioned. "There, was, uh, a slight hiccup in the process."

"Oh, dear. Did the washing machine break, too?"

He should be so lucky! "No, it works fine," he said heavily. "The clothes got clean. They're dry."

Oh, be a man, Halloran. Confess. "They're just— pink. I turned a whole load of your…your things pink." Jack braced himself for an explosion. That would be the good reaction. He wondered if she could sue him for misrepresentation of domestic skills?

Mel reached up and touched his forearm. Some sort of electric current arced from her hand straight to his personal power tool.

"I don't care what color they are," she said softly, and it grew even more electrified. "Thank you."

"You're welcome, I guess," Jack choked out, fighting off visions of those minuscule remnants of silk and lace. Of Mel in them.

Or not.

Releasing Jack's arm, which continued to conduct phantom electric tingles directly to his gender-specific appendage, Mel jabbed her fork into the brownish blob in the center. "Oh! I asked about the health plan. I'll pick up the forms tomorrow before surgery."

Jack sank into the chair across from Mel. He'd have bet his 401(k) that there wasn't a woman on earth who wouldn't freak out if some moron redyed her underwear. Then again, he'd never imagined one who'd just toss her silk-chocolate hair over her shoulder and consume unrecognizable food squares with apparent pleasure.

Melinda Burke was like no other woman he'd ever…*married.*

For business reasons. Which didn't include monkey business—that obviously only interested him.

"Dr. Bowen has a committee meeting at the med school tomorrow." After that non sequitur, Mel slid her tongue along the tines of the fork.

Jack's throat went dry. That other, electrified part— far south of his throat—went titanium rigid.

"If you can meet me at the hospital around eleven, I'll put you on my checking account so you can pay all our expenses out of there."

What a woman! Gorgeous, easygoing and generous.

If he ever changed his mind about falling in love, Jack mused, he ought to look for someone like Melinda to do it with.

Sanity reasserted itself as he recalled his sister's lingering unhappiness. *Love's too painful.* But for the next six months, he'd get to play house, no strings attached.

No sex, either.

That wasn't carved in stone, Jack reminded himself.

No reason he couldn't, ahem, raise the issue at some future date.

In fact, once the stove was fixed, laying the ground-work would be easy.

She'd come home, he'd have dinner ready, maybe open some wine. They'd talk while they ate, get to know each other—

"Just…" A little furrow peeped above the bridge of Mel's glasses. "Don't wait up for me anymore, okay?"

Nodding reluctantly, Jack told himself to buck up. His CFP courses had taught him there was more than one way to build a nest egg.

He'd just have to come up with Plan B. "Okay, then."

She didn't even look up.

"Well, good night."

"Good night, Jack."

THEY TIPTOED around each other for the next ten days.

The appliance repair service—who turned out to be a guy named Lenny—didn't show up until Thursday. An expensive fifteen minutes later, he left, claiming he'd have to order a part.

From Afghanistan, apparently. Lenny couldn't say when he'd be back and Jack wasn't convinced the damned range would operate properly even after the Second Coming.

Sherry gave him a list of good take-out places and Tess—the one time he managed to get hold of her—stayed on the phone only long enough to offer nutrition advice—something about vegetables and no fries. When he asked how she was doing, his sister hung up. Hard.

Taking Tess's advice, Jack brought home salads piled high with grilled chicken and cheese, and ordered pizzas with weird gourmet toppings like tuna and fruit.

Mel got to sleep on clean, if crumpled, sheets and wear her own clothes again—most of the time they were the right color and had all their buttons—while Jack absorbed the latest changes in estate tax laws. Conversations were so limited, they could have been texted. Morning. Bye. Drive safe. Don't wait u—I know, I won't.

Ten days married and it was working out as expected. Each knew they should be happy. Both would insist—if asked—that they were.

Liars, both of them. They weren't happy. For reasons neither could grasp, they were both miserable.

And damned if either of them knew what to do about it.

ONCE AGAIN, Mel dragged herself out of her car and into the silent house. She dropped her bag on the breakfast table, then dropped herself into one of the chairs surrounding it.

Wouldn't it be nice if— Mel chopped off the fantasy that had dogged her constantly the past ten days: Jack meeting her, feeding her, listening to her, touching her...

Stop acting like such a girl, *Burke!* It was almost two and she was beat. And frustrated. The endoscopy had taken longer than it should have, and Bowen had let her know it.

Worse, he'd let everyone in the OR know it.

And had she ever performed an endoscopy before?

Didn't matter to Bowen, she reflected glumly.

Simmons could lacerate a kid's liver without receiving any criticism harsher or more public than a hissed "You imbecile! Step back before you kill somebody."

Bowen's treatment of her in the OR had been outrageous. Which wasn't news and didn't bother her except at times like this, when she was hungry, angry, lonely and tired.

So, h-a-l-t, goofball.

Taking her own advice, Mel pulled a box from the

freezer and carefully read the instructions, since last night she'd just punched numbers and turned the sofa chicken—no, *divan,* chicken *divan*—into a desiccated block of rock.

While the meal heated, she wandered into the den to look at her brother's portrait. To remember why she put up with the extreme pressure and the incredibly long hours and the constant, often unearned criticism.

As always, Mel's chest tightened and her eyes filled with tears as she studied the smiling boy on the tricycle. To this day, she missed Harry. Since she couldn't bring him back, she'd do everything in her power to save other little kids.

Even put up with Bowen's constant ragging and a personal non-life that was beginning to feel…unsatisfying.

Aw, quit griping, she told herself.

But dammit, clean clothes and hot meals notwithstanding, the few minutes she saw Jack in the morning only seemed to fuel a desire for more.

Which wasn't mutual. Mel could tell that their brief moments together had a very different effect on him than on her.

He popped in to deliver the coffee, which tasted way better now than that first morning. Probably she'd just gotten used to it.

He sat through breakfast, even microwaved eggs, which yesterday he'd called the stupidest food ever. But maybe that was because they were crunchy. He stuck around for housekeeping requests, then vanished the minute she stood to leave.

Who could blame him? He certainly saw her at her worst: bed-headed, heavy lidded, likely sporting dried drool at the corner of her mouth.

Her spouse, on the other hand, always looked great. Sexy beard stubble, shirttails hanging loose, barefoot…

Face it, Burke. Five minutes of exposure to Jack contained the maximum dose of male sensuality safe for a woman with her underdeveloped resistance levels.

The timer on the microwave emitted its high-pitched summons, but Mel didn't respond in her usual Pavlovian manner. Food could wait a sec while she searched for Jack's note.

Tonight she really needed one. Contact with the normal world. *With him.*

Where was it?

Usually she found it under the salt shaker on the table in the breakfast nook. Or taped to the microwave. Or stuck to the refrigerator with a magnet that looked like a hamburger.

Not that they were love notes or anything. Just pragmatic questions or brief status reports on the apparently still incapacitated stove.

Stamps?

In the desk in the study.

Where's the vacuum?

She'd guessed on that one.

Repairman didn't show. That was last Tuesday.

The stove guy finally came—at 4:00! Needs to order a part!

How pathetic was she? Notes about dysfunctional cooking equipment were the major highlight of her day. As for her relationship with her spouse—they didn't have one. Except as pen pals.

Poor baby! Break out the violins. Mel collected her dinner, carried it into the family room and deposited it on the coffee table.

Thirty seconds after collapsing onto the sofa, she shot upright. Performing a perfect half-gainer double take.

Because her gluey lasagna was actually resting *on* the coffee table.

Mel looked around frantically. What had he done with the journals that had covered the thing like a California rockslide on Highway 101 since the week she'd moved back into her parents' home?

"Whew." *—rnal of Pediatric Medi—*peeked coyly past her lasagna from the lower shelf of the coffee table. It lay there with its buddies, all fanned out like a deck of cards.

Awestruck, she gazed admiringly at the rest of the room. The man must work like a dog. The place was looking like a decorator's showroom.

Jack's study materials, a neat pile of booklets, manuals and notebooks featuring the word "Financial" in their titles, sat beside her dad's recliner.

No note in here, either. Jack had nothing to say to her today.

Ignoring another of those little pangs of arrested femininity or whatever thoughts of the man caused, Mel powered on the TV and ate her dinner to the soothing accompaniment of a forensic science docudrama.

When she went upstairs, she stood in the hallway for a long minute, looking at the closed door at the end of the hall.

Forget it. Who needed a life or personal relationships when they could have clean clothes?

Mel went into her room and hit the sack.

RECEIVER PRESSED TO HIS EAR and his aching back pressed against the cool door of the refrigerator, Jack felt his patience ebbing as fast as most dotcoms had.

Unbelievable. He was listening to the radio. On the phone.

An obvious ploy to discourage customers.

Won't work this time, Jack vowed. No way he was giving up just because he'd burned twenty minutes on hold again. This time he'd outwait them. He'd listen to this infuriating "soft rock" crock until he got an answer to the question he'd been trying to ask for a week now.

When was Lenny the repairman bringing over the bleepin' part to fix the stove?

Finally, Torquemada's—aka Lenny's—receptionist came on the line. Jack asked. She put him back on hold while she "checked." Seventeen more minutes later, she gave him Lenny's decision.

"Another week!" He was supposed to keep letting Melinda survive on tired takeout and frozen junk chunks for seven more days?

The geezer across the street, Old Bob, had warned him between WWII stories: guys like No-Show Lenny who wore their names on their shirts thought they were God.

Jack hadn't believed him. Not until he'd called a dozen other repair services and they'd given him the same runaround.

"Fine," he sighed into the phone, then hung up.

His spirit momentarily as broken as his back felt, Jack schlepped into the den to slump in the leather chair he'd commandeered. For studying. Because of its ergonomics, of course.

Still too shocked by Lenny's arrogance to focus on work at the moment, he thumbed on the tube and surfed absently until he hit the Chef Channel or whatever it was called.

Jack's thumb left the remote. He hated this channel but found himself watching it like car-wreck videos.

There was nothing but cooking programs on it. 24/7.

Hosted, of course, by chefs. Ninety percent of whom were male, just to rub it in a little deeper.

They cooked alone, in groups, indoors, outdoors, on location. They barbecued, they baked, they demoed regional dishes. Created whole meals for niche special occasions like Icelandic Eruption Day or Easter. The weirdest show he'd seen so far featured chefs competing in a frenzied timed contest. Complete with instant replay and sideline color announcers!

He'd learned one thing from his viewing: it didn't much matter whether Lenny fixed Mel's stove or not. 'Cuz he couldn't cook worth beans.

Jack slid deeper into the overstuffed leather. He especially disliked the bozo on now. He had curly red hair and a weird name. Something like Jewels, which only reminded Jack of Mel's emerald eyes.

And he didn't need any reminders. The woman totally haunted his thoughts as it was.

Ol' Red expounded on today's creation. Looked like flour water in a dirty pan but he called it rue.

"I know all about rue," Jack muttered. He was full of it.

The bottom line was that he owed ol' Deb—and every other woman who "just stayed home"—an apology.

Because in the past ten days, he'd learned a sheetload about housewifery.

Prime example, Jack thought as Chef Jewels broke away for commercials and he flipped to a golf rerun—it had taken him days but he'd cleaned and straightened and dusted the den. Then he'd walked in here today and—poof! There it was again, microscopic fluff all over the place. And Mel's magazines were rioting again, too.

Nothing was working as he'd expected. Not even the dust!

Or helping his sister rebuild her life. Tess continued to refuse his invitations, pretending she was busy. Doing what? Sitting alone in her apartment night after night he was sure.

And what sadist had designed the vacuum cleaner? Jack wondered, flipping back to watch the cooking genius chop onions with debonair flair. Hours of pushing the thing back and forth, dragging it upstairs, stopping to release every throw rug, curtain hem and loose sock it sucked up, winding and unwinding the stupid cord—no wonder his back hurt.

Laundry? That never seemed to go away. And once you keyed into reading the labels—and quit fantasizing about where they'd been and what *he* could do there—*bo*-ring! The only parts he hadn't quite mastered yet were ironing and sewing on missing buttons. Mrs. Bob had agreed to tutor him if he ever mastered sticking the floppy thread end through the needle hole.

Broodingly, Jack watched the redheaded kahuna shout accolades to himself while the audience clapped and oohed.

Even if Lenny ever did heal the stove, nobody'd ooh over *his* cooking.

And Mel wouldn't come home to eat it even if he could give Chef Gemstone or whatever-his-name-was a run for his money.

"Want some snacks with your whine?" he asked himself, climbing out of the recliner to pace the room. He had to get out of this mood. He hadn't quit work to sit around feeling lousy about himself.

Maybe he was just tired of being cooped up.

He had plenty to do outdoors, but every time he went outside, either Geezer Bob or the ancient mariner next door, Preston Something, showed up. They'd offer to help. And start chatting. And giving him unsolicited advice. And chatting.

Jack extended his pacing path to the formal living room, which was still serving as a federal repository for native airborne particulates. He'd start on that tomorrow. Hopefully, he'd remember not to use the polishing spray on the lampshades in there.

Not that Mel would care. Or even know.

The routine they'd developed since their little discussion that first Sunday could be summed up in three little words.

Do Not Disturb.

Or in two: Passing Ships.

He wasn't complaining. Exactly. Sure he had to do that ghoulish crack-o'-dawn thing, but otherwise he had all the free time he could ask for.

And after all, it wasn't as if they were real newly-weds, crazy in love and hot to hop in bed and dying to talk with each other for hours.

Aside from the bed-hopping part, he didn't want to be married. Not for real. Not forever.

But a little personal contact with Melinda would be nice.

Only not the kind he'd caught himself making this morning.

He'd gone in as usual. Set down the coffee as usual. Whispered her name, but she'd just smiled in her sleep and wiggled that enticing body under the bedclothes. She'd looked so…vulnerable. So tired.

So damned beautiful.

Without thinking, he'd reached down and smoothed her hair off her face. God! Those chocolate strands felt as soft and silky as they looked.

She still hadn't stirred and before he could stop him-self, he'd bent and brushed his lips against her temple.

He'd wanted—like he'd never wanted with any woman before—to crawl into bed with her and wake her up the old-fashioned way.

Instead, he'd dialed the radio to some hideous rap music, cranked the volume to deafening and parachuted out of there.

Jack circled back to the den and headed for the framed pictures cluttering the shelves of the built-in bookcases.

He liked looking at them. At Melinda as a child. Adorable in a little dance costume. Proudly posing on a beach in shorts that revealed the promise of long legs to come. His favorite was an exuberantly grinning Mel on a bike with training wheels, pulling a younger kid in a wagon. Her brother, he supposed.

Were any of those facets of her still there under the dedicated-doc disguise? They should be. And Jack's personal experience told him that Melinda should re-model her lifestyle to make room for them again.

With a sigh that came from his toes, Jack reslumped in the recliner. It was up to him to convince her of that wisdom before she burned out on doctoring the way he had on stock trading. But how?

Not by touching and kissing her while she slept.

Turning to a sitcom so old it was in black and white, Jack worked through the logic. Carefully, although it was pretty straight-line when you laid it out.

Melinda Burke fascinated him.

Because—*only* because he didn't know her well enough to get past that gorgeous face, sweet smile and sexier-than-sin body and see her as an ordinary person.

Therefore, to overcome Melinda's allure, he must spend time with her.

Once he did, he'd have no trouble giving her brotherly advice—or controlling her riveting effect on his male anatomy.

Perfect. The only stumbling block was the time-together thing.

And there, he mused as the laugh track roared at marginally funny antics, his pal Lenny might prove useful after all.

As promised, he wouldn't wait up; he'd just…go on the offensive. Drop in at the hospital. An in-the-neighborhood kind of thing. As long as he's there… Take Mel out to dinner. Not on a date or anything. Just to eat.

Inspired, Halloran, Jack congratulated himself just before he spotted the weak link: Mel's boss.

That Bowen guy ought to be reported to Amnesty International—the jerk detained her till all hours.

Not that Jack accosted her in the kitchen anymore, but he sure as hell didn't go to sleep until he heard her coming upstairs.

"I've gotta do something about that, too," Jack muttered as the sitcom doofus'd its way through the predictable plot.

Tess, no doubt, would call him bossy and interfering; Sherry'd likely go with her usual sneer about the evils of caretaking.

But Jack figured he'd been nominated by marriage, so... Leaping from the chair, he jabbed the remote to cut off the TV. "What's the point of wasting time?"

Yeah. Action. That's what he needed.

And any excuse besides grocery shopping to get out of the house!

6

MEL DROPPED HER GLOVES into the disposal bin while Bowen continued reviewing Dan Blabbermouth's performance. Not very flatteringly.

Unlooping the mask she'd worn and pulling off the papery gown that covered her scrubs, Mel dropped them, too, into the bin. It would be her turn next.

The only good thing about getting reamed out now, she reflected as she exited the surgical suite behind the others, was that she was too damned tired to care.

They'd just finished seven hours of surgery. At this moment, all she wanted to do was flop on a gurney and be fed intravenously.

In front of her, Bowen and Dan turned left. A civilian peeled himself off the wall opposite the double doors. *Nice*-looking man, Mel thought, but the family waiting area was one corridor over.

Wait. *That's no* nice-*looking civilian, that's*—

"Jack?"

He came forward. Smiling warmly. At her. "Hi, Melinda!"

Mel's flagging energy quit flagging. Had to, with all the endocrine activity going on internally. Her temp flashed skyward, heading rapidly for the delirium zone.

If a smile could do that, what would actual contact cause? An embolism?

"Friend of yours, Dr. Burke?" Bowen dropped ol' Dan like a used surgical sponge and spun around; without a second's hesitation, the cowardly gossipmonger sped away. "Perhaps you'd care to introduce us."

Perhaps she'd care to leap off a highway overpass at rush hour, too.

"Uh, sure. Dr. Bowen, Jack Halloran. Jack, Dr. Leo Bowen."

The two men shook hands as briefly as possible. Jack, Mel noticed smugly, towered over her boss by a good eight or ten inches.

"Pleased to meet you, Dr. Bowen." Ha! Jack didn't *sound* very pleased.

"Pleasure's mutual, Mr. Halloran." Bowen's declaration didn't resonate convincingly, either. "I take it you're the new husband?"

Jack nodded while Mel smothered a smile at the idiocy of her own shocked reaction to the term. Only a she-geek would keep thinking of a man this commanding, this masculine as a wife. *Self-defense,* she pleaded silently. If Jack was the husband, that made her the wife. The nerdy Melinda Burke would be clueless about that role—or about how to handle having a husband like Halloran.

Shoot, she didn't even know how to handle him showing up at work.

"What, what are you doing here, Jack?" Mel asked, then realized she should have herded him away first. Damn her interpersonal ineptitude!

"Waiting for you, Burke," Bowen said, grimacing at having to explain the obvious to her. "The question is why?"

Jack blinked those dark blue eyes at her, then at her boss.

"I thought we could grab some dinner," he said finally, letting his gaze return to settle on Mel's face. "You hungry?"

For the warm concern floating in those incredible sapphire eyes and the erotic touch of that deep, husky voice? Hell, yes. She was *starving*.

"According to the lady out front, y'all were in there a long time."

Bowen shouldered Mel aside to stand toe-to-toe with Jack. "Surgical procedures take as long as they take," the program chief snapped. "We're not paid by the hour, you know."

Oh-oh. Jack's jaw was jutting. Not used to Bowen's hostility, Mel realized.

"Neither is Jack," she said in a rush. "He's a stockbroker. At least, he was. Now, he's…well, he's—"

Dammit. She couldn't recall the name of that test he was studying for. Some kind of financing…. "He's—"

An arm as hard as the titanium plates they'd screwed onto the skateboarding teen's shattered femur clamped around her waist. "I'm a lonely husband who's here to rescue his wife."

"Rescue, Mr. Halloran?"

Mel cringed. She'd heard Bowen called every name in the book, but nobody'd ever accused him of being slow on the uptake.

"From—?"

Without thinking, Mel wrapped her arms around Jack. *Wow, what a great fit,* the unoccupied part of her brain thought.

"From malnutrition," she supplied quickly, while that other brain part became feverishly occupied imagining how they'd fit together making love. "Jack thinks I don't eat right when I'm working and I guess he's all freaky 'cuz the stove doesn't work. But the microwave does, so there's really no reas—"

"Melinda's too dedicated for her own good," Jack said, mercifully cutting off her babbling. "These outrageous hours she works, skipping meals…. It's appalling the way she comes home dead on her—"

Now it was Mel's turn to disrupt the flow of babble. "Isn't he sweet?" She laughed brightly. "Being so concerned about my welfare." Weird, Bowen looked startled. Then…*embarrassed?*

Nah. She must be hallucinating.

"Somebody ought to be," Jack insisted. "Any fool

knows that your own health and well-being affect your job performance. And it's not like you're rotating tires here, you're patching up people.''

Uh-oh. Bowen looked ready to stroke out. *Intervene, Burke—now!*

''Oh, 'fess up, honey.'' Acting like some ditzy car-show bimbo, Mel poked her cutie's six-pack abdomen playfully. ''You're the one who's tired of frozen dinners, right? Hungry for something with real taste?''

Jack's hand captured hers, pressed it against the warm, hard flesh beneath his starched cotton shirt. His eyes darkened, which Mel hadn't even realized was possible. ''Damned right I am,'' he growled softly. His head bent toward hers.

''Now that you mention it, I could use some refueling, too,'' Bowen piped up just as their lips met.

Jack lifted his head, breaking physical contact, but kept his gaze on Mel's mouth.

Which felt exactly the way it had after the ceremony, when he'd actually kissed her. Hot and tingly, spreading delicious aching need through her interior like seismic waves.

After a moment as charged as one of those Russian delivery rockets lifting off for the International Space Station, Jack turned his attention to Dr. Bowen. ''Then don't let us keep you,'' he said with a faint smile.

When Bowen's eyebrows reached for his hairline, Mel wanted to groan, then just…slip into a nice coma or something. But after a second, he gave a little shrug.

''Tomorrow, Burke,'' he said, and walked away without another word.

Jack turned her in the opposite direction. ''I'm surprised he took the hint,'' he muttered. His arm still around her waist, he guided her down the sterile, nausea-green hallway under the harsh fluorescent lights.

Mmm, what a romantic place for a stroll, Mel thought dreamily.

No. That wasn't right.

Carefully detaching herself from Jack's embrace, Mel stalked onward, shaking herself mentally.

She was losing it! This morning, she'd awakened dreaming of being kissed—but lightly, on the temple. Wasting good dreamtime on chaste, preteen swoony stuff. And now, here she was getting all mushy about walking arm-in-arm with Jack down a hospital corridor.

What next, Burke? Ask him to the prom?

Nuts. She was too close to achieving her dream for such nonsense. She couldn't afford to start missing things she'd given up years ago. Like a social life. Physical intimacy. *All* that male-female stuff.

Mel knew that one false step could prove fatal at this point.

She doubted Bowen would take offense at tonight's rebuff, but rhino-skinned or not, the man delighted in his program's high dropout rate. He'd exploit any weakness he found to test his residents' dedication.

As the corridor ended in a T and she automatically turned right, Mel reminded herself that she'd have the rest of her life to make up for lost time. Years ahead of her to get out and meet people. Maybe get married for real someday, have a child…even learn how to tell for herself when a stove didn't work.

But for now, she needed to stay focused. Undistracted by navy eyes, a breathtakingly masculine body *or* concern for her welfare.

"I can see you're hungry," Jack said, catching up and letting his arm steal around her again. Damn, the man's touch drained all her willpower and determination. "But what for?"

The answer wasn't Chinese or Cajun or mac 'n' cheese.

The answer was a little human kindness. And a certain man's touch, his smile, some nonmedical conversation.

Mel looked at her watch. She had thirty minutes. *Why not?*

"If we hurry, we can get to the cafeteria before they quit serving supper entrées." For the next half hour, she could have her Jack and eat dinner, too.

"Cafeteria?" Jack halted his forward progress. And Mel's. "I was thinking more like one of the new places in Uptown. Or maybe the Enclave."

Someplace way more intimate, relaxing and upscale than some freaking hospital cafeteria.

The Enclave, of course, topped his list since it offered the greatest potential return on investment. As in, dancing. He figured a little vertical touching, twining and twisting might cure his obsession with the horizontal version.

Mel chuckled. "Good luck getting a table at one of those trendy places without a reservation." Moving onward, she turned left at the next hallway intersection.

Jack stared after her in dismay. She was right, dammit. How the hell had he forgotten that? Maybe he was exposing his brain cells—at least the ones that remembered how to date—to too many strong cleaning chemicals.

"And I'm due back in Recovery in thirty, anyway."

"What?" He hurried to catch up. It's not a date, he reminded himself. It's getting over his strange obsessive fascination with this woman. That's why a leisurely dinner in a conducive atmosphere was so important.

Mel pushed through a metal door and began descending stairs. Jack clattered behind her. "You have to go back to work? Tonight?" Unbelievable.

Unacceptable, too. If she didn't know the cost of this kind of work schedule, he did.

Without waiting for her answer, Jack double-clattered past her, then stopped at the next landing. Mel halted one step above it.

Looking straight into the soft green depths of her eyes, Jack recognized the irony of what he was about to say, but made a note to appreciate it on tape-delay. Right now, he had to make this woman who'd accepted—no, actively solicited—his caretaking understand just how much she needed it.

"Sweetheart…" Manfully he uttered The Phrase. The phrase normally delivered by females, the four words guaranteed to strike terror in the hearts of unsuspecting males. "We have to talk."

"Okay." She pushed past him. "But we've got three minutes to do it over dinner. Otherwise, we'll have to ingest our protein as eggs and *theirs* are runny."

Well, who was he not to be swayed by such a persuasive argument?

"Right. Lead on, babe."

THEY AVOIDED the runny ovoids with a minute-nineteen to spare, but—Jack examined the contents of his tray while the cashier rang it up—he wasn't so sure they'd gained much.

Mystery meat under glutinous white gravy. Green gelatin cubes. Corn bread so dry it crumbled when he lifted its plate from the service table.

Mel's selections looked equally unappetizing.

After paying for the "food," he threaded his way through a sea of mostly empty tables to join Melinda. Who nodded but remained silent as he offloaded his dishes and she doctored her salad with dressing packet glops.

Okay, Halloran. This was your idea, start your pitch.

"So that's your boss?"

Good choice, buddy. As an opening gambit, it only earned him another nod.

"Does he diss everybody who works for him or just you?"

Well, that got her attention.

Mel's head jerked up, sending her dark hair sliding back over her shoulder like a stream of chocolate syrup.

"He was actually pretty civil back there," she insisted.

Jack hardly heard her ridiculous claim. Too caught up in speculating how that shoulder would feel, naked beneath his fingertips. As silky as her hair? As smooth and creamy as the enticing curves of her back had looked?

Lifting and lowering the shoulder in question, Mel went on, "His concern is increasing our proficiency, not projecting joviality."

"Yeah, I got that," Jack said as he tried to cut through the breading on the mystery meat. "Your boss has the personality of pond scum."

Mel gave him one of her high-beam smiles. "Can't argue with you on that."

"But why do you have to go to wherever-that-was in a few minutes instead of coming home?" He wasn't whining, just implementing his brilliant plan to get to know the woman he'd married so he'd get over being attracted to or interested in her. Sort of like real spouses.

"After surgery, patients go to Recovery. It's an area near the OR suites, where they're monitored while they come out of the anesthetic."

Jack gave up sawing on the impenetrable breading. "I watch TV," he informed her. "What I meant was—why you?"

"Huh?"

Her soft, full lips almost distracted him from the dark circles under her eyes and the lousy food. Almost.

"Why isn't Bowen doing the monitoring?" Jack spelled it out slowly. "Or that other guy who came out with you? Why are you the one staying late, and coincidentally the one shoving down this ghastly stuff?" His fork encompassed every item on the table. Even the iced tea tasted bitter and powdery.

"I volunteered."

"You what?" Jack pushed aside his plate. "Come on, Melinda! Look, if it's me...if I'm the reason you stay here night and day, just tell me what I'm doing wrong. I'm not pestering you. I've got the bills caught up. I'm doing my best as far as the housework goes...."

Okay, he'd been studying some, too, but that was part

of the agreement. "I can do better," he admitted. Quit napping, for one thing. Cut back on the cooking shows. And limit the old geezers to fifteen minutes when they dropped by, instead of putting on a pot of coffee and letting them yak while they snacked him out of house and home.

"It's not you, Jack."

Man, he loved the sound of his name on her lips. He loved his lips on hers. He'd love his lips on...*her.*

Moron! What happened to his aversion-therapy program?

So far, it wasn't working worth squat.

"I intend to be the best pediatric surgeon Bowen has ever trained," Mel said quietly, but even he could hear the determination. "That means taking every opportunity to gain experience, to learn, to practice what I've learned."

"How much are you learning when you're asleep on your feet?"

Mel narrowed her eyes at him as she sat up straighter. "I'm not tired."

Somebody else might have bought it, but Jack knew better from personal experience. "Bull-oney. You're so exhausted you don't even feel it anymore."

One side of Mel's mouth quirked up. "Oh, I feel it," she assured him. "I just can't pander to it." She spread her hands palms up. "This is just part of the price you pay to be a doctor."

Jack sat back, crossed his arms over his chest. Mostly to keep from reaching for her. Plucking her out of her seat and carrying her off someplace private—especially if it contained something, anything resembling a bed big enough for two.

"Well, it's too high a price," he declared.

Mel shook her head. "No, it's not. *No* price is too high if I can save the lives of kids like Harry."

Her head stilled; her eyes met his. "Jack, try to understand. My dad's in the oil exploration business, so we moved around. A lot. Lived in towns one block long, in campers—once we spent months in a tent in the middle of nowhere, North Africa. Maybe that's why my little brother and I were so close.'' She gazed past him at something only she could see.

"Just before he turned six, Harry got…sickly. We were in a little town on the Alabama coast then. The only doctor available couldn't figure out what was wrong.''

Jack could see she was fighting back tears; he ached to gather her into his arms. To hold her. Even his desire to help his sister past her grieving couldn't hold a candle to how he felt about taking care of Melinda. Protecting her from all this pain and discomfort, from any hint of sorrow.

"So, didn't your parents take him to a bigger town? Another doctor?''

A tear spilled from each of those brimming green eyes and rolled unchecked down her cheeks. "Not soon enough. And the guy was a specialist, but not in pediatrics. Children aren't just small adults, you know. He operated on Harry, but…

"When they came out and told us he'd died on the table, I vowed then and there to do something useful with my life, so his wasn't wasted.'' Wadding up her paper napkin, Mel blotted the errant tears, then dropped it atop her barely eaten meal. "And that's what I'm doing. That's why I married you. Not to talk me into slacking off just as I'm about to achieve that goal.''

The woman had a great sense of timing, Jack admitted ruefully as he watched her move around the table in preparation for stalking off.

But if she expected to make such a dramatic speech and exit stage left without a peep out of him, then she bought that whole Easter Bunny thing, too.

In one move, Jack rose and stepped in front of her, leaving less than a centimeter between them. "You're seriously mistaken, Melinda,'' he purred, his hands curling around the shoulders made for them. "I'm not trying to discourage you. I'm trying to help. You need a more balanced life."

He stared down at Melinda. They were so close, almost touching. He could feel her breath on his neck, just above his collarbone.

He'd have to plead insanity for what came next. His fingers were kneading those soft, yielding shoulders. She made a low sound in her throat as her chocolate hair swept over his hands like satin fire.

He kissed her. Down to her tonsils. Right there in the deserted hospital cafeteria.

And if her pager hadn't gone off, he might have followed up with one of those movie moves: sweeping dishes off the table and laying her back, coming down over her....

But the pager buzzed. And either Jack let her go or Mel wrenched herself free.

Whatever, she took off like a jet-fueled dragster. Heading for the recovery room, he assumed.

Jack staggered off to recover, too. Melinda Burke might need some instruction on attaining balance in her life.

But she could give master classes on kissing. *And sign me up for a few.* As in, a few thousand.

Yeah, a few thousand of those kisses and he'd have Melinda right out of her clothes—

Jack shook his head to clear it. No, no kisses. No clothing removal. What he ought to be trying to get Melinda out of was his system.

Good luck, pal. There wasn't a shower icy enough to cool down the feverish desire she generated in him.

His usual practice of loving and leaving by mutual consent had hit a road bump, Jack realized as he wandered the rabbit warren of anonymous corridors in search of one leading to the hospital's parking garage.

Melinda was a whole new country. In her case, absence didn't make abstinence any easier. But intercourse required interaction. And why would Mel interact with a guy who tried to jump her bones almost every time he got near her?

So now he not only had to pry her away from her damned surgery fellowship, he had to reassure her he wasn't Jack the Ripper.

Only one sure way to accomplish that: the courtship thing.

Funny, the idea didn't seem as unpalatable as it always had in the past. In fact, he could picture himself and Mel as a couple.

Well, he could picture them coupling....

FORGET EVERYTHING that just happened, Mel advised herself as she stormed down to Recovery. The guy was well-meaning but misguided; his advice irrelevant. And his kiss—

Whew! Jack Halloran's kisses turned her to mush. Unfortunately, right now she was a doctor on duty, not a woman. She'd have to save the mushy business for later.

Mel flat-handed the gray metal door and walked into Postop.

One of the two nurses working there looked up from adjusting an IV drip. "You checking on Bowen's kid?"

"Yes. How's he doing?"

Dammit, she could practically hear Jack whispering, *See? Even the nurses think of him as Bowen's case. So why isn't* Bowen *here monitoring his patient's post-op progress?*

"BP's good and he's breathing well."

"Is he coming around yet?" Mel asked, crossing the room to reach the unconscious teen, taking his wrist to check his pulse. Strong and steady.

"Not that I've noticed," the nurse answered as he checked another patient. "Who did the anesthetic?"

"Kronsky."

Both nurses laughed. "Grab a magazine," the one

who'd hailed her advised. "Kronsky puts 'em under deep. Thinks she's doing the surgeons a favor."

Maybe she was, while they were in the operating room. But now... Mel looked at the big clock above the desk in the corner. Already after ten.

She'd be pulling her Cinderella act again. A yawn cracked her jaw. Jack was right about her putting in outrageous hours.

Not Bowen. He's probably home by now. Asleep.

Well, maybe she could sleep in one day soon. Weekends were generally a little slower. No morning rounds on Saturday, for one thing.

In fact, Mel realized suddenly as she tucked the boy's blanket around him, some Saturdays she didn't see Bowen until late afternoon.

The nurse turned around. "Dr. B.'s orders for the kid are in his chart."

"Brian," Mel said softly, looking down at the still-unconscious boy. "His name is Brian."

Picking up the chart, Mel flipped it open to scan the orders. No surprises. Monitor and update vitals. Report condition to family.

As she closed the chart, the nurse working the other side of the room said, "Oh! As he was leaving, Dr. Bowen said to tell you he wants someone—meaning one of you doctors, not a lowly nurse—to check the kid again at 7:00 a.m."

Mel clenched her pager, cursing silently. "Were those his exact words?" she asked. "Have *someone* check on Brian tomorrow morning?"

The male RN grinned and nodded. "Uh-huh, but he didn't use the boy's name."

The order-reciting nurse made a rude noise. "Because he didn't know it," she contributed. "Bowen never bothers with unimportant details like that."

"What do you mean?" Mel asked, before any inopportune professional etiquette discouraging gossip about colleagues could rear its ugly head.

"Leo Bowen's one of those old-fashioned surgeons," explained the male nurse, whose name tag read Jesse Ordonez. "You know, the kind who don't think of their patients as human beings."

"Yeah, they're just procedures to perform," the other nurse—Mary Chan—agreed as she came over and patted Mel on the shoulder. "Bowen doesn't remember his residents are humans, either. You have to remind him."

Nurse Ordonez laughed. "Right, but don't do it tomorrow. I heard he's scheduled to play golf with some neurosurgeons. I made the mistake of paging him once when I first started here. He was on the tenth hole. Putting. I almost lost my job." He shuddered in mock horror at the memory.

The two nurses went back to checking vital signs, joking about other doctoral quirks they'd observed over the years.

Mel stood there, looking down at Brian, the teenage skateboarder with more bravado than sense.

A sudden fury swept over her. She'd been killing herself—never letting up. Working 24/7 to keep up with her reading, to write precise, thorough and exhaustive reports, fill out the endless parade of hospital forms, do patient follow-up...while Bowen played golf!

She owed Jack an apology.

After checking Brian again, Mel went over to the wall phone, snatched up the receiver and paged ol' Blabbermouth. She owed him something, too.

As for herself...

Jack was gonna find a little note on the coffeemaker when he came down in the morning.

The doctor would be sleeping in. Maybe even as late as six o'clock.

The sheer rebelliousness of the decision made her dizzy. Or was that fatigue? Or the lingering aftereffects of a kiss so astonishing, so incapacitating, it made an F-5 tornado feel like a soft spring breeze?

JACK RAKED HIS HAIR. Glared viciously at the clock, then back at the note.

That was the real problem with 4:30, he reflected. There was nobody else awake if you needed to vent.

Nice that Mel had seen the light after their discussion last night, but an extra hour in the sack wouldn't give her the balanced life she needed.

Too restless to go back to bed, too sleepy for TV, Jack parked at the breakfast table.

He tried to focus on Mel's imbalanced life and what he could do about it for her, but he could swear he heard tapping. Now what? he wondered. Aural hallucinations, or another appliance getting ready to give up the ghost?

No, that was definitely tapping. At the kitchen door.

Jack strode over and wrenched it open. Felt his jaw sag.

"Bob?"

The old man from across the street grinned apologetically. "I know. It's too early for a social call, but...I saw your light on. 'Severything okay over here?"

"Oh, yeah. Just fine, thanks." Jack smothered a sigh and started to close the door. When the oldster's face fell, he reversed the motion, inviting Bob in. "Want some coffee?" he asked. Might as well shoot the breeze with the senior till it was time to rouse Mel. Better than sitting here confused, frustrated and...frustrated.

Within minutes, Bob was happily slurping coffee and accepting Jack's offer to pop a frozen waffle in the toaster, since he'd finally learned how to not turn the rectangles into charcoal briquettes.

"Got a partiality for blueberry muffins," geezer Bob said a minute later, while he drowned the waffle in syrup and dug in.

"I'll make a note of that," Jack promised dryly. "In case the repairman ever returns to fix the blankety-blank range."

He'd swear the old man's ears actually perked up. "Say what? Your stove still don't work?"

Anything to break his obsession with Mel. Jack spilled the whole sorry Lenny story.

"Told you 'bout those sanctimonious service guys, didn't I?" Bob crowed, then jabbed his fork in Jack's direction. "Joe Donaldson's the man you oughta call," he said as seriously as an SEC regulator. "He retired from Big D's Appliance World. Likes to keep his hand in. Wouldn't charge you an arm and a leg, neither."

Taking a small notepad and ballpoint from his shirt-pocket, ol' Bob scribbled down a phone number, ripped off the sheet and handed it to Jack. "Joe lives a block over. He'll be glad to come over 'n see what he can do—his wife's always wanting him out from under-foot."

Repocketing his writing tools, the oldster mopped up syrup with the last piece of waffle. "It ain't easy on us old coots, just sitting around. A man likes to feel useful, ya know?"

Jack nodded absently. Yeah, he knew. He looked at the scrawled number. What the heck. If Joe wasn't the genius Bob thought he was, Lenny could fix whatever the retiree messed up—if he ever showed up.

Meanwhile, the term "asset reallocation" floated through Jack's head. Less time on the house equaled more time to solve the Mel-balance problem, right?

"Any of you 'old coots' work on pool pumps?" He'd detected the reason for the green water, but after the Lenny experience had hesitated cold-calling a phone book listing.

Ol' Bob nodded happily. "Right next door. Preston St. Clair. Used to own a pool company. An' if you want some help takin' the dead limbs off that tree out front, Charlie Rodriguez's your man."

"Give me their numbers, too," Jack said as he got up to refill Bob's coffee. Was the whole neighborhood retired and hot to do odd jobs? Why didn't they play golf? Or cruise around in RVs or whatever old people did?

Well, if they showed up and got the job done…
"How much do you guys charge?" he asked. Couldn't
be more than Lenny.

"Why? You need to check this out with the little lady
first?" Bob asked with a funny expression. Oh, he was
eyeing the toaster.

Jack snorted as he heated another waffle. "The little
lady—I mean, Mel—doesn't care what I do or how I
do it."

"She said that?" At Jack's nod, it was Bob's turn to
snort. "And you believed her? You *are* new at this,
aren't ya?"

Well, yes, he was. "So what? I'm the houseperson
around here. I don't have to ask her permission," Jack
warned the self-proclaimed old coot.

"Heck no," Bob agreed. "But women don't think
the way we do. That's why ya gotta be…subtle, ya
know? Best way to handle 'em is to make 'em think
whatever it is, it's their idea."

"What? Aw, come o—"

The geezer cut Jack off. "Come on yourself, son.
You ever told your woman somethin' she didn't want
to hear? Did she listen? Hell no." He answered his own
questions.

"Women're wired different, son. So we gotta learn
different ways t'deal with 'em."

After a third waffle and the rest of the coffee, the
wizened know-it-all finally went home.

Thoughtfully, Jack made a new pot of coffee.

Bob's view of females sounded a tad outdated, but…

The direct approach to Mel and her brutal work
schedule had been about as successful as fortifying cereal with baloney.

So maybe Bob had a point. Think different.

A brilliant plan leaped fully formed into Jack's brain.
A *genius* of a plan. He smiled at this latest proof of
restored creativity. Quitting work to stay home was the
smartest move he'd made in years.

"Oh! I didn't know you were up." Mel's cloud-soft voice came from the doorway.

She'd tied her hair back in a ponytail, but the robe she wore dipped low enough in front to taunt him with the cleavage it revealed that it concealed. His hands ached to slo-owly push aside that soft peach material...to stroke those smooth creamy breasts...to take their weight in his palms...to rub his thumbs over Mel's nipples and feel them grow as taut with arousal as he already was.

Jack wrenched his gaze from Melinda and looked at the clock. Just after 5:30.

"It's too early to be up," he said, taking a deep breath. Trying to think, not imagine. No luck. Before the oxygen reached his brain, he blurted, "Where we need to be, Mel, is back in bed."

7

"TOGETHER?" Oh, that sounded good…!

No, it didn't. Mentally, Mel ka-whammed herself upside the head. Where were these wild thoughts coming from?

"Of course not."

Jack's quick answer confirmed her ka-wham.

"Of course not," Mel echoed. No doubt she was the only one around here interested in something more. Like consensual conjugal congress.

And she'd better get over it. Quick. Unless she wanted to scare off the best thing that had ever happened to her.

Clean underwear. That's what she meant. Not a great-looking, genuinely caring male whose physical presence seemed to rev her female hormones into high gear.

"I need some coffee," she declared, aiming herself at the cabinet holding the mugs instead of the man she wanted to hold her. Touch her the same intense way he kissed her.

Whoa. Jack was right. Working so much *was* affecting her. Like being frightened affected the adrenal system.

"What you need is a day off," Jack corrected her as if he could read her mind while he shouldered her aside to grab the mug and fill it with freshly brewed java.

Maybe he was right about that, too. A little time off to clear her head of these crazy ideas about him and her.

"Do something different," he suggested. "Get some fresh air. It'll give you a whole new perspective."

Talk about sounding good....

Reality crashed in. "Can't." Blabbering Dan hadn't answered his page, so she had to do the follow-up Dr. Bowen had ordered on Brian. *While he plays golf.*

Jack *is* right, she realized as hot caffeine slid down her throat. *Everybody else is finding a way to have a life. Even Bowen.*

"At least...not today."

"When, then?" Jack grabbed a waffle box off the counter, upended it and shook it. Nothing happened. With a muttered curse, he stuffed the box into the trash.

Why's he getting all stressed? Mel wondered. *Afraid I'll disrupt his secret life of leisure if I'm around for a few hours?*

"I don't kn—"

"What would you like to do?" The question came out muffled: Jack had his head deep in the freezer while he rooted around for something.

"Well, I don't kn—"

"Aha!" He waved a box of pancakes around like an athlete hoisting some big trophy. Tearing it open and plating a couple, he programmed the microwave, then poured a glass of juice and directed her to sit.

"Plenty to do in the Metroplex," he continued, leaning on one hand near the nuker. "I know!" he exclaimed. "Six Flags just opened—we'll go there. Then do dinner and a movie."

Mel's blood froze. "But, but that would be—" *Like a date,* she finished silently. Appalled. Mostly at how much she wanted to—when she knew how much of a disaster it would be. She hadn't been on a real date in years. Talk about a fish out of water! More like completely off the planet.

"We're married, Melinda," Jack pointed out gently.

"Married people can go places together. It's in the fine print," he added with a teasing purr.

But this wasn't a teasing matter. As limited as their contact might be, it meant a lot to Mel. Too much to risk screwing up by enhanced exposure.

Better he think she's a workaholic than a pathetic loser. "No. We...we can't, that's all."

Jack got a strange look on his face. His jaw jutted.

Mel braced herself for some domineering macho pronouncement, but "Your pancakes are ready" was all he said.

So she ate the round breakfast products—stuffing down her disappointment at his easy capitulation with every bite. Trying to ignore the male heat coming off his body as he sat watching her. Scowling faintly.

It occurred to her as she swallowed juice that he could be taking her refusal to go out with him personally. Misinterpretation seemed to be a male hobby. It was certainly easier than paying attention and thinking.

"It's not that I wouldn't like to," Mel said, trying to make the truth sound like a lie trying to sound like the truth.

Aargh! This male-female interacting got convoluted faster than Bowen found fault. "I thought about what you said last night...." Only between reliving that stellar cafeteria kiss over and over! "And you're right—I could use a little time off, but you're busy."

"So?"

"So I don't expect you to keep me company."

She could grab a bite and go to a movie by herself and enjoy it, couldn't she?

Mel scooped pancake onto her fork and delivered it to her esophagus. Normally, she'd noticed, food tasted better with Jack's company, but this morning the cooked batter tasted like packing pellets. "You've got better things to do."

"Like?"

"I don't know—sleep? Study? Take a bubble bath? Wait for Godot the repairman."

He twinkled those sapphire eyes at her and instantly she lost her train of thought, dammit. Oh. Yeah. Better things to do.

Oh, *yeah*, she could think of a few! None of which were solitary pursuits.

Downing the last of the juice, Mel pushed back her chair. "Thanks for breakfast. I can't tell you how much I appreciate everything you do for me. I'll call when I know how late I'll—"

"Mel."

Oh, God! The way he was looking at her—heat simmering in his sapphire eyes. She wanted to crawl up in his lap, nuzzle his neck, open her mouth for one of his hypersensual kisses and return the favor to the best of her ability.

"You remember my sister?"

She didn't remember *anybody's* sister at the moment. Oh. "T-Tess?"

Jack nodded, the little strand of cowlick hair wiggled—and Mel felt swoonier than ever. "She's become a hermit since Pete...well, it's not healthy." For some reason, he was speaking to either the napkin holder or the salt shaker in the center of the table. "I'm worried about her."

Now he lowered his gaze to his lap. A destination Mel's optic nerve centers would enjoy perusing, too. "I've been trying unsuccessfully to coax her out of that apartment, but..."

He shared a sly look with one of the kitchen machines whose purpose Mel had never grasped. "If she thought it was for somebody else's benefit..."

Good thing the guy liked financial planning; he'd starve as a double agent. "You mean, we invite her somewhere and tell her I won't go unless she comes along?"

Mel bit her lip when Jack nodded, obviously pleased with his clumsy manipulation.

She was beginning to think men weren't some strange species after all, just simple-minded women with optional equipment below the belt.

"Okay," she said, putting her dishes in the sink before heading upstairs to dress for work. Tess knew her brother even better than Mel did; let her see through him and say no. Or say yes, thus giving Mel an opportunity to relax, enjoy Jack's company and attempt the art of casual conversation—with the help of a nice woman who might become a friend. "I'll try to get half a day off next week."

What would she rather do with some free hours? Mel wondered as she donned black pants. Sleep or be with Jack and his sister?

Pulling on a lavender tee she thought used to be long sleeved and hip length but now sported three-quarter sleeves and barely covered her waist, she told her raging-hormonal self to chill on the alternate leisure activity it championed: sleeping with Jack.

A foolish idea. A tantalizing fantasy.

About as likely as Leo Bowen praising her surgical technique.

"DAMMIT, TESS!" Jack yelled—er, pleaded. "I'm begging you." A basket holding four gallons of milk and two screaming toddlers zoomed past him.

He raised an eyebrow at the speeding mom, but continued scanning the shelves of snack crackers and cookies.

Aha. Jack snagged a box of graham crackers. He'd discovered that Mel liked them with peanut butter, so now he put a little sack of peanut butter on grahams and an apple in her purse every morning. Otherwise, she'd drop in at a Stop & Shop on the way to or from work, buy a Moon Pie and claim she'd eaten.

He'd caught on to that when he'd taken her car in to get the oil changed the day after she'd agreed to try to take some time off, which so far—three days later—she hadn't "remembered" to schedule. The kid changing the oil had joked about all the wrappers he'd found when he'd cleaned the car's interior.

Another little known aspect of the housewife's job description: must be part detective, part psychologist and part saint. "Come on, Tess. Help me out here."

"Help you out?" his sister squawked.

Jack dropped the crackers into his basket and passed a lady who ducked her head as he rolled by. Ha. *Cookie junkie!* He gave her an Elvis lip twitch and she scurried away. But she'd be back. He knew it, she knew it.

"Forget it! I'm not falling for another of your *pathetic* ploys to trick me into a blind date!"

Holding the phone away from his face, Jack shot it a look of disbelief. Here he was, just trying to be helpful, caring, considerate, and this was the grief he caught?

"It's not a ploy, Tess." Well, yes, it was. But it was diabolically clever, not pathetic! "And I promise, no dates—blind or otherwise. Just you and me dragging Melinda off and giving her something to look at, do and think about besides the messed-up insides of little kids."

"Why?"

"Because she works too—"

"No, idiot-boy. Why drag me into it?"

Negotiations had reached a delicate phase. Seeking privacy, Jack turned down the first deserted aisle he came to. Good—just him, lightbulbs and motor oil.

"Because she won't go unless she thinks we're doing it for you." He sighed. It shouldn't be so hard to get people to do what was good for them, even if it was the last thing they felt like doing.

"Why? Is the honeymoon over?" Tess asked.

Never got started. But Jack was too smart to spill that tidbit, especially to his sister.

"You two aren't having problems, are you?"

Dammit. He sensed some leverage there, but all this subtle intrigue made his head spin worse than single-premium variable annuities did.

Calling on every particle of noble character and self-control he possessed, Jack growled, "None of your beeswax, Sis! But I figure it wouldn't hurt to spend a little time together on neutral ground. So are you gonna help me or not?"

"Oh, okay," Tess said. *Grudgingly!* After all he'd done for her. "I'll be your co-conspirator—but only to protect poor Melinda from your steamrolling."

Wounded by the unfounded accusation—he never steamrolled!—Jack shook his head as he resumed shopping. There was something he needed from sundries…toothpaste, that was it.

"…your plan?"

Huh? Oh. "Well, I want her out in the fresh air, out of pager range and thoroughly distracted. I'm open to suggestions, but a neighbor's wife mentioned a giant flea market, east of Dallas somewhere."

"A flea market?"

"I think that's what she said." Flea market, flea circus. Who cared? As long as he got to be with Mel and she got to see him taking care of her.

He could practically hear Tess drumming her fingers as she considered the idea. No, that was somebody tapping the store mike. Alerting shoppers to an impending announcement about the usual special on fried chicken from the deli. Which Jack dared anyone to reheat without turning it into rubber chew toys.

"Do you mean the Canton First Monday Trade Days?"

How did women know these things? Jack wondered as he picked up a carton of orange juice, then exchanged it for one with calcium. Mel needed all the nutritional assistance he could give her. "That's it. So you're on-board?"

"Sounds like fun. When are we going?"

"Depends on Mel. It's held the four-day weekend before the first Monday of every month. I'll call you if she takes off one of those days. And when I do, just play along, okay?"

Jack thought Tess muttered something about an imbecile and his double-helix twisted plot, but it was probably a glitch in the cell reception.

"Play along?" Tess barked, her tone threatening renewed resistance. "How?"

"Back up my story." Jack double-parked at the bread. "Pretend you don't really want to come."

"Well, I don't!"

Selecting a loaf loaded with healthy nuts and twigs, Jack grinned as he rolled it off his fingertips into the basket. "So see? You won't even have to lie."

ONCE SHE'D DECIDED to do it, fortune smiled on Mel. Bowen announced a three-day absence the following week for a conference in Belize. Simmons's wife had just informed him she was pregnant again, so he volunteered to take Mel's shift in the Pediatric Screening Clinic on the Bowen-less Thursday.

"Don't rush into motherhood, Burke," he advised glumly. "Having kids is unbelievably expensive."

She wouldn't know. Too busy feeling like one herself.

Like a kid at Christmas. Forget an afternoon—she had a whole day off! The evening, too, if she wanted. With Jack.

And his sister.

Which was okay. Safer. Mel wasn't sure she trusted herself to be alone with her spouse. *Just me, Jack and my feminine side—locked and loaded?* A recipe for disaster. Especially if she was the only partner wanting to get closer than cloth allowed.

"SORRY TO BOTHER YOU again, Mrs. P." Jack cradled the phone between his neck and shoulder, squinting at the recipe card he held. "But now it says 'knead until smooth and elastic.'"

A minute later, Jack thanked the woman for her clarification and hung up, pretending not to hear her laughing at his expense.

Thanks to Joe Donaldson, he now had a functioning stove capable of producing home-cooked meals. Tonight, he'd be wowing Mel with meat loaf, smashed potatoes from a box and—ta-da!—homemade bread.

The phone rang just as his hands sank into the dough. He let the machine get it while he squished more flour into the sticky mixture.

"Hey, Halloran, it's Sher. Call me. I want a status report on the joys of married life." *Sardonic snicker.* "Oh! You don't happen to know anything about ceiling fans, do you? Mine's weirding out on me and Maintenance can't get to it for weeks. Later."

When he finished kneading the dough—at least, he thought he was finished, although what elastic flour paste looked like, who knew?—Jack consulted the recipe again, then put the blob in a greasy bowl, covered it with foil and "put it in a warm place to rise." The warmest place he could find was the cement apron ringing the pool.

Which Preston had back in pristine condition. That clear blue water looked inviting.

While he waited for the dough to double in size, he called ol' Bob and set up a time for him to fix Sherry's fan.

Heading back into the den to pick up where he'd left off with bond ratings bases, Jack considered the significance of that exchange.

He stood at the nexus of a cheap, reliable supply of help and an endless demand for it. It didn't take Financial Planner Certification to figure out that somebody should take advantage of the situation. But how, exactly?

The phone rang again. Jack snatched it up. "What?" he snarled at whatever telemarketer was disturbing his peace this time.

"J-Jack?"

"Melinda! Sorry. I thought you were calling about siding or had a truck on my street." Through sheer force of will, he made himself shut up. "How are you?" he asked, trying to sound sane, when just hearing her breathe made him nuts. He couldn't remember even his first crush hitting him as hard as she did.

"Busy." Icicles hung from both syllables. "I just...I've got next Thursday off."

Mel had no idea what response she expected. Not the "Fantastic!" she got. It made her feel so warm and giddy, she smiled at a passing administrator, who of course looked shocked and scurried away.

"What time can you get home tonight?" Jack asked eagerly. Mel got warmer, giddier. "I want to call Tess when you're here," he explained, dashing her silly adolescent hopes to microscopic shards. "In case I need you to substantiate my li—er, story. She's a suspicious broad," he added peevishly.

Summoning her professional persona, Mel answered coolly, "I'll try to be home before ten."

Another "Fantastic!" followed by a purring promise, "There'll be a surprise waiting for you."

With a muttered curse word, Mel crashed the receiver onto its cradle. She had an appendix to remove in ten minutes; she couldn't be mooning around, imagining, in a profoundly erotic manner, the nature of Jack's surprise.

Next Thursday's expedition—*not* date—was becoming increasingly necessary. She *had* to get over her obsession with her husband!

"HEY, TESS, how's it going?" Jack smiled at Mel as he played out his side of the phone call.

"So, are we on?"

"Good, good. Work okay?"

"Skip the BS," Tess snapped. "I'm in the middle of a show."

"That's great. Say...I was wondering if I could interest you in a proposition."

"Absolutely not! First Monday, you and Mel. That was the deal."

"Well, you see, I've finally browbeaten Mel into going to Canton on Thursday. But she'd like you to go with us."

"What time?"

Jack covered the mouthpiece to address his audience. "She's hesitating," he whispered. "What should I say?" Without waiting for Mel's answer, he withdrew his hand and spoke coaxingly into the phone. "She's really looking forward to getting to know her sister-in-law. Please don't disappoint her."

"This is ridiculous," Tess said. "When should I be ready?"

"Pretty please?"

His sister used a word forbidden in the Halloran childhood home.

"Great, great," Jack said, pretending he'd persuaded his sister at last. "How about if we pick you up about nine?"

He turned his back on Mel, to block the dial tone, and kept talking. "Oh, just wear something comfortable.... Yes, she's looking forward to spending time with you, too. Okay, Tess. Bye-bye."

Turning around again in time to see his spouse dispose of her bread into the trash can, he faked oblivion.

The dough hadn't doubled in the hot sun. It hadn't risen a bit. He'd baked it anyway—and ended up with a brick. He'd only served it as proof he did things around here.

"She fell for it?" Mel asked.

Jack nodded. Dammit, he did work hard. Unfortunately, most of what he did got undone immediately or was otherwise unnoticeable. No wonder women jumped into the corporate trenches seeking power and recognition. Didn't appeal to him anymore—been there, done that—but he could see the attraction of tangible, external rewards.

"Good. Well...thanks for dinner, Jack. The meat loaf's wonderful!" Mel disrupted—and disproved—his thoughts with her velvet-voiced praise.

Face it, Mel in any format disrupted his thinking. He couldn't concentrate on squat when she was around. And when she wasn't, her clothes were. Her childhood pictures. All the symbols of her dreams and drives—the drives that threatened to overwhelm her. The dreams that had brought them together. Except they weren't. Which was why he spun so many fantasies about her.

This flea market trip couldn't happen soon enough for Jack. He needed to get to know the real, true, actual Melinda Burke. Then she wouldn't bother him anymore. Hot-and-bother him, that is. Like he'd never been hot and bothered before.

THURSDAY ARRIVED about as quickly as campaign-financing reform.

Jack let Mel sleep until seven. Just as he was about to take her coffee upstairs, she showed up at the breakfast table in a pair of long legs—er, shorts and a barely sleeved shirt he must have overdried because it clung like skin to...well, her skin, clearly outlining her world-class luscious curves in the process.

Jack poured her some OJ; he missed the glass by a

good five inches. After wiping up the mess, he mumbled something about neighbor assignments and disappeared.

While she ate her egg taco—were those reddish-brown specks cinnamon?—Mel wondered if she should change. Her clothes, that is. Too late to change her personality. But what did one wear to a giant flea market?

After breakfast, Mel fled upstairs to brush her teeth, fighting a losing battle against the nervous anticipation that filled her insides.

She could cut open a child's chest and repair his or her heart, but she couldn't think of a single thing to say to her husband...wife...*whatever* during the twenty-minute trip to Tess's apartment.

At least Jack's sister appeared to be ready to enjoy herself. She sat in the back of the Jeep trading stories with him about their misspent youth. Stories that revealed as much mutual affection as mischief.

Mel simply listened, breathed non-hospital air and watched the scenery and the other traffic—gambling buses headed for Shreveport, NAFTA trucks and... "Why are there so many boats being towed?" she asked.

"Lots of lakes around here," Jack replied as he passed a van packed with kids. They waved, Mel waved back. Out of the corner of her eye, she saw Jack wave, too.

For some undoubtedly foolish reason, warmth rippled through her at his gesture. The heat loosened her tongue and she took a stab at prolonging the conversation.

"Are they fishing lakes or waterskiing?"

"Mostly fishing, I think," Jack said.

Tess added, "You know skiers though—they'll try it anywhere."

If "it" involved Jack's mostly bare body covered with glistening water droplets, Mel thought, she'd sign up with the skiers. *Chill, Burke.* This was a G-rated outing, remember.

"We, ah, we used to go fishing," she blurted. "My dad, my brother and me."

They'd had fun, too.

"Your mother didn't fish?" Jack asked, nodding as Tess tapped him on the shoulder and pointed to the exit sign.

Mel laughed. "No, she'd stay home and read or do needlepoint. She said the only good way to catch a fish was on a plate brought by a waiter."

There was a moment of silence at that boring bit of information. *Lame-O!* Mel berated herself. She'd never get this conversation thing.

"Jerk," Jack muttered to a semi barreling past. Then as he signaled and changed lanes, he said, "Those pillows in the formal living room—your mom made those?"

Ten minutes later, as Jack followed the signs from the interstate to a huge and already highly packed gravel parking area, they were still talking.

We're having a real conversation! Mel grinned at her ridiculous sense of accomplishment. She and Jack were actually chatting about something other than laundry and broken appliances.

"Y'ALL READY?" Jack asked as they piled out of the car. They joined the crowd of people streaming toward a huge open-air pavilion area containing what seemed to Mel to be hundreds of booths selling everything from hand-painted duster coats to "miracle" cleaning products to homemade candy to eight-track tapes.

In addition to a second large outdoor area, they discovered, there were two buildings, too, that contained sales booths. "And don't miss the civic center," someone advised when they'd made their first rest stop. "That's where the antiques and such are."

And apparently, there were more acres of unofficial flea market on the north edge of town.

"Let's check out the rest of this place first," Jack suggested as they wandered through the second pavilion.

Mel nodded politely, continuing to feign curiosity. Her feigning had begun the minute they'd entered the first Trade Days Pavilion and Jack had put his arm around her. She'd been so busy reveling in his touch, she'd lost all interest in the merchandise and the crowd surrounding them.

And not one person had pointed and jeered. Or snatched them apart and ordered her back into her normal role as dedicated Loner Doc/Bowen's Bashee.

Today she was just another woman strolling with her man through bright May sunshine, along row after row of merchandise, most of which seemed destined for future individual garage sales.

"Thank you, Jack," she said, halting between a T-shirt display and a fresh-squeezed lemonade stand. She knew she ought to explain her gratitude, but his dark blue eyes were gazing into hers and words…words just failed her.

Jack's mouth curved in a gentle, sexy smile that seemed to say he understood all she couldn't express verbally. He pulled her closer.

"Tess! Is that you?" Mel heard a male voice say somewhere in the haze beyond her and Jack.

She found herself teetering, her balance upset by Jack's abrupt removal—of his embrace and his attention. She grabbed at the nearest stationary object. Unfortunately, it was a plastic bucket perched on the corner of the lemonade wagon. A bucket filled with lemons.

Reflexes and her trauma-rotation training came into play: Mel managed to catch three of the lemons in midair. As she scrambled after the rest of the rolling citrus, Jack—who'd dropped her like last year's boy band the second Tess's name had been called—joined the salvage efforts. Physically, at least.

Squatting, he scooped up yellow fruit without taking his eyes off his sister and the guy who'd hailed her, a tall, dark-haired man accompanied by a young girl.

Mel apologized to the lemonade vendor and continued collecting the escaping citric inventory.

Real smooth, Burke, she told herself. She guessed she could add klutz to her list of reasons why Jack seemed more interested in acting like a Doberman on his sister's behalf than in kissing the woman he'd married. Obviously, Jack remembered she was no ordinary woman. And no wife. No way.

As a wake-up call, it ought to help her remember why losing her focus on her professional goals—throwing away all those years of hard work for a possible broken heart—would be a totally boneheaded move.

Tess, meanwhile, was looking puzzled, then surprised, then pleased.

"Dale? Dale Reilly?" Absently handing Mel a recaptured lemon, she stepped around her brother to greet the man who'd called her name. "Oh my gosh!"

Mel was standing close enough to Jack to hear him growl when his sister hugged the other man. She also saw the little girl with the newcomer raise her eyebrows, then grimace.

Tess introduced the man as an old friend she'd lost track of; then commenced the reconnection dance. Where are you living now? What are you doing jobwise?

Inevitably, the subject of spouses arose. Dale was divorced.

"What about you?" he asked Tess.

Jack's growl became louder. Mel put a hand on his arm; he shook it off. Gave her a "you don't understand" look and opened his mouth to deflect the man's nosy, insensitive question.

"Oh, be quiet, Jack," Tess said sweetly before telling Dale that she was a widow.

I'm gonna rip his head off, Jack thought when the jerk asked for details. He cleared his throat as menacingly as possible. "She'd rather not talk about it," he informed Doofus Dale.

Tess turned on him. "No, you'd rather I don't talk about it. You can't grasp that I loved Pete too much to pretend he never happened."

"I'm trying to spare you painful memories," Jack retorted while Mel and Dale looked uncomfortable but stood their ground. Dammit. He appealed to Melinda, "I swear, I don't get it, do you? If losing him hurts so much for so long, why fall in love in the first place?"

They were beginning to draw a crowd. Jack didn't care. He planted his fists on his hips and glowered at...somebody. Anybody. Everybody.

His crazy sister just looked at him. *Sorrowfully?* "You really don't get it, do you? I thought...when I saw you and Mel at your wedding, I thought you'd finally understand." Tess shook her head. "It isn't love that hurts, Jack, it's life. Life is painful sometimes. Love is what makes the pain bearable."

The bystanders drifted away, losing interest when the shouting stopped.

Jack remained perplexed, but gave up on discussing the subject—whatever it was—here and now.

Dale's kid tugged on her father's sleeve. "Dad? You promised."

"Okay, honey," the guy told his daughter, but his eyeballs still targeted Tess. So did his next sentence. "I promised Carrie she could spend her birthday money here, but what she wants to buy..."

"All my friends have one," the kid insisted.

Shyly, but immediately, Tess offered to mediate. Smiling at Dale the whole time, like some preteen getting goofy over the latest boy band.

Look, he was glad his sister was acting interested in something, okay, someone other than her late husband, but an insensitive jerk like Dale wasn't what he'd had in mind.

"I don't think—" Jack began.

"Darling!" Mel cried, dragging him away to a deserted area behind an unoccupied booth before a fistfight broke out.

"Hey, I was just try—" Jack didn't get another syllable out.

Desperate to distract him, Mel obliterated the rest of his sentence with a kiss that halted all higher brain function involving distant relatives.

He started to pull away, but Mel's lips moved beneath his. Her tongue penetrated his mouth and began contradancing with his. Jack's mental activities suddenly descended to pure primitive level. *Melinda...taste her.*

Reluctantly parting company with hers, his tongue found her ear and flicked erotically over its delicate whorls. From there, he nuzzled his way past her velvety lobe, down the side of her neck, then traced the little hollow above her breastbone.

Touch her.

"Ja—"

Get the damned clothes off....

His fingers worked buttons free, then slipped along the lacy edge of her bra, then inside. The smooth roundness of one perfect breast filled his palm. *Mmm. Made for each other....*

Then he was stroking, kneading, kissing her breasts, his mouth wetting the nipples, his warm breath shivering over her sensitive skin as he sighed, "Ah, Mel, you're perfect."

"Jack."

Who cares name...?

Mel moaned softly.

Jack stilled, then gently drew back his hand.

"'Sokay," she whispered. "We're alone here."

"I'm sorry," Jack stammered, slowly coming to his

senses. "I...I didn't mean to get so carried away." This wasn't some casual pick up. This was Mel. His wife. A woman he respected.

Jack looked down at Mel's blouse, half-unbuttoned. Her lips were pink and puffy. A tiny pulse beat rapidly in her neck.

Better cool it. No sense making things awkward between us.

He turned away to give Mel time to pull herself together while they both recovered from...whatever had just happened.

Mel had dragged him into this private little oasis and kissed him, that's what. Man, had she kissed him!

What was it with him and her? One touch of her lips to his, one caress of her beautiful, satiny breasts and he torched like C-5 explosive detonating an oil refinery. No woman had ever aroused him so fast, so hard, so often—not even when he was seventeen and the very letters *s-e-x* could set him off.

"No, I'm the one who should apologize," Mel said, softly adding, "probably," as she slid the last button into place and turned to leave.

"Wait! Where's Tess?" he demanded as Mel began walking away. Some caretaker he was. He'd misplaced his own sister!

"I'm sure she'll be along in a minute," Mel said calmly over her shoulder. She looked as cool as she sounded. Cool, contained and completely unaffected by what had just transpired between them.

He didn't know whether to accept the inherent challenge or breathe a sigh of relief at his close escape from that kiss taking him and Mel to a deeper level.

Tess's earlier statement echoed through his head. *"Love is what makes pain bearable."* But love involved commitment. Real commitment. Long-term commitment. And that was what made you vulnerable to the kind of pain his sister now suffered.

He didn't want to go there, did he? Jack wasn't sure...except of one thing: Melinda was the only woman who'd ever made it look tempting.

"I'm starving," Mel announced stiffly as she led the way down the narrow alleyway between two booths and back into the open, public area, where a minute later, Tess joined them. "Let's get something to eat and then I want to buy a souvenir."

The two women linked arms and headed for the nearest food-vending area, on the hunt for gummy nachos. Jack followed, mentally reconstructing himself, downplaying the effect Melinda Burke had on his male physiology.

But she did affect him. And one of these days, he decided, they should explore the full extent of that effect. Taste, touch and take each other. Listen to their hearts beat in rhythm. Feel their bodies melt together.

But not before he had this whole commitment, love, pain thing worked out in his head.

8

MEL BOUGHT a pair of peanut shell earrings, hand decorated with bluebonnets, then shellacked to a high shine. A silly souvenir for a silly day.

That's all it was.

That's what she told herself, anyway. Trying to be sensible, objective, logical.

Failing spectacularly. Face it, she wanted Jack—all of him. Maybe she hadn't dated half the population of Plano, but even she knew that few kisses—few *kissers*—actually shorted out the kissee's neural activity.

Jack's kiss did. Not to mention what his touch did to her. And not just physically.

It was the other ways Jack affected her—when he wasn't even present—that concerned her. Difficulty concentrating—never on patients, but some of her billing sheets got kicked back these days.

Occasional irritability, too. Especially during the week following their day in Canton. Because, aside from that toe-sizzling interlude behind the booths, Jack had pointed out a hundred different hobbies and interests turned into part-time businesses.

Mel got his point: there were lots of ways to spend your time. And that, even if one could, maybe it wasn't *good* to work at life-and-death stress levels all the time.

She'd concede that seeking balance was as desirable as more caresses from her spouse.

But Mel knew one thing about balance: it couldn't be found anywhere under Bowen's supervision. The two short—fourteen-hour—days she'd worked while he conferenced in Belize—the meetings must have been held outdoors, judging by his sunburn—she'd nearly caught up on her reading *and* her casework.

Only to be dumped on again the minute Bowen returned. She pulled a thirty-six. Followed by another.

Before Jack, she'd thrived on the heavy workload. Before Jack, she hadn't thought about anything but surgery. Saving lives.

Now she found herself thinking about the quality of the lives she was saving. And about the quality of *her* life.

It's pretty rank, Burke. Pretty lonely, too.

Which was pretty silly. She had a spouse at home— a spouse who might not be interested in true love or a real marriage, but whose body seemed interested enough.

In what, though? Her? Or generic sex? And did she want to find out? If so, how could she if she was stuck here at the damned hospital?

She was still pondering possible answers on Friday night, a week after the trip to Canton, as the residents gathered around a video monitor to view a surgical tape.

Dobson and Svoboda had performed a cleft palate repair; now Bowen had the whole group reviewing their performance. Dissecting every slice and suture. Puhleeze.

"Well, Burke? Care to join the discussion?" Bowen snapped.

"Not really," Mel snapped back. No, she just *snapped.* In a going-postal kind of way. "I'd rather go home and get some rest, so I can be fresh tomorrow."

"This is a training program, Burke," Bowen shot back. Mel had heard it before. More than often enough.

"Supposed to be," she agreed, "but we're not discussing surgical techniques here. We're just second-guessing the surgeons. Why? They're good doctors. They had to make decisions on the fly—and they did.

"So I might have done one or two things differently—so what? The girl's palate is fixed, her condition is stable. End of story.''

You could cut the tension in the room with a dull scalpel. None of the other residents would even look at her.

Bunch of cowards, Mel thought as she waited for Bowen to go ballistic.

He looked at his watch first. Then, after a longish—geologic-era longish—pause, the program chief said, ''You're right. It is late. Good night, everyone.''

Like zombies, the shocked residents filed silently out of the room. Except they moved a whole lot faster than movie zombies, Mel thought as she started to follow the last one out.

''Burke.'' Dr. Bowen halted her exit. ''A word with you.''

Since it wasn't a request, Mel simply turned around and waited. Interesting that he'd restrained himself until the others left. Public humiliation was Bowen's usual method.

''I know I work you residents hard.''

And since that wasn't an apology or a question, Mel just nodded.

''I'm trying to prepare you not only technically, but for life as a pediatric surgeon. It's not just tonsillectomies and fat fees, you know.''

Bowen stuffed his hands into his pockets. ''I screen my residents for dedication as well as skill. My approach is designed to let you know what you're getting into, the sacrifices you'll be required to make....''

He'd made those perfectly clear, thank you. But he was right, too, so Mel bit her tongue before she snarled herself out of the program.

''I have two sons,'' Bowen said, scowling at the shiny linoleum floor. A scowl, Mel realized as he went on, not of anger, but of guilt. ''And an ex-wife. All of whom blame me for the breakup of our family.''

Was that why he drove them all like slaves building

Pharaoh's pyramid? Not so much obsessed with surgical perfection, but defending his own *im*perfections?

Nah. Couldn't be.

Bowen looked up at her. His facial muscles spasmed—no, that was a smile. "I don't think their complaint is valid, of course. But maybe I'd better make sure I don't get the blame for your marriage crumbling, too.

"You're a superb surgeon, Burke. You've also worked harder than any of the others. So why don't you take the weekend off?" he suggested. "Take Monday, too."

She was stunned, but not stupefied. "O-okay," Mel said. "Th-thanks."

"I'll rearrange the call schedules," Bowen offered. "See you Tuesday." He strolled out, leaving Melinda alone to contemplate something she hadn't thought about in years: her immediate future.

A whole weekend with Jack. Just the two of them. In the same house for days. And married, though not...involved.

Could that change in three days?

Mel's pager buzzed. The readout sent her rushing for the Pediatric ICU. Jamison's heart valve was crashing and she *was* on call tonight. Her near-term personal life would have to wait.

JACK FROWNED at the cubs frolicking around the mother cheetah.

Again, he thought disgustedly, his frown turning to a scowl as he gazed at the sofa and its sleeping occupant. What kind of moron was Mel's boss—and how was overworking his students till they fell in their tracks considered brilliant training?

Bowen and Jensen should be exiled to the same desert island.

"They could cook rats together," Jack muttered, powering off the TV and steeling himself to just pick the woman up—like she's a sack of groceries, pal—and carry her up to bed.

Again.

Where he'd leave her. Alone. Again. In *her* bed.

He'd leave her there fully dressed, too.

Because damned if he was undressing any part of Melinda Burke's exquisite body again unless she was awake—and returning the favor. He was already taking too many cold showers.

Another unobstructed look at his spouse's frontal curves would have him instantly and urgently ready to commit an act that'd be classified a felony without her prior consent.

Which she couldn't give when she was passed out from sheer exhaustion.

Dammit.

He'd heard her come in around one; he'd pulled on knit lounging pants around two and traipsed down at two-thirty to find her collapsed on the sofa in the den. Again.

Lifting her gently, Jack crossed the carpet and mounted the stairs with his burden's silky hair rubbing erotically against his bare upper body.

"Mmm."

Was that him or her?

"Jack?" Mel's sleepy murmur against his skin sent hot tingles straight to the appendage stirring below his drawstring.

Until he wondered who else she thought might be carrying her sleeping self around. "Yeah, it's me," he growled.

"Don't wake me up," she purred. Her lips curved into a smile that tickled the sensitive skin of his—huh. All his skin was sensitive right now, as sensitive as a hair trigger on a semiautomatic.

"I'm not. I'm just putting you to bed."

"'Sgood." Her arms curled around his neck. "Think I'll sleep all day."

Right. Like she'd suddenly take another day off. Just for clarity's sake, though, he said it aloud. "You're kidding, right?"

Her chocolate hair slid over him, back and forth. Jack almost dropped her as the sensations rippled through him. He wanted her, damned straight. But carrying her like this—he also wanted to take care of her, protect her, bring her the world on a platter.

Oh, hell, he sounded like a Hallmark card! He didn't feel that way about Melinda Burke. Did he?

Jack pushed open the door to Mel's room with his foot. The soft jolt halted her head movements.

"Not kidding," she declared sleepily. "Got th'whole weekend off. So'm not waking up till I feel like it. No coffee t'morrow, Jack—'kay?"

"Okay," he agreed as he reached down awkwardly to pull back the bed covers. "Sleep as long as you want." He laid Mel down, removed her shoes and tucked her in.

"'M not sleeping all weekend," she insisted, burrowing into her pillow. "Jus' morning. Then I wan' t'get t'know you better. *Much* better...." Eyes closed, she flashed a satisfied smile—and flopped onto her other side.

After a long look at her blanket-covered back, Jack retreated. From her room, down the hallway, finally stumbling downstairs to finish the cheetah documentary while he assimilated this surprise development.

And contemplated how soon they could start.

"YOU'RE EATING BREAKFAST."

Jack looked up, milk dribbling from his suspended-in-midair spoon. "Ye-es," he said cautiously.

"But it's seven o'clock at night."

"So it is, sleepyhead," he said with a grin that practically seared her insides. "Welcome back to the land of the living."

At a loss on how to respond—defensively? Or with

an expression of gratitude for not being disturbed while she racked up the zees?—Mel spied the coffeepot and helped herself to some caffeine.

After a sip to clear her head, she managed to say, "Breakfast at night, interesting idea. Guess I'll join you." As she turned around, her nose flattened against a steel plate.

No, that was her spouse's chest.

"Oh!" The gasp of surprise came out more squeak like. Mel tried again. "E-xcuse me." Great. *That* sounded breathlessly ridiculous.

Okay, her intergender skills were adolescent, but *she* was twenty-eight. Why couldn't she act like it whenever Jack was within three feet of her? She was around men all day; none of them turned her to jelly.

"Sorry." His deep voice, well, deepened. His body was an inch from hers. "The bowls...for the...cereal..."

Mel's mouth curved into what had to be a fatuous smile, but she couldn't stop herself. Lordy! Her lips, her breasts, her pelvic region—everything was zinging.

Until Jack broke away to hurtle across the kitchen to the pantry.

"I—uh, here. Try this," he said, returning to shake a cereal box at her like a Native American dance rattle. "If you like it, I've got a coupon. It's supposed to be low sugar and all-natural fiber and..."

While he continued lauding the flaky stuff, he swooped past her to grab a bowl, tore open the box and tipped it up so far that the cereal cascaded not only into the bowl but all over the counter.

Mel stood there, wide-eyed, until the significance of his antics hit her. Then she started to laugh.

Jack froze in the act of sweeping the spilled cereal back into the box.

The man was as flustered as she was.

"The counter's clean," he said defensively, and she laughed harder.

What a weekend this was going to be! She could feel it. Right in her pelvic region. "Forget the cereal," she said with a grin. "Let's order a pizza!"

WHILE SHE WAITED for extra-pepperoni, extra-cheese to arrive, Jack sped to the video store to rent a movie. He had no idea what to get, so he picked flicks from three completely different genres: martial arts, action-adventure and supernatural–space terror.

Anyone would like at least one of those categories, but to be sure, Jack called his sister as he left the store.

"What are they again?" Tess asked, once he'd convinced her he wasn't inviting her to watch them. Sheesh! The woman was paranoid—came from spending too much time alone.

"*Hong Kong Hoopla,* with the great Jackie C. *Bombs Over Terre Haute.* And *Galactic Ooze.*"

"Gosh, Jack, you sure know how to put a woman in the mood, don't you?"

Before he could inform her that these were very mood- and thought-provoking films, Tess went on, "Of course, the way Mel looked at you on our little outing, I think I could show her the home movies of you making mud pies, wearing only your diaper, and she'd be in the mood."

"The way she looked at me or the way I looked at her?" Jack stepped out of the way of a gaggle of giggling teens while he waited for Tess's answer. It was, he realized, an essential piece of information.

Ever since Canton, he'd been thinking of "getting to know her" in biblical terms; he'd wondered if Mel being so serious minded might mean trying that dating routine again first. Finding out her favorite color and political leanings and stuff.

"Yes," his smart-aleck sister replied. "Oh! I've got another call," she added, then with a quick goodbye, she clicked off. Hmm. She sounded almost…excited. Over a phone call?

Who was calling Tess on Saturday night? Jack wondered as he headed for the car. He had to spend more time with her. Definitely. But not this weekend.

This weekend he and Mel were going to become better acquainted.

But…he was damned well moving slowly. Carefully.

Mel had certainly participated enthusiastically that day in Canton, but was she interested in anything more? How much more? Getting naked together? Naked and horizontal? More than once? And how soon?

He'd bet she wasn't the most experienced woman in the world. If he moved too far too fast, she might feel obligated to throw him out, and then what would he do until he took the CFP exam?

More importantly, who'd take care of her and the house and the yard and the old geezers and…?

Jack looked down at the video boxes in his hand. There was a lot riding on this unexpected weekend.

Meaning, dammit, he'd better be on his best behavior.

"I HONESTLY DON'T think a human could jump through plate glass, fall three stories into a bomb blast and just walk away," Mel said seriously. The last video was over and the silence in the den deafening. And what the heck did she know about post-movie chat?

"The percussive effects alone would—" She looked over at Jack, who'd been hugging the far end of the sofa all night. His head had fallen back and his mouth was open.

A tiny snore came from him. How darling, Mel thought, then realized it was probably a comment on the exhilarating company.

Well, what did she know about watching movies with a guy?

About as much as she did about seducing him. Mel sighed. Jack's attention had been riveted on the TV all night; she'd taken that to mean he wasn't interested in talking. To her, anyway. Or cuddling, either.

Of course, the movies' plots had been somewhat confusing; she'd had to watch carefully, too, to follow the stories.

Which seemed to be less important than the body count, the number of fires and explosions and the inclusion of high-speed auto—or as the case may be, spaceship—chases at regular intervals.

"Jack?"

"Yeah!" His head jerked up, his eyes flew open. Surreptitiously, he wiped the corner of his mouth with the back of his hand. "Classic Chan, right? And *Ooze*—great effec—" A yawn interrupted his discourse.

"They were all…" Mel searched for a polite term that wouldn't commit her to a lie. "Interesting," she finished.

Jack nodded, smothering another yawn. "You should see the one where he takes on a Russian Mafia smuggling operation on an island with a volcano about to erupt. Incredible!"

"I'm sure it is," Mel said dryly, watching a third yawn form. "Why don't you go on up to bed?" she suggested.

For some reason, he went perfectly still.

"I, uh, think I'll read a little. I'm not, ah, sleepy yet," she assured him. "I'd better decide what to do with the rest of my time off, too. I've got two whole days to fill. Wow! I can't remember the last time…"

Mel quit listening to her own babbling. It was like a conversational bleeder. She had to clamp it off somehow, but how?

"If you have any ideas for things to do, let me know, okay?" she heard herself say. She was groaning silently over her infantile idiocy when Jack leaped to his feet.

"Tired!" he exclaimed. "Right. Really tired. Going to b—my room. G'night." Three long strides took him to the foot of the stairs. As he grasped the banister like a drowning man clutching a lifesaving rope, he added,

"Shopping. You should go shopping tomorrow. Mall. Sales. Relax."

Taking the stairs two at a time, he climbed out of sight.

"Guess you got your answer," Mel muttered to herself as she rewound and boxed the video for return. Maybe he was right, though. All Jack wasn't much different than all work, if you were trying to build a balanced life.

And she was. That was her goal, not dancing and romancing the weekend away with a hunky husband she craved the way chocoholics obsess over Godiva truffles.

Fine. She'd go shopping tomorrow. Spend a little of the money she'd been making. Get some exercise walking the mall. Hmm…if she could find a swimsuit, she could do a few laps in the revitalized pool.

Maybe that would ease some of this odd, antsy feeling jittering through her insides like confetti fluttering above Times Square at midnight on New Year's Eve.

JACK HIT THE POWER SWITCH and jerked the cord from the outlet as the vacuum whined down.

A few dust bunnies probably remained free to lurk beneath furniture, but, like dirty dishes, he'd learned they were always going to be part of his life.

Today, though, the repetitive nature of housework was driving him nutzoid.

No, Jack admitted with a sigh as he wound the cord and shoved the vac into its resting place, what was driving him bonkers was Melinda. Within reach.

Like a monarch butterfly to those trees in Mexico, irresistible forces drew Jack through the house to the French doors leading to the backyard.

She'd gone shopping, as agreed—while Jack blitzcleaned the house and wondered what OSHA-approved activity he ought to suggest tonight.

But now…now it was four o'clock and Melinda lay

on one of the chaises that he and Old Man Lopez and his pal Edgar had scrubbed clean just this week.

She was wearing the sexiest one-piece bathing suit Jack had ever seen. Maybe because it was on the most enticing—okay, Garden of Eden level tempting—female body he'd ever seen.

Jack wanted to do more than see it. He wanted to experience it, every inch of it, every curve…. He wanted, in the process, to taste her, touch her, inhale her scent and hear her moan with pleasure.

He voted for a duet of pleasure-moaning.

Voting was still in progress when Mel looked up and waved. She turned a page in the book she'd brought home from the mall and went back to reading.

As she did, Jack caught a glimpse of the cover. Huh. Looked like those books his sister used to read—the ones he and his brothers would steal in order to study the juicy parts.

He was no earl or pirate or whatever, but he'd sure as heck like to act out one of those steamy scenes with Mel!

Vivid recollections of their intimate encounters flashed through his mind. They hadn't exactly been one-sided. And with the book maybe getting her in the mood…

The hell with good behavior. Let's go back to getting her out of your system by thorough indulgence.

Jack cracked the door and stuck his head through. Well, no sense air-conditioning the whole neighborhood. "How about a frozen margarita?"

Mel's smile almost knocked him on his keester. From fifteen feet away. "That'd be great, Jack." Her smile faltered as she added, "Would you like to join me?"

The wattage kicked up again when he said, "Sure! Be right out."

He should have been planning his moves while he got out the blender and mixed the drinks, but all he could think about was the sheer domesticity of the scene. Last night, too: middle-class married American weekend.

He pictured himself repeating such homey experiences weekend after weekend, year after year.

Weird. Instead of revolting him, the picture—and repeating it—attracted him.

Even now, Jack thought, as he poured his slushy tequila concoctions into tall, salt-rimmed glasses, set them on a tray and added a bowl of tortilla chips and some salsa, he was looking forward to more than a little sensual romping.

For the first time in his life, no-strings sex wasn't all he wanted. Picking up the tray and balancing it on one hand, Jack walked through the house and out the French doors.

But it was a helluva place to start.

YOU CAN DO THIS, Mel told herself as she accepted the margarita and swirled the straw. She'd thought about it all day. Rehearsed her lines.

Too bad Jack didn't seem to know his part. She'd broiled out here for almost an hour already while he puttered around inside. She'd been just about ready to march in and haul him outside herself when he'd offered to bring her something cold to drink.

Nervously Mel took a sip of margarita. Thinking about a successful outcome to her plan of action made her so hot she was surprised the frozen drink didn't start boiling right there in her hand!

Quit stalling, Burke. "Um, Jack…" Oh great, that came out like a gerbil's chirp. "Would you mind—"

Jack said, "What?" at the same time.

Mel slugged back half her drink, then blurted out her request. "Wouldyourubsomelotiononmybackplease?"

"Huh?"

She made herself say it slower, but to do that, she

had to stab her straw repeatedly into her margarita. "Would you rub some lotion on my back, please?"

It seemed to require some thought, but eventually, in a strangely tight voice, Jack said, "Sure."

Mel put down her glass before she dropped it, handed him the bottle of suntan oil she'd bought earlier for this very purpose and flipped over onto her stomach. She almost flipped back over at Jack's sharp intake of breath.

And then his hands, slippery and smelling of childhood summers and swimming and lighthearted fun, began to move, trembling with banked power, in sensuous patterns over her back. Warm, slow, caressing strokes over her shoulders, then below the strap across the middle of her back. From thorax to pelvis, Jack massaged, stroked, aroused her backside.

She almost came off the lounger when his hands moved to one leg, then the other. From ankle to upper thigh, anterior to interior, his magical touch heated her insides. Not knowing what to do about it, exactly, Mel lay perfectly still.

What she wanted to do was writhe. Writhe and wriggle. And touch him the same way.

"Melinda." His hoarse whisper cut through her sensually induced fog. "Turn over."

She did, then curled her fingers around the chaise's armrests to keep from grabbing him, stroking him, pulling him down on top of her....

No worries. Apparently, Jack had the same idea. He didn't bother to pour oil in his palm; he just leaned over and lowered his hands to her thighs.

Then he covered her lips with his and while their tongues danced and mated and thrust and explored, his hands slid upward to pull down her top, then cup her breasts. When his thumbs brushed the tips and circled their sensitive flesh, she thought she'd levitate off the planet.

His mouth followed the path blazed by his fingers. His lips, his tongue, even his teeth—gently—driving her wild and wilder. Afraid she'd come off the lounger as he laved her beaded nipples, her hands came up to clasp his rib cage and the hard sheath of muscles covering it.

Jack moved his hands, too. Lower…and higher again.

Mel moaned with pleasure. The man knew exactly where and how and what to touch. He was playing her like a Stradivarius—and she was singing!

"O-ooh!" She couldn't help gasping as his fingertips teased along the lower edges of her suit.

Yes, she thought through the delicious haze encompassing her. *Touch me. Deep. Hard. Touch my feminine core with your—*

Jack's hands jerked away, leaving her body humming like an eight-hundred-person kazoo band. His head swiveled, aiming his face skyward. He appeared to be jutting his jaw and clenching it at the same time. "Are, are you sure about this?" he asked hoarsely. "I—I don't want to rush you into anything, Mel."

He didn't? Because he didn't want to rush or because he wasn't as hot to go as she was?

Either way, it's time to hit the pause button, Burke.

As she waited for her pulse rate to drop to mere stroke-out levels, Mel restored her suit to its appropriate location.

Once she had herself decently covered again, she looked over at Jack. He had his eyes closed and both hands in his hair.

"Hey, Halloran!"

Who the—?

"You out here?"

An elderly man's face, topped with silver hair, appeared above the side fence. "Well, hi, Melinda. I didn't know you were home today." Without waiting for her to reply, the neighbor addressed Jack. "I found that pension notice you were talking about," he announced cheerfully, waving a sheet of paper above the wooden slats. "You wanna see it now?"

After throwing a helpless, pleading look in her direction, Jack called out, "Sure, Pres. Why not."

Mel slid off the lounger, stood on still-shaky legs and started walking away. Carefully, like a drunk trying not to show it.

Neighborly interruption or not, she knew they ought to stop here. At least for now. Until at least one of them thought through the whole sex question. Consciously. Sensibly.

Mel hoped she'd make it into the house before her bones liquefied completely. She definitely needed to think before they went any further, but all she wanted to think about was going all the way. With Jack.

"Go over and see Mr. St. Clair," she encouraged him when her hand gripped the door leading inside. "I'll—" *take a cold shower* "—make dinner."

"No!" Jack leaped to his feet. "I mean, let's go out. Get some Mexican food to go with our margaritas." Still agitated, he practically skipped around the pool and across the grass to tell her parents' neighbor they'd talk tomorrow.

Mel frowned as the reason for his agitation came to her: maybe he didn't want to have to consume her cooking.

That frosted her. At least until they were sharing a single serving of flan for dessert and she realized they'd been talking, easily, honestly and nonstop for almost three hours.

Part of the comfortable mood derived, she thought, from not having to wonder who was playing what role. El Mirador's chef cooked, the waiter waited—and she and Jack just ate their chicken enchiladas and enjoyed each other's company.

Well, there'd be other meals…like breakfast, tomorrow. She'd show Jack she wasn't completely undomestic—just in case that mattered.

A HOLIDAY MONDAY MORNING. Jack ruffled his hair as he strolled into the kitchen. Wow. Almost nine already. It was great getting a break from the predawn coffee patro—what the hell was that smell?

And what the hell was he seeing? Jack rubbed his eyes and gave it another try. Same image: someone crouched over the trash can, cradling the toaster under one arm, wielding a knife with the other hand.

Not someone. "Mel?"

She spun around. Guilt, then something else flashed across her features. As she straightened, she tried to hide the toaster behind her.

She looked upset. Dammit, he didn't want her upset. Jack hurried forward to make it better. "Whassup, darlin'?" he asked as he pried the knife and the toaster from her.

Whew! He still didn't know what the smell was, but he'd found its source. "Get something stuck in here?" He peered into the bread slots.

A yellowish, plastic-looking substance covered most of the heating wires and filled the bottom of the slots.

Jack looked up from the strange mess admiringly. He'd never thought of using the toaster to melt stuff. "What happened?"

"I was trying to make French toast," Mel said stiffly, which Jack didn't know how she managed to do with her lower lip quivering like that. It was making his primary male part quiver, too. "I wanted to make you breakfast and I thought…"

Hellfire. Her beautiful green eyes were dripping tears. "Don't," Jack murmured as he dropped the toaster on the counter and gathered her in his arms. *Where she belongs.*

"Don't cry," he soothed. "I'm not big on French

toast anyway. And breakfast is still my job. Nobody expects you to turn into Donna Reed the minute you have a day off.''

He put bacon in a skillet, turned the burner to the right temp, then rushed off to buy cinnamon rolls at the supermarket bakery while she ''cooked'' the strips of cured pork.

After breakfast, they took turns showering. Jack considered suggesting a water-saving technique, but forced himself to hold that one back for now.

You've got all day, he told himself as he shaved. *Take it slow and easy.*

MEL CAME DOWNSTAIRS, rosy from her bath, her silky chocolate hair now turned to black satin—er, damp. Her hair was wet.

The hell with slow and easy.

Jack plucked her from the third stair, twirled her around and let her slide slowly down his body.

Just as her feet touched the floor, every phone in the house shrilled, breaking the moment's spell like divine intervention.

''I...I'll answer tha—'' Mel started to say, moving backward until they broke contact.

No way. ''I'll get it.'' Jack strode over to snatch up the nearest receiver. No distractions allowed today.

''Burke residence,'' he said, trying to lock her gaze with his.

''Then put Burke on the phone!'' snapped the caller. Male, irate, obnoxious.

Bowen, Jack mouthed without thinking, then showed Mel a palm to keep her back.

''Oh, never mind!'' Dr. Congeniality snarled. ''Just give her a message. Tell her Zunica broke an ankle skydiving, the imbecile. Tell her if she wants to scrub in on a liver transplant, she's got seventeen minutes to get her tail down here.''

Dial tone.

"Nice talking to you, too," Jack told the dead receiver before replacing it in the charging dock.

He ought to lie like a lawyer, he thought darkly, but relayed Bowen's message to Mel. Who immediately started flurrying around looking for her beeper, scraping her hair back with one of those zigzag torture bands and wishing aloud she'd eaten something more substantial than sugared bread.

Jack slapped together a turkey and Swiss on oat bran, threw some baby carrots into a zip baggie and filled a travel mug with milk.

"Here." He handed the lunch off resignedly as she darted past. "Eat in the car. See you when I see you."

"I have to go," she said softly. "I *want* to go. This is too big to pass up. You have to understand that."

Jack shrugged graceless acceptance. His gaze shifted to the refrigerator.

Then Mel cupped his cheek with her free hand. Her palm urged his face downward, toward her.

"But I also want to stay here," she whispered, her lips curving into that sweet smile that just fried him. "With you."

"Go!" Jack insisted hoarsely. "Now!"

Mel went.

As he listened for her departure, Jack made himself—and Melinda—a promise. One of these days, they'd finish what they'd started this weekend. One of these days soon.

And if his vote got counted, that would be just the beginning.

9

SINCE IT WAS NOW just another Monday, Jack tossed in a load of clothes and started loading the dishwasher. As he did, he continued to ponder what he'd learned during the Bowen-shortened weekend.

He wanted to live with Mel. For more than six months. And not as her wife. And mostly not because she needed him as her housekeeper.

He wanted to care for, protect and help Melinda. He wanted to do everything he could to make her life easier. And what he wanted in return was affection, not gratitude.

Well, hell. Wasn't that *l-o-v-e?*

Sure felt like it.

The idea stunned him. Then stunned him some more. Love was the last result he'd expected from this crazy arrangement, but he hadn't expected this arrangement in the first place. He'd seized an opportunity.

Now…he had a choice to make: reclaim his former disdain for the mushy L-emotion—or turn himself into a personal investment opportunity too good for Mel to pass up.

Jack checked the time. Hmm, he had about twenty minutes before the boys would be showing up. Better get the Danish warmed up and the assignments compiled.

By now, most daily household tasks had become second nature, though he still had to check himself when he used the oven. To broil or to bake, that was the question. He still couldn't see what difference it made where the heat came from, but after that smoke-alarm disaster... Who knew mac-n-cheese could actually explode? Choosing Bake on a hunch, he popped in the pastry.

As he went back to fill the dishwasher soap dish and flip the lid down, Jack wondered how to convince Mel she needed a husband, not a wife, and that he'd be the best candidate for the job.

"What exactly does a husband do in this millennium, anyway?" Jack asked the dust bunny who lived under the table in the breakfast nook.

He'd made his gender-equality statement and he stood by it. But maybe racking up a few traditional male-role accoutrements, like a decent income—and a mortgage to match?—would raise his attractiveness quotient.

He could take the next Certified Financial Planner's certification exam, scheduled for July, instead of waiting until November. Was he ready? Butterflies rioted in his stomach.

Luckily for Jack, the old guys arrived to tell a few war stories and kaffeeklatsch until, calmed by their distraction, he handed out job slips and made sure O'Banyon had a ride. Despite the geezer's insistence, Jack wasn't about to let those cataract-clouded eyeballs navigate Dallas streets.

Ever since ol' Bob fixed Sherry's ceiling fan by replacing the switch, she'd been circulating Jack's phone number as Handyman Central. It didn't take a genius to jot down addresses and problems and match them up with a retiree having the needed skill. And the men loved the extra money.

They were always offering him a cut of their earnings, but so far, he'd traded his clearinghouse act for their financial info, using it as practice problems for his test.

Once he had the oldsters situated for the day, Jack shuffled the laundry into the dryer, got something out for dinner and paid bills.

"Guess I'll work up Preston's profile," he decided as he peered around the stack of sheets and towels before starting up the stairs. And he'd send in his registration form and fee for the July test.

Just in case his wife preferred an old-fashioned, breadwinner mate.

As Mel clamped off a blood vessel and stepped back, she acknowledged the thrill of participating, even so secondarily, in a transplant operation. But while Dr. Patel and the main team removed the child's diseased liver—to be replaced by part of a donor organ being shared with an adult recipient—she couldn't help cursing the personal opportunity she'd lost this morning.

Her hunger had been reflected in Jack's eyes. A few more minutes and they'd have been out of earshot from Earth. She could have let nature take its course then.

Now one of them would have to make a play for the other. But who?

Not that it mattered. They were both consenting adults with no other exclusive relationships. They even had a marriage license to legitimize such activity.

She'd do the asking, Mel decided. Because surgeons treat aggressively rather than dose and wait. Besides, Jack made her feel like a woman, but she didn't have the faintest idea how to play the more traditional female role and get him to ask.

Jack's feelings were a complete mystery, but she knew what *she* wanted: one wonderful, womanly memory of union with her husband.

If they could get to it before he booked.

And he would. A guy like Jack Halloran had better things to do than stay married to a geeky doctor with little free time and—Mel recalled her French toast fiasco—no wifely skills at all.

Tonight. When the surgery ended, she'd go home and proposition her hottie husband. Get it over with. Get on with it. Get it on.

Oh, *yeah*. If Jack agreed to revise the no-sex clause, they'd explore each other thoroughly tonight. Listen to their hearts beat in rhythm. Let their bodies join together. Melt and mold, meld and mingle.

The thought of going to bed with Jack made Mel so giddy, she laughed at one of Bowen's stupid Texas A&M Aggie jokes.

The ancient one about the Aggie being so proud of his Olympic gold medal, he had it bronzed.

HOURS LATER, still awed by Dr. Patel's skill and the human body's amazing intricacy, Mel walked into the kitchen.

Empty.

Hmm. His car was here. "Jack?"

She walked through into the family room. Also empty. A quick circuit of the rest of the downstairs yielded the same results.

Maybe he'd gone somewhere. In someone else's car. Without leaving a note.

Not that she was disappointed, discouraged, distraught, depressed or anything. She was just…tired.

So crash, Burke.

Good advice. Also frustrating as hell. Glumly she climbed the stairs.

Dammit, she'd geared up for a confrontation that would end in consummation, not another night alo—

Mel paused with her hand on the doorknob to her room. What was that sound? And was it coming from Jack's room?

She moved down the hallway swiftly and silently, like a SWAT team closing in on a crack house. His door was ajar. Holding her breath, she put her ear to the narrow opening between door and frame.

Hmm. Either someone was torturing a small animal during a rainstorm or Jack was singing in the shower.

Refusing to let herself stop and think, Mel slipped into the room, climbed over the clothing strewn across the floor and stepped into Jack's bathroom—just as the water and the caterwauling cut off.

When he swooshed open the shower curtain, Mel had her hands on the hem of her pullover tee. "Oh," she said as calmly as she could, which wasn't very, since she'd never seduced anyone before. "I was just coming to join you."

Jack grabbed the shower curtain and covered his, ah, assets.

Which, Mel had time anyway to see, were quite substantial.

She tried to remember even *one* of the logical points she'd thought up on the drive home to convince Jack there was no reason they shouldn't add sex to their approved-marital-activities list.

Hopeless. That gorgeous male body, slick and flushed, drove everything out of her mind. Sent it all rushing south.

"You…" Jack's voice raveled the word into about three syllables. "Mel…" With a visible effort, he swallowed. His sapphire eyes darkened to midnight-navy. Finally he managed a complete sentence. "I'm wet."

Mel smiled. Here goes. "Me, too," she murmured, releasing her shirt hem and closing the distance between them.

MAKING LOVE WITH MELINDA was everything he thought it would be. And more. Much more.

He knew they should probably talk first. Establish ground rules, clarify what the sex meant, all that stuff. Or at least exchange some sweet compliments.

But when a naked man gets propositioned, then kissed and caressed by the woman he's been wanting forever—only a very dead, very crazy person would refuse to respond.

Jack wasn't dead or crazy. Not yet, anyway.

Freeing the towel she'd jerked from the rack and stroked him with, he dropped it in the tub. "I'm dry enough," he said, not caring now how ragged his voice sounded. He wanted her—so much, he'd be lucky to get her undressed first. "Let's get some of these clothes off you."

"Yes," she breathed.

With her help, Jack set a record for disrobing a female. He set another record carrying her to his bed.

That's where he slowed the pace. He wanted her as aroused as he was. He thought he'd torture her the way she tortured him, making her teeter for days on the edge of orgasm until she begged him to take her over.

And it might have worked that way. Turning down the comforter and pulling back the sheet, arranging the pillows—and her hair on them—Jack got himself under enough control to kiss her slowly, thoroughly. He cupped and fondled and suckled her breasts. Concentrating on control and technique.

But somewhere along in there, Mel moaned with pleasure.

He was already at peak capacity or he'd have swelled with pride. He throbbed, instead. Then he suckled more. He licked, he used his teeth to gently scrape her sensitive flesh. He moved his hand between her thighs, threading his fingers through her damp curls, blazing a path to...

She moaned again.

That's when Jack quit worrying about technique. Since she seemed to like it—and he sure as hell did—he just kept doing what he was doing. Somehow he still clung to his control.

Until she twisted out from under him, rolled him onto his back. "Please," she whispered as she rose above him. Her green eyes glowed like burning emeralds. "I can't...wait...any longer."

The hot, hard tip of his arousal touched her hot, wet entrance. "Please."

With a groan, Jack put his hands on her hips and guided her down.

She took them to paradise in less time than it would take even someone as succinct as Madonna to say it.

Not that Jack minded the speed of the trip, but the next time, he stayed in charge—and made it last.

And last. And last. Until they both begged for release and found it together.

Afterward was almost as good as during. Sated, languid, warm. Their bodies still entangled, they drifted to sleep.

Sometime later, Jack awoke. They'd left the lights on; the sky visible through the window was dark. Propping his elbow on one of the pillows and his head on his hand, he watched Mel doze on.

And wondered how anything so right could feel so...wrong.

Damn. He sure as hell wasn't ready to give up the best sex he'd experienced in his life, but...

Jack sighed and let his free hand play with Mel's silky chocolate hair.

He wanted more. Sex without love seemed wonderful but, for the first time ever, incomplete. And all Hallorans knew that love without commitment was just talk.

Was that what had him squirming inside? Some antiquated sensibility that a woman as special as Mel deserved more than casual, uncomplicated sex?

She hadn't asked for anything more! And maybe she didn't want more.

Or maybe, with her life devoted to medicine, she didn't know there was more to want.

Should he keep his mouth shut, take what she offered and slowly try to show her what more they could have together?

Or should he refuse to get back in the sack with her until she agreed to a long-term commitment?

Oh, right, like he'd hold out for more than an instant if she so much as bared a toenail or fluttered her eyelashes suggestively!

Momentarily conclusionless, he stole out of bed, tucked Mel in carefully and dressed in the hallway. Then he went downstairs to whip up some energy-boosting dinner. Chicken with raspberry-balsamic sauce, steamed broccoli and jasmine rice.

"Take that, Red Chef!" he muttered as he finished the low-fat but flavorful sauce.

He served Mel dinner in bed. When she shivered from the air-conditioning, he gave her one of his shirts to put on; it sure looked better on her than it ever had on him.

And he wanted to take it right back off her.

THIS IS, Mel decided as she accepted another bite of saucy chicken, *the height of decadence.*

And she was savoring every minute of it.

Jack had to be the reigning lovemaking champion. Not that she had enough experience to judge that for herself, but she couldn't imagine anyone needing to be any better than he'd been. Than they'd been.

Twice!

Then he'd brought her this delicious meal and practically fed it to her, bite by bite. And now...was that just a gratuitous bulge in his jeans or was Jack's interest in applied erotica reviving?

Hers was. Rapidly.

"Do you—?"

"I want to—" Jack cleared his throat. "Sorry. Go ahead."

Mel signaled him to go first. She didn't mind a bit sharing the aggressor role. "No, you."

Before Jack could speak, something buzzed. Mel looked around, her heart suddenly pounding. Was there a rattlesnake loose in the room?

The buzzing came again.

With a disgusted expression, Jack got up, dug through the clothes on the floor, removed something and handed it to her.

"You're being paged, Dr. Burke," he said heavily, then muttered something that sounded like an offer to disembowel Bowen while she checked the readout.

"Sorry about that," Mel said as she scooted to the edge of his bed. "It's not the hospital," she added, reaching for the phone. "Probably a wrong number—I don't recognize it. Let me check. Otherwise, we might get paged every ten minutes."

She smiled across the rumpled sheets. "And I'd rather not be disturbed again tonight. How about you?"

His dark blue eyes blazing, Jack corralled the tray. "I'll remove the breakables while you take the page. And no," he added as he crossed the room, "I don't want to be disturbed by anyone tonight. Except you, Melinda. But you disturb me all the time."

"Good or bad?" Mel asked.

"In a bad, very bad way," he said with a deep chuckle that set her insides tingling. "And, believe me, that's way good."

As Jack departed and Mel punched in the phone number showing on her pager display, she admitted she felt a smidge of relief at the interruption.

All she needed was a little bit of breathing room. A fingersnap's worth of time to make sure her head was still on straight. And that her heart wasn't wandering down any blind, dead-end, no-win alleys.

Jack made her body sing. He made her laugh. He gave her attention, consideration and care.

None of which meant she'd give up her career for him. Not that he'd asked, of course, but…

Medicine was her life. Trading pediatric surgery for the role of Jack Halloran's wife would make her brother's death meaningless.

She couldn't do that to Harry. To her parents. To herself.

"Or to Jack," she whispered as the phone rang again. So she'd just have to make sure he never asked.

The ringing stopped as someone picked up. "Hello?" The voice sounded vaguely familiar.

"Hello. This is Melinda Burke."

Before she could say anything more, the voice on the other end gave a heartfelt "Thank God," then added, "It's Bobby. Noreen's husband."

Mel listened as he went on—the words spilling out, full of panic and terror and pleading.

JACK PRACTICALLY TELEPORTED back upstairs. Good to go didn't even begin to cover his condition! Well, he was married to an insatiable goddess. How lucky could a guy get?

He started to race down the hall then screeched to a halt.

"Mel? What are you doing?" She'd relocated to her room, which was okay, but she didn't appear to be prepping for a long night of love. She looked to be—

"Packing."

Jack thought about clamping his arms around her ankles and refusing to let go. Instead, he asked, "Why?"

She ceased wadding up clothing and looked at him, clearly distressed. "The page…my cousin's been in an accident. She's in surgery at Presbyterian. It sounds pretty bad."

"But why are you taking clothes?"

"Because I'm meeting Bobby at the hospital and taking the baby home. He wants me to keep her until Noreen's out of—'' Mel plunged her hands into her hair and pulled outward. ''I don't know what to do with a baby!'' she wailed.

''Of course you do,'' Jack said. Was she nuts? ''You're a—''

''If you say 'woman,''' Mel warned him conversationally, ''I'll relocate your cowlick.''

''—pediatrician. That was my call all along,'' he insisted firmly. ''You're a pediatrician.''

''That doesn't mean I like kids enough to get along with them,'' Mel informed him.

It doesn't?

''I went into pediatric surgery so Harry's life wouldn't be wasted.''

Jack stared at her. This was *so* not right. ''Why build a career around kids if you don't like them? That seems like a waste of *your* life.''

Mel's soft green eyes turned to serpentine. ''I didn't say I don't like them.''

''What?!'' She'd drive him crazy if he wasn't already so close he could walk.

''I don't know how I feel about kids! I've only been around sick ones—and I'm too busy getting them well to worry about feelings.'' She wadded up another cotton T-shirt and slam-dunked it into the soft-sided bag she was packing. ''And making my brother's death count is *not* a waste of my life.''

She didn't add ''you jerk,'' but Jack could hear it. Okay, an issue for another time.

''This'll be a good experience then,'' he said with the hard-edged cheerfulness of an elementary school phys ed teacher. ''Nothing like a day or two with a baby to find out whether you—'' Oops. He almost said ''want one.'' And that would be putting the layette before the trousseau. Or whatever.

''—like them,'' he finished quickly before changing, sort of, the subject. ''Let me grab a few things, then we'll go. You drive, I'll call Bowen so he can't tell you no.''

"*We'll* go? Y-you're coming with me?''

"Of course. We're in this together, Mel."

She didn't say anything, but he'd bet big that lowering her shoulders like that spelled relief.

Was that sweet or what? The woman could transplant a liver, but baby-sitting a normal, healthy infant scared her to death.

SOMEWHERE NEARBY, a baby whimpered. Reflexively Mel got to her feet and looked around. Huh. She'd slept in her clothes again. In a chair in Noreen's minuscule living room.

They'd been baby-sitting less than three days, but she felt as exhausted as she had after her first week of internship.

The parallel was exact. Overwhelming demands meeting inexperienced uncertainty. It took everything out of you—faster than the latest annoying behavior became a syndrome with a Web site.

Another whimper. Proof that babies were tougher than they looked. Swiping her hair off her face, Mel went in search of her niece.

So far, she'd managed to diaper, feed and burp the five-month-old without harm. This, though, was her downfall: the soothing stuff. She just didn't have the patience for it.

Luckily for them all, Jack did. His magic touch extended to babies, too. He'd hoist the kid up against his shoulder and walk her to sleep.

And while Amber slept… Mmm.

Not that they made love in Bobby and Noreen's bed.

Just everywhere else they could think of—and what an imaginative partner Jack was! Athletic, too. Great flexibility, strength, endurance. And a very well developed, ah, circulatory system.

''What time is it?'' Mel asked as she entered the bedroom and intersected Jack's path.

''Morning.'' He stopped patting the baby he held long enough to tuck a strand of Mel's hair behind her ear and smooth his thumb over her eyebrow, cheekbone, and lip. ''Thursday morning,'' he clarified, twinkling his blue eyes at her and smiling.

As if he didn't care that she wasn't very good with babies. Or cooking. Or anything domestic, when it came down to it.

But the question haunted her. Stopped her from bringing up the topic of making their arrangement permanent.

What if—when it came to the long haul—Jack wanted a wifely wife? After her French toast disaster, he'd said something about not expecting her to be Donna Reed on her first day off.

Did that mean he'd expect Donna-like behavior from her later?

Later, like now?

''Bobby called,'' Jack said over the baby's continuing whimpers. ''Noreen's still in SICU, but he thinks she'll be moved to a regular bed this afternoon''

''Good.'' Mel breathed a sigh of relief. Bobby could take the baby with him then. And they could go home.

''Waaa!''

''Here.'' Mel made herself hold out her arms. ''Let me have her. You've done your tour.''

Jack didn't bother disguising his relief as he handed Amber over. ''We've been awake and fussing since three.''

Mel couldn't blame his eagerness. Amber was her niece and adorable when she slept, but...

''Are you sure she isn't sick?'' Jack asked. '''Cuz she's leaking.''

''What do you mean?'' Mel's hand went to Amber's diaper.

''Not there,'' Jack answered, as crankily as she'd ever

heard him. Which, compared to Bowen, sounded like Emily Post on her best behavior. "Her nose is running. She's drooling like a fountain. Maybe she's got rabies."

After putting the infant down for a quick visual examination, Mel absently chewed on her lip as she considered symptoms and diagnoses.

Aha. A possible explanation occurred to her. Gently she rubbed a fingertip over Amber's gums. Yep. Score one for the doc.

"What's wrong?" Jack demanded.

Smiling now, Mel said, "Noreen's really going to be chapped about this." She bent to kiss the baby's soft, fat cheek, then picked her up. As she turned her smile on Jack, she said, "I just hope Bobby's home before—"

"Before what?" Jack shouted, ramming fingers through his hair. He knew they taught doctors to remain calm in crises, but this was ridiculous! Shouldn't they be calling 911 or rushing to the nearest doc in the box or something!

"Before Amber's first tooth comes in. I know they'll want to see it right away."

Jack sank into a chair, cradling his head in his hands. My God. He'd just gone to hell on a high-speed train and now...

He looked up at Mel holding the baby in one arm, letting the kid gum her other forefinger and resting her puckered-up lips against Amber's temple.

Now I understand what Tess means. About life and love and pain.

He also understood what Melinda meant to him. What he wanted—no, needed—for his life and hers.

"Would you see if we've got any ice?" Mel asked him, still getting chewed on and drool-soaked. "I've heard that numbing the gums makes babies less uncomfortable when they're teething."

He wanted to say, "I'll remember that for our

babies," but he cautioned himself not to get too far ahead of himself. Not yet.

Right now, he just drank in the sight of his woman—his dear, sweet, smart, sexy woman cradling the tiny, quiet, cuddly baby.

Without thinking, he blurted, "I gotta tell you, Mel—I don't intend to be your house spouse much longer."

Meaning, of course, that he wanted to be her adoring husband. The father of her undoubtedly adorable children. Her co-mortgage holder. The guy who brought home at least half the bacon and saved for the kids' college and took Mel on romantic getaways whenever possible.

Before he could get it all said—hell, before he could get any of it said, Mel whirled close to him. Close enough to poke his chest with her drool-covered finger.

"Too bad, buster," she grated, glaring at him between rapid eye blinks. "We made a deal and you're going to honor it. Either you continue to be the house spouse for the rest of the six months or you arrange for a substitute housekeeping service to take over before you bail."

Mel whirled away. Then whirled back to plop Amber in his arms. "Here. Try the ice, but don't give her frostbite. I'm going to check on Noreen, then I'm going to work. I'll be back…later."

Congratulations, moron, Jack saluted himself as he watched Mel gather her doctor paraphernalia and almost run from the apartment. *You certainly handled that well.*

Gingerly he let Amber grab his finger and stick it in her mouth. *Now what, brainiac?*

10

"Is that clear, Dr. Burke?"

Bowen referred to…something. Mel nodded anyway. Everything *was* clear now. All it took was seeing her with Amber for Jack to realize just how little he wanted to do with her. And why.

"I don't intend to be your house spouse much longer."

"Damned hypocrite," Mel muttered, which had Bowen turning back, ready to rumble again. She fended him off with a not-applicable, ignore-me gesture.

Jack Halloran could talk a good equal-rights line, but when push came to shove, when real life happened along, he turned into just another damned chauvinist. Wanting a wife who stayed home cooking, cleaning and child rearing, while he went out and managed other people's money.

Big deal. She'd devoted her whole life to medicine. To saving lives.

That's what she'd studied and worked and sacrificed for. That's why she'd survived when Harry had developed the heart problem that cut his life short.

She refused to give up her career to serve Jack's fantasies—or his beer.

Very righteous, Burke. Except he hadn't asked her to do anything.

Mel's fingers squeezed her pager. She didn't want him to ask. She knew her answer if he did. Saving lives was more important than *having* one.

Or making love. Or—

She started over. Lecturing herself again on the wisdom of concentrating on her surgical career instead of wallowing in a diaper-induced and Jack Halloran-enhanced sea of female inadequacy.

"SOUNDS GREAT."

"Count me in!"

Jack breathed a short sigh of relief as the men filling the den verbally jumped on his bandwagon.

"Bet the wife'd like ta sign up, too," Bob said. "Think there'd be any call for handy women?"

"I don't see why not," Jack replied while other seniors volunteered their wives. "I can't mend hems or wrap presents worth spit. And I'm sure there are packs of executives with busy families, working couples strapped for time and—"

He looked at Chester, a recent widower newly recruited by Preston. They'd keep him too busy to get lonely. Chester was a retired carpenter.

"—ah, suddenly single home owners who've never cleaned a gutter, planted flowers or caulked a window in their lives," Jack finished. "Rent-a-Spouse is practically a success already."

Leave it to Preston to locate the black cloud in the silver lining. "What about the Social Security earnings limits?" he asked.

"He's all over it, Pres." Bob came to Jack's rescue. They'd discussed the plan in exhaustive detail before presenting it to the larger group. "Jack's brother is writing some software to track each Spouse's earnings, tax bracket, preferred work area—everything.

"This is gonna be the sweetest deal since the GI Bill. For us, for our neighbors, for Halloran. Everybody wins."

Jack nodded agreement. He had no doubts about Rent-a-Spouse's appeal. Where else could one find rea-

sonably priced, dependable, skilled workers to do all
those little tasks that piled up around the house? The
oldsters would have more work than they could handle
in no time.

And Jack, who'd agreed to set up and run the business, foresaw a decent income stream while he built his
financial consulting business, giving him the freedom to
take only clients he really wanted to work with.

Most importantly, running Rent-a-Spouse would
leave him with plenty of time to lavish on his own home
and family.

The only unknown was just who would constitute that
family.

In five years, would he be living with a surgeon
named Melinda and maybe a kid or three? Or would he
be keeping tabs on his brother Mike between SEAL
missions and nagging Tess to go on a damned date?

After Mel's reaction two days ago, when his heart
had puddled at the sight of her, looking like a Madonna,
holding her niece... Some kind of primitive, possessive,
totally macho urge had just overtaken him and he'd
blurted out, well, whatever he'd blurted out. Something
about wanting to be her man.

All he knew for sure was it had ticked Mel off. Roy-
ally.

Okay, he'd made a mistake. It happened. But Jack
was too intelligent to let his mouth try to fix the trouble
it had gotten him into in the first place.

Not without some tangible assets to back him up, anyway.

Hence, Rent-a-Spouse. And he'd pass the next CFP
exam or die trying. He'd offer both accomplishments as
proof he was worthy of consideration as a husband.
Spouse. Life partner. Legally recognized significant
other.

Terminology didn't matter. Only one thing did: sharing a life with Mel. A home. A bed.

Love. Meals. Chores. Vacations. Extended families. Sickness. Savings. Shopping. Gray hair. Midlife crises. Everything.

Nothing about love and commitment scared him anymore as long as they went through it all together.

They could divide up the damned housework, the bookkeeping, the child care any way she wanted.

As long as he ended up with Mel. For the rest of their lives.

Dammit, he needed her! Without Mel, his life wasn't meaningful enough to get him out of bed every morning.

Of course, *with* Mel—he'd be uninterested in getting out of bed any morning. But he'd do it. For her. Hell, he'd get up at four-thirty every day for the rest of his life, if that's what it took. Love made the painful bearable, the irritating unimportant.

"Let's hook it up, guys," Jack spoke over the group's rising chatter level. "I've gotta get going."

Noreen remained in the hospital and Amber remained fussy, so Jack continued to baby-sit during the day while Bobby pulled vigil with his wife.

Yesterday Mel had stopped off on her way home, first at Presbyterian to check on Noreen, then at the apartment to take a baby shift. She'd gotten back to her folks' house about thirty minutes after the nurses kicked Bobby out and gone right up to bed. Hers. Alone.

Looked like they were doing that passing ships thing again.

Which even Jack realized was not conducive to romance. And romance, he decided as he headed toward Amber and the apartment, was probably his best bet to regain lost ground. Some big Romeo-style gesture to get Mel back and keep her.

But what? Imaginative ideas were not his strong suit.

FINALLY. Six days after her accident, Noreen went home.

After enduring a flood of gratitude, so did Jack and Mel. Together at last. But not for long.

Dr. Burke dodged dinner and locked herself in her room "to read."

Halloran ate two corn dogs and paced his room half the night, coaching the televised Rangers, then telling Chef Jewels where to get off.

The next morning, though, he woke with a plan and leaped out of bed to put it into action. ASAP.

After dispatching the day's rent-a-spouses, Jack went shopping.

He bought candles, flowers, a bottle of Oregon's finest pinot gris and a point-84, square-cut carat of native crystalline carbon—that's dictionary for "diamond"—mounted in platinum. Matching wedding bands to follow.

Then he enlisted Dr. Bowen to send Mel home at a decent hour. Okay, he lied. Told the grouch it was Mel's birthday and her dying grandmother had a surprise party planned.

As Jack tested the pecan-crusted cornish hens for doneness, he glanced at the microwave's clock.

Took a deep breath. It was almost the "decent hour" he and Bowen had agreed on. Mel might be home any minute. Let's see…the ring was in his pocket. Candles and flowers on the dining table. The wine chilled.

Quickly Jack checked on the roasted garlic for the mashed potatoes, the baby yellow squash and the nasturtium blossoms to garnish them.

Okay. Now, was it time to mash the potatoes, sauté the squash or start the orange-cranberry sauce for the cornish hens? Or should he wait ten more—?

Phones shrilled.

Better not be Bowen reneging or Mel detouring to visit her cousin. "I've got a totally romantic evening planned, complete with bended-knee proposal," he muttered as he crossed the kitchen. A proposal nobody was going to defer.

He couldn't stand another day of not knowing where they stood with each other. He wanted their life together to begin now.

The phones rang again.

Jack snatched up the receiver. "What?"

"Hey, bro, it's Tess. Just thought I'd call and see how you're—"

"Get to the point," Jack suggested. Okay, he barked it.

Tess pretended to be hurt by his brusqueness. That took forever.

"Whatever, Sis. Why'd ya call?" Jack eyed the clock. He really needed to get back to his cooking.

"Well, you know how you've been pushing me to date?" Tess began, her voice growing more hesitant with every word. "Um, well, I wondered what you'd say if I…ah, if a guy asked me—"

Jack cut her off. "You're an adult, Tess. If you think you're ready, you're ready." Sisters. Sheesh. "I really have to go now." He hung up just as Mel walked in.

"Wait! I'm not ready!" Dammit, he didn't want her in here watching him run around like a crazy person finishing up the meal. "I mean, hi. Say, you look tired. Why don't you go take a bubble bath while I finish dinner? I'll call you when it's ready."

GET IT, BURKE? He didn't ask you to stay and help, did he? You've been dismissed as useless. Again. "Okay," she said, moving toward the stairs. "I'll be in the tub if you…need me."

She'd almost said *want to join me.* But even three or four days after the fact, Jack's pronouncement still rang in her ears, amplified by years of insecurity about her femininity. Insecurity masked by hard work and studying medicine instead of moisturizers.

"I don't intend to be your house spouse much longer."

They'd been great in bed together. So the problem had to lie beyond the sheets. And it had to be her. Jack Halloran was all man—as masculine with a dust rag in his hand as with a Harley between his legs.

She had to be the problem: not being woman enough for a man like Jack. How could she be? She'd needed a wife herself.

Upstairs Mel ran the water, tossed in a handful of scented bath crystals and disrobed. After pinning up her hair, she stepped into the tub and lowered her body into the warm, soothing, bubble-topped water.

Where she sat soaking—and admitted, finally, to wishing with all her heart that she could transform herself into a woman Jack Halloran *would* want as his wife.

Could she? If she knew what kind of woman that was, could she become it? Mel wondered, gazing at her toes peeking through the mounds of frothy bubbles.

"You won't know what he wants till you ask," she advised herself. "So go ask."

Before she could chicken out, Mel left the tub, dried off, pulled on her peach silk robe and unpinned her hair.

As she brushed out the tangles, she heard that small-animal torture again.

"That's a good sign, isn't it, if he's singing while he cooks?" Heart pounding with equal parts hope and anxiety, Mel edged down the hallway to the staircase.

JACK TWEAKED the squash arrangement on Mel's plate and tried to pull together a speech. Something about undying love and staying married happily ever after.

A series of strange sounds disturbed his ruminations. First, clicking, then a snick, a creak, then—ba-aam!

Someone was coming through the front door! Jack looked around for a weapon.

An unknown male voice muttered, "Damn! I always forget how easy that door swings open."

"My, it's good to be home." Another voice. Female. Tired.

Home? Jack was still processing that information when a sunburned couple appeared in the doorway of the kitchen.

The man—big, beefy, sixtyish—dropped most of the suitcases he carried. His hands, Jack noticed, were ham sized. "Who the hell are you?" the hulk demanded. "And what the hell are you doing in my house?"

"Aah…" Jack stared at what had to be Mel's parents. *Go ahead, Halloran. Tell them you're sleeping with their daughter. That you married her to quit work.*

No way. Even caught off guard he wasn't that stupid.

"Hello!" Jack said as heartily as possible. "You must be the Burkes." He plastered on a big doofus smile. "Jack Halloran. I'm…ah, here just, ah, helping out. You know, cooking, yardwork…." He fiddled with the dinner plates to prove his point. "Surgeons work awfully hard. Long hours. I'm just, just studying. Financial planner stuff. So when good ol' Mel couldn't get everything done, she asked me…"

Jack prayed to be struck by lightning. Run over by a monster truck. Anything. "…strictly as a friend, of course, to…help…out."

He shot a glance at Mel's parents to see how they were taking it. Not very well. Then Jack's glance shot right past them to Mel's pale, stricken face. He groaned.

"Uh, here's Mel now." In her robe. Great. Any other time…

"Hi, Mom, Dad." Mel greeted her parents dully. She'd be happier to see them once she removed the big no-commitment, no-thanks stake Jack had just driven into her heart. "I see you've met Mr. Halloran. I believe he's just leaving."

"Mel, no!" Jack cried. Then he pushed between her

parents and grabbed her wrist. "Excuse us," he said to her mom and dad as he pulled Mel past them, then through the kitchen and into the utility room. "We'll just be a minute," he said, and shut the door.

Plapf! The fold-out ironing board snapped down like a guillotine, separating Mel from her—*her nothing.* He wanted to be nothing to her.

He was going to get his wish.

"How much did you hear?" Jack asked. The lock of hair that sprouted from his cowlick was bobbing around like a drunk on a pogo stick.

"All of it." Enough to answer every question she'd had. Enough to shatter any stupid dreams she'd had, too. She might learn to be more traditionally female, but she couldn't make a man want what he didn't want. And damned if she'd try.

"I just didn't want to shock them," Jack claimed, waving his hands around, the hands that had stroked her so intimately. "I thought we'd sort of break it to them gently. 'Cuz, you know, the whole 'I married a stranger' thing might sound too, ah, bizarre for parental units to handle."

Come on, Burke. Make a clean excision. "There's nothing to break." *Except my heart.*

She could live without it as long as she didn't lose her purpose. "We were never really married. Legally but not really."

Mel stuffed her hands into the pockets of her robe and concentrated on not showing Halloran how hurt she felt. If all she had left was her pride, she'd protect it.

"I think you'd better go," she said, looking down at one of the things separating them. *Surgeons don't iron.* "I'll explain you to my folks…later."

Jack moved toward her, to hug away whatever was bothering her—and got a nice shot to the groin from the barricading ironing board.

Then her words hit him even harder.

"Explain me? How?" Dammit! He didn't know what to say, what to do. How to get the damned ironing board out of the way.

Or how to convince her he really was serious about her, committed to their relationship—after his little tap dance around the pop-up parents.

"You're right," Mel interrupted his desperate search for a strategy. "There's nothing to explain. Because you—this whole marriage has been nothing but a fantasy all along."

"Right and I'm not interested in fantasizing," Jack snapped. He wanted a real, forever marriage. "Not anymore."

Didn't their time together mean anything to Mel? Their incredible lovemaking? The baby-sitting trials? Their shared taste in videos? "I don't understand. I thought what we had was real. Was I alone out here?"

Mel didn't respond. Just stood there. Looking more and more remote.

Fear overwhelmed him, like waves washing over a drowning man, which was what he felt like. He fought it with bluster. "Okay. I see. Well, with your parents home now, you don't need me any longer, do you?" He paused, waiting, hoping for a dissenting opinion.

Nothing. Survival instinct sent in the Halloran temper with orders to override the pain crushing him.

"Fine. Go back to that hospital, then, Melinda! Hide behind your patients!" Jack shouted. "But let me tell you one thing before I go."

Of course, even a six-year—okay, a female six-year-old—would know that the "one thing" he should tell her ought to be something along the lines of "I love you, just the way you are, and I'm nothing without you."

But Jack being a man, he bumbled on instead. "Your life's a precious gift, Mel. A gift to you. Don't waste it trying to make up for your brother's death. You can't replace Harry. You don't need to! The way to honor his memory is to live your life, to fill it with joy and love and—''

"Go to hell, Jack." Mel's quiet instruction stopped the rest of his words in his throat. It was hopeless. "Now, please."

"Your wish, my command," he replied, digging in his pocket for the ring. Slamming it down on the ironing board. "Here. I won't be needing this." Jack pushed himself out of the utility room, then stormed out of the kitchen, shouting instructions as he went, if anyone cared to listen, to dry the clothes in the washer on delicate and only for ten minutes.

By the time that ten minutes would have been up, Jack was packed and downstairs. Nobody tried to stop him, so he left the house, the marriage and, he realized before he'd gone a block, his damned heart in Mel's keeping.

Since he was suddenly technically homeless, Jack drove to Tess's.

"It's just until I find my own place," he said. And put his meaningless life back together.

Though he doubted Tess was thrilled with her new roommate, at least she didn't throw him out. He was family. And no trouble.

No energy, either. He could barely field the forwarded Rent-a-Spouse calls.

Tess kindly took over a lot of the business stuff. She said he was grieving and she felt a duty to help him past it.

Grieving—like hell. He had the flu or something. What could he be grieving about—other than his heart being broken in a kazillion pieces and his body aching, aching, aching for his sweet surgeon spouse, who didn't want him.

Who, with her parents home, probably didn't even miss him.

Jack lay on the sofa, the TV tuned to the Who Cares? Channel, and slipped back into his fog of funk.

If Jack felt depressed, Mel felt nothing.

At least, she tried very hard to feel nothing. She reverted to her old schedule: working, pulling a lot of thirty-sixes. If Bowen hadn't banned her from 24/7s, she'd have worked continuously. As it was, she only went home occasionally to eat, sleep—and change pink underwear.

Her mother hadn't asked a single question since the utility room showdown. Just patted her arm while saying, "It'll all work out, dear" every chance she got.

Mel's father kept trying to ask questions her mom wouldn't let him finish. She'd switch the conversation to their adventures in Oman and why they'd been sent home so early.

Why *had* they come home the very night Jack—?

Here's a better question, Burke. He'd prepared that fancy meal and had a ring in his pocket, but he'd bailed the minute she agreed their marriage wasn't real. What was that about?

She didn't know the answer, so Mel went back to work. No, she was already there—catnapping in one of the residents' rooms until her hip vibrated. Trauma calling.

Lab coat flapping, Mel raced down to the trauma center. This was what she did. What she'd trained for. She wasn't sacrificing herself to—what had Jack implied?— relieve her survivor's guilt.

She *wasn't*. Was she?

As she consulted with the attending physician and studied the X rays, Mel wondered if that idiot Jack Halloran could just possibly be right.

Had she given up her own life for Harry? And was that wrong? Jack had shown her so many things she'd missed while she focused on pediatric surgery: afternoons in the sun, really dumb movies, earth-shattering kisses, laughter....

She suddenly recalled one of her fondest memories of her brother—his belly laugh making everyone who heard it smile. Sharing his joy. Reveling in his aliveness.

That was Harry's true legacy, Mel thought as she went in search of the trauma patient's parents. His own bright spirit. Finding the anxious pair, she explained the procedure their son needed and got the waiver forms signed, assuring the parents that, barring unforeseen problems, they'd save the child's life.

From that point on, she thought to herself, what he did with it only he could choose. His choices would shape his life; his life would be *his* gift to the world.

And my life should be mine, Mel realized as she introduced the chaplain. Thanks to Jack, she knew that the most meaningful thing a person could do was to choose life. All of it.

Which made the rest simple. Choosing life meant just one thing: love. And, for Mel, love meant just one man.

As she sketched the spleen's location and explained its removal, Mel made a new commitment.

No way she was giving up medicine, but if winning Jack back required more time at home, she'd drop the surgical fellowship for a well-baby practice with saner hours and fewer traumas. She'd use what she'd learned so far to catch potential health problems before they became crises.

Good plan, she congratulated herself as she returned to the trauma room and prepped her patient to go upstairs.

Maybe she could convince Jack to give their marriage another shot if she signaled her willingness to renegotiate terms and responsibilities.

How?

Hmm. Perhaps she ought to consult some experts with more experience in the ways of men and the wiles of women. Mel had a feeling she'd need all the wiles she could get.

ABOVE THE TELEVISION'S soothing noise, Jack heard his sister on the phone. Again.

That's all she'd done since he got here. Talk. To him. About him. Mostly bashing him for walking out on his marriage.

He was supposed to stay when Mel didn't want him?

"Nope, other than run Rent-a-Spouse, he's still just imitating a large houseplant. Eat, mope, sleep. That's it."

It's Sherry, she mouthed when he looked up from the TV; he'd apparently been watching a documentary about termites.

Jack shook his head. He didn't want to talk to bright, brittle Sherry. Or to ol' Bob except about the business. Or even to Tess, who'd inexplicably chosen his darkest hour to become cheerful and outgoing again.

"Yes, I think so, too," Tess told Sher.

Since nobody was asking him a direct question, Jack's attention drifted to its usual subject: Melinda. Why hadn't she listened to him?

I should have dragged Mel upstairs and loved her into listening to me. Loved her till she believed *me.*

"Don't worry. I'll get him there." Tess again.

Now what? Jack wondered when she hung up and struck a confrontation pose: hands on hips, feet apart.

"Come on, bro, snap out of it. You've been in my hair—er, here two weeks. Time to get on with your life!

"This brainchild of yours," Tess went on, "is turning into a huge success. So huge, in fact, that if you pass that CFP test and get even halfway busy with financial planning, I'm going to have to quit my other job to help you out."

"You'd do that?" A faint shock rippled through him.

He'd always been big brother the caretaker. When had the tables turned?

"Sure," Tess said, then lifted her chin. "And it looks like sooner rather than later. We need more Spouses already," she declared, and before Jack could even finish a nod, she extended an index finger in his direction. "Sherry knows someone who'd be a real asset to the business."

"So hire 'em." Jack sighed. He should be happy Rent-a-Spouse had taken off, but no matter how busy he stayed, he also stayed miserable. Without Mel, nothing mattered. Not one thing.

"No," Tess said with a firm headshake. "Your business, you hire." She punched his upper arm. "Sherry's setting up an interview for tomorrow."

Whenever. Time no longer mattered. He'd lost Mel two weeks ago, but it'd take more like two hundred years to get over her. To stop remembering the feel of her silky chocolate hair sliding over his skin. To stop hearing her velvety voice breathing his name. To stop reliving her heat and tightness surrounding him.

"I'm sorry." Jack gazed up at his sister. "I'm sorry I tried to rush you past your grief. I didn't understand. Now I do."

Tess patted the top of his head. "Bygones, bro. I appreciated the concern behind your insensitivity. Now be sure to look nice tomorrow."

Why? Oh. Jack sighed. "Better write down the time and address."

WEIRD, HE THOUGHT the next day as he confirmed the address against Tess's slip of paper. The Mansion on Turtle Creek—Dallas's preeminent luxury hotel? One of the housekeeping staff must need extra money.

His sister's instructions said to give his name to the desk clerk. When he did, the guy smirked.

"Welcome, Mr. Halloran. You're in the Presidential

Terrace Suite." The clerk smirked harder as he handed over a key card. "Your party's waiting for you."

Jack's heart pounded in his chest. Sherry was his best friend; Tess his sister. They couldn't, they wouldn't be this cruel. "H-how do I get there?"

"Ninth floor, follow the signs."

He took off for the elevator bank at a dead run. Leaping into an empty car, he punched the requisite button. And started praying before the doors closed.

Please let her be there. Let it be okay. Let it be forever.

MEL PACED the huge suite, oblivious to its size, its color scheme or its opulence. All she could think about was the gamble she was taking with her heart, her happiness, her whole future.

Okay, surgeons are bold, she told herself, but what if Jack—provided he even showed—just laughed his posterior off, then retreated as fast as humanly possible?

Maybe she should retreat from the extreme position she'd taken.

Get dressed, at least.

She shook her head and lifted her chin. No. She had to give Jack a clear message of what she was prepared to do if he'd come back. And stay. That's wh—

Mel froze in mid-thought and mid-pace as the door to the suite flew open.

And there stood Jack. God, he looked good! His hair disheveled, his jaw stubble covered, his khakis rumpled.

His eyes the color of the midnight sky. Glowing hotter by the second. With what?

Time to find out. Clearing her throat, Mel began her prepared speech. "H-hi. I asked you here—"

"What are you doing—?" Jack's hoarse voice interrupted her. He extended a shaking index finger in her direction, moved it up and down. "—in that?"

Reflexively Mel's hands touched the ruffled edge of

the gauze-thin French maid's apron she'd rented from a costume shop. It and a couple of pieces of her sexiest pink underwear were all she wore. And a pair of sky-scraper-high heels.

"Applying for a job." Here came the tough part, but nothing was tougher than living without the man she loved. "As your wife."

"You—"

Mel held up her hand, palm out. "Let me finish." Reaching behind her, she began untying the apron. "Now, my résumé isn't very strong in some of the traditional wife areas." She removed the apron. Her hands went to her bra closure. "But I'm highly motivated. In fact, I'm making arrangements to join a well-baby practice so I'll be able to spend more time at home. With you. And I'll do my best to acquire the necessary skills to become the wife you want."

Jack was tearing off his clothes. "Melinda, darlin', I'll be happy if you're happy. We don't have to spend every minute of the rest of our lives together, as long as we spend every minute we've got left loving each other.

"So let's throw out the role rules and just figure out who does what as we go along." He picked her up and carried her into the suite's bedroom, to the huge canopied bed.

"You already are my perfect wife," he told her between hot, tender kisses, "just the way you are, as long as you love me the way I love you."

"Which is?" Mel asked, when he'd lowered her onto the bed.

"Totally, completely, forever," Jack said as he followed her down.

"That's exactly how I love you," Mel assured him happily.

Jack covered her mouth with his for a long, satisfying

moment, then he promised, "I'll do my best, darling, to be your perfect husband, too."

Mel grinned as her hands reached for him. "Maybe I'd better review your qualifications for the, ah, position," she purred.

They quit talking then. After all, they'd have a life-time together for things like that.

Now...ah, now they compared résumés, made and accepted partnership offers and signed up for a perma-nent, full-time, forever benefit package called love.

Bestselling Harlequin® author

JUDITH ARNOLD

brings readers a brand-new,
longer-length novel based on her
popular miniseries *The Daddy School*

Somebody's Dad

If any two people should avoid getting
romantically involved with each other, it's
bachelor—and children-phobic!—Brett Stockton
and single mother Sharon Bartell. But neither
can resist the sparks...especially once
The Daddy School is involved.

"Ms. Arnold seasons tender passion with a dusting
of humor to keep us turning those pages."
—*Romantic Times Magazine*

*Look for Somebody's Dad
in February 2002.*

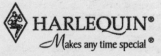

HARLEQUIN®
Makes any time special ®

If you enjoyed what you just read,
then we've got an offer you can't resist!

Take 2 bestselling
love stories FREE!
Plus get a FREE surprise gift!

Clip this page and mail it to Harlequin Reader Service®

IN U.S.A.	IN CANADA
3010 Walden Ave.	P.O. Box 609
P.O. Box 1867	Fort Erie, Ontario
Buffalo, N.Y. 14240-1867	L2A 5X3

YES! Please send me 2 free Harlequin Duets™ novels and my free surprise gift. After receiving them, if I don't wish to receive anymore, I can return the shipping statement marked cancel. If I don't cancel, I will receive 2 brand-new novels every month, before they're available in stores! In the U.S.A., bill me at the bargain price of $5.14 plus 50¢ shipping & handling per book and applicable sales tax, if any*. In Canada, bill me at the bargain price of $6.14 plus 50¢ shipping & handling per book and applicable taxes**. That's the complete price—what a great deal! I understand that accepting the 2 free books and gift places me under no obligation ever to buy any books. I can always return a shipment and cancel at any time. Even if I never buy another book from Harlequin, the 2 free books and gift are mine to keep forever.

111 HEN DC7P
311 HEN DC7Q

Name	(PLEASE PRINT)
Address	Apt.#
City	State/Prov.	Zip/Postal Code

* Terms and prices subject to change without notice. Sales tax applicable in N.Y.
** Canadian residents will be charged applicable provincial taxes and GST.
All orders subject to approval. Offer limited to one per household and not valid to current Harlequin Duets™ subscribers.
® and ™ are registered trademarks of Harlequin Enterprises Limited.   DUETS01

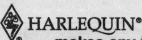